新多益
高分核心字彙

◀ 3000個一定要記住的必考單字 ▶

尤菊芳—著

學英文（或學習任何一種語言）難不難？聽、說、讀、寫、單字、發音、文法，哪樣最難？要我說，樣樣都難，各有不同的難點和不同的難法。不過，根據學者的研究，學習外語一段時間後卻放棄的人中，有百分之二十五的原因是：字彙量一直上不來！無法累積足夠的字彙量，就很難體會多懂一種語言的好處，最終選擇放棄，讓過去學習的時間與心血付諸流水！

大家都知道學單字不等於學英文，但不學單字絕對學不好英文。像「超強單詞記憶術」這類省力又快速的記憶法，讓每個學生多少都心嚮往之，然而「超強記憶術」的存在只是個迷思，就算有也只適合原本底子就很好或天生有超強記憶力的人。對你我這般「正常人」而言，一步一腳印的走比較實在。

學習的第一階段：留下印象

背英文字彙的法門眾說紛紜，有人說要聽發音，用「耳」；有人說要朗誦，用「口」；有人說你應該聽你應該拿起筆來寫一寫英文拼法、寫一寫中文意思；這是用「手」；也有人說只要多瞄幾眼，用「眼」就夠了。此外，還有拆解字根、字首、字尾的記憶法，或是諧音轉換、故事情境式的聯想法。但無論如何，這些都只是資訊進入記憶管道的第一步：留下印象。

二十世紀有學者提出「多元智能理論」的說法，原來每一個人學習方式的偏好不同，對張三有用的方法，對李四未必能夠產生同樣的效果，王二麻子甚至可能永遠學不來！背單字亦是如此，如果問一問周圍好學生怎麼學有效、怎麼學沒效，毋庸置疑會得出相互矛盾的答案。

其實，每個單字本身的內、外在結構和涵意深淺各不相同，每次出現在教材或生活裡的情境也不同，很難只用一兩種方法就能學好所有類型的字彙。想要讓單字留下印象，最好的方法就是多管齊下，也就是綜合果汁法（或許你喜歡用洋名兒「雞尾酒法」），挑好幾種喜歡的方式背誦。但要記住，這只是第一步——如果在一個星期到一個月間不再複習，我們註定會忘記這些資訊。

一般人都能勉力達成第一個學習階段「留下印象」，然而，更艱鉅的任務其實在後頭：怎麼維持第一階段日日擴大的學習成果。通常，當學習者發覺自己前一段時間所付出的努力所剩無幾的時候，挫折感油然而生，便會產生放棄的念頭。

學習的第二階段：鞏固印象，化為記憶

「強化」或「鞏固」這些已經留下印象的字彙，是學習的第二步，換句話說就是要「複習」。但複習的概念不只是透過學習管道（眼、耳、口、手、情意、思索）再接觸一遍那麼簡單，而是要看複習的目的才能決定成效。

舉例來說，如果是為了要聽懂，就得用聽的方式複習；如果是想確定再看見這些字在文章裡的時候能夠認得，複習時就要確定這些字不在熟悉的情境出現的時候自己還認得；如果是為了能夠把字彙拼寫出來，複習時就要確認自己能夠有機會去拼寫這些單字。

坊間字彙學習的書籍，多半很少關注學習的第二個階段；即使部分書本提供了少許複習測驗，其篇幅及型式都非常有限。《新多益必考高分字彙》所附的光碟提供了多種快速複習方式，學習者可以從最簡單的「含中譯的選擇題」做起，建立對字彙的熟悉度，逐漸增加學習的掌握度。已有英語根基的學習者，也可直接使用符合考試方式的模式來複習。

同樣隨書附贈的學習遮色片，則可在每頁閱讀完畢後立即使用，檢驗自己的學習成效，有助於將短期記憶轉化為長期記憶。更重要的是，這種作法能夠不斷維持「學習有成」的樂觀情緒。

正向回饋促進學習動力

憑良心說，我教書那麼久，沒碰過幾個能夠好好啃完一本傳統單字書的學生。歸根究柢，這都是大腦面對的情緒問題。當我們決定開始一個有意識的活動（如：開始啃單字學習的書），大腦就開始評估其功效，以便持續或中斷執行計畫。當我們遇到困難（如：單字可能不好記），大腦除了想方設法尋找更好的解決之道，還會評估是否該繼續這項投資（如：萬一單字才背過就忘了）。大腦需要不停的有成功經驗，來肯定自己的努力是值得的。

單字書若以傳統編排，學習者會太早碰到困難的進階單字，大腦會為避免太多挫折感而想放棄。此外，字彙量特別多的兩個字母，被我稱為「邪惡的A」和「更邪惡的C」，會讓大腦有看不到盡頭的無力感而想放棄。就算撐了下來，因為不瞭

解單字記憶和遺忘是同出同入的攣生兄弟，當越死命記憶、遺忘越多的時候，大腦會不願再無謂地付出而想放棄。除了學習情緒的問題，大多數人還有惰性和鴕鳥心理，這些種種都促使學生拋下單字書，放棄背誦。

「成也大腦、敗也大腦」！看多、聽多學生這些類似的抱怨，我終於看清一半的問題出在學生身上，一半的問題出在單字書的編排上。字彙學習的書不該長得像大堆頭的賀歲片，明星越多越好，這種電影從沒聽過哪齣成為經典。字彙的選擇也是同理，要各司所職、恰如其分，適當區分難度，才能最有助於加深記憶。當然，一本字彙學習書裡不可能全部都是「生」的，如果偶爾碰到當天的目標字中熟悉的比較多，可以增加學習的量，當然也可以當作彩頭，輕鬆一點。保持愉快的心情，路可以走得更長。

如果你已經打開這書，都到這裡，請多再翻一兩頁，一定要好好看完使用說明，讓這本字彙書發揮最大效用。即使你沒有時間唸完整本書，只複習完精挑的基礎字彙，也會有一定的效用。請充分應用光碟裡的測驗功能，用實際的測驗成果來肯定自己對學習的掌控，增加對學習的信心。請記住：信心是建立在成功的經驗上。祝福你不只在多益考試中取得高分，更希望這個成功經驗能開啟你對英語學習的興趣。

多益測驗TOEIC代表Test of English for International Communication（國際溝通英語測驗），乃針對英語非母語人士所設計之英語能力測驗，測驗分數反映受測者在國際職場環境中與他人以英語溝通的熟稔程度。參加本測驗毋需具備專業的知識或字彙，因為測驗內容以日常使用之英語為主。

多益測驗台灣地區自2008年3月起，在多益公開測驗中採用新版多益聽力與閱讀測驗新題型，稱之為「新版多益測驗」或「新多益」（NEW TOEIC）。測驗題的內容，從全世界各地職場的英文資料中蒐集而來，題材多元化，包含各種地點與狀況。

多益測驗是以職場為基準點的英語能力測驗中，世界最頂級的考試。2012年在全球有超過七百萬人報考多益測驗，並在150個國家中有超過14,000家的企業、學校或政府機構使用多益測驗，同時在全球超過165個國家施測，是最被廣泛接受且最方便報考的英語測驗之一。

本書編排特色

●科學方法選字

《新多益高分核心字彙》中挑選的所有單字，不僅包括數個多益推薦字表中重複出現的字，更與其他語言檢定測驗的常見字彙表交叉比對，抓出真正在英語中、高頻率出現的核心單字，並透過編者多年鑽研英語學習領域的專業涵養進一步微調，確保讀者在背誦單字時，能以最有效率的方式入門，迅速掌握學習關鍵。

●原創例句

單字離不開句子，考慮到學習者的理解能力，句子的複雜度只能略高於學習者目前的水準，使他們能專注於目標字彙的學習。本系列的所有例句，均為在美國任教的母語人士或專業英語教師所原創，以保證例句的語言更加道地，同時涵蓋更多元化的主題。

● 難度分級

《新多益高分核心字彙》將字彙由易到難分為三個級別：基礎、核心、進階。基礎字彙共一千餘個，紙本書中以「字彙能力檢查表」形式呈現，完整介紹收錄於光碟電子書之中；兩千多個核心字彙與一千多個進階字彙，則在紙本書中盡數呈現。分級原則採字彙學研究中的字頻分佈，字頻越高表示越常見，學習者越容易也越需要記憶。

編者還分析了字彙的可學度（learnability），以決定某個單字應該歸入哪個級別。字彙可學度涉及的因素包括：是否容易記憶（比如合成字較簡單，音節數少的字較簡單，拼法越規律的字越簡單）、是否容易與其他單字混淆（字形、字音、字義）、是否包含複雜的理解（比如actual, genuine, authentic雖有相似的字義，但其字義內涵的複雜度並不相同）。

大體說來，基礎字彙學習者可輕鬆過關。核心字彙學習者可能本來就有印象，只需留意其使用情境，加強記憶即可。進階字彙的識記難度較高，需反覆練習。為滿足大多數學生的需求，編者在字彙選擇方面儘量擴大範圍，以便把字彙的精義一次性完整呈現，學習者可斟酌自身學力程度，充分利用光碟內含的測驗軟體所提供的多種題型進行強化。

● 字彙標籤

本書每個單字均配有字彙標籤：托、雅、學，分別代表托福考試字彙（TOEFL）、雅思考試字彙（IELTS）和學術英語字彙（Academic Word List）。提供這些標籤的目的，是要消除學習者學習英語單字的恐懼，讓他們知道學習英語單字並不可怕，重要的字彙只有那些，背完一組便有助於其他檢定測驗，任何努力都將為下一個階段的學習奠定基礎。

● 詞性說明

全書使用的詞性縮寫意義如下：

vi 不及物動詞	adj 形容詞	prep 介系詞
vt 及物動詞	adv 副詞	conj 連接詞
n 名詞		

●測驗光碟

　　《新多益高分核心字彙》附有測驗光碟一張，可按照學習者的要求隨機出題進行測驗。此光碟提供自我檢查表，以及五種由易到難的測試方式：選擇題含中文翻譯、選擇題不含中文翻譯、配合題含中文翻譯、配合題不含中文翻譯、填充題。

　　學習者可以從最簡單的「選擇題含中文翻譯」做起，以便逐漸掌握。由於測試是隨機出題，每次的試卷都不相同，即使是選字範圍、題型和題數相同，試題出現的順序也不一樣，選擇題的選項也不一樣。光碟電子書收錄的基礎字彙，也包含進隨機出題的模式，讓各種學力差異的學習者皆可找到適合的練習難度。

●字彙編排規則

　　《新多益高分核心字彙》將部分拼法相同、詞性不同的單字分條列出，選字的取捨與呈現方式大致遵循下列規則：

1. 單字的動詞和名詞拼法相同，且字義沒有差異或只有些許差異時，會在中文解釋中標記全部詞性，例句以單字的動詞形式呈現。

blaze
[blez]

托　雅　學

n 火焰；閃光；vi 燃燒，冒火焰；閃光　　　　　b1023
When she found her husband had cheated on her, her eyes were blazing with fury.
當她發現丈夫出軌時，她的眼中冒著憤怒之火。

2. 單字的動詞和名詞拼法相同，但字義不同時，會分條列出。

blast
[blæst]

托　雅　學

n 一陣（風）；爆炸；衝擊波；管樂器聲　　　　b1021
The blast of the bomb destroyed the entire building.
炸彈的爆炸把整棟建築物都毀了。

blast
[blæst]

托　雅　學

vt 爆炸；徹底毀掉　　　　　　　　　　　　　b1022
Randy's bad test scores blasted his chance to get into college.
蘭迪極差的考試成績徹底毀掉了他進入大學的機會。

3. 容易混淆的詞性變化，會分條列出。

presumably
[prɪˈzuməblɪ]

托 雅 學

`adv` 推測起來，大概

Presumably, all lives were lost at sea when the ship sank.
推測起來，船沉沒後所有人都在大海中喪生了。

p2061

presume
[prɪˈzum]

托 雅 學

`vi`/`vt` 擅自行動；設想；假設，揣測；濫用；擅自做

I would never presume to know why you are upset, but good friends can sometimes guess when you are in trouble.
我從來不去揣測你心情不好的原因，但是作為你的好友，我有時候可以猜到你是有麻煩了。

p2062

presumptuous
[prɪˈzʌmptʃʊəs]

托 雅 學

`adj` 冒昧的，放肆的

It is extremely presumptuous to sit at the head of a table when you are a guest in someone's home.
身為客人卻去坐在餐桌的主位是一種非常冒昧的行為。

p2063

4. 某些單字的用法較難理解，即使不同詞性拼法相同，字義也相同，還是會分條列出。

premise
[ˈprɛmɪs]

托 雅 學

`n` 前提，假設；房屋

The premise for the story is original but it is up to the writer to execute his ideas well.
這個故事的假設是很具原創性的，但是也要看作者如何詮釋自己的觀點。

p2053

premise
[prɪˈmaɪz]

托 雅 學

`vi`/`vt` 提出前提；預設，假定

The assumption was premised upon our major findings across all the studies.
這項假設的提出是以所有研究的重大發現作為前提的。

p2054

5. 「字彙能力檢查表」因搭配電子書中單字呈現，故會有部分字彙重複出現，代表其字義、詞性或用法符合上述四點，值得讀者再次複習。

儘管中英文間常常不該逐字翻譯，但本書的例句中文翻譯，皆將關鍵字彙明確地翻譯出來，這是為了配合測驗光碟中的題目，方便讀者學習。例如：

Nathan was confined to his bed until his broken leg healed.（vt. 限制；使不外出，禁閉）

　　較好的翻譯是「在腿部骨折痊癒前，南森都必須臥床」，但為了配合測驗題：

Nathan was _____ to his bed until his broken leg healed.

　　該句子的中文翻譯必須是「南森被困在床上，直到骨折的腿痊癒」。

　　此外，本書英文句子並不追求譯到信達雅的境界，目標在於讓學習者清楚瞭解其用法；中譯之美感與奧妙，需要學習者自己體會。

學習指導與建議

　　字彙的習得基本上分為兩個階段：一是學習，即通過學習管道（眼、耳、口、手……等），讓新的單字在腦中留下印象。二是複習，即通過反覆演練，強化或鞏固這些已經留下印象的單字。

　　《新多益高分核心字彙》提供高頻率出現的單字，學習者有了這些基本素材，能順利進行第一個階段的學習。然而，更艱鉅的任務是怎樣維持第一階段的學習成果。一般的字彙書很少關注學習的第二個階段，雖然有些也隨書提供了複習測試，其篇幅及形式也非常有限。

　　購買本書的學習者，建議從「核心字彙」開始，先確認是否瞭解各字母起始「字彙能力檢查表」的單字；若仍有不懂的字，便開啟光碟中的電子書加深印象。其後，每天以學習40～50個單字為目標，每讀完一頁，便立刻使用隨書附贈的學習遮色片，確認自己是否已記住單字；當日學習完畢後，再透過光碟中的「自我檢查表」進行檢測。

　　按照這種方式學習四五天之後（約學習了150～200個單字），就應該暫停一兩天，運用光碟中的五種題型，對學過的單字進行複習和檢測。在學完600～800個單字以後，停下來再做一次總複習。「進階字彙」的難度更高，建議以每天20～30個單字為目標。當然，學過之後同樣要定期反覆進行複習，並建議適時地印出試卷，測驗後保留下來，作為日後複習的依據。

PART 1 核心字彙

A

字彙能力檢查表

先自我檢驗是否瞭解以下初階單字，若有不清楚者，請先開啟光碟中的電子書複習。

☐abroad
☐absence
☐absolutely
☐accident
☐accidental
☐accomplish
☐according to
☐achieve
☐actual
☐additional
☐address
☐admire
☐admit
☐adult
☐advance
☐advance
☐advance
☐advanced
☐advantage
☐advice
☐advise
☐advisory
☐afford

☐agency
☐agenda
☐agreement
☐aid
☐aid
☐aim
☐aim
☐aim
☐aircraft
☐aisle
☐alarm
☐alarm
☐album
☐alongside
☐aluminum
☐amuse
☐amusing
☐announce
☐annoy
☐annual
☐annually
☐anxiety
☐apart

☐apologize
☐apology
☐appearance
☐applicant
☐application
☐apply
☐apply
☐appoint
☐appointment
☐approve
☐argue
☐argument
☐arise
☐arithmetic
☐arrange
☐arrangement
☐article
☐ashamed
☐aside
☐aspirin
☐assignment
☐assistant
☐athlete

☐atlas
☐attack
☐attack
☐attend
☐attend
☐attendance
☐attendant
☐attention
☐attentive
☐attract
☐attraction
☐audio
☐automatic
☐avenue
☐average
☐average
☐avoid
☐award
☐award
☐aware
☐awareness
☐awful
☐awkward

A

abandon
[ə'bændən]

vt 離棄，拋棄，放棄

a1001

They abandoned their broken car on the side of the highway and walked to the gas station.

他們把拋錨的車丟棄在高速公路邊，步行去加油站。

abbreviation
[ə,brivɪ'eʃən]

n 節略，縮寫，縮短

a1002

NASA is the abbreviation for the National Aeronautics and Space Agency.

NASA是美國國家航太空署的縮寫。

abnormal
[æb'nɔrml]

adj 不正常的，反常的，不規則的，異乎尋常的，例外的

a1003

It was abnormal for it to snow at this time of year.

一年裡在這個時候下雪是不正常的。

abrupt
[ə'brʌpt]

adj 出其不意的；（行為等）粗魯無禮的

a1004

Their disagreement led to his abrupt departure from the party.

他們的分歧導致他突然離開宴會。

absorb
[əb'sɔrb]

vt 使全神貫注

a1005

The new employee absorbs information quickly and has been promoted to the group leader position.

那個新的員工學得很快，已經被提拔為小組長。

absorb
[əb'sɔrb]

vt 吸收

a1006

She used a paper towel to absorb the spilled drink.

她用一張紙巾吸乾打翻的飲料。

abstract
['æbstrækt]

adj 抽象的

a1007

Nathan preferred geometry because he liked abstract concepts.

南森更喜歡幾何學是因為他喜歡抽象的概念。

abstract
['æbstrækt]

n 摘要

a1008

After reading the abstract, there is little need to read through the entire journal article.

讀完摘要之後，幾乎不需要讀整篇期刊文章了。

abstract
[æb'strækt]

vt 提取；摘錄要點

a1009

I do not want you to copy the whole article; I want you to abstract the main points.

我不要你把整篇文章抄下來，我要你擷取要點。

absurd
[əb'sɝd]
托 雅 學

adj 荒謬的，荒誕的，荒唐可笑的；不合理的
Everyone always looked forward to Steven's absurd Halloween costumes.
每個人都很期待史蒂芬可笑的萬聖節服裝。

a1010

abuse
[ə'bjus]
托 雅 學

n 濫用；惡習；弊端
Terence worked to help end abuse against children and teens.
特倫斯致力於幫助停止虐待兒童和青少年的行為。

a1011

academic
[ˌækə'dɛmɪk]
托 雅 學

adj 學院的；學術性的；理論的
This university has a reputation for academic excellence.
這所大學因學術卓越而聞名。

a1012

academy
[ə'kædəmɪ]
托 雅 學

n 專科院校；學會；研究院
Gina was thrilled by her acceptance into the Royal Academy of Sciences.
皇家科學院錄取了吉娜，她激動萬分。

a1013

access
['æksɛs]
托 雅 學

n 進入；享用權
The card gave him access to the university library.
那張卡片使他能夠進入大學圖書館。

a1014

access
['æksɛs]
托 雅 學

vt 存取
Please tell me how to access the information for the computer stores.
請告訴我如何取得這電腦裡儲存的資訊。

a1015

accessible
[æk'sɛsəbḷ]
托 雅 學

adj 可接近的；可進入的
The control room is accessible to staff only.
控制室只有員工可以進入。

a1016

accessory
[æk'sɛsərɪ]
托 雅 學

n 配飾品，附件；同謀，從犯
Diane loved earrings, purses, and other fashion accessories.
戴恩喜歡耳環、包包和其他時尚配件。

a1017

accompany
[ə'kʌmpənɪ]
托 雅 學

vi/vt 陪伴，伴隨；伴奏
Joan asked if her brother could accompany her to the dance.
瓊恩問她哥哥是否可以陪她一起去參加舞會。

a1018

accordingly
[ə'kɔrdɪŋlɪ]

adv 相應地，照著辦；於是
If the situation is not as good as expected, we should reassess our plan and act accordingly.
如果情況不如預期的好，我們應該重新評估我們的計畫，並且照著行動。

`a1019`

account
[ə'kaʊnt]

n 敘述，說明；帳目，帳戶；**vi** 說明，解釋
Kathy had three different bank accounts to help her run her businesses.
凱西有三個不同的銀行帳戶，用以幫助她經營生意。

`a1020`

account
[ə'kaʊnt]

vi 說明，解釋
The poor weather may have accounted for the small crowd.
天氣不好可能可以解釋為什麼人來得少。

`a1021`

accountant
[ə'kaʊntənt]

n 會計人員，會計師
The accountant is doing the bookkeeping and breaking down the traveling expenses of the last month for her boss.
會計正在做帳，給她的老闆分別列出上個月的旅行支出。

`a1022`

accounting
[ə'kaʊntɪŋ]

n 會計；財務
She took her tax return to an accounting office.
她把報稅資料帶到會計公司去。

`a1023`

accurate
['ækjərɪt]

adj 正確的；精確的
My prediction of the experiment's outcome was not accurate.
我對這個實驗結果的預測是不準確的。

`a1024`

accuse
[ə'kjuz]

vi/vt 控告，指責
Laura was accused of lying to cover up her mistake.
蘿拉因撒謊掩蓋自己犯的錯誤而遭到指責。

`a1025`

acid
['æsɪd]

adj 酸的，酸味的；尖刻的
The acid taste of the tomato soup was too much for me.
番茄湯的酸味對我來說太重了。

`a1026`

acid
['æsɪd]

n 酸；酸性物質
The teacher taught the students how to handle acid safely.
老師教了學生們如何安全地處理酸性物質。

`a1027`

acknowledge
[ək'nɑlɪdʒ]

托 雅 學

vt 認知；告知（信件等的）收到；答謝
She acknowledged that she'd seen the photograph before.
她承認之前就已經看過這張照片。

a1028

acquire
[ə'kwaɪr]

托 雅 學

vt 獲得；學到（知識等）；養成（習慣）
It will take some time to acquire the professional skills you need to take the job.
獲取這份工作需要的專業能力需要一些時間才能學會。

a1029

acquisition
[ˌækwə'zɪʃən]

托 雅 學

n 學到，養成（習慣）；獲得的東西
He dedicates most of his free time to the acquisition of specialized knowledge.
他把大部分閒置時間都用於學習專業知識。

a1030

adapt
[ə'dæpt]

托 雅 學

vi/vt 使…適應（新用途、新情況）
An employee has to easily adapt to changing demands from the supervisors.
一個員工必須順暢地適應主管們不斷變化的要求。

a1031

adapt
[ə'dæpt]

托 雅 學

vt 改編，改寫
The television program was adapted from a novel written by a retired FBI agent.
這個電視節目改編自一本由退休聯邦調查局探員所寫的小說。

a1032

adaptation
[ˌædæp'teʃən]

托 雅 學

n 適應；改編；改編本，改寫本
The play is an adaptation of the classic movie.
該劇是一部經典電影的改編本。

a1033

adequate
['ædəkwɪt]

托 雅 學

adj 充足的，適當的
Her supply of flour was adequate to make the cake.
她的麵粉足夠拿來做蛋糕。

a1034

adjust
[ə'dʒʌst]

托 雅 學

vi/vt 調節，調整；適應
It would be nice of you to adjust the volume levels when you listen to music at night.
當你晚上聽音樂的時候，如果能調整音量就太好了。

a1035

adjustment
[ə'dʒʌstmənt]

托 雅 學

n 調整，調理；調節器
Kris has a sore back so he's seeing his chiropractor for an adjustment.
克里斯背痛，所以他正在看脊椎按摩師，以做個調理。

a1036

administer
[əd'mɪnəstə]

vi/vt 施行，實施；掌管，料理…的事務；給予
We will administer the test next Wednesday.
我們將在下星期三實施考試。

a1037

A

administration
[əd,mɪnə'streʃən]

n 管理；行政機關，管理部門
When you're done with the registration form, please take it to the administration office.
註冊表填完之後，請你交到行政辦公室。

a1038

admission
[əd'mɪʃən]
托 雅 學

n 允許進入，入學；入場券，入場費
Numerous students have been trying to gain admission to this prestigious school.
許多學生一直在努力獲得這所名校的入學許可。

a1039

admittance
[əd'mɪtəns]

n 准許進入
Don't be late as admittance to the theater is prohibited after the play begins.
不要遲到，因為在戲劇開演之後不能再進場。

a1040

adopt
[ə'dɑpt]
托 雅 學

vt 採用；收養
The government should adopt a better way to avoid the spread of the disease.
政府應該採取一個更好的方法來避免疾病的擴散。

a1041

adore
[ə'dor]

vt 崇拜，敬慕，愛慕；非常喜歡
Jamie adored the paintings of Van Gogh.
傑米非常喜歡梵谷的畫作。

a1042

advantageous
[,ædvən'tedʒəs]
托 雅 學

adj 有利的，有幫助的
His high SAT scores were advantageous to him as he applied to colleges.
學術能力測驗和學術評估測驗獲得高分有助於他申請大學。

a1043

adventure
[əd'vɛntʃə]
托 雅 學

n 冒險；奇遇
Justin regarded life as a long adventure.
賈斯汀認為生命就是一次長長的冒險。

a1044

adventure
[əd'vɛntʃə]
托 雅 學

vt 大膽行進
They spent two months adventuring across the tropical forest.
他們花了兩個月在熱帶雨林中冒險行進。

a1045

adventurous
[əd'vɛntʃərəs]

托 雅 學

adj 喜歡冒險的；大膽創新的；驚險刺激的   a1046

Our tour guides planned an adventurous day at the national park.

我們的導遊計畫了國家公園內一天非常冒險的行程。

advertise
['ædvə,taɪz]

托 雅 學

vi/vt（為…）做廣告；廣告   a1047

The company only advertised its products online.

這個公司只在網路上為產品做廣告。

advocate
['ædvəkɪt]

托 雅 學

n 擁護者，鼓吹者   a1048

William Wilberforce was an outspoken advocate for enslaved Africans in Britain.

威廉·威伯福斯是釋放在英國被奴役的非洲人直言不諱的宣導者。

advocate
['ædvəket]

托 雅 學

vt 擁護，提倡，主張   a1049

The non-profit organization advocates buying food from local markets.

這個非營利組織提倡購買當地的食材。

affect
[ə'fɛkt]

托 雅 學

n 情感   a1050

Her lack of affect to anything explains why she has few friends.

她對什麼事都缺乏情感，這解釋了為何她沒有什麼朋友。

affect
[ə'fɛkt]

托 雅 學

vt 影響；感動；（疾病）侵襲   a1051

The romantic story affected most of the audience.

這個浪漫的故事感動了大多數觀眾。

affection
[ə'fɛkʃən]

托 雅 學

n 情感；喜愛；愛慕；患病   a1052

Affection is very important for young children.

愛對於小孩子來說非常重要。

agreeable
[ə'griəbl]

托 雅 學

adj 一致的   a1053

Some of the terms stated in the contract were not very agreeable to my needs.

合約裡陳述的有些條款並不符合我的要求。

agreeable
[ə'griəbl]

托 雅 學

adj 愜意的；令人愉快的   a1054

Kevin, being the most agreeable companion I know, is always so considerate, friendly, generous and helpful.

凱文是我所認識最窩心的同伴，他體貼、友善、慷慨又樂於助人。

agriculture
['ægrɪ,kʌltʃɚ]

托 雅 學

n 農業，農耕
a1055
Agriculture is the main industry in the American Midwest.
農業是美國中西部的主要產業。

alert
[ə'lɝt]

托 雅 學

adj 警覺的；機靈的；n 警戒，警報
a1056
Jack wasn't very alert because he had only 2 hours of sleep the night before the accident.
傑克不是很警覺，因為他在發生車禍的前一晚只睡了兩個小時。

alert
[ə'lɝt]

托 雅 學

vt 使…警覺；通知
a1057
The teacher alerted the parents to the fact that their child had been smoking.
老師讓家長警覺一個事實：他們的小孩一直抽煙。

alien
['elɪən]

托 雅 學

n 外僑，外國人；外星人；adj 外國的；相異的
a1058
Many of this director's movies are about space aliens.
這導演執導的許多作品跟外星人有關。

alienate
['eljən,et]

托 雅 學

vt 使疏遠，離間；（與某群體）格格不入
a1059
He slowly alienates his peers because of the different opinions they all hold.
由於意見上的不和，他漸漸與他的同輩疏遠了。

allowance
[ə'lauəns]

托 雅 學

n 津貼，補助費
a1060
The company's benefits include medical insurance and housing allowance.
公司的福利包括醫療保險以及住宿補貼。

allowance
[ə'lauəns]

托 雅 學

n 零用錢；允許
a1061
I don't get very much allowance from my parents.
我父母沒有給我很多零用錢。

altitude
['æltə,tjud]

托 雅 學

n 高度，海拔；複數＝高處，高地
a1062
Airplanes typically fly at an altitude of 20,000 feet.
飛機通常在海拔2萬英尺的高空中飛行。

amateur
['æmə,tʃur]

托 雅 學

adj 業餘（水準）的；n （在運動、藝術等方面的）業餘玩家
a1063
These beautiful photos were taken by an amateur photographer.
這些美麗的照片是由一位業餘攝影師拍攝的。

amaze
[ə'mez]

vi/vt 使驚奇，使驚愕；使困惑

a1064

The fireworks amazed the children.

煙花使孩子們感到驚奇。

amazing
[ə'mezɪŋ]

adj 驚人的

a1065

It is amazing that the 5-year-old boy can play the piano so well.

5歲大的男孩鋼琴彈得這麼棒，實在令人驚奇。

ambassador
[æm'bæsədɚ]

n 大使；（派駐國際組織的）代表

a1066

The ambassador from France arrived early this morning.

法國大使今天一早就到了。

ambitious
[æm'bɪʃəs]

adj 有抱負的；有野心的

a1067

Allan was ambitious and climbed the corporate ladder quickly.

艾倫很有抱負，他在公司晉升得很快。

ambulance
['æmbjələns]

n 救護車／船／飛機

a1068

First aid should be given to the injured people before an ambulance arrives.

在救護車到來之前，必須要對受傷者採取急救措施。

ample
['æmpl]

adj 足夠的，充分的；富裕的；寬敞的，寬大的

a1069

The food at Aunt Dorothy's Thanksgiving dinner was always ample and delicious.

桃樂絲阿姨家感恩節晚餐的食物總是充足又美味。

analysis
[ə'næləsɪs]

n 分析；分解

a1070

The doctor's analysis of his illness was very thorough.

醫生對於他疾病的分析相當透徹。

analytical
[ˌænə'lɪdɪkəl]

adj 分析的；解析的；善於分析的

a1071

Michael is very smart and has a sharp, analytical mind.

麥可非常聰明，擁有一顆敏銳、善於分析的大腦。

analyze
['ænḷˌaɪz]

vt 分析；分解

a1072

He analyzed his notes from their session and determined that she would need more counseling.

他分析了他們會談的筆記，確定她需要更多的輔導。

A

anchor
['æŋkə]

n 錨；危難時可依靠的人或物 a1073
The anchor of the boat became trapped in the reef, and they were forced to abandon it.
船錨陷入了暗礁中,他們被迫棄船。

anchor
['æŋkə]

vi 用錨泊船；使固定,繫住 a1074
After drifting on the ocean for several days, those sailors finally anchored near a small island.
在海上漂流了幾天後,水手們終於停泊在一座小島附近。

anniversary
[,ænə'vɜ-səri]

n 周年,周年紀念日 a1075
Their anniversary was always a special treat for Jean and Thomas.
吉恩和湯姆斯一直把周年紀念日當作是對自己的特殊待遇。

annoyance
[ə'nɔiəns]

n 煩惱；生氣；令人不快的事 a1076
Missing the train today was such an annoyance.
今天錯過了火車,真是讓人不愉快。

anthem
['ænθəm]

n 聖歌；國歌 a1077
America's national anthem is considered one of the most difficult to sing.
美國的國歌是公認的最難唱的國歌之一。

antibiotic
[,æntibai'ɑtik]

adj （含）抗生素的 a1078
Remember to apply an antibiotic cream to the open cut on your finger.
記得在你手指頭那個開放傷口上抹抗生素藥膏。

anticipate
[æn'tisə,pet]

vt 預料,期望；預先考慮；搶先 a1079
The children were eagerly anticipating Christmas.
孩子們在熱切地盼望著耶誕節的到來。

anticipation
[æn,tisə'peʃən]

n 盼望；預期,期待；預料,預測 a1080
Taylor's family waited in anticipation of his safe return.
泰勒的家人在期待中等待他平安歸來。

antique
[æn'tik]

adj 古式的；過時的 a1081
My grandmother showed me some nice antique furniture kept in the attic.
奶奶給我看了存放在閣樓裡的一些很好的古董傢俱。

antique
[æn'tik]
托 雅 學

n 有價值的古物，古董
Jenny was delighted to find that her jade bracelet was a valuable antique.
珍妮欣喜地發現自己的玉鐲是一件值錢的古董。

a1082

anxious
['æŋkʃəs]
托 雅 學

adj 焦慮的，擔心的；（急切）渴望的
She was anxious to make a good dinner in order to impress her mother-in-law.
她急於做一頓像樣的飯菜，以便給婆婆留下一個好印象。

a1083

apparent
[ə'pærənt]
托 雅 學

adj 表面上的；顯然的
The impact of global warming on climate change has become more and more apparent.
全球暖化對氣候變化的影響已經越來越明顯了。

a1084

appeal
[ə'pil]
托 雅 學

n 呼籲；申訴；吸引力
Van Gogh's bright colors and dramatic brush strokes explain a lot of his enduring appeal to art lovers.
明快的色彩和誇張的畫法是梵谷的畫作能夠長期吸引藝術品愛好者的主要原因。

a1085

appeal
[ə'pil]
托 雅 學

vi 懇求；訴諸；有吸引力，迎合愛好
The lawyer appealed to sympathy of the jury, trying to make them feel sorry for the victim.
律師訴諸陪審團的同情心，試圖讓他們為受害者感到難過。

a1086

appendix
[ə'pɛndɪks]
托 雅 學

n 附錄，附屬物；闌尾，盲腸
The book contained a helpful appendix on the history of botany.
這本書包含了一個非常有用的植物學歷史附錄。

a1087

appetite
['æpə,taɪt]
托 雅 學

n 食欲；欲望，性欲；愛好，趣味
Her appetite returned suddenly after her fever broke, and she ate a large breakfast.
她燒退以後突然有了食欲，早餐吃了很多。

a1088

applaud
[ə'plɔd]
托 雅 學

vi/vt 鼓掌歡迎；贊同
The performance was so good that the audience applauded for 15 minutes.
表演如此精彩，以至於觀眾鼓掌長達15分鐘。

a1089

appliance
[ə'plaɪəns]
托 雅 學

n 電器；器械，裝置；應用，適用
A washing machine and drier are usually a young couple's first large appliance purchase.
洗衣機和烘乾機通常是年輕夫婦首先購買的大型電器。

a1090

A

appreciable
[əˈpriʃɪəbl]

`adj` 可估價的；可察覺的

Real estate, bonds, stocks and gold, to name a few, are good examples of appreciable assets.

房地產、債券、股票與黃金等都是可估價資產很好的例子。

a1091

appreciate
[əˈpriʃɪˌet]

托 雅 學

`vt` 為⋯表示感激；欣賞，評價

Jonathan could appreciate fine wines and cheeses.

喬納森會鑑賞名酒和起司。

a1092

appreciation
[ə͵priʃɪˈeʃən]

托 雅 學

`n` 感激

We showed our appreciation to our teacher with flowers.

我們對老師獻上鮮花表示感謝。

a1093

appreciation
[ə͵priʃɪˈeʃən]

托 雅 學

`n` 欣賞；鑒別

The audience showed their appreciation for the extraordinary performance.

觀眾表達了他們對精彩演出的欣賞。

a1094

approach
[əˈprotʃ]

托 雅 學

`n` 接近；途徑，方式

Jane's approach to teaching violin differed a great deal from the norm.

珍教授小提琴的方法和一般標準大不相同。

a1095

approach
[əˈprotʃ]

托 雅 學

`vi/vt` 靠近，接近；找⋯商量；著手處理，開始對付

I always approached my father when I had difficulty in life.

當我在生活中遭遇困境時，總是找爸爸商量。

a1096

appropriate
[əˈproprɪˌet]

托 雅 學

`adj` 適當的，恰當的

Bathing suits are only appropriate in the pool or on the beach.

泳裝只適合在泳池或海灘穿。

a1097

appropriate
[əˈproprɪˌet]

托 雅 學

`vt` 撥給；挪用（資源）

The board of directors appropriated funds for the research project.

董事會撥了資金給研究計畫。

a1098

approval
[əˈpruvl]

托 雅 學

`n` 批准，通過；贊成

The politician's approval rate fell sharply after the scandal.

醜聞過後，這位政界人士的支持率急劇下降。

a1099

approximate
[ə'prɑksəmɪt]

adj 近似的

He calculated the approximate number of drinks they would need for the family picnic.

他計算了一下全家野餐大約需要的飲料數量。

a1100

approximate
[ə'prɑksəmɪt]

vi 接近

The results of the study approximated to what was expected.

研究的最後結果接近原先的預期。

a1101

approximately
[ə'prɑksəmɪtlɪ]

adv 近似地，大約

There are approximately 300 international students in the school.

這所學校大約有三百名國際學生。

a1102

aquarium
[ə'kwɛrɪəm]

n 水族館

The new aquarium held salt-water fish.

新的水族館裡養著鹹水魚類。

a1103

arch(=arc)
[ɑrtʃ= (ɑrk)]

n 拱門

There is a wooden arch over the entrance of the church.

教堂的入口處有一個木質拱門。

a1104

arch(=arc)
[ɑrtʃ= (ɑrk)]

vt 用拱連接；拱起

A cat hisses and arches its back to make itself appear larger when faced with a threat.

貓在面對威脅時，會嘶叫並將背部拱起，好讓自己看來更大。

a1105

archaeology
[ˌɑrkɪ'ɑlədʒɪ]

n 考古學

Archaeology involves the search for material evidence of ancient groups and tribes.

考古學包含尋找古代族群和部落的實質證據。

a1106

architect
['ɑrkə,tɛkt]

n 建築師；設計師；創造者

The architect redrew the plans to account for the changes in topography.

建築師重新繪製了規劃圖，以說明地形上的變化。

a1107

architecture
['ɑrkə,tɛktʃɚ]

n 建築學；建築式樣（或風格）；建築物

Morgan loved the architecture of old churches.

摩根喜歡古教堂的建築風格。

a1108

arena
[ə'rinə]
托 雅 學

n （體育比賽或表演用的）場地，競技場；劇場　　a1109
My son is learning to ice skate at the hockey arena.
我兒子在曲棍球場上學習溜冰。

array
[ə're]
托 雅 學

n 佇列，排列　　a1110
The Oscar Show featured an array of famous guests and impressive performances.
奧斯卡晚會以著名的嘉賓和精彩的演出為特色。

array
[ə're]
托 雅 學

vt 列陣；裝扮；排列　　a1111
She has always arrayed herself in her best clothes for the most important events of the year.
她向來在年度重要場合盛裝赴會。

artificial
[ˌɑrtə'fɪʃəl]
托 雅 學

adj 人工的；虛偽的，做作的　　a1112
His artificial leg had a specially designed spring that helped him walk more normally.
他的義肢上裝有專門設計的彈簧，使他走起路來更像正常人。

artistic
[ɑr'tɪstɪk]
托 雅 學

adj 藝術的，美術的；善於藝術創作的　　a1113
You need to be artistic enough to create this piece.
要很有藝術氣息才能創造出這樣的作品。

aspect
['æspɛkt]
托 雅 學

n 外表，面貌；（問題等的）面向　　a1114
He'd never encountered this aspect of her character before.
他以前從未發現她性格的這一面。

assign
[ə'saɪn]
托 雅 學

vt 分配；指定（時間、地點等）　　a1115
Gary never assigned too much homework to his students.
蓋瑞從不給學生指派過多作業。

assist
[ə'sɪst]
托 雅 學

vi/vt 協助；促進　　a1116
She assisted him with his chores so they could go play sooner.
她幫他做些家事，這樣他們就可以早點兒去玩了。

assistance
[ə'sɪstəns]
托 雅 學

n 協作；援助　　a1117
Your professional teaching assistance improved the class a lot.
你專業的教學協助使這個班級進步很多。

associate
[ə'soʃɪet]

托 雅 學

adj 聯合的；副位的
Wendy works as an associate attorney at that law office.
溫蒂在那家律師事務所當助理律師。

a1118

associate
[ə'soʃɪet]

托 雅 學

n 夥伴
James and I have been business associates for over 20 years.
詹姆士和我是二十多年的業務夥伴了。

a1119

associate
[ə'soʃɪet]

托 雅 學

vi/vt 聯想；聯結；交往
Bob is a business partner that everyone wants to associate with.
鮑伯是個大家都想結交的工作夥伴。

a1120

association
[ə,sosɪ'eʃən]

托 雅 學

n 聯想；聯結；交往
They joined a professional association to gain new opportunities for professional development.
他們加入了職業協會，以便獲得新的職業發展機會。

a1121

assorted
[ə'sɔrtɪd]

托 雅 學

adj 各種各樣的；混雜的；組合的
Please pick up some assorted pastries for the party tonight.
請為今晚的派對挑選各種不同口味的酥皮點心。

a1122

assume
[ə'sjum]

托 雅 學

vt 假想；承擔；採取
Dave assumed that the game would be on later that evening.
大衛猜想比賽會在那晚遲些時候開始。

a1123

assumption
[ə'sʌmpʃən]

托 雅 學

n 假設；承擔；採取；推測
He made a bold assumption that his girlfriend would agree to his proposal however he did it.
他大膽地設想無論怎麼求婚，他女朋友都會答應。

a1124

assurance
[ə'ʃʊrəns]

托 雅 學

n 保證，擔保；財產轉讓書；確信，斷言；信心，信念
Cindy's self-assurance was one of her most attractive features.
辛蒂的自信是她最迷人的特點之一。

a1125

assure
[ə'ʃʊr]

托 雅 學

vt 使確信，使放心；向…保證
Who can assure me of the safety of this new high speed rail?
誰能向我保證新高鐵的安全性呢？

a1126

astronomy
[əs'trɑnəmɪ]

a1127

n 天文學

We explored astronomy and other space related topics in the science camp.

我們在科學營探索天文學和其他與太空相關的話題。

attach
[ə'tætʃ]

a1128

vt 連接，連為一體；使依戀

He attached a small letter to the package.

他在包裹上附了一封短信。

attachment
[ə'tætʃmənt]

a1129

n 連接物；附件

A computer virus can spread via an attachment that is included in an e-mail.

電腦病毒可以通過電子郵件的附件散佈。

attempt
[ə'tɛmpt]

a1130

n/vt 企圖，試圖

The thief attempted to run away from the police.

小偷試圖從警方手中逃跑。

attitude
['ætətjud]

a1131

n 態度，看法；姿勢

Her attitude improved enormously after her vacation.

她度假回來後態度有了很大的改變。

attractive
[ə'træktɪv]

a1132

adj 引人注意的；迷人的

Most people thought Kayla was exceptionally attractive tonight.

大多數人認為凱拉今晚格外迷人。

audience
['ɔdɪəns]

a1133

n 聽眾，觀眾；讀者

The audience sat in rapt attention to the ballerina's dance.

在座觀眾全神貫注地欣賞著芭蕾舞者的舞蹈。

auditorium
[,ɔdə'torɪəm]

a1134

n 觀眾席，聽眾席；會堂，禮堂

The auditorium was large enough for the whole class to watch the performance.

那觀眾席足以容納整個班級觀賞表演。

authentic
[ɔ'θɛntɪk]

a1135

adj 真實的；可靠的，有根據的；真正的

Authentic leather may be more expensive, but the quality is higher.

真皮可能會更貴一些，但品質也更好。

author
['ɔθɚ]
托 雅 學

n 作者，著作人
The author wrote seven books in the series, with each one becoming more popular than the last.
這個系列作者共寫了七本書，一本比一本暢銷。

a1136

authority
[ə'θɔrətɪ]
托 雅 學

n 權力；權威（人士）；職權
She had studied her subject well, so she spoke with authority.
她學習成績好，所以說話很有權威。

a1137

authorize
['ɔθə,raɪz]
托 雅 學

vt 授權；批准，認可
Their boss had authorized the purchase of the materials beforehand.
他們的老闆事先批准了材料採購。

a1138

automobile
['ɔtəmə,bɪl]
托 雅 學

n 汽車，機動車
His automobile was at least 20 years old.
他的車至少買了二十年了。

a1139

availability
[ə,velə'bɪlətɪ]
托 雅 學

n 有效（性）；可得性
The senior and elderly populations are on the rise nowadays thanks to the availability of better medical treatment and care.
由於獲得更好的醫療與照顧，中年人口近年來持續增長。

a1140

available
[ə'veləbl]
托 雅 學

adj 可用的，可得到的
That brand of paper towel is no longer available.
那個品牌的紙巾已經買不到了。

a1141

28

B

字彙能力檢查表

先自我檢驗是否瞭解以下初階單字，若有不清楚者，請先開啟光碟中的電子書複習。

☐ bachelor	☐ basic	☐ blank	☐ bouquet
☐ background	☐ basis	☐ blanket	☐ bowl
☐ bacon	☐ bathe	☐ bleed	☐ brain
☐ badge	☐ battery	☐ bless	☐ breathe
☐ balance	☐ beat	☐ bless	☐ breeze
☐ bald	☐ beforehand	☐ blink	☐ breeze
☐ ballet	☐ behave	☐ block	☐ brief
☐ band	☐ belly	☐ bloom	☐ briefcase
☐ bandage	☐ belongings	☐ blossom	☐ brilliant
☐ bang	☐ beloved	☐ boil	☐ broaden
☐ bankrupt	☐ bend	☐ bold	☐ bubble
☐ banner	☐ beneficial	☐ bonus	☐ bucket
☐ bar	☐ bet	☐ book	☐ buckle
☐ barbecue	☐ bill	☐ bookkeeper	☐ bud
☐ bare	☐ billion	☐ booklet	☐ buffet
☐ bare	☐ bind	☐ boom	☐ bull
☐ bargain	☐ biography	☐ boom	☐ bump
☐ bargain	☐ bite	☐ booth	☐ bundle
☐ bark	☐ bitter	☐ bore	☐ bundle
☐ barn	☐ bitterness	☐ bore	☐ bush
☐ basement	☐ blame	☐ bother	☐ buzz

bait
[bet]
托 雅 學

vt 安裝誘餌

Tommy said he would bait his fishing hook with a worm.

湯米說他要用蟲子給魚鉤安裝誘餌。

b1001

balcony
['bælkənɪ]
托 雅 學

n 陽臺；表演廳等的樓座、包廂

They enjoyed watching the sunset on the balcony.

他們喜歡在陽臺上看落日。

b1002

ban
[bæn]
托 雅 學

n 禁止，禁令；**vt** 取締，查禁，禁止

Some countries ban alcohol consumption.

某些國家禁止酒精消費。

b1003

bankruptcy
['bæŋkrəptsɪ]
托 雅 學

n 倒閉；破產

Edward declared bankruptcy four times before he finally succeeded in business.

愛德華曾四次宣佈破產，之後才最終在生意上取得了成功。

b1004

banquet
['bæŋkwɪt]
托 雅 學

vi/vt 參加宴會；宴請；**n** （正式的）宴會

The guests banqueted on the delightful food prepared for them.

參加宴席的客人享用著為他們準備的美味佳餚。

b1005

barcode
['bɑrkod]
托 雅 學

n 條碼

A barcode is a machine-readable representation of data, most often used to mark the price of an object for sale.

條碼是機器可讀取的數據標示，最常用於標記銷售物品的價格。

b1006

barely
['bɛrlɪ]
托 雅 學

adv 無遮蔽地；僅僅，勉強（湊數）

She barely managed to finish her homework before the due date.

她勉強在截止日期前完成了她的家庭作業。

b1007

barrel
['bærəl]
托 雅 學

n 桶；槍管，炮管

She stored the apple harvest in barrels in the barn.

她把收穫的蘋果儲藏在穀倉的桶裡。

b1008

barrier
['bærɪr]
托 雅 學

n 柵欄；屏障，障礙（物）

The levees acted as a barrier to the increasing water levels in the river.

這些防洪堤是河裡不斷升高的水位的一道屏障。

b1009

B

batch
[bætʃ]
托 雅 學

b1010

vt 分批次處理；**n** 一批，一組，一群
Ed, please batch all the chicken eggs and box them.
艾德，請將所有的雞蛋分批次處理並裝盒。

beam
[bim]
托 雅 學

b1011

n（橫）梁，桁條；光束；**vi** 發光，發熱
The beam of the car headlights are preventing me from
seeing clearly.
車的前大燈的光讓我看不太清楚。

beam
[bim]
托 雅 學

b1012

vi 微笑
Her proud mother beamed at her daughter at the award
ceremony.
她自豪的母親在頒獎典禮上對著她的女兒微笑。

bean
[bin]
托 雅 學

b1013

vt 擊中（人的頭部）
Peter was beaned on the head with a broom.
彼得被掃帚戳中了頭部。

bear
[bɛr]
托 雅 學

b1014

vi 忍受，容忍；負擔
I can't bear to see you being laughed at like this.
我不忍看你像這樣被嘲笑。

behalf
[bɪ'hæf]
托 雅 學

b1015

n 利益；代表
The spokesman apologized to the public on behalf of the
company.
這個發言人代表公司向大眾道歉。

benefit
['bɛnəfɪt]
托 雅 學

b1016

n 利益，好處，恩惠；**vt** 有益於；受益
Throwing garbage in the ocean benefits no one.
把垃圾丟進海裡對任何人都沒有益處。

beverage
['bɛvərɪdʒ]
托 雅 學

b1017

n（水、酒等之外的）飲料
She made a hot beverage to help calm herself after all the
excitement.
她給自己沖了杯熱飲，幫助平復激動的情緒。

bid
[bɪd]
托 雅 學

b1018

n 出價，投標；**vi** 報價，投標
Quite a few construction companies are bidding for the
contract.
很多家建築公司都在參與這個合同的競標。

bin
[bɪn]

托 雅 學

n （貯藏食物等用的）箱子

A storage bin helps me keep my paint supplies organized.

儲存箱讓我將繪圖工具整理的井然有序。

b1019

biology
[baɪˈɑlədʒɪ]

托 雅 學

n 生物學

Cellular biology has taken several huge leaps in the last century.

細胞生物學在過去的一百年裡已經有了幾次重大飛躍。

b1020

blast
[blæst]

托 雅 學

n 一陣（風）；爆炸；衝擊波；管樂器聲

The blast of the bomb destroyed the entire building.

炸彈的爆炸把整棟建築物都毀了。

b1021

blast
[blæst]

托 雅 學

vt 爆炸；徹底毀掉

Randy's bad test scores blasted his chance to get into college.

蘭迪極差的考試成績徹底毀掉了他進入大學的機會。

b1022

blaze
[blez]

托 雅 學

n 火焰；閃光；vi 燃燒，冒火焰；閃光

When she found her husband had cheated on her, her eyes were blazing with fury.

當她發現丈夫出軌時，她的眼中冒著憤怒之火。

b1023

blend
[blɛnd]

托 雅 學

n 混合（物）

Cafes often have their own special blend for their coffee.

咖啡廳經常有他們特別調製的咖啡。

b1024

blend
[blɛnd]

托 雅 學

vi/vt 混合，混雜

Red and blue blend to make purple.

紅色和藍色混合會變成紫色。

b1025

blur
[blɝ]

托 雅 學

n 模糊不清的事物；汙點

If I forget to wear my glasses, everything is a blur.

如果我忘了戴眼鏡，所有東西看起來都一片模糊。

b1026

blur
[blɝ]

托 雅 學

vt 使模糊；玷污

We should not let personal factors blur our judgments.

我們不應該讓個人因素模糊了自己的判斷。

b1027

B

blush
[blʌʃ]
托 雅 學

n 臉紅；**vi** 臉紅，害臊　　　　　b1028

She blushed when her friend pointed out that she had her shirt inside out.

當她的朋友指出她衣服穿反了時，她臉紅了。

board
[bord]
托 雅 學

vi/vt 供…膳食，住宿　　　　　b1029

She finally decided on which homestay family she will board with when she went to Canada.

她終於決定去加拿大時要寄宿的家庭。

bond
[bɑnd]
托 雅 學

n 結合力，黏結劑；公債，契約；鐐銬；束縛　　　b1030

The bond of friendship can be tested if you and your friend are in times of need.

如果你與朋友共患難，就可以檢測出你們友誼的凝聚力。

boost
[bust]
托 雅 學

n 提升，增加；抬高（價格）；支援　　　b1031

Can you please give my dead car battery a boost with your jumper cables?

可以請你用充電電線幫我沒電的汽車電瓶快速增電嗎？

boost
[bust]
托 雅 學

vt 提升，增加；抬價；支援　　　b1032

Jenny boosted her business by selling her merchandise overseas.

珍妮通過販賣商品至海外來增加她的業務。

border
['bɔrdə]
托 雅 學

n 邊界，國界；邊沿；**vt** 交界，與…接壤；接近　　b1033

Lisa's yard was bordered with fences and vines.

莉莎的後院用籬笆與藤蔓圍住了。

bounce
[baʊns]
托 雅 學

n 彈力　　　　　b1034

The soccer ball was so old that it had no bounce left.

那個足球太舊了，以至於沒有剩下任何彈力。

bounce
[baʊns]
托 雅 學

vt 彈起，彈回；跳起　　　　　b1035

Jimmy bounced the basketball between his legs.

吉米在兩腿間反復拍著籃球。

bound
[baʊnd]
托 雅 學

adj 被束縛的；一定的　　　　　b1036

You are bound to tell only the truth in the court.

你一定要在法庭上說出實話。

bound
[baʊnd]
托 雅 學

n/vi 跳躍
Deer can often bound over fences and bushes.
鹿經常能跳過籬笆與灌木。

b1037

bowel
['baʊəl]
托 雅 學

n 腸；排便
Horses develop a condition known as colic when their bowels become obstructed.
當馬的排便受阻時，它們便患了一種被稱作疝氣的病。

b1038

brace
[bres]
托 雅 學

n 托架，支柱；vi/vt 使防備；使…繃緊，撐牢
I braced the bench with four more legs; it should be firm and solid now.
我在長凳上加裝了四條腿來支撐；它現在應該堅固緊實了。

b1039

brake
[brek]
托 雅 學

n 閘；煞車；抑制
He slammed on the brakes as a deer jumped to the front of his car.
他猛踩了一下煞車，因為一隻鹿跳到了他的車前面。

b1040

branch
[bræntʃ]
托 雅 學

n 分支，支流；分店；分科，部門
The company has branches all over the world.
這家公司在全世界都有分公司。

b1041

breakdown
['brek,daʊn]
托 雅 學

n 崩潰；衰竭；中斷；倒塌；失敗
She had a mental breakdown when she received her husband's death news in a letter.
當她在信中收到丈夫的死訊時完全精神崩潰了。

b1042

breakthrough
['brek,θru]
托 雅 學

n 突破；突破性進展
It was a delightful breakthrough for my dad to improve his health by quitting smoking.
我父親令人高興的突破是透過戒煙來改善他的健康。

b1043

breathtaking
['brεθ,tekɪŋ]
托 雅 學

adj 驚人的，令人驚歎的，驚艷的
The Canadian Rockies attract many tourists every year because of the breathtaking scenery.
加拿大落磯山脈以其令人驚嘆的優美風景每年都吸引著大量遊客。

b1044

breed
[brid]
托 雅 學

n 品種
My cat is the same breed as yours.
我的貓跟你的是同一個品種。

b1045

B

breed
[brid]
托 雅 學

b1046

vi/vt 使…繁殖；產生；教養，撫養
Many animals breed only once a year.
很多動物一年只交配繁殖一次。

brew
[bru]
托 雅 學

b1047

vt 釀造，泡，調製
Marianne will brew a nice pot of hot tea.
瑪麗安要泡壺熱騰騰的好茶。

bribe
[braɪb]
托 雅 學

b1048

n 賄賂（物）
The official was involved in the scandal of taking bribes.
這官員深陷收受賄賂的醜聞中。

bribe
[braɪb]
托 雅 學

b1049

vt 向…行賄，買通
They bribed the customs officers in order to bring in more alcohol and cigarettes.
他們為了帶更多的煙酒入境而賄賂了海關人員。

brittle
['brɪtl]
托 雅 學

b1050

adj 易碎的；脆弱的；冷淡的；（聲音）尖利的
Crystal ware is very brittle and must be handled with care.
水晶器皿非常易碎，必須小心使用。

broadcast
['brɔd,kæst]
托 雅 學

b1051

n 廣播；廣播節目；**vt** 廣播
This radio station broadcasts the news for 15 minutes every hour.
這個電臺每個小時廣播十五分鐘的新聞。

brochure
[bro'ʃʊr]
托 雅 學

b1052

n 小冊子
All of the information, along with the photos, is included in the printed brochure.
所有的資訊及相片都包含在印刷的小冊子上。

bronze
[branz]
托 雅 學

b1053

n 青銅（色），古銅色；青銅製品，銅牌
He won the bronze medal in swimming in the Olympics.
他在奧林匹克游泳項目裡得到銅牌。

browse
[braʊz]
托 雅 學

b1054

vi/vt （牲畜）吃（草或嫩枝）
The giraffes reached upward to browse the bushes.
長頸鹿向上伸長頸子在樹叢上吃嫩草。

browse
[braʊz]
托 雅 學

vi/vt 瀏覽
More and more people browse through the Internet with their smart phones while they wait.
愈來愈多的人在等待的時候用智慧型手機上網瀏覽網頁。

b1055

bruise
[bruz]
托 雅 學

n 青腫；挫傷；傷痕；**vt** 使…受瘀傷；挫傷
That nighttime job had hurt his health and bruised his ego.
那個夜間工作損害了他的健康，也傷害了他的自我。

b1056

brutal
['brutl]
托 雅 學

adj 殘酷的；不講理的，野蠻的
Boxing is a brutal sport and only for the brave.
拳擊是一項只適合勇敢者的殘酷的運動。

b1057

buck
[bʌk]
托 雅 學

n 莊家標誌，責任
Sam said he wasn't going to pass the buck so he fixed the problem.
山姆說他不想推卸責任，所以他解決了那個問題。

b1058

budget
['bʌdʒɪt]
托 雅 學

vi 做預算
By budgeting carefully, we can afford the house.
如果小心謹慎地做預算，我們能買得起這棟房子。

b1059

bug
[bʌg]
托 雅 學

n 臭蟲；小毛病；竊聽器
If you don't clean up the kitchen regularly, there will be little bugs living everywhere.
如果你沒有定時地打掃廚房，就會有小蟲子到處住在裡面。

b1060

bug
[bʌg]
托 雅 學

vt 裝置竊聽器；困擾
The telephones in the Mayor's office were bugged.
市長辦公室的電話被竊聽了。

b1061

bulk
[bʌlk]
托 雅 學

n 體積；主體；大批，大量
The bulk of participants agreed to attend the banquet that evening.
大批參與者都同意參加那天的晚宴。

b1062

bulletin
['bʊlətɪn]
托 雅 學

n 公報，公告
She added his announcements to the bulletin.
她把他的告示加入到了公報中。

b1063

B

bully
['bʊlɪ]

托 雅 學

n 恃強欺弱者，小流氓；vt 威脅，欺侮

b1064

Wilson finally stood up to the bully and made him stop picking on his friend.

威爾森最終站出來面對惡霸，讓他不要再欺負他的朋友。

burial
['bɛrɪəl]

托 雅 學

n 埋葬，埋藏

b1065

Victoria flew to attend the burial of her grandfather.

維多利亞乘飛機去參加她祖父的葬禮。

butcher
['bʊtʃə]

托 雅 學

n 屠夫，賣肉者

b1066

The butcher measured out 5 pounds of steak for her.

屠夫給她秤了五磅牛排。

C

字彙能力檢查表

先自我檢驗是否瞭解以下初階單字，若有不清楚者，請先開啟光碟中的電子書複習。

☐cabin	☐charge	☐collective	☐couple
☐cabinet	☐charge	☐college	☐coupon
☐cabinet	☐charm	☐colonial	☐courier
☐cable	☐chart	☐colonial	☐coverage
☐cable	☐checkup	☐colonialism	☐coward
☐cafeteria	☐chef	☐colony	☐coworker
☐calculate	☐chic	☐column	☐crack
☐calculation	☐chief	☐column	☐crack
☐calculator	☐chief	☐combine	☐cradle
☐calendar	☐chill	☐comet	☐craft
☐campus	☐chill	☐comic	☐crane
☐cancel	☐chip	☐common	☐crash
☐cane	☐chip	☐communicate	☐crawl
☐cannon	☐choir	☐communication	☐create
☐canvas	☐choke	☐company	☐creation
☐capable	☐choppy	☐comparative	☐creative
☐cape	☐chord	☐compare	☐credit
☐cape	☐chore	☐compare	☐credit
☐capital	☐chorus	☐comparison	☐credit
☐capsule	☐chunk	☐compass	☐credit
☐captain	☐circus	☐complain	☐creep
☐cardinal	☐citizen	☐complaint	☐creep
☐carpenter	☐citizenship	☐complete	☐cricket
☐carton	☐civic	☐concentrate	☐cripple
☐cartoon	☐civil	☐concentration	☐cripple

C

- carve
- cast
- cast
- cast
- casual
- casually
- catalog
- catching
- category
- cater
- catering
- caution
- caution
- cautious
- cavity
- cavity
- cellar
- cement
- cement
- cemetery
- century
- ceramic
- cereal
- ceremony
- certainty
- certificate
- certification
- chant
- chapel
- charge

- clam
- clamp
- clash
- clasp
- classic
- classic
- classical
- clay
- clearance
- click
- client
- climate
- climate
- cling
- clinic
- clinical
- clip
- clip
- closet
- closet
- clue
- clumsy
- coach
- coarse
- cocaine
- coin
- colleague
- collect
- collection
- collective

- concern
- conclude
- conclude
- conclusion
- concrete
- concrete
- confidence
- confidence
- confident
- confuse
- confusion
- congratulate
- congratulation
- conquer
- conqueror
- consent
- consider
- considerable
- considerably
- considerate
- consideration
- considering
- constant
- constantly
- container
- contribute
- contribution
- corner
- couch
- couch

- crisp
- crooked
- crossing
- crowd
- cruel
- cruelty
- cruise
- cruise
- crumb
- crush
- crush
- crust
- crystal
- cube
- cucumber
- cupboard
- curb
- curb
- curiosity
- curious
- current
- current
- currently
- curse
- curve
- cushion
- cute
- cycle
- cyclist
- cylinder

campaign
[kæm'pen]
托 雅 學

n 戰役；運動
Working on the campaign was one of the most exciting experiences in her life.
為競選活動出力是她一生中最令人激動的經歷之一。

c1001

canal
[kə'næl]
托 雅 學

n 運河；（溝）渠
The Panama Canal greatly shortened the shipping routes between the Atlantic and Pacific Oceans.
巴拿馬運河大大縮短了大西洋和太平洋之間的航線。

c1002

capacity
[kə'pæsətı]
托 雅 學

n 容量；能量；能力；接受力
The capacity of the ship was only large enough to transport half the cargo.
輪船的承載量只夠運載一半貨物。

c1003

capture
['kæptʃə]
托 雅 學

n 俘虜；戰利品；獎品
The capture of the burglar was recorded by the police video.
警方的錄影記錄了小偷被抓的整個過程。

c1004

capture
['kæptʃə]
托 雅 學

vt 捕獲，俘虜；奪得，攻佔
The scientists were able to capture several specimens of the new species.
科學家們收集到了這個新物種的幾個標本。

c1005

career
[kə'rır]
托 雅 學

n （終身的）職業；經歷
Whatever career you decide on, please make sure you use your best talents.
不論你最後選擇什麼職業，都請你充分發揮自己的才能。

c1006

cargo
['kargo]
托 雅 學

n 船貨，貨物
Ben secured the cargo in the ship's hull.
本把貨物放在船身以確保安全。

c1007

carnival
['karnəvḷ]
托 雅 學

n 狂歡（節）；嘉年華會
They spent the afternoon at the carnival.
他們下午在狂歡節上度過。

c1008

carrier
['kærɪə]
托 雅 學

n 搬運人，送信人；載體，媒介物；航空母艦
Rats are often carriers of infectious diseases.
老鼠經常是傳染病的載體。

c1009

cashier
[kæ'ʃɪr]
托 雅 學

n 收銀員，出納員
She worked as a cashier for a few months before she moved up to manager.
她先當了幾個月的收銀員，然後才晉升為經理。

c1010

casualty
['kæʒjʊəltɪ]
托 雅 學

n 傷亡人員；受害人；損失的東西；急診室
The colonel was thankful that the casualty reports weren't high.
傷亡人數不算高，上校對此表示感恩。

c1011

cease
[sis]
托 雅 學

n 停止，中止
John worked on his biology project all night without ceasing.
約翰整晚都在做他的生物研究專案，沒停下來過。

c1012

cease
[sis]
托 雅 學

vt 停止，中止
The loud noise coming from the neighbor's house had ceased before the police arrived.
鄰居房子裡傳來的巨大噪音在員警到達之前就停了。

c1013

celebrate
['sɛlə,bret]
托 雅 學

vt 慶祝，過節；頌揚，讚美
Let's all celebrate the New Year together with some singing and dancing.
讓我們一起唱歌跳舞來慶祝新年吧。

c1014

celebration
[,sɛlə'breʃən]
托 雅 學

n 慶祝，過節；頌揚，讚美
Best Teacher nomination was the reason for celebration.
最佳教師提名是慶祝的原因。

c1015

celebrity
[sɪ'lɛbrətɪ]
托 雅 學

n 名人，名流；著名，名聲
Daniel Radcliffe became an international celebrity after starring in the Harry Potter movie series.
在主演「哈利波特」系列電影後，丹尼爾·雷德克裡夫變成了一位國際名人。

c1016

challenge
['tʃælɪndʒ]
托 雅 學

n 挑戰（書）；艱巨任務，難題；vt 向…挑戰
He was sure the boxing champion would challenge him to a rematch.
他很確定拳擊冠軍會挑戰他，要求再賽一場。

c1017

chamber
['tʃembɚ]
托 雅 學

n 室；會議室；議院；（動物體內的）腔室
The judge ordered both lawyers to meet him in his chamber.
法官命令兩位律師都到他的法官室去見他。

c1018

champagne
['ʃæm'pen]

托 雅 學

n 香檳酒；微黃色
They ordered champagne for their anniversary.
他們為周年紀念日訂購了香檳。

c1019

champion
['tʃæmpɪən]

托 雅 學

n 冠軍，得勝者；擁護者，鬥士
They won the final series and became world champions.
他們贏了最後的系列賽，成了世界冠軍。

c1020

channel
['tʃænl]

托 雅 學

n 海峽，水道；頻道，波段；路線，途徑
She became so interested in the program that she never changed the channel.
她對這個節目太感興趣了，從不換頻道。

c1021

chaos
['keɑs]

托 雅 學

n 混亂；雜亂的一團
The mother told her sons to go back and straighten up the chaos in their bedroom.
媽媽告訴兒子們回去把臥室裡亂七八糟的東西整理一下。

c1022

chaotic
[ke'ɑtɪk]

托 雅 學

adj 混亂的，紊亂的
The meeting became chaotic, and they had to take a break to gather their thoughts.
會議陷入一片混亂，他們需要休息片刻整理一下思路。

c1023

character
['kærɪktə]

托 雅 學

n 性格；角色；字元
A man of good character would not be mean to others.
品德好的人是不會對別人刻薄的。

c1024

characteristic
[,kærəktə'rɪstɪk]

托 雅 學

adj 特有的，獨特的
This town is proud of the characteristic dish often associated with it.
小鎮以常與之聯想在一起的特色食物為豪。

c1025

characteristic
[,kærəktə'rɪstɪk]

托 雅 學

n 特徵，特性
A successful person must have the characteristic of being able to meet challenges.
成功人士必須具備的特徵是能夠面對挑戰。

c1026

characterize
['kærəktə,raɪz]

托 雅 學

vt 表示…的特性；描述…的特性
Friendliness and kindness are two traits that characterize the people in this unique town.
友善以及和藹是這個獨特小鎮裡居民的特性。

c1027

C

charity
['tʃærətɪ]

c1028

n 慈善（團體）；仁慈；施捨
He donated half of his lottery winnings to charity.
他把彩券獎金的一半捐給了慈善機構。

chase
[tʃes]

c1029

n 追逐，追求；**vi/vt** 追趕
If my horse escapes from the stable, I will have to chase after it immediately.
如果我的馬兒從馬廄中逃脫，我就必須立即追趕它。

cherish
['tʃɛrɪʃ]

c1030

vt 珍愛；懷有（感情）
Paul cherished the pictures of his kids and he carried with him on long business trips.
保羅珍視自己孩子的照片，他出差到很遠的地方時都隨身攜帶。

circuit
['sɝkɪt]

c1031

n 環行；周線；電路；**vi/vt** 環行，繞行
Light rail trains that circuit the city take you to most-visited tourist attractions.
環城的輕軌火車帶你到最常被造訪的觀光地點。

circular
['sɝkjələ]

c1032

adj 圓（形）的，環形的；迴圈的
Do you prefer the square table over the circular one?
你更喜歡方桌還是圓桌？

circulation
[,sɝkjə'leʃən]

c1033

n 迴圈；（貨幣等）流通
His blood circulation has improved a great deal since he began exercising.
他開始鍛煉之後，血液迴圈得到了很大改善。

circumstance
['sɝkəm,stæns]

c1034

n 情況；境遇
Circumstances had prevented him from going to college until now.
先前的條件不允許他上大學，直到現在才有所改變。

claim
[klem]

c1035

n 權利，所有權；索賠
She has a legitimate claim to the property.
她對那塊土地擁有合法所有權。

claim
[klem]

c1036

vt 要求；聲稱
He claimed that his child was innocent and not a criminal in any way.
他聲稱他的孩子是無辜的，無論如何絕非罪犯。

clarify
['klærə,faɪ]

vt 淨化   c1037

It is time consuming to clarify olive oil as it involves a long cold-press process.

淨化橄欖油很花時間,因為它包含了一個很長的冷壓過程。

clarify
['klærə,faɪ]

vt 澄清,闡明   c1038

Please clarify your instructions so that the group can fully understand your request.

請澄清你的指令,這樣小組成員才完全明白你的要求。

clarity
['klærətɪ]

n 清晰,明晰   c1039

She spoke with such clarity that many were convinced by her arguments.

她的講話非常清晰,許多人都對她的論據表示信服。

classification
[,klæsəfə'keʃən]

n 分類,分級   c1040

You can find the file under the classification of "current students".

你可以在「在讀學生」的分類下找到這個檔案。

classified
['klæsə,faɪd]

adj 分類的;機密的;**n** 分類廣告   c1041

Who is going to be responsible for the unauthorized disclosure of the classified document?

誰該為未經授權就揭露機密文件而負責?

classify
['klæsə,faɪ]

vt 分類,分等(級)   c1042

Please classify the reports based on whom they will be sent to.

請根據最後這些報告寄送的對象把他們分類出來。

clause
[klɔz]

n 條款;從句,分句   c1043

The landlord can't force you to abide by the lease if there is an illegal clause in it.

如果租房條約裡面有違法條款,房東就不能強制你遵守租約。

climax
['klaɪmæks]

n 頂點,高潮   c1044

Her aria was the climax of the opera.

她的詠歎調把歌劇推向了高潮。

cohesion
[ko'hiʒən]

n 凝聚;結合;內聚力   c1045

The church embodies an enviable cohesion of spiritual devotion and fellowship.

教堂體現出一種令人羨慕的精神奉獻和友誼的凝聚。

comedy
['kɑmədɪ]
托 雅 學

n 喜劇；喜劇性事件　　c1046
He chose to go to see a comedy with her on their first date.
第一次和她約會，他選擇去看喜劇片。

comment
['kɑmɛnt]
托 雅 學

n 注釋；評論，意見；vi 注釋；評論　　c1047
The news station will not comment on the situation until they confirm all the facts.
在他們確認所有事實前，新聞台不會對這個情況作評論。

commerce
['kɑmɝs]
托 雅 學

n 商業，貿易；社交　　c1048
The city council voted to spend more money on fixing the roads to increase commerce downtown.
市議會投票決定將更多的錢用於修建道路，以便促進市中心的商業發展。

commercial
[kə'mɝʃəl]
托 雅 學

adj 商業的，商務的；可獲利的　　c1049
Peter secured a commercial loan to make improvements to his restaurant.
彼得獲得了一筆商業貸款，以改善他的飯館。

commercial
[kə'mɝʃəl]
托 雅 學

n 廣告節目　　c1050
Did you see the commercial on television? It was so funny!
你在電視上看到了這個廣告嗎？它太搞笑了！

commission
[kə'mɪʃən]
托 雅 學

n 傭金　　c1051
Every sale Susan makes in the store will earn her a 10% commission.
在這個店裡，由蘇珊完成的每筆交易，她都能抽取10%的傭金。

commission
[kə'mɪʃən]
托 雅 學

n 委員會；委任；委託（書）　　c1052
The commission concluded that the politician had not violated ethics rules during the business transaction.
委員會的結論是，這位政治家在公司交易上沒有違背倫理道德。

commit
[kə'mɪt]
托 雅 學

vt 信奉；支持；獻身　　c1053
The artists committed themselves to the restoration of the old palace.
這些藝術家致力於這座古老王宮的重建。

commit
[kə'mɪt]
托 雅 學

vt 犯（錯誤），幹（壞事）　　c1054
More and more crimes are committed by young people.
越來越多的罪行都是年輕人犯下的。

commitment
[kə'mɪtmənt]
托 雅 學

n 承諾，保證，投入，獻身，承諾
James was known as a man who frequently honored his commitments.
大家都知道詹姆斯是個經常能兌現承諾的人。

c1055

---

committee
[kə'mɪtɪ]
托 雅 學

n 委員會，全體委員
The committee reached the final agreement after arguing for hours.
委員會在爭議了數小時後終於達成了最後共識。

c1056

---

community
[kə'mjunətɪ]
托 雅 學

n 同一地區的全體居民；社會，社區；共同體
Valerie enjoyed the company of the other inhabitants in her retirement community.
瓦萊麗喜歡她的退休社區其他居民的陪伴。

c1057

---

commute
[kə'mjut]
托 雅 學

vi 通勤
The young man is willing to commute long distances because he needs a job now.
這個年輕人願意長途通勤，因為他現在急需工作。

c1058

---

commute
[kə'mjut]
托 雅 學

vt 減（刑）；補充
The judge commuted his sentence towards the end of his life in view of his poor health.
考慮到他健康狀況很差，法官在他臨終前對他減輕了判刑。

c1059

---

comparable
['kɑmpərəbl]
托 雅 學

adj 可比較的；類似的；比得上的
As for the quality of life, Tokyo is not comparable to Helsinki given the drastic difference between both cities.
至於生活的品質，東京和赫爾辛基是無法比較的，因為兩座城市之間差異太大。

c1060

---

compensate
['kɑmpən,set]
托 雅 學

vt 補償，賠償
The family was compensated by the government for the damage to their property.
這家人財產受到的損失得到了政府的補償。

c1061

---

compensation
[,kɑmpən'seʃən]
托 雅 學

n 補償（或賠償）的款物；賠償
A generous insurance plan was included in his compensation package.
他的補償金計畫裡包括了一個數額不小的保險計畫。

c1062

---

competition
[,kɑmpə'tɪʃən]
托 雅 學

n 競爭，比賽；角逐，較量
The competition for the senior sales job was fierce.
高級銷售的職位競爭激烈。

c1063

---

competitive
[kəm'pɛtətɪv]

`adj` （價格等）有競爭力的 　　　　　`c1064`
Our competitive price is the major reason why our company ranks top in this industry.
具有競爭力的價格是我們公司在這個產業裡佔據龍頭老大的主要原因。

complementary
[ˌkɑmplə'mɛntərɪ]

`adj` 補充的；互補的，相配的 　　　　`c1065`
Given its flight cancellation, the airline offered me a free hotel stay as a complementary service.
因為取消班機，航空公司給我提供了免費的旅館住宿作為補償服務。

complex
['kɑmplɛks]

`adj` 複雜的；合成的，綜合的 　　　　`c1066`
Paul loved to figure out complex riddles.
保羅喜歡猜複雜的字謎。

complex
['kɑmplɛks]

`n` 聯合體 　　　　　　　　　　　　`c1067`
The apartment complex is now fully occupied.
這棟公寓大樓已經全數住滿。

complexion
['kɑmplɛks]

`n` 面色；面容 　　　　　　　　　　`c1068`
Ginny was able to clear her complexion by using a new brand of soap.
金妮用了一款新香皂，對膚色有所改善。

complexity
[kəm'plɛksətɪ]

`n` 複雜（性） 　　　　　　　　　　`c1069`
Due to the complexity of the dance, it took the performers several days to master it.
因為舞步複雜，舞者花了幾天才掌握它。

complicate
['kɑmplə,ket]

`vt` 使…複雜；使…難懂；使（疾病等）惡化 `c1070`
The afternoon was complicated by the breakdown of the car.
下午由於車子壞掉而麻煩不斷。

complicated
['kɑmplə,ketɪd]

`adj` 錯綜複雜的；麻煩的；難解的 　　`c1071`
It is a complicated mathematical equation.
這是一個很複雜的數學公式。

complication
[ˌkɑmplə'keʃən]

`n` 複雜，混亂 　　　　　　　　　　`c1072`
Breaking up with my boyfriend is just one more complication for me to deal with in my life.
和男朋友分手只是我生活中要處理的另一件難事罷了。

complication
[ˌkɑmpləˈkeʃən]
托 雅 學

n 併發症 `c1073`

Post-op complications are unpredictable, so all we can do now is pray for the best outcome.
手術後併發症是無法預測的，此時我們只能祈禱有最好的結果。

compliment
[ˈkɑmpləmənt]
托 雅 學

vt 讚美，祝賀 `c1074`

Amy blushed when Mark paid her a heartfelt compliment.
馬克衷心讚美了艾美，艾美紅了臉。

compose
[kəmˈpoz]
托 雅 學

vt 創作（詩歌等） `c1075`

He loved to compose poetry under his favorite tree.
他愛在最喜歡的樹下創作詩歌。

compose
[kəmˈpoz]
托 雅 學

vt 由…組成 `c1076`

The investigation committee is composed of four professors and four doctors.
這個調查委員會由四位教授和四位醫生組成。

compound
[ˈkɑmpaʊnd]
托 雅 學

adj 混合的，化合的；**n** 混合物，化合物 `c1077`

High fences and armed guards kept the secret compound secure.
高圍牆再加上武裝警衛保障了秘密化合物的安全。

compound
[kamˈpaʊnd]
托 雅 學

vi/vt 混合，摻和；使惡化 `c1078`

The accrued interest will compound with the principal on a mortgage debt.
應計利息將會隨著抵押貸款的本金而增加。

comprehend
[ˌkɑmprɪˈhɛnd]
托 雅 學

vt 瞭解，理解，領會 `c1079`

Randle comprehended things quickly and made good grades as a result.
蘭度理解事情很快，結果取得了好成績。

comprehensive
[ˌkɑmprɪˈhɛnsɪv]
托 雅 學

adj 內容廣泛的；總括性的，綜合的 `c1080`

We need a comprehensive survey before the goods go on sale.
在商品上市之前，我們需要一個廣泛的調查。

compromise
[ˈkɑmprəˌmaɪz]
托 雅 學

n 妥協，折衷；**vi/vt** 妥協，折衷，放棄（原則等） `c1081`

Okay, let's just agree to come to a fair compromise on the price difference.
好吧，我們合理地妥協價差吧。

C

compromise
['kɑmprəˌmaɪz]

托 雅 學

c1082

vt 危及

The company claims that they will not compromise safety in their search for cheaper auto parts.

這家公司強調，在尋求低價的汽車零件時絕不會犧牲其安全性。

---

compulsory
[kəm'pʌlsərɪ]

托 雅 學

c1083

adj 強迫的，義務的

The basic exams were compulsory for entering the college.

上大學必須參加基礎測試。

---

conceal
[kən'sil]

托 雅 學

c1084

vt 隱藏，隱瞞

Irene couldn't conceal her delight in the result of the game.

愛琳知道比賽結果後，難以掩飾自己的喜悅。

---

concept
['kɑnsɛpt]

托 雅 學

c1085

n 概念，觀念；設想

The concept for the car was simple and elegant.

此車的設計概念是古樸典雅。

---

conception
[kən'sɛpʃən]

托 雅 學

c1086

n 構思，理解

From its conception, the business plan was too complicated to implement successfully.

從構思上看，此商業計畫太複雜了，難以成功付諸實施。

---

concern
[kən'sɜ·n]

托 雅 學

c1087

vt 關注；擔憂

Our lack of preparation for the change really concerns me.

我們對事態的變化缺乏準備著實讓我擔心。

---

concise
[kən'saɪs]

托 雅 學

c1088

adj 簡潔的，簡短的

The economist gave a concise business report.

那位經濟學家做了一個簡潔的商業報告。

---

condemn
[kən'dɛm]

托 雅 學

c1089

vt 譴責；判刑，宣告有罪

Despite the damage the thief had caused to her house, she forgave him rather than condemned him.

儘管小偷對房屋造成了破壞，她還是原諒他而不譴責他。

---

condition
[kən'dɪʃən]

托 雅 學

c1090

n 條件；狀況，環境

Her fragile condition prevented her from being transferred to a bigger hospital.

她虛弱的身體狀況不允許她轉到大醫院。

condition
[kənˈdɪʃən]
托 雅 學

vt 決定；支配；訓練
His final payment is conditioned on whether he receives good service.
他最終的款項支付由他是否得到良好服務來決定。

c1091

conditioning
[kənˈdɪʃənɪŋ]
托 雅 學

adj 調節的，護理的
The hairdresser said to use this conditioning shampoo to make your hair soft and glossy.
髮型師說用這種潤絲洗髮精能夠使你的頭髮柔軟亮澤。

c1092

conduct
[ˈkandʌkt]
托 雅 學

n 行為，品行
His conduct was becoming of an officer of his rank.
他的行為逐漸與他高級職員的身份相稱。

c1093

conduct
[kənˈdʌkt]
托 雅 學

vt 引導；管理；指揮（樂隊）；傳導；表現，為人
She conducted herself with a great deal of dignity and courtesy at all times.
她行事一向端莊而謙恭。

c1094

conference
[ˈkanfərəns]
托 雅 學

n （正式）會議；討論，商談
Ben made a lot of new connections at the writers conference.
班在作家會議上建立了很多新的聯絡。

c1095

confess
[kənˈfɛs]
托 雅 學

vt 承認，坦白，懺悔
After being confronted by the witness, the suspect confessed his crime.
在受到目擊者的指證後，嫌疑犯供認了他的罪行。

c1096

confidential
[ˌkanfəˈdɛnʃəl]
托 雅 學

adj 秘密的；表示信任的
The medical records were kept strictly confidential.
醫療檔案嚴格保密。

c1097

confirm
[kənˈfɝm]
托 雅 學

vt 使更堅定、堅固；（進一步）證實；確認
Further testing confirmed that she had skin cancer.
進一步的檢測證實她患了皮膚癌。

c1098

confirmation
[ˌkanfəˈmeʃən]
托 雅 學

n 證實，確定；確認
You will get an e-mail confirmation shortly after completing the booking process.
在完成訂票手續之後不久你會接到一封電子郵件確認。

c1099

C

conflict
[ˈkɑnflɪkt]

n 鬥爭，抵觸，衝突　　c1100
The counselor was adept at helping his clients defuse conflicts and learn to work together.
顧問善於協助客戶解決爭端，學會與他人合作。

conflict
[kənˈflɪkt]
托 雅 學

vi 抵觸，衝突，矛盾　　c1101
The results of this research conflict with earlier findings.
這些研究結果與早期的發現相矛盾。

confront
[kənˈfrʌnt]
托 雅 學

vt 使面臨，使遭遇；面對（危險等）；使對質　　c1102
The reporter confronted the mayor about bribery at the city council meeting.
記者在市議會會議上就行賄問題向市長提問。

connect
[kəˈnɛkt]
托 雅 學

vi/vt 連接；與…聯繫，接通（電話）　　c1103
All the small towns in the mountain area are connected by bus services.
所有山區的小鎮都由公共汽車服務連接起來。

connection
[kəˈnɛkʃən]
托 雅 學

n 親戚；社會關係　　c1104
I got your name from one of my business connections.
我從生意上的一個客戶那裡知道了你的名字。

connection
[kəˈnɛkʃən]
托 雅 學

n 聯繫，連接　　c1105
The poor phone connection kept them from speaking long on the phone.
電話連接不暢使他們沒有打很久的電話。

conquest
[ˈkɑŋkwɛst]
托 雅 學

n 征服；征服地，掠取物　　c1106
The conquest of Britain cost the Romans many troops.
征服英國耗掉了羅馬人許多軍隊。

conscious
[ˈkɑnʃəs]

adj 意識到的，自覺的；神志清醒的　　c1107
He was conscious during the process since the doctor only used local anesthetic.
由於醫生只進行了局部麻醉，他整個過程都意識清醒。

consciousness
[ˈkɑnʃəsnɪs]

n 意識，覺悟；知覺　　c1108
Fred regained consciousness quickly after the surgery.
手術過後，福瑞德很快恢復了知覺。

consequent
['kɑnsə,kwɛnt]

adj 作為結果的；必然的　　　　　　　　　　c1109

After the rise in unemployment, there was a consequent decrease in foreign investments.

失業率上升後，外資減少是必然的結果。

consequently
['kɑnsə,kwɛntlɪ]

adv 結果，因此，所以　　　　　　　　　　c1110

The restaurant has increased the number of cooks and consequently they can serve faster now.

這家餐廳請了更多的廚師，因此現在上菜更快了。

conservative
[kən'sɝvətɪv]

adj 保守的，守舊的　　　　　　　　　　　c1111

She was very conservative in the way she dressed.

她穿衣服的風格非常保守。

conservative
[kən'sɝvətɪv]

n 保守主義者　　　　　　　　　　　　　c1112

The British politician is a conservative who opposes the reform bill.

這位英國政治家是一個反對改革法案的保守派分子。

conserve
[kən'sɝv]

vt 保存；保護；保守；守恆　　　　　　　c1113

The park rangers developed a plan to help conserve the native plant species.

公園管理者們推出一項計畫，幫助保護本地植物物種。

consist
[kən'sɪst]

vi 由…組成，由…構成　　　　　　　　　c1114

The salad consisted of seven different kinds of beans seasoned with vinegar.

沙拉由七種不同的豆子與醋調和而成。

consistent
[kən'sɪstənt]

adj 前後一致的，一致的，符合的　　　　c1115

His work was consistent with his previous reputation.

他的工作與他之前獲得的讚譽相符。

constitution
[,kɑnstə'tjuʃən]

n 構成，構造，組成（方式）；體格；憲法　c1116

The Constitution is the founding document of the United States of America.

美國憲法是美利堅合眾國的立國之法。

constrain
[kən'stren]

vt 強迫；限制，束縛；拘禁；壓制，抑制　c1117

The Navy Seals had to constrain their emotions while on their mission.

海豹部隊出去執行任務時須抑制他們的感情。

C

constraint
[kən'strent]

n 強迫，約束；強制力；限制

c1118

A mortgage puts somewhat of a constraint on most people's monthly budget.

抵押貸款對大部分人每個月的預算都造成了或多或少的限制。

construct
[kən'strʌkt]

vt 建設，建造，創立；**n** 概念

c1119

The boy constructed a house of cards while he waited for his father to return.

男孩等爸爸回來的時候，用卡片搭了座房子。

construction
[kən'strʌkʃən]

n 構造；建築物

c1120

During the summers, Will worked on construction sites to pay the bills.

夏天的時候，威爾在建築工地工作來支付帳單。

consult
[kən'sʌlt]

vi 與人商討

c1121

He needs to consult with his colleagues on the new project.

他需要和同事商討這個新項目。

consult
[kən'sʌlt]

vt 請教，向…諮詢；查閱

c1122

They consulted a lawyer about the proposal before writing the contract.

在起草合約之前，他們就提案內容先諮詢了律師。

consultant
[kən'sʌltənt]

n 顧問

c1123

We need to hire a consultant to improve our stock system.

我們應該聘一位顧問來改進我們的倉儲系統。

consume
[kən'sjum]

vt 消耗；吃完，喝光

c1124

The boys consumed all of the stew she'd made that afternoon.

男孩們把她那天下午燉的所有燉菜都吃光了。

consume
[kən'sjum]

vt 燒毀，毀滅

c1125

The fire quickly consumed the connected apartments.

大火很快就燒毀了相連的公寓。

consumer
[kən'sjumɚ]

n 消費者，用戶

c1126

Consumers are always looking for the best deal.

消費者總是想要最好的交易。

consumption
[kən'sʌmpʃən]
托 雅 學

c1127

n 消耗（量）
Modern motor technology has a strong focus on reducing petrol consumption.
現代汽車技術都注重減少油耗。

---

contemporary
[kən'tɛmpə,rɛrɪ]
托 雅 學

c1128

adj 現代的，當代的；同時代的；同時代的人
George Washington was considered one of the most humble men of all his contemporaries.
喬治·華盛頓被認為是所有同僚中最謙恭的人之一。

---

contend
[kən'tɛnd]
托 雅 學

c1129

vi 競爭；全力對付
Our school basketball team is expected to contend for the championship this season.
我們學校的籃球隊被認為可以角逐本賽季冠軍。

---

contend
[kən'tɛnd]
托 雅 學

c1130

vt 堅決主張，聲稱
The defense lawyer at the press conference contended that the evidence was inadmissible.
被告律師在記者會上聲稱那些證據法庭是不會接受的。

---

content
[kən'tɛnt]
托 雅 學

c1131

adj 滿意的；甘願的；vt 使滿足，使滿意
What I answered did not seem to content him.
我的回答好像不能令他滿意。

---

content
['kɑntɛnt]
托 雅 學

c1132

n 容量；內容
The content of the driveway was a mix of sand and gravel.
這條馬路的鋪路材料是沙和碎石的混合。

---

contented
[kən'tɛntɪd]
托 雅 學

c1133

adj 滿足的；知足的；滿意的
He was contented with the way his life had turned out.
他滿足於自己的生活現狀。

---

contest
['kɑntɛst]
托 雅 學

c1134

n/vt 競爭，比賽；爭論
The lawyer advised that he would not contest the court verdict.
律師建議他最好不要去爭議法庭上的判決。

---

context
['kɑntɛkst]
托 雅 學

c1135

n （文章等的）前後關係；（事件等發生的）背景
We can often infer the meaning of an unknown word from the context.
我們可以從上下文推斷出生詞的詞義。

C

continual
[kən'tɪnjʊəl]
托 雅 學

adj 不斷的，連續的；頻繁的
`c1136`
The noise from the football game was continual.
足球賽場的吵鬧聲不斷傳來。

contract
['kɑntrækt]
托 雅 學

n （承包）合同，契約
`c1137`
They drew up a contract to govern their shared property.
他們起草合約監管他們共有的財產。

contract
[kən'trækt]
托 雅 學

vi/vt 使⋯縮小
`c1138`
The heated steel will contract when it cools down.
加熱的鋼鐵降溫時會縮小。

contract
[kən'trækt]
托 雅 學

vt 訂合同、契約
`c1139`
I will contract a builder to start working on my new home.
我會和建築商簽訂契約來開始建蓋我的新家。

contrary
['kɑntrɛrɪ]
托 雅 學

adj 相反的，矛盾的
`c1140`
Her views were usually contrary to popular opinions.
她的觀點通常和常人相反。

contrast
['kɑn,træst]
托 雅 學

n 對比；**vi/vt** 形成對比，比較差異
`c1141`
The history teacher told the students to compare and contrast World War I with World War II.
歷史老師讓學生們把兩次世界大戰比較和對比一下。

controversial
[,kɑntrə'vɝʃəl]
托 雅 學

adj 引起爭論的，有爭議的
`c1142`
The issue concerning abortion has always been controversial.
關於墮胎的議題一直都具有爭議。

controversy
['kɑntrə,vɝsɪ]
托 雅 學

n 爭論，辯論；爭吵
`c1143`
She greatly enjoyed debating about political controversies.
她非常喜歡參與跟政治有關的論辯。

convenience
[kən'vinjəns]
托 雅

n 便利；複數＝便利設備
`c1144`
He enjoyed the convenience of the local corner store.
他盡享當地住宅區附近商店的便利。

convenient
[kən'vinjənt]

adj 便利的，方便的
His hotel was convenient to the airport and several restaurants.
他的旅店到機場和幾家飯館都很方便。

c1145

convention
[kən'vɛnʃən]

n 習俗，慣例；公約；大會
He left the sales convention with a lot of new ideas about how to run his business.
他離開展銷會，對怎樣經營自己的公司有了很多新點子。

c1146

conventional
[kən'vɛnʃənl]

adj 慣例的，常規的
Chopsticks are conventional eating utensils for Chinese food.
筷子是中餐慣用的餐具。

c1147

convert
[kən'vɝt]

vt 變換，轉換；改變（信仰等）；兌換（錢）
In order to convert milliliters to liters, divide by 1,000.
要把毫升轉換成公升，需要除以1000。

c1148

convey
[kən've]

vt 運送，轉運；傳達
He conveyed how desperately he needed to get the loan.
他表達了自己如何迫切需要貸款。

c1149

convince
[kən'vɪns]

vt 使…信服，使…確信
I convinced her to come with me to the dance.
我說服她和我一起來參加舞會。

c1150

cooperate
[ko'apə,ret]

vi 合作；相配合
Penny and her sister cooperated to plan the family reunion.
潘妮和她的妹妹合作策劃了家庭聚會。

c1151

coordinate
[ko'ɔrdnɪt]

n 同等者；座標
Let's look at the coordinate on the map and we will be able to locate our exact position.
查一下地圖上的座標我們就能夠找到確切的位置。

c1152

coordinate
[ko'ɔrdnɪt]

vi 搭配；協調
This shade may coordinate with a range of other colors.
這種深淺的顏色可與很多顏色搭配。

c1153

C

coordinate
[ko'ɔrdnɪt]

vt 協作，協調；整合
Sandra coordinated 800 volunteers to help rebuild the burned building.
桑德拉協調指揮800名義工幫助重建燒毀的建築。

`c1154`

corporate
['kɔrpərɪt]

adj 法人（組織）的，合為一體的；企業的
Time-honored traditions are handed down to new members who join a corporate culture.
經過時間洗禮的傳統被傳給加入企業文化的新成員。

`c1155`

corporation
[ˌkɔrpə'reʃən]

n 市鎮自治機關；法人；公司，企業
The corporation hosted their new product launch at their flagship store.
企業在自己的旗艦店主辦了他們的新產品發佈會。

`c1156`

corps
[kɔr]

n 兵團；（經專門訓練或有特種使命的）團隊
After finishing med school, my brother joined a medical corps to help cure sick people in thirdworld countries.
在念完醫學院之後，我弟弟加入了一個醫療團，以幫助治療第三世界國家的病患。

`c1157`

corrupt
[kə'rʌpt]

adj 腐敗的，貪汙的
At times politics can be a very corrupt mind game.
有時候政治是極度腐敗的心智遊戲。

`c1158`

corrupt
[kə'rʌpt]

vi/vt 使...腐敗，使...墮落；賄賂，收買；篡改
Oh dear, the online file is corrupted, so all the data has been lost.
天啊！線上檔案被篡改了，所有的數據都遺失了。

`c1159`

costume
['kɑstjum]

n （流行的）服飾；戲裝，（特定場合的）套裝
Her costume was an exact replica of Dorothy's dress in the Wizard of Oz.
她的服裝是《綠野仙蹤》中桃樂絲的裙子的完整翻版。

`c1160`

council
['kaʊnsl]

n 理事會，委員會；議事機構
The school council will discuss the budget of the graduation trip next Monday.
校理事會下週一會討論畢業旅行的預算。

`c1161`

counter
['kaʊntɚ]

adv 相反地，逆向地；**vt** 反對，反擊；逆轉
The company decided to counter the multi-million dollar offer.
公司決定不接受這數百萬的開價。

`c1162`

counter
['kaʊntə]
托 雅 學

n 櫃檯；計數器　　　　　　　　　　c1163

Please pay your bill at the counter near the entrance.
請在入口附近的櫃檯付費。

courtesy
['kɝ·təsɪ]
托 雅 學

n 禮貌，謙恭；請安　　　　　　　　c1164

She considered occasional visits to her neighbors only a common courtesy.
她認為不時地去拜訪下鄰居是起碼的禮節。

credible
['krɛdəbl]
托 雅 學

adj 可靠的，可信的　　　　　　　　c1165

The jury did not think the young lady was a credible witness.
陪審團認為這名年輕女子不是個可靠的證人。

crime
[kraɪm]
托 雅 學

n 罪（行）；犯罪　　　　　　　　　c1166

It is reported that the crime rate has been rising sharply in this city.
據報導，這個城市的犯罪率一直在極速上升。

criminal
['krɪmənl]
托 雅 學

adj 犯罪的，刑事的；n 罪犯，刑事犯　c1167

The captain of the Italian cruise ship that ran aground was charged with criminal negligence.
那艘擱淺的義大利郵輪的船長被指控犯有刑事疏忽罪。

crisis
['kraɪsɪs]
托 雅 學

n 危機，緊要關頭　　　　　　　　　c1168

The bank survived the financial crisis by conserving funds and investing in safe commodities.
銀行通過保存資金並投資到安全的產品上而逃過了金融危機。

criterion
[kraɪ'tɪrɪən]
托 雅 學

n 標準，準則，尺度；複數＝criteria　c1169

Excellence was her only criterion for accepting work for publication.
稿件品質好是她收稿出版的唯一標準。

critical
['krɪtɪkl]
托 雅 學

adj 批評的，評論的；緊要的；臨界的　c1170

He was critical of their farming methods, but pleased with the results.
他對他們的耕作方法持批評態度，但對結果還滿意。

criticism
['krɪtə,sɪzəm]
托 雅 學

n 評論，批評，非難　　　　　　　　c1171

Film criticism was his favorite subject in college.
電影評論是他大學裡最喜歡的科目。

C

criticize
['krɪtɪ,saɪz]
托 雅 學

vt 批評，評論 c1172
Her mother rarely criticized her cooking.
她媽媽很少批評她的廚藝。

crucial
['kruʃəl]
托 雅 學

adj 決定性的，重要的；嚴酷的，艱難的；十字形的 c1173
It is crucial that you read the material before class to understand the lecture.
課前閱讀材料對於理解講座是非常重要的。

cue
[kju]
托 雅 學

n 暗示，信號；線索；vt 暗示，提示 c1174
The conductor will cue the orchestra to start playing their instruments.
指揮會提示管弦樂隊何時該吹奏樂器。

cultivate
['kʌltə,vet]
托 雅 學

vt 耕作，栽培；養殖；教養，磨煉 c1175
The purpose of this seminar is to cultivate the loyalty of the staff.
這次研討會的目的是討論如何培養員工的忠誠度。

cultural
['kʌltʃərəl]
托 雅 學

adj 修養的；文化的；人文的；種植的，培養的 c1176
The university's Indian cultural festival took place every spring.
這所大學的印度文化節在每年春天舉辦。

culture
['kʌltʃə]
托 雅 學

n 文化，文明；修養；耕種，培育 c1177
Jim was a dedicated fan of English culture.
吉姆非常熱衷於英國文化。

currency
['kɝənsɪ]
托 雅 學

n 流傳，流通；通貨，貨幣 c1178
She changed her currency at the airport.
她在機場兌換了貨幣。

custom
['kʌstəm]
托 雅 學

n 風俗，慣例 c1179
It was his custom to drink tea in the morning.
上午喝茶是他的習慣。

customary
['kʌstəm,ɛrɪ]
托 雅 學

adj 通常的；照慣例的 c1180
He stopped at the bar for his customary after-work beer.
他停在酒吧外，按照慣例他下班後都在這裡喝杯啤酒。

customer
['kʌstəmə·]

托 雅 學

n 顧客，主顧

c1181

The customer inspected the produce carefully for defects.
顧客認真查看農產品，看有沒有瑕疵。

customs
['kʌstəmz]

托 雅 學

n 海關，關稅（通用複數）

c1182

Customs duties are business taxes that are paid on imported goods.
關稅是對進口商品所付的商業稅。

cynical
['sɪnɪkl̩]

托 雅 學

adj 憤世嫉俗的；悲觀的；冷嘲的

c1183

Her cynical attitude prevented her from enjoying the amusement park.
她憤世嫉俗的態度使自己在遊樂園裡沒能盡興。

D

字彙能力檢查表

先自我檢驗是否瞭解以下初階單字，若有不清楚者，請先開啟光碟中的電子書複習。

- ☐ dairy
- ☐ dam
- ☐ damp
- ☐ dampen
- ☐ dart
- ☐ dash
- ☐ dash
- ☐ data
- ☐ database
- ☐ dawn
- ☐ dawn
- ☐ deadly
- ☐ debate
- ☐ debt
- ☐ decade
- ☐ decisive
- ☐ deck
- ☐ decrease
- ☐ define
- ☐ definite
- ☐ definition
- ☐ definitive
- ☐ degree
- ☐ delay
- ☐ delicious
- ☐ deliver
- ☐ delivery

- ☐ delivery
- ☐ dense
- ☐ density
- ☐ dental
- ☐ dentist
- ☐ department
- ☐ depend
- ☐ dependant
- ☐ dependence
- ☐ dependent
- ☐ deposit
- ☐ deposit
- ☐ deposit
- ☐ depth
- ☐ describe
- ☐ description
- ☐ description
- ☐ desert
- ☐ desert
- ☐ despite
- ☐ dessert
- ☐ destiny
- ☐ detail
- ☐ detail
- ☐ detergent
- ☐ determination
- ☐ determine

- ☐ develop
- ☐ develop
- ☐ development
- ☐ dialect
- ☐ diet
- ☐ diet
- ☐ digital
- ☐ digital
- ☐ dim
- ☐ dine
- ☐ dip
- ☐ direct
- ☐ direction
- ☐ director
- ☐ disable
- ☐ disagree
- ☐ disagreement
- ☐ disappearance
- ☐ disappoint
- ☐ disappointing
- ☐ disc(k)
- ☐ discount
- ☐ discuss
- ☐ discussion
- ☐ disgust
- ☐ disgusting

- ☐ display
- ☐ disposal
- ☐ distance
- ☐ distant
- ☐ district
- ☐ ditch
- ☐ dizzy
- ☐ dock
- ☐ dose
- ☐ dose
- ☐ dot
- ☐ doubtful
- ☐ doubtless
- ☐ download
- ☐ draft
- ☐ drama
- ☐ dramatic
- ☐ dread
- ☐ dreadful
- ☐ dreamy
- ☐ dull
- ☐ dumb
- ☐ dump
- ☐ duration
- ☐ dwarf
- ☐ dye

damage
['dæmɪdʒ]
托 雅 學

n/vt 損害，毀壞
The damage to the car in the accident was only superficial.
事故中的汽車只是表面受到了損害。

d1001

deadline
['dɛd,laɪn]
托 雅 學

n 最後期限
This list contains several strategies to help you successfully meet deadlines.
這張列表包含了幾個能夠幫助你在期限內成功完成事情的策略。

d1002

dean
[din]
托 雅 學

n （大學）院長；主持牧師；（基督教）教長
The dean has given clear instructions to the future direction of the department.
院長對於系所未來的方向給予了明確的指示。

d1003

deceive
[dɪ'siv]
托 雅 學

vi/vt 欺騙；蒙蔽
Even though she forced herself to smile, she couldn't deceive him for long.
即使她強迫自己微笑，也騙不了他多久。

d1004

decent
['disn̩t]
托 雅 學

adj 體面的；正派的，合乎禮儀的；合適的
They decided to pay a little more to stay at a decent hotel.
他們決定多花一點兒錢去住一個體面的賓館。

d1005

declaration
[,dɛklə'reʃən]
托 雅 學

n 宣言，聲明；申訴
The flowers were a clear declaration of his love.
那束花是他愛的明確宣言。

d1006

declare
[dɪ'klɛr]
托 雅 學

vi/vt 宣佈，聲明；斷言，宣稱
She declared that she would never fly on an airplane again.
她宣佈她將永遠不再乘坐飛機。

d1007

decline
[dɪ'klaɪn]
托 雅 學

n 下降，衰落；斜面；**vi/vt** 下降，衰落；拒絕
She declined his offer to go dancing this weekend.
她拒絕了他這個週末去跳舞的邀請。

d1008

decorate
['dɛkə,ret]
托 雅 學

vi/vt 裝飾，裝潢，佈置
The children helped their mother decorate the tree.
孩子們幫助他們的母親裝飾那棵樹。

d1009

decoration
[ˌdɛkəˈreʃən]

托 雅 學

n 裝飾，裝潢；獎章
d1010
It is January and you can take down those Christmas decorations.
都已經一月了，你可以把那些耶誕節的裝飾取下來了。

decorative
[ˈdɛkərətɪv]

托 雅 學

adj 裝飾的，可作裝飾的
d1011
The handmade cushions of an ornate design are highly decorative in the living room.
風格華麗的手工製抱枕在客廳的裝飾效果很好。

dedicate
[ˈdɛdəˌket]

托 雅 學

vt 奉獻，獻身於
d1012
She dedicated the rest of her career to finding a cure for the virus.
此後的職業生涯中，她致力於尋找治癒這種病毒的方法。

dedication
[ˌdɛdəˈkeʃən]

托 雅 學

n 奉獻，供奉；致力，獻身
d1013
Her dedication to the company has earned her much respect from colleagues over the years.
這麼多年來，她對公司的貢獻贏得了同事們對她的尊敬。

deduct
[dɪˈdʌkt]

托 雅 學

vt 扣除；演繹（推理）
d1014
The referee deducted a point from his team.
裁判從他的球隊減掉了一分。

defeat
[dɪˈfit]

托 雅 學

n/vt 擊敗，戰勝；使失敗
d1015
The Romans defeated the Persians and won the war.
羅馬人打敗了波斯人，在戰爭中獲勝。

defend
[dɪˈfɛnd]

托 雅 學

vi/vt 防守，保衛；為……辯護
d1016
He hired the best lawyer he could afford to defend him.
他聘請了他請得起的最好的律師來為他辯護。

defendant
[dɪˈfɛndənt]

托 雅 學

adj 辯護的；**n** 被告
d1017
The defendant tried to prove his innocence and defend his reputation.
那名被告試圖證明他的清白並為自己的名譽辯護。

delete
[dɪˈlit]

托 雅 學

vt 刪除；擦掉
d1018
He deleted last year's files in preparation for new classes.
為了準備新課程，他把去年的文件刪除了。

D

delight
[dɪ'laɪt]

托 雅 學

n 快樂，高興；**vi/vt**（使……）高興，（使……）欣喜 d1019
Let me delight you by taking you to go shopping.
我帶你去購物，讓你高興高興吧。

demand
[dɪ'mænd]

托 雅 學

n/vt 要求；需要（量）；查問 d1020
This judge demanded that the prisoner be released immediately.
法官要求那個囚犯立即被釋放。

demanding
[dɪ'mændɪŋ]

托 雅 學

adj 苛求的；使人吃力的；高要求的 d1021
Steve always made time in his demanding work schedule for his family.
史蒂夫總是從他吃力的工作行程中為家人騰出時間。

democracy
[dɪ'mɑkrəsɪ]

托 雅 學

n 民主，民主制；民主國家 d1022
The ancient Greek was one of the first civilizations to practice democracy.
古希臘是實行民主制的第一批文明古國之一。

demonstrate
['dɛmən,stret]

托 雅 學

vi 示威 d1023
The union demonstrated outside the company headquarters for six hours.
工會在那個公司總部外面示威了六個小時。

demonstrate
['dɛmən,stret]

托 雅 學

vt 論證；演示 d1024
He demonstrates how the espresso machine makes espresso.
他示範說明濃縮咖啡機如何製作濃縮咖啡。

demonstration
[,dɛmən'streʃən]

托 雅 學

n 論證；演示；示威 d1025
The police used the tear gas to stop the crowd in demonstration.
警方用催淚彈來阻止示威群眾。

denial
[dɪ'naɪəl]

托 雅 學

n 否認；拒絕；否認某事或某事實的聲明 d1026
Her mother thought she was in denial about her financial problems.
她母親認為她在否認她的財務問題。

deny
[dɪ'naɪ]

托 雅 學

vt 否認，否定；拒絕 d1027
She denied all of the charges against her.
她否認了所有對她的控告。

depart
[dɪ'pɑrt]
托 雅 學

d1028

vi 離開，起程
Erin departed from her house at 6:30 this morning.
愛琳今天早上六點半從家裡起程。

---

departed
[dɪ'pɑrtɪd]
托 雅 學

d1029

adj 過去的，逝世的
Let us toast to the departed soldiers who gave their lives to protect us.
讓我們向那些犧牲自己的生命來保護我們的已故士兵們敬酒。

D

---

departure
[dɪ'pɑrtʃɚ]
托 雅 學

d1030

n 離開，起程
Hannah delayed her departure as long as possible.
漢娜盡可能長地推遲了她的起程時間。

---

depict
[dɪ'pɪkt]
托 雅 學

d1031

vt 描繪，描述
These novels depict how a smart detective solves mysterious cases.
這些小說描述了一個非常聰明的偵探是如何偵破神秘案件的。

---

depress
[dɪ'prɛs]
托 雅 學

d1032

vt 壓抑；使沮喪；壓下
She didn't watch the news because it depressed her.
她沒有看那個新聞，因為它讓她感到很沮喪。

---

depression
[dɪ'prɛʃən]
托 雅 學

d1033

n 消沉；不景氣，蕭條期
Her depression finally lifted when her son returned from the war.
當她的兒子從戰場回來時，她的消沉終於煙消雲散了。

---

deputy
['dɛpjətɪ]
托 雅 學

d1034

adj 副的；代理的；**n** 代理人，代表
We are heading to the deputy mayor's office right now.
我們現在要去副市長的辦公室。

---

deserve
[dɪ'zɝv]
托 雅 學

d1035

vi/vt 應受，值得
He felt his wife deserved a break, so they went on a vacation.
他感覺他的妻子應該好好休息一下，所以他們就去度假了。

---

design
[dɪ'zaɪn]
托 雅 學

d1036

n 設計；圖樣
His design for the new building won in the architecture contest.
他的新大樓設計在建築大賽中獲勝了。

desirable
[dɪˈzaɪrəbl̩]
托 雅 學

adj 值得做的；合意的；期望得到的   d1037
It is desirable to eat a balanced diet to stay healthy.
均衡飲食以保持健康是人們都想要的。

despair
[dɪˈspɛr]
托 雅 學

n 絕望；令人失望的人（或事物）；**vi** 絕望   d1038
So long as you help me, I shall never despair.
只要你幫我，我就絕不會感到失望。

desperate
[ˈdɛspərɪt]
托 雅 學

adj 絕望的；危急的；極度渴望的   d1039
After working in the cold all day, he was desperate for a hot bath and some dinner.
在嚴寒中工作了一整天後，他極度渴望洗個熱水澡並吃些晚餐。

destination
[ˌdɛstəˈneʃən]
托 雅 學

n 目的地，終點   d1040
They arrived at their destination two hours earlier than expected.
他們比預期時間早兩小時到達了目的地。

destructive
[dɪˈstrʌktɪv]
托 雅 學

adj 破壞性的，危害的   d1041
The destructive force of the explosion brought down the building.
爆炸的破壞性威力摧毀了那棟樓。

detect
[dɪˈtɛkt]
托 雅 學

vt 察覺，發覺；偵察，探測   d1042
The chef was famous for being able to detect all the ingredients in a dish just by taste.
那位大廚以僅憑味覺就能探測出一道菜裡所有的配料而著稱。

detection
[dɪˈtɛkʃən]
托 雅 學

n 察覺，發覺；偵察   d1043
Early detection and treatment are vital for cancer patients.
及早察覺和及早治療對癌症患者是很重要的。

detective
[dɪˈtɛktɪv]
托 雅 學

n 偵探，密探   d1044
She hired an excellent detective to find her missing husband.
她雇了一個極好的偵探來尋找她失蹤的丈夫。

device
[dɪˈvaɪs]
托 雅 學

n 裝置，設備，儀錶；方法，設計   d1045
The piano tuner had a range of devices in his tool chest to help him fix pianos.
那個鋼琴調音師的工具箱裡有一套器械，以幫助他調整鋼琴。

D

devote
[dɪˈvot]

vt 奉獻，致力於

d1046

She devoted a whole week to writing the report.

她用了整個星期的時間撰寫那個報告。

diagnose
[ˈdaɪəgnoz]

vt 診斷（疾病）；判斷（問題）

d1047

The patient was saddened that he was diagnosed with diabetes.

病人因為被診斷出患有糖尿病而感到很難過。

diagnosis
[ˌdaɪəgˈnosɪs]

n 診斷；調查分析，判斷

d1048

Her symptoms were so clear that he had no difficulty making a diagnosis.

她的症狀很明顯，因此他做出診斷沒有任何困難。

diagonal
[daɪˈægənl]

adj 對角線的

d1049

Hannah cut the pattern along the diagonal line she had drawn.

漢娜按照她畫的對角線切割了樣板。

dictate
[ˈdɪktet]

vi/vt 口述；（使……）聽寫；指示，命令

d1050

She dictated her letters to her secretary.

她向她的秘書口述了她的信。

digest
[daɪˈdʒɛst]

n 文摘，摘要

d1051

My wife enjoys reading this digest in the morning.

我的太太喜歡早上閱讀這個文摘。

digest
[daɪˈdʒɛst]

vi/vt 消化；領會，融會貫通

d1052

Antacids can help you digest a spicy meal.

抗酸劑能夠幫助你消化辛辣的食物。

dignity
[ˈdɪgnətɪ]

n （舉止、態度等的）莊嚴，端莊；尊貴

d1053

She carried herself with great dignity.

她舉止端莊。

dilemma
[dəˈlɛmə]

n （進退兩難的）窘境，困境

d1054

The conflict between her father and her brother put her in a dilemma.

她父親和她弟弟之間的衝突使她置身於一個進退兩難的困境。

dimension
[dɪ'mɛnʃən]
托 雅 學

n 尺寸，尺度；維（數），度（數）；面積
The dimensions of the house were nearly square.
這個房子的尺寸比例差不多是方形的。

d1055

diploma
[dɪ'plomə]
托 雅 學

n 畢業文憑，學位證書
She has made many significant sacrifices and she finally received her diploma from school.
她做出了很多重大犧牲，最終從學校拿到了文憑。

d1056

diplomat
['dɪpləmæt]
托 雅 學

n 外交官
The diplomat represented his country at the meeting.
那位外交官在會議上代表他的國家。

d1057

diplomatic
[ˌdɪplə'mætɪk]
托 雅 學

adj （從事）外交的；策略的，有外交手腕的
The embassy received several diplomatic communications from the home country.
大使館收到了幾封來自本國的外交通信。

d1058

disapprove
[ˌdɪsə'pruv]
托 雅 學

vi/vt 不贊成，不同意
Her mother disapproved of loud music at home.
她母親不喜歡家裡有鬧哄哄的音樂。

d1059

disaster
[dɪ'zæstə]
托 雅 學

n 災難，大禍；徹底的失敗
New Jersey has an excellent disaster management plan.
紐澤西州有一個極好的災難管理計劃。

d1060

disastrous
[dɪz'æstrəs]
托 雅 學

adj 災難性的；完全失敗的
His changing the type of flour in the cake turned out to be disastrous.
他更改了做蛋糕的麵粉，其結果是完全失敗的。

d1061

discard
['dɪskɑrd]
托 雅 學

vi/vt 拋棄，遺棄
She discarded the wrapper in the trash can.
她把包裝紙丟棄在垃圾桶裡。

d1062

discipline
['dɪsəplɪn]
托 雅 學

n 紀律；學科
Her discipline and work ethic made her one of the most valuable members of the team.
她的紀律和職業道德使她成為這個小組裡最有價值的成員之一。

d1063

discipline
['dɪsəplɪn]

托 雅 學

vt 訓練，管教   d1064
I will discipline all the soldiers to get ready for war.
我會訓練所有的士兵，讓他們為戰爭做好準備。

disciplined
['dɪsəplɪnd]

托 雅 學

adj 受過訓練的，遵守紀律的   d1065
Professional ballet dancers must practice a well-disciplined schedule.
專業芭蕾舞者必須接受嚴格的訓練日程。

discourage
[dɪs'kɝɪdʒ]

托 雅 學

vt 使洩氣，使失去信心   d1066
His mother discouraged him from joining the army at such a young age.
他母親阻止他在這樣小的年紀就參軍。

discriminate
[dɪ'skrɪmə,net]

托 雅 學

vi/vt 區別，辨別；（against）有差別地對待，歧視   d1067
His perfect palate could discriminate easily between different wines.
他那充分開發的味覺很容易鑒別不同的葡萄酒。

discrimination
[dɪ,skrɪmə'neʃən]

托 雅 學

n 辨別，識別力；歧視   d1068
She fights against people's discrimination by teaching people about the power of empathy.
她通過教導人們同理心的力量來反抗歧視問題。

disgrace
[dɪs'gres]

托 雅 學

n 失寵；恥辱；**vt** 使失寵；玷辱，使蒙羞   d1069
She disgraced herself by continually gossiping in public about her friends and loved ones.
她不停地在公開場合說她親朋好友的閒話，使她自己蒙羞。

disgraceful
[dɪs'gresfəl]

托 雅 學

adj 不名譽的，可恥的，失體面的   d1070
It was quite disgraceful that the coach belittled the players.
這個教練藐視球員，這是非常丟臉的。

dismay
[dɪs'me]

托 雅 學

n/vt 使⋯沮喪；使⋯驚慌；使⋯失望，使⋯絕望   d1071
He had to control his feelings of dismay after he received more bad news about his father's illness.
在他知道更多他父親健康情況的不好消息後，他必須控制自己沮喪的心情。

dismiss
[dɪs'mɪs]

托 雅 學

vt 免職，解雇，開除；解散；消散   d1072
She dismissed her mother's fears with a gentle smile.
她輕輕一笑就消除了母親的恐懼。

dismissal
[dɪsˈmɪsl̩]

托 雅 學

n 解散；解雇

d1073

The sudden dismissal of hundreds of employees revealed the company's deepening crisis.

數百名員工突然被解雇，暴露了那家公司不斷深化的危機。

disorder
[dɪsˈɔrdɚ]

托 雅 學

n 失調（疾病）；身體功能障礙

d1074

The ballerina has suffered from an eating disorder for many years.

這個芭蕾舞星已經患有進食障礙很多年了。

disorder
[dɪsˈɔrdɚ]

托 雅 學

n 騷亂，騷動，混亂

d1075

Mounted troops were called out to put an end to the disorder in the streets.

騎兵部隊被召集來平息街頭的騷亂。

dispatch
[dɪˈspætʃ]

托 雅 學

n 急件

d1076

He sent a dispatch to the head office in Alaska to inform them about their shipping schedules.

他寄了一份急件到阿拉斯加的總公司，告知他們的運輸計畫。

dispatch
[dɪˈspætʃ]

托 雅 學

vt 派遣；調度，發送

d1077

She dispatched a letter to her lawyer requesting a new will.

她發送了一封信件給律師，要求辦理新的遺囑。

dispute
[dɪˈspjut]

托 雅 學

n 爭論，爭執

d1078

The longstanding family dispute over the inheritance was finally resolved.

那場曠日持久的家庭遺產紛爭最終得到了解決。

dispute
[dɪˈspjut]

托 雅 學

vi/vt 爭論；反駁；懷疑；阻止

d1079

The two countries disputed for years over a small strip of land on their border.

這兩個國家為了邊界上的一小塊土地已經爭執多年。

disregard
[dɪsrɪˈgɑrd]

托 雅 學

n 忽視，漠視

d1080

Because of his disregard for his parental duties, his son began misbehaving in school.

因為他忽視了做父母的責任，他的孩子在學校裡開始有不良行為。

disregard
[dɪsrɪˈgɑrd]

托 雅 學

vt 不理會，忽視，漠視

d1081

The kids totally disregarded what their parents had just told them to do.

孩子們完全漠視父母剛才告訴他們要做的事情。

dissertation
[ˌdɪsɚˈteʃən]

n 論文；學術演講　　d1082
That graduate student completed his dissertation in two years.
那位研究生在兩年之內完成了他的論文。

D

dissolve
[dɪˈzalv]

vi/vt 使…溶解，使…融化；解散，取消　　d1083
The cleaner dissolved the build-up on the tub.
清潔劑溶解了浴盆上堆積的污垢。

distinct
[dɪˈstɪŋkt]

adj 清楚的；截然不同的　　d1084
Her voice was so distinct that he recognized it instantly.
她的聲音如此與眾不同，以至於他一下子就辨認出來了。

distinction
[dɪˈstɪŋkʃən]

n 區別，差別　　d1085
What is the distinction between butterflies and moths?
蝴蝶與飛蛾有什麼不同之處？

distinction
[dɪˈstɪŋkʃən]

n 特性；聲望；顯赫　　d1086
He was considered a man of distinction and culture.
他被認為是一個有聲望和有文化的人。

distinctive
[dɪˈstɪŋktɪv]

adj 有特色的；特殊的　　d1087
We need to come up with a distinctive name for our new product, so people will remember it.
我們必須為新產品想出個有特色的名稱，這樣人們容易記住。

distinguish
[dɪˈstɪŋgwɪʃ]

vi/vt 區別，辨別；辨認出；使傑出　　d1088
Children are often unable to distinguish reality from fantasy.
孩子時常無法分辨現實與幻境。

distort
[dɪsˈtɔrt]

vt 歪曲，曲解，扭曲　　d1089
The ripples in the glass of the window distorted his view of the garden.
玻璃窗戶內的波紋扭曲了他眼裡的花園景觀。

distortion
[dɪsˈtɔrʃən]

n 弄歪，歪曲；畸變　　d1090
The intense heat from the sunlight caused the distortion of the plastic model.
日光劇烈的熱度造成塑膠模型扭曲變形。

distract
[dɪ'strækt]

托 雅 學

vt 分散；使分心；使心情煩亂

d1091

She was distracted from her work by the music from the neighbor's house.

她被鄰居屋裡的音樂打擾，使她在工作中分心了。

distraction
[dɪ'strækʃən]

托 雅 學

n 注意力分散；消遣；心煩意亂

d1092

Listening to good music is a welcome distraction to life's hustle and bustle.

聽好音樂是一種很受歡迎的消遣，用以應對生活的忙碌和喧囂。

distress
[dɪ'strɛs]

托 雅 學

n 苦惱；危難；不幸，痛苦

d1093

The counselor worked quickly to soothe the accident victim's distress.

輔導老師迅速地展開了工作，撫慰事故受害者的悲傷。

distress
[dɪ'strɛs]

托 雅 學

vt 使苦惱；使悲傷

d1094

All the stories he's been telling her distressed her greatly.

他對她所說的所有的故事都讓她非常悲傷。

distribute
[dɪ'strɪbjʊt]

托 雅 學

vt 分發；分佈；配（電）；散佈

d1095

She distributed packs of warm socks, hats, and gloves to people at the homeless shelter.

她向流浪收容所裡的人們分發了好幾包保暖的襪子、帽子和手套。

distribution
[ˌdɪstrə'bjuʃən]

托 雅 學

n 分發；分佈

d1096

After the disaster, helicopters were sent into the area for distribution of food and other supplies.

災難發生後，直升機被派入災區分發食物及其他用品。

disturb
[dɪs't3·b]

托 雅 學

vi/vt 擾亂，妨礙；使不安

d1097

She didn't like to watch scary movies because they disturbed her at night.

她不喜歡看恐怖片，因為它們會使她夜裡不安。

disturbance
[dɪs't3·bəns]

托 雅 學

n 動亂，騷亂；干擾

d1098

The disturbance caused by the cats outside did not last long.

外面那些野貓造成的騷動並未持久。

diversify
[daɪ'v3·səˌfaɪ]

托 雅 學

vt 使多樣化，增加種類；分散投資

d1099

The couple decided to diversify their investments before retirement.

那對夫婦決定在退休之前就分散投資。

diversion
[daɪˈvɝˈʒən]

n 轉向，轉移；牽制；解悶，娛樂　　　d1100
They went to the movies for some light diversion.
他們去看電影作為輕鬆消遣。

diversity
[daɪˈvɝˈsətɪ]

n 多樣性；差異　　　d1101
I enjoy the cultural diversity of metropolitan cities.
我喜歡都市的文化多樣性。

dividend
[ˈdɪvəˌdɛnd]

n 紅利，股息；回報，效益；獎金；被除數　　　d1102
The company declared a large dividend at the end of the year.
年底，公司宣佈獎金優渥。

divine
[dəˈvaɪn]

adj 神的，神授的，天賜的；極好的，極美的　　　d1103
The ancient Egyptians thought that cats, alligators, and even the Nile River were divine.
古埃及人認為貓、鱷魚，甚至尼羅河都是神靈。

document
[ˈdɑkjəmənt]

n 公文；文獻；證件　　　d1104
The secretary circled all the typos in the document.
秘書把公文中所有的排印錯誤都圈出來了。

documentary
[ˌdɑkjəˈmɛntərɪ]

n 紀錄片　　　d1105
She filmed her first documentary on the story of the Hubble Space telescope.
她拍攝了她的第一部關於哈勃太空望遠鏡的紀錄片。

dodge
[dɑdʒ]

vt 躲開，避開，規避，設法或施計回避　　　d1106
I told my boss that I would dodge the bullets from any disgruntled customers.
我告訴我老闆，我會躲開不滿顧客的攻擊。

dome
[dom]

n 圓屋頂，拱頂　　　d1107
The dome of the chapel was decorated with gold and jewelry.
教堂的圓屋頂用黃金與珠寶裝飾。

domestic
[dəˈmɛstɪk]

adj 本國的，內政的　　　d1108
The meeting concerns both foreign and domestic policies.
會議關係到外交和對內政策。

domestic
[də'mɛstɪk]

托 雅 學

adj 馴養的，家畜的
This is a domestic cat, not a wild cat.
這是一隻家貓，不是野貓。

d1109

donate
['donet]

托 雅 學

vt 捐獻，捐贈
The rich man donated all his land to the church.
這個有錢人把他所有的土地都捐給了教會。

d1110

donation
[do'neʃən]

托 雅 學

n 捐獻，捐贈
She made a generous donation to the children's charity.
她向兒童慈善機構進行了慷慨的捐贈。

d1111

doom
[dum]

托 雅 學

n 命運；毀滅；**vt** 註定
Not surprisingly, that construction project was doomed to be heavily criticized by the public.
不出意料，那個建築工程註定要被大眾嚴厲地批判。

d1112

drastic
['dræstɪk]

托 雅 學

adj 激烈的，嚴厲的；（藥性等）猛烈的
The drastic change in her appearance shocked her friends.
她外表的激烈變化使她的朋友們都感到震驚。

d1113

dreary
['drɪərɪ]

托 雅 學

adj 沉悶的，枯燥的
She spent the dreary rainy day at home reading.
她在家讀書來打發枯燥的雨天。

d1114

drill
[drɪl]

托 雅 學

n 操練，練習；鑽孔（機）；**vi/vt** 練習，操練；鑽孔
He needed to drill a hole through the tiles in order to insert a pin to hang a picture.
他需要在瓷磚上鑽一個孔並裝上一個掛鉤，以便掛一幅畫。

d1115

drown
[draʊn]

托 雅 學

vi/vt 溺死；淹沒
If he drowned, the whole town would go to the funeral.
如果他淹死了的話，全城的人都會去參加葬禮。

d1116

dubious
['djubɪəs]

托 雅 學

adj 懷疑的，無把握的；有問題的，靠不住的
He was dubious about the authenticity of the recently discovered scrolls.
他懷疑最近發現的畫卷的真實性。

d1117

due
[dju]

adj 應支付的；（車、船等）預定應到達的；到期的　d1118

The paper was due next week, but she hadn't even started researching.

論文下周就要到期了，但是她都還沒開始研究。

due
[dju]

n 應有權力；應付款；會費　d1119

All members are required to attend the monthly meeting and pay dues on time.

所有成員都必須參加月會，準時繳納會費。

duplicate
['djupləkɪt]

adj 複製的；二重的；**n** 複製品　d1120

It is common to make a duplicate key in case the original one gets lost.

為了避免原來的鑰匙不見，製作一把備份鑰匙是很平常的。

duplicate
['djupləkɪt]

vi/vt 複寫；複製；使...加倍　d1121

He had a distinctive singing voice that was difficult to duplicate.

他有獨特的歌喉，他的聲音是獨一無二的（難以複製）。

dwell
[dwɛl]

vi 凝思，細想　d1122

She dwelled upon negative things that happened in the past too often to move forward.

她太常回想著過去發生過的不好的事情，以至於無法向前進。

dwell
[dwɛl]

vi 居住　d1123

Alice regrets that she dwelled in that little town with her parents for twenty years.

愛麗絲後悔她與雙親在那個小鎮住了二十年。

dwelling
['dwɛlɪŋ]

n 住宅，寓所　d1124

It's not entirely fair to judge a person's wealth by the type of dwelling in which he or she lives.

由一個人的住宅去推斷他的財富並不完全是公平的。

dynamic
[daɪ'næmɪk]

adj 有生氣的，有活力的　d1125

I just had a very dynamic aerobic exercise at the gym.

我剛才在健身房做了活力十足的有氧運動。

dynamical
[daɪ'næmɪkəl]

adj 機能上的；動力的，動能的　d1126

Scientists continue to work on the dynamical system in that research project.

科學家們持續研究那個研究計畫中的動力系統。

E

字彙能力檢查表

先自我檢驗是否瞭解以下初階單字，若有不清楚者，請先開啟光碟中的電子書複習。

☐ease
☐Easter
☐echo
☐edge
☐edit
☐edition
☐editor
☐education
☐elbow
☐elderly
☐electrical
☐electrician
☐electronic
☐electronics
☐elementary

☐elevator
☐enable
☐engage
☐engagement
☐engineer
☐engineering
☐enroll
☐enrollment
☐equal
☐equal
☐equal
☐erase
☐essay
☐establish

☐establish
☐establishment
☐event
☐exact
☐examine
☐exchange
☐exchange
☐excitement
☐excuse
☐exist
☐expand
☐expansion
☐expect
☐expense

☐expensive
☐experience
☐explanation
☐express
☐express
☐expression
☐expressive
☐extend
☐extension
☐external
☐extra
☐extreme
☐extreme
☐eye

economic
[ˌikə'namɪk]

adj 經濟（上）的，經濟學的   e1001

Our nation's economic problems have put a lot of people out of work.

我們國家的經濟問題已經使很多人失業了。

economical
[ˌikə'namɪk!]

adj 節約的，經濟的   e1002

She was economical in her grocery shopping.

她在日常開銷方面很節約。

economically
[ˌikə'namɪkḷɪ]

adv 節約地，在經濟上   e1003

Some studies show that the more economically developed a country is, the later in life its people get married.

有些研究顯示，經濟上越發達的國家，人們通常越晚婚。

economics
[ˌikə'namɪks]

n 經濟學；經濟情況   e1004

The economics of small countries differ greatly from those of large ones.

小國家的經濟情況與大國家的有很大不同。

economize
[ɪ'kanəˌmaɪz]

vi 節約，節省   e1005

A good way to economize is to buy generic brands and to shop for weekly store specials.

一個節約的好方法是購買大眾品牌以及商店的每週特價商品。

economy
[ɪ'kanəmɪ]

n 節約；經濟   e1006

The economy recovered slowly that summer.

那年夏天經濟緩慢復甦。

editorial
[ˌɛdə'tɔrɪəl]

adj 社論的；編輯上的；**n** 社論   e1007

The editorial railed against the current administrations.

社論譴責執政政府。

effective
[ɪ'fɛktɪv]

adj （法律和規則）生效的，有效果的   e1008

This law is effective immediately after the holiday.

此法律在假期過後立即生效。

efficiency
[ɪ'fɪʃənsɪ]

n 效率；功效   e1009

The efficiency of the new system is impressive.

這個新系統的效率令人讚歎。

efficient
[ɪˈfɪʃənt]

托 雅 學

adj 效率高的；有能力的，能勝任的
She was an efficient statistic data analyst.
她是個工作效率很高的統計資料分析員。

e1010

ego
[ˈigo]

托 雅 學

n 自我，自負，利己主義；（心理學）自我意識
An overinflated ego usually indicates that a person exudes too much confidence.
過分膨脹的自我意識通常暗示一個人散發出過多自信。

e1011

elaborate
[ɪˈlæbəˌrɪt]

托 雅 學

adj 精心製作（的）
An elaborate hoax was carried out to scare off the tourists from visiting the local shrine.
一個精心設計的騙局被用來嚇跑參觀當地神社的遊客。

e1012

elaborate
[ɪˈlæbəˌret]

托 雅 學

vi/vt 精心製作；詳細闡述
A man in the audience asked the professor to elaborate on her point.
一位聽眾請教授詳細闡述她的論點。

e1013

elaborately
[ɪˈlæbərɪtlɪ]

托 雅 學

adv 精心地，苦心經營地
I decorated elaborately for my good friend's surprise birthday.
我為我好朋友的生日驚喜精心地裝飾著。

e1014

election
[ɪˈlɛkʃən]

托 雅 學

n 選舉，選擇權；當選
The presidential election will be held next month.
總統選舉即將在下個月舉行。

e1015

elegant
[ˈɛləgənt]

托 雅 學

adj 優雅的，高雅的
She had elegant tastes in decorating.
她在裝飾方面品味高雅。

e1016

element
[ˈɛləmənt]

托 雅 學

n 元素；要素；成分
Helium is one of the most abundant elements in the universe.
氦是宇宙中最豐富的元素之一。

e1017

embarrass
[ɪmˈbærəs]

托 雅 學

vi/vt 使困窘；阻礙，麻煩
The teenager was embarrassed by her Dad's fashion sense.
少女被父親的時尚品味搞得非常窘迫。

e1018

emergency
[ɪˈmɝˌdʒənsɪ]

 e1019

n 緊急情況，突然事件
When she saw the accident, she quickly called for emergency services.
她看到發生事故後，迅速撥打了急救電話。

---

emigrant
[ˈɛməgrənt]

e1020

adj 移民的，移居的；n 移民，僑民
The Lin family has been planning to become emigrants in New Zealand.
林家人正計劃成為紐西蘭移民。

---

emigrate
[ˈɛməˌgret]

e1021

vi 自本國移居他國；（反義）immigrate
He emigrated from Spain to Costa Rica.
他從西班牙移民到了哥斯大黎加。

---

emotion
[ɪˈmoʃən]

e1022

n 情緒，情感
She wasn't able to keep her cheerful emotions off her face.
她無法讓自己興奮的情緒不在臉上表露出來。

---

emotional
[ɪˈmoʃənl]

e1023

adj 感情的，情緒的；情緒化的，感情用事的
He was too emotional to speak clearly after the funeral.
葬禮過後他太過激動，話都說不清楚了。

---

emphasis
[ˈɛmfəsɪs]

e1024

n 強調；重要性
Eventually, his students were grateful for the emphasis he had placed on concise writing.
最終，他的學生們感激他強調簡約寫作。

---

emphasize
[ˈɛmfəˌsaɪz]

e1025

vt 強調，著重
The coach emphasized the importance of focusing to his players.
教練向隊員們強調集中注意力的重要性。

---

employ
[ɪmˈplɔɪ]

e1026

vt 雇用；使用
Jeff hasn't been employed since he graduated from university.
傑夫自從大學畢業後就沒被雇用過。

---

employee
[ˌɛmplɔɪˈi]

e1027

n 雇員
The employees are thinking about having a protest next month to express their anger.
員工們正考慮下個月進行抗議以宣洩不滿。

employer
[ɪm'plɔɪɚ]
托 雅 學

n 雇主 e1028
The employer is not satisfied with the sales number this year.
雇主對今年的銷售數字不滿意。

employment
[ɪm'plɔɪmənt]
托 雅 學

n 雇用；使用；工作 e1029
He is looking for overseas employment.
他在找海外的工作。

enclose
[ɪn'kloz]
托 雅 學

vt 圍住；封入 e1030
She enclosed $50 in the birthday card for her son.
她把五十美元封到給兒子的生日賀卡裡。

encounter
[ɪn'kaʊntɚ]
托 雅 學

n 遇到，遭遇 e1031
This encounter with the bear in the woods many years ago was never forgotten.
多年前在森林中遇見熊的遭遇永不曾被忘記。

encounter
[ɪn'kaʊntɚ]
托 雅 學

vi/vt 遇到，遭遇 e1032
We encountered many strange sights on our trip.
我們在旅途中遇到了很多奇怪的景象。

endurance
[ɪn'djʊrəns]
托 雅 學

n 耐久力，持久力 e1033
As a runner, she was known for her endurance.
作為一個賽跑運動員，她以耐力而著稱。

endure
[ɪn'djʊr]
托 雅 學

vi/vt 忍受；持久，持續 e1034
She endured the opera because her husband loved it.
因為她的丈夫喜歡看歌劇，她也就忍受了。

energetic
[ˌɛnɚ'dʒɛtɪk]
托 雅 學

adj 精力旺盛的；積極的；有力的 e1035
He was known for being energetic and full of humor.
他以精力旺盛和富有幽默感而聞名。

energize
['ɛnɚˌdʒaɪz]
托 雅 學

vt 給予⋯能量；對⋯供以電壓；激勵 e1036
His passionate speech energized the crowd.
他熱情的演說激勵了群眾。

E

energy
['ɛnədʒɪ']

n 活力，精力；能量
e1037

He played soccer with energy and enthusiasm.
他踢足球時活力四射，熱情高漲。

enforce
[ɪn'fors]

vt 實施，執行；強制；支持，堅持（要求、主張等）
e1038

The teacher enforced the rules gently but firmly.
老師執行規章時雖和善卻很堅決。

enhance
[ɪn'hæns]

托 雅 學

vt 提高，增強；誇張
e1039

The lemon juice enhanced the natural flavor of the steak.
檸檬汁增強了牛排的天然風味。

enlighten
[ɪn'laɪtn]

vt 啟發，啟蒙；教導
e1040

Would you please enlighten the business team as to what your current thoughts are regarding this matter?
可以請您教導那個商業團隊您現在對這件事的想法嗎？

enormous
[ɪ'nɔrməs]

托 雅 學

adj 巨大的，龐大的
e1041

Mom brought back an enormous pumpkin from the market.
媽媽從市場帶回一個巨大的南瓜。

ensure
[ɪn'ʃʊr]

托 雅 學

vt 確保；使安全
e1042

She walked her daughter to school to ensure that she made it to the right class.
她陪女兒走到學校，以確保她能找到正確的班級。

entertain
[ˌɛntə'ten]

托 雅 學

vt 懷有（想法、希望、感覺等）
e1043

She often entertained the thought of someday becoming famous.
她常懷抱著有朝一日成名的想法。

entertainment
[ˌɛntə'tenmənt]

n 招待；娛樂節目
e1044

Last night's live entertainment was performed by a band of musicians.
昨天晚上的現場娛樂節目是由一群音樂家演出的。

enthusiasm
[ɪn'θjuzɪˌæzəm]

n 熱情；積極性
e1045

Her enthusiasm for the theater was infectious.
她對戲劇的熱情富有感染力。

enthusiast
[ɪn'θjuzɪˌæst]

托 雅 學

e1046

n 狂熱分子
The company's high-definition cameras are targeted at extreme sports enthusiasts.
該公司的高畫質相機的目標族群是極限運動愛好者。

enthusiastic
[ɪnˌθjuzɪ'æstɪk]

托 雅 學

e1047

adj 熱衷的，熱心的
He is very enthusiastic about becoming a heart surgeon.
他非常熱衷於成為一名心臟外科醫生。

entry
['ɛntrɪ]

托 雅 學

e1048

n 記載；條目
This record contains over 6,000 entries on rare insect species.
這個記錄包含了6000多個稀有昆蟲種類條目。

environment
[ɪn'vaɪrənmənt]

托 雅 學

e1049

n 環境，外界；圍繞
The students picked up aluminum cans to help protect the environment.
學生們撿鋁罐來幫助保護環境。

environmental
[ɪnˌvaɪrən'mɛntl]

托 雅 學

e1050

adj 環境的，環境產生的
Environmental protection is one of the most important concerns that require the attention of the entire human race.
環境保護是最重要且需要全人類關注的議題之一。

envy
['ɛnvɪ]

托 雅 學

e1051

n/vi/vt 羨慕，忌妒
I envy her beauty and success in life.
我羨慕她的美貌和人生中的成功。

equation
[ɪ'kweʃən]

托 雅 學

e1052

n 平衡；平均；反應式；方程式
I would like to ask my math teacher to show me how to solve this equation.
我想去問數學老師怎麼解這個方程式。

equipment
[ɪ'kwɪpmənt]

托 雅 學

e1053

n 設備，器材；才能
The technical equipment did all that it was supposed to do during the conference.
技術設備完成了所有應該在會議中完成的事。

erosion
[ɪ'roʒən]

托 雅 學

e1054

n 腐蝕，磨損；削弱，減少
Natural erosion in the desert has created some beautiful canyons.
沙漠中的天然風化形成了一些美麗的峽谷。

errand
[ˈɛrənd]

n 差使，差事
e1055
She went out that evening on a couple of errands.
那天晚上她外出去辦了一些雜事。

escalator
[ˈɛskəˌletə]

n 電梯，升降機
e1056
Amanda was happy to take the escalator instead of hiking up all the stairs.
艾曼達很高興能夠乘上電梯而不用一步一步爬樓梯了。

essence
[ˈsəns]

n 本質，本體；精華，精髓
e1057
The freedom to choose is the essence of democracy.
民主的精髓就是人有選擇的自由。

essential
[ɪˈsɛnʃəl]

adj 本質的；基本的；精華的；n 本質；要素
e1058
Olive oil is an essential ingredient in Italian cooking.
橄欖油是義大利烹飪的基本原料。

estate
[ɪsˈtet]

n 房地產，不動產；所有權
e1059
The grandfather willed all his estates to his first son.
這位爺爺立遺囑把他的所有地產都給了長子。

estimate
[ˈɛstəˌmet]

n/vt 估計，估價；評估
e1060
Have you finished the estimate for tomorrow's presentation?
你做完了明天報告用的估價表沒有？

eternal
[ɪˈtɝnl]

adj 永久的，永恆的
e1061
Christians believe that God is eternal, having no beginning and no end.
基督徒認為上帝是永恆的，沒有起始和結束。

ethics
[ˈɛθɪks]

n 倫理學；倫理觀；道德
e1062
Everyone knew her ethics were impeccable.
每個人都知道她的道德是無可挑剔的。

evacuate
[ɪˈvækjʊˌet]

vi/vt 疏散，撤出；排泄
e1063
They evacuated the children from the school when the fire alarm went off.
當火災警鈴聲響起時，他們把孩子從學校裡疏散。

83

evaluate
[ɪ'væljʊ,et]

托 雅 學

vi 估價，評價；**vt** 求…的值

She evaluated the horse from all sides before she purchased it.

她在買馬前從各個方面對馬進行了評估。

e1064

evaporate
[ɪ'væpə,ret]

托 雅 學

vi/vt （使）蒸發

By the time she found a cloth, the spilled alcohol had evaporated from the counter.

等她找到一塊布的時候，灑出來的酒精早已從櫃檯蒸發了。

e1065

eventual
[ɪ'vɛntʃʊəl]

托 雅 學

adj 最終的，最後的

She waited for his eventual apology.

她等著他最後的道歉。

e1066

eventually
[ɪ'vɛntʃʊəlɪ]

托 雅 學

adv 終於，最後

I hope to eventually pass all my exams if I can keep up with my homework assignments.

如果我可以跟上我的功課的話，我希望自己最終可以通過所有的考試。

e1067

everlasting
[ɛvə'læstɪŋ]

托 雅 學

adj 永久的，持久的

The teacher believed that educating students was the best way to make an everlasting contribution to the world.

那位老師相信，教育學生是她對世界做出永久貢獻的最佳方式。

e1068

evidence
['ɛvədəns]

托 雅 學

n 明顯，顯著；根據；證據

The lawyer submitted ten pieces of evidence to the court before the trial started.

審判開始前律師向法庭提交了十項證據。

e1069

evidence
['ɛvədəns]

托 雅 學

vt 證明；顯示；表明

He evidenced his approval by promising his full support.

他以全力支持的承諾來表明他的認可。

e1070

evident
['ɛvədənt]

托 雅 學

adj 明顯的，明白的

It was evident that the students had not studied hard enough for the test.

很明顯學生們考試準備得不夠認真。

e1071

evoke
[ɪ'vok]

托 雅 學

vt 喚起，引起

His landscape paintings evoked the peace of the country.

他的山水畫喚起了鄉村寧靜的感覺。

e1072

E

evolution
[ˌɛvəˈluʃən]

n 進化；演變，發展，進展
Many environmental factors, such as temperature and rainfall, can affect the evolution of living organisms.
許多環境因素，如氣溫和降雨，會對生物的進化產生影響。

e1073

evolve
[ɪˈvɑlv]

vi/vt （使）發展；（使）進化；（使）進展
The idea for the screenplay evolved out of his childhood experiences.
電影劇本的想法是從他的童年經歷中發展而來的。

e1074

exaggerate
[ɪgˈzædʒəˌret]

vi/vt 誇大，誇張
He had a tendency to exaggerate his feelings.
他傾向於誇大自己的情感。

e1075

excel
[ɪkˈsɛl]

vi 勝過其他；**vt** 勝過，優於；擅長
She excelled at classic ballet dancing.
她擅長古典芭蕾舞。

e1076

excellence
[ˈɛksḷəns]

n 優秀，卓越
The medical specialist was awarded a prize for excellence in his field.
那位醫學專家因為在他的領域中表現優秀而獲獎。

e1077

excellent
[ˈɛksḷənt]

adj 優秀的，卓越的
She studied diligently and that's why her grades were excellent.
她學習勤奮，因此她的成績很優秀。

e1078

exceptional
[ɪkˈsɛpʃṇḷ]

adj 例外的；優越的；獨特的，異常的
He is famous for his exceptional talent playing the piano.
他以異常的鋼琴彈奏天分聞名。

e1079

exclusive
[ɪkˈsklusɪv]

adj 獨佔的，唯一的；高級的
He had exclusive rights to develop the novel into a movie.
他獨享把小說翻拍成電影的權力。

e1080

exclusively
[ɪkˈsklusɪvlɪ]

adv 專門地，專有地，排外地
Sports stars sign contracts to play exclusively for their teams.
運動明星們簽署合約以專門為其團隊效力。

e1081

execute
['ɛksɪˌkjut]
托 雅 學

vi/vt 實行；執行；完成；履行；處死
They executed the general's order quickly.
他們迅速執行了將軍的命令。
e1082

---

execution
[ˌɛksɪ'kjuʃən]
托 雅 學

n 實行，執行；處死刑
The project's execution was simply faultless and I would highly recommend the team for future assignments.
這計畫的執行非常完美，我強烈建議分派日後工作給這個團隊。
e1083

---

executive
[ɪg'zɛkjʊtɪv]
托 雅 學

adj 執行的，實施的
I would like to speak to the executive director of your company.
我想與貴公司的執行董事談談。
e1084

---

executive
[ɪg'zɛkjʊtɪv]
托 雅 學

n 總經理，董事，行政負責人
The executive spent much of the year traveling the country.
總經理花了大半年時間周遊全國。
e1085

---

exhaust
[ɪg'zɔst]
托 雅 學

n 排氣裝置；廢氣；**vi/vt** 使筋疲力盡，耗盡；抽完
The smoke from the car exhaust made him cough.
汽車廢氣的煙霧使他咳嗽起來。
e1086

---

exhaustion
[ɪg'zɔstʃən]
托 雅 學

n 疲憊，筋疲力盡；竭盡
Her signs of exhaustion were obvious near the end of the marathon.
她疲憊的樣子在馬拉松接近結束時很明顯地顯露了出來。
e1087

---

exhibit
[ɪg'zɪbɪt]
托 雅 學

n 展覽品，陳列品；**vi/vt** 展出，陳列
The museum only exhibits his sculptures once a year.
博物館每年只展出一次他的雕刻作品。
e1088

---

exhibition
[ˌɛksə'bɪʃən]
托 雅 學

n 展覽會；陳列
The artist attended the first exhibition of her paintings.
藝術家參加了她的第一次畫展。
e1089

---

experiment
[ɪk'spɛrəmənt]
托 雅 學

n 實驗；試驗；**vi** 做試驗
The students are excited about doing experiments in the laboratory tomorrow.
學生們對於明天要去實驗室做實驗都感到非常興奮。
e1090

expert
[ˈɛkspɚt]

托 雅 學

e1091

adj 熟練的，有經驗的；專門的
We need your expert opinion regarding the explosion.
我們需要您對於爆炸事件的專家意見。

expert
[ˈɛkspɚt]

托 雅 學

e1092

n 專家，能手
He was an expert in French literature.
他是研究法國文學的專家。

expertise
[ˌɛkspɚˈtiz]

托 雅 學

e1093

n 專門知識（或技能等），專長
Shanghai has been valued as a major hub for attracting capital and financial management expertise.
上海被珍視為吸引資金和金融管理專門人才的主要樞紐。

explode
[ɪkˈsplod]

托 雅 學

e1094

vi/vt （使）爆炸，（使）爆發
The soda exploded all over his shirt.
汽水爆炸了，濺得他襯衫上四處都是。

exploration
[ˌɛkspləˈreʃən]

托 雅 學

e1095

n 考察，勘探，探查
Lewis and Clark carried out the first exploration of the Louisiana Purchase.
路易士和克拉克進行了路易斯安那購地的首次考察。

explore
[ɪkˈsplor]

托 雅 學

e1096

vi/vt 勘探，探測；探究，探索
She explored the library until she found the Mystery Section.
她在圖書館裡仔細探索，直到找到神秘小說區才甘休。

explosion
[ɪkˈsploʒən]

托 雅 學

e1097

n 爆炸，爆發
The sound of the explosion really panicked the crowds.
爆炸的聲音真的嚇壞了群眾。

explosive
[ɪkˈsplosɪv]

托 雅 學

e1098

adj 爆炸（性）的，爆發（性）的；n 爆炸物，炸藥
The explosive device failed to detonate after the timer was set.
在計時裝置設定後，那個爆炸性的裝置未能成功引爆。

expose
[ɪkˈspoz]

托 雅 學

e1099

vt 使暴露；使曝光
The journalist exposed the corruption of the large accounting firm.
記者將這家大型財務公司的腐敗曝光了。

E

exposition
[ˌɛkspə'zɪʃən]

n 說明，解釋；陳列；展覽會

She prepared her company's display table for the electronics exposition.

她為了電子展覽會佈置公司的展示桌。

e1100

exposure
[ɪk'spoʒə]

n 暴露；遭受（危險）；揭露

Protect your skin by limiting your exposure to the harsh sun.

你要通過減少皮膚暴露在強烈陽光下的時間來保護它。

e1101

extensive
[ɪk'stɛnsɪv]

adj 廣泛的，大規模的

When investigating the cause of the blaze, the fire inspector noticed extensive smoke damage.

當調查烈火的成因時，那位火災調查員注意到有大規模的煙霧損害。

e1102

extent
[ɪk'stɛnt]

托 雅 學

n 廣度；程度；限度，範圍

We were able to see the full extent of the city from the window of the hotel.

從這個飯店的窗戶我們可以看見整座城市的範圍。

e1103

exterior
[ɪk'stɪrɪə]

adj 外部的，外面的；n 外部

The seed has a hard exterior covering to protect itself.

種子有堅硬的外殼來保護自己。

e1104

F

字彙能力檢查表

先自我檢驗是否瞭解以下初階單字，若有不清楚者，請先開啟光碟中的電子書複習。

☐face
☐fairly
☐fairy
☐faith
☐familiar
☐fare
☐farewell
☐fault
☐favor
☐favor
☐fee
☐female
☐ferry
☐festival

☐festival
☐field
☐field
☐file
☐file
☐filling
☐final
☐firm
☐firm
☐fist
☐fit
☐fit
☐fitness
☐fitting

☐fix
☐fix
☐fixture
☐flavor
☐flight
☐float
☐float
☐flour
☐fluent
☐focus
☐focus
☐fold
☐fold

☐force
☐force
☐foreign
☐forward
☐frame
☐frame
☐frank
☐frequent
☐fridge
☐fruitful
☐furniture
☐further
☐furthermore

fabric
['fæbrɪk]
托 雅 學

n 織物，布料；結構，構造；建築物
The dress was made of imported fabric.
這條裙子是用進口布料製成的。

f1001

fabulous
['fæbjələs]
托 雅 學

adj 極好的；極為巨大的
You look fabulous in your new dress.
你穿那件新裙子看起來是極好的。

f1002

facet
['fæsɪt]
托 雅 學

n 小平面，方面，刻面
His keen intellect was only one facet of his charming personality.
他的睿智只是他迷人個性的一個方面。

f1003

facilitate
[fə'sɪlə,tet]
托 雅 學

vt 使變得（更）容易，使便利，使順利；推動；促進
He facilitated the discussion between the two diplomats.
他使這兩個外交官的討論順利進行。

f1004

facilitation
[fə,sɪlə'teʃən]
托 雅 學

n 推動；促進
The teacher association is committed to facilitation of effective learning.
教師協會致力於有效學習的推動。

f1005

factor
['fæktə]
托 雅 學

n 因素，要素
Finances were only one factor in her decision not to buy the house now.
資金只是她決定現在不買房子的一個因素。

f1006

factory
['fæktərɪ]
托 雅 學

n 工廠
The new factory produces 1,000 toys each week.
新的工廠每週生產一千個玩具。

f1007

faculty
['fækl̩tɪ]
托 雅 學

n 才能；學院，系；（學院或系的）全體教職員工
The faculty always meet on the second Tuesday of every month.
全體教職員工總在每月的第二個星期二開會。

f1008

fade
[fed]
托 雅 學

vi 褪色；衰減，消失
The color of the chair began to fade from the harsh sun over time.
在酷日下曬久了，這把椅子褪色了。

f1009

failure
['feljə]
托 雅 學

n 失敗，不及格；失敗者；故障，失靈；未能 f1010
He attributed his failure to poor judgment and foolish behavior.
他把自己的失敗歸因於糟糕的判斷和愚蠢的行為。

faint
[fent]
托 雅 學

adj 微弱的，模糊的；不明顯的 f1011
Since Jason's grandmother raised him from a toddler, his memory of his parents was faint.
傑森從學步時就由他的祖母撫養，因此他對親生父母的記憶是模糊的。

faint
[fent]
托 雅 學

n/vi 昏倒，昏暈 f1012
I think she will faint when I kiss her.
我想當我吻她的時候她會昏倒。

faithful
['feθfəl]
托 雅 學

adj 守信的；忠實的；如實的，可靠的 f1013
Dogs are generally considered the most loyal and faithful pets to own.
大家普遍認為狗是人們可擁有的最忠誠、最可靠的寵物。

fake
[fek]
托 雅 學

adj 假的，冒充的 f1014
The bank manager is said to have issued fake certificates.
這個銀行經理據說出具過偽造的憑證。

fake
[fek]
托 雅 學

n 假貨，贗品 f1015
The art appraiser said the expensive painting was a fake and completely worthless.
那個藝術鑒定人說那幅昂貴的畫作是贗品，而且毫無價值。

fake
[fek]
托 雅 學

vt 偽造；偽裝；做假 f1016
The football quarterback faked a pass to his wide receiver during the playoff game.
在加時賽進行時，那個足球四分衛做假動作傳球給他的外接員。

fame
[fem]
托 雅 學

n 名聲，名望；傳說；vt 使出名；傳揚……的名；稱道 f1017
The fifty-year-old restaurant has been famed for its seafood.
這家有五十年歷史的老餐廳以海鮮著名。

famous
['feməs]
托 雅 學

adj 著名的 f1018
Every student dreams of entering this famous university.
每一個學生都夢想要進入這所著名的大學。

F

fancy
['fænsɪ]
托 雅 學

adj 花式的，奇特的，精美的
The snake skin is used to make fancy bags.
蛇皮被用來製作精美的包。

f1019

fancy
['fænsɪ]
托 雅 學

n 愛好，迷戀；想像（力）
Perfect love can exist only in your fancy.
完美的愛情只存在於你的想像中。

f1020

fancy
['fænsɪ]
托 雅 學

vt 想像；幻想
Do you fancy yourself being the boss someday?
你是否想像過有一天自己做老闆？

f1021

fantastic
[fæn'tæstɪk]
托 雅 學

adj 奇異的，幻想的，異想天開的；了不起的
He thought the artist's newest piece was fantastic.
他認為這個藝術家的最新作品是很了不起的。

f1022

fantasy
['fæntəsɪ]
托 雅 學

n 幻想，空想，夢想；空想的產物，幻想作品
A fantasy came true for the young bride when she married a real-life prince.
對那個年輕的新娘而言，當她嫁給了一位現實生活中的王子時，她的夢想就成真了。

f1023

fascinate
['fæsən,et]
托 雅 學

vt 迷住，強烈吸引
As a young boy, Jason was fascinated by sharks.
傑森小時候很迷戀鯊魚。

f1024

fascinating
['fæsən,etɪŋ]
托 雅 學

adj 迷人的；極美的；極好的
I just could not put down the fascinating book until I had read it from beginning to end.
我在從頭到尾都讀過之後，才把那本吸引人的書放下。

f1025

fashion
['fæʃən]
托 雅 學

n 流行式樣（或貨品）；風氣，時尚
The wealthy lady is always dressed in the latest fashions.
那個富有的女士總是穿著最時尚款式的衣服。

f1026

fashionable
[fæʃənəbl̩]
托 雅 學

adj 流行的，時髦的
He admired her fashionable choices in clothing.
他欣賞她在穿著上的時尚選擇。

f1027

fasten
['fæsn̩]
托 雅 學

vi/vt 繫牢，（使）固定　　　　　f1028
She made sure that they all fastened their seat belts.
她確認他們全都扣上了安全帶。

fatal
['fetl]
托 雅 學

adj 致命的，毀滅性的，災難性的　　　f1029
The reporter rushed to the scene of the fatal accident.
記者火速趕到災難性事件的現場。

F

fatigue
[fə'tig]
托 雅 學

n 疲勞　　　　　f1030
Despite her fatigue, the nurse continued to care for her patients during the disaster.
儘管這個護士非常疲勞，她還是堅持在災難中照顧病人。

fatigue
[fə'tig]
托 雅 學

vt 使⋯疲勞　　　　　f1031
The intensive schedule of the conference fatigued all the participants.
本次會議的緊湊安排讓所有與會者都感到疲憊。

faucet
['fɔsɪt]
托 雅 學

n 龍頭，旋塞　　　　　f1032
Her son had accidentally left the faucet dripping.
她的兒子無意間把水龍頭留在那兒一直滴水。

faulty
['fɔltɪ]
托 雅 學

adj 有錯誤的；有缺點的，不完善的　　f1033
He returned the faulty product to the supplier.
他將有瑕疵的商品退回給供貨廠商。

feature
['fitʃɚ]
托 雅 學

n 特徵；容貌；特色；特寫　　　f1034
Her blue eyes were one of her most striking features.
藍眼睛是她最惹人注目的特徵之一。

feature
['fitʃɚ]
托 雅 學

vt 展示；刻畫，勾勒；以⋯⋯為特色　　f1035
The program will feature highlights from recent games.
這個節目將重點展示最近的比賽亮點。

federal
['fɛdərəl]
托 雅 學

adj 聯邦（制）的；聯合的；同盟的　　f1036
The federal judge overturned the decision of the lower court.
聯邦法官推翻了下級地方法院的決議。

feedback
['fid,bæk]
托 雅 學

n 回饋；反應；回授

The company used questionnaires to gather feedback about its products from the customers.

公司利用問卷收集客戶對產品的回饋。

f1037

fertile
['fɝtl]
托 雅 學

adj 肥沃的，富饒的；能繁殖的

The Nile floods twice a year depositing a rich layer of fertile soil for later crop growth.

尼羅河一年兩次的氾濫沉積了一層豐富肥沃的土壤，有利於日後的穀物生長。

f1038

fetch
[fɛtʃ]
托 雅 學

n 取得；拿；**vi/vt** 取來；引出；售得

My dog always enjoys fetching the ball I throw.

我的狗很愛撿回我丟的球。

f1039

fiction
['fɪkʃən]
托 雅 學

n 虛構，編造；小說

The Joy Luck Club is categorized as historical fiction.

《喜福會》被歸為歷史小說一類。

f1040

fierce
[fɪrs]
托 雅 學

adj 兇猛的，殘忍的；狂熱的，強烈的，激烈的

Several local talented performers faced fierce competition from a multitude of overseas contestants.

一些當地有才藝的表演者面臨著眾多來自海外參賽者的激烈競爭。

f1041

figure
['fɪgjɚ]
托 雅 學

n 人，人物；體形，輪廓；數字；圖形

Did you see the familiar figure standing at the corner last night?

你昨晚看到站在角落裡的熟悉的人影了嗎？

f1042

figure
['fɪgjɚ]
托 雅 學

vi/vt 描繪；計算；推測；想，覺得

She figured that she had learned a lot from the experience.

她覺得自己從那次經歷中學到了許多。

f1043

filter
['fɪltɚ]
托 雅 學

n 濾紙；**vt** 過濾

The best prevention for cholera is to boil or filter water.

預防霍亂最好的辦法是把水煮沸或者過濾。

f1044

finance
[faɪ'næns]
托 雅 學

n 財政，金融

He is a major player in the world of finance.

他是金融界的一個大玩家。

f1045

finance
[faɪˈnæns]

托 雅 學

vt 為…提供資金　　　　　f1046

He was able to finance his education by working part-time during the summer.

他靠暑期兼職打工為上學提供資金。

financial
[faɪˈnænʃəl]

托 雅 學

adj 財政的，金融的　　　　f1047

Hong Kong is one of the key financial cities in the world.

香港是世界上主要的金融城市之一。

finding
[ˈfaɪndɪŋ]

托 雅 學

n 發現，發現物；複數＝研究調查結果　f1048

He presented his market research findings to his manager for review.

他把市場調查的結果給經理審核。

flake
[flek]

托 雅 學

n 片，薄片；肌膈　　　　f1049

Snow flakes fall from the sky during winter.

雪花在寒冬裡從天而降。

flame
[flem]

托 雅 學

n 火焰，火苗；熱情；光輝；**vi/vt** 發火焰，燃燒　f1050

Her cheeks flamed an angry red very quickly.

他的臉很快氣得通紅，像燃燒起來一樣。

flap
[flæp]

托 雅 學

n 垂下物；帽檐；口袋蓋；（信封的）封蓋　f1051

Most envelopes include an adhesive under the flap that you must moisten first.

大部分信封在封蓋下都有黏合劑，但你必須先打濕它。

flap
[flæp]

托 雅 學

n 拍打；**vi/vt** 拍打，拍動　f1052

The chicken flapped its wings, but no matter how hard it tried, it just couldn't fly.

那隻雞拍打它的翅膀，但無論它如何努力嘗試，就是無法飛起來。

flash
[flæʃ]

托 雅 學

adj 閃光（的）；炫耀的，花稍的　f1053

You can go for a system, which sounds flash but quite cheap.

你可以弄一個系統，聽上去很花稍，其實很便宜。

flash
[flæʃ]

托 雅 學

n 閃光；閃光燈　　　　f1054

You should use a flash when taking pictures on cloudy days to brighten up people's faces.

陰天拍照時你應該開閃光燈，讓人的臉看起來光亮些。

flash
[flæʃ]
托 雅 學

vi/vt 發閃光，閃亮；閃現
The figures flash up on the scoreboard.
數字在記分牌上閃現。

f1055

flask
[flæsk]
托 雅 學

n 保溫瓶；燒瓶
Flasks are used to do chemical experiments in a laboratory.
燒瓶在實驗室裡是用來做化學實驗的。

f1056

flaw
[flɔ]
托 雅 學

n 裂縫；缺陷；**vt** 使…破裂；使…有缺陷，使…有破綻
The villain's evil plan was flawed by an awkward start.
反派角色的邪惡計畫在笨拙的開場就露出破綻。

f1057

flesh
[flɛʃ]
托 雅 學

n 肉；肌肉
Human flesh decomposes in the first few months after death.
人類的肉體在死後幾個月就會分解。

f1058

flexibility
[ˌflɛksəˈbɪlətɪ]
托 雅 學

n 易彎曲性；適應性，靈活性；彈性
Her flexibility increased daily as she practiced her gymnastics.
當她練體操時她的靈活性每天都在增加。

f1059

flexible
[ˈflɛksəbl]
托 雅 學

adj 柔韌的，易彎曲的，靈活的，能變形的
The doctor kept a flexible schedule in case he received an emergency call.
醫生維持著彈性的時間表以防他接到緊急的電話。

f1060

fling
[flɪŋ]
托 雅 學

vi/vt （用力）扔，拋
Could you please fling the manual over to me so I can read about the product?
可以請你把手冊扔給我嗎？這樣我可以讀取產品資訊。

f1061

flip
[flɪp]
托 雅 學

n 拋，彈；筋斗；空翻
The gymnast made a perfect flip at the end of the performance.
在表演的最後，體操選手做了一個完美的空翻。

f1062

flip
[flɪp]
托 雅 學

vi/vt 擲，彈，輕擊；蹦跳
That boy didn't know what to do, so he flipped a coin to make a decision.
那個男孩不知道要做什麼，所以他擲硬幣來做決定。

f1063

flock
[flɑk]
托 雅 學

n 群，（禽、畜等的）群；大量；vi 群集，成群 `f1064`
All of the students flocked to the beach party.
所有的學生都群集至海灘派對。

flush
[flʌʃ]
托 雅 學

adj （短暫）手頭寬鬆 `f1065`
I don't mind paying for this meal because I'm rather flush at the moment.
最近我的手頭比較寬鬆，所以我並不介意付這頓餐費。

flush
[flʌʃ]
托 雅 學

vi （臉）發紅 `f1066`
The boy's sweet words caused the girl's cheeks to flush with embarrassment.
男孩的甜言蜜語讓女孩尷尬得臉發紅。

flush
[flʌʃ]
托 雅 學

vt 沖洗 `f1067`
To keep the pipes clean, flush them with fresh water every day.
為保持水管乾淨，請每天用乾淨的水沖洗。

foil
[fɔɪl]
托 雅 學

n 陪襯物；陪襯者 `f1068`
The actress played as a comedic foil to the queen in that play.
女演員在那部戲劇裡扮演諧星的配角，作為女王的陪襯者。

foil
[fɔɪl]
托 雅 學

vt 貼箔於…；挫敗，阻止 `f1069`
The citizens foiled the bank robber's plan by taking his gun away and calling the police.
市民奪過搶匪的槍並通知員警，借此阻止了他搶銀行的計畫。

folk
[fok]
托 雅 學

adj 民間的；n 人們；民族；親屬 `f1070`
Many old people like traditional Chinese folk medicine.
很多老年人喜歡中國傳統的民間醫療。

folklore
['fok,lor]
托 雅 學

n 民間傳說，民俗；民俗學 `f1071`
According to Irish folklore, there is a pot of gold at the end of a rainbow.
根據愛爾蘭的民間傳說，在彩虹的盡頭有一缸黃金。

forecast
['for,kæst]
托 雅 學

n 預測，預報 `f1072`
He delivered his election forecast quickly.
他很快發表了他的選舉預測。

forecast
['for,kæst]

托 雅 學

vi/vt 預測，預報
The weatherman forecasted two days of rain.
氣象播報員預測會下兩天雨。

f1073

forgive
[fə'gɪv]

托 雅 學

vt 原諒，饒恕
She asked him to forgive her for breaking her promise.
她求他原諒自己違背承諾。

f1074

form
[fɔrm]

托 雅 學

n 形狀；形式；表格；**vi/vt** 組成，構成；形成
He was determined to form a new pop music band.
他決心要組建一個新的流行樂隊。

f1075

formal
['fɔrml]

托 雅 學

adj 正式的；形式的
She wore a blue satin gown to the formal dance.
她穿著藍色緞面的禮服去正式的舞會。

f1076

formality
[fɔr'mælətɪ]

托 雅 學

n 禮節；程式，正式手續；拘謹
Westerners may not understand the formalities for Asian weddings.
西方人可能不瞭解亞洲婚禮的禮節。

f1077

forthcoming
[,forθ'kʌmɪŋ]

托 雅 學

adj 即將到來的；準備好的；樂意幫助的
Tina is worried about the forthcoming examination because she is still not prepared for it.
緹娜對於即將到來的考試感到很擔心，因為她仍舊沒有準備好。

f1078

fortunately
['fɔrtʃənɪtlɪ]

托 雅 學

adv 幸運地，幸虧
Fortunately, the rain started after we arrived at the house.
幸運的是，我們到家後才開始下雨。

f1079

forum
['forəm]

托 雅 學

n 論壇，討論會
He made the meeting an open forum for hearing new ideas for the company.
他把會議弄成為公司聽取新點子的開放式討論會。

f1080

foster
['fɔstə]

托 雅 學

adj 收養的
Many foster children live in that community building.
很多收養的小孩住在那個社區大樓裡。

f1081

foster
['fɔstɚ]
托 雅 學

vt 養育，收養；懷抱；鼓勵 ▸ f1082

We fostered the puppy after we found him wandering around our neighborhood.

這隻小狗在社區裡遊蕩的時候我們收養了牠。

---

foul
[faʊl]
托 雅 學

adj 污穢的；邪惡的 ▸ f1083

The room smells a bit of foul because of all the trash put outside the window.

因為窗戶外頭的垃圾，這個房間聞起來有點臭。

---

foul
[faʊl]
托 雅 學

n 犯規 ▸ f1084

It was an obvious foul when the player hit his opponent in the head with his elbow.

那個球員用手肘撞對手的頭部，那是明顯的犯規。

---

foul
[faʊl]
托 雅 學

vt （以廢物、排泄物）弄髒 ▸ f1085

You should not allow your dog to foul the grass in the park.

你不應該允許你的狗污染公園的草地。

---

found
[faʊnd]
托 雅 學

vt 使有根據；鑄造，熔制；建立，創辦 ▸ f1086

The prosecutor was able to found a theory on firm evidence.

檢察官能在確鑿證據的基礎上建立一套理論。

---

foundation
[faʊn'deʃən]
托 雅 學

n 基礎，地基；創立；基金，基金會 ▸ f1087

She had repairmen come and check the foundation of her house for cracks.

她因爆裂聲請了維修工人過來並檢查房子的地基。

---

founder
['faʊndɚ]
托 雅 學

n 創建者；締造者 ▸ f1088

The company's founder retired after fifty years as CEO.

在擔任了50年的CEO後，這位公司的創建者退休了。

---

fountain
['faʊntən]
托 雅 學

n 泉水，噴泉；源泉 ▸ f1089

The little girls played near the fountain while their mothers were chatting.

小女孩們的媽媽在閒聊時，她們在噴泉附近玩耍。

---

fragile
['frædʒəl]
托 雅 學

adj 易碎的，脆的，易損壞的；虛弱的，脆弱的 ▸ f1090

He carefully picked up the fragile pieces of the ancient parchment.

他小心謹慎地拾起易損壞的古代羊皮紙文獻。

fragrance
['freɡrəns]
托 雅 學

n 芬芳，香味；香，香料

He knew the fragrance that she liked and bought it for her.

他知道她喜愛的香料，並給她買了。

f1091

fragrant
['freɡrənt]
托 雅 學

adj 香的；芬芳的

The babysitter rubbed fragrant oil on the baby's chest and belly.

褓姆把芳香精油塗抹在嬰兒的胸部和肚子上。

f1092

framework
['frem,wɝk]
托 雅 學

n 框架；結構；組織

You are required to apply the theoretical frameworks taught in the class in your thesis.

你必須在你的論文裡運用課堂上教授的理論架構。

f1093

fraud
[frɔd]
托 雅 學

n 欺詐；欺騙（行為）；騙子；假貨

The investor tricked his clients out of their life savings and he's being investigated for tax fraud.

那個投資者騙光了客戶的畢生積蓄，他現在正因詐欺稅額被調查。

f1094

freak
[frik]
托 雅 學

vt 胡鬧，開玩笑；崩潰

Please don't freak out when I tell you what it cost!

當我告訴你它花了多少錢時，請千萬別崩潰！

f1095

frost
[frɑst]
托 雅 學

n 霜凍；嚴寒

He cleans the condensed frost on the windshield off his car before taking it out.

他在開車前將車子擋風玻璃上的厚霜清除了。

f1096

frown
[fraʊn]
托 雅 學

n/vi 皺眉；蹙額

I haven't told her the bad news, because I really don't want to see her frown.

我還沒告訴她這個壞消息，因為我真的不想看見她皺眉頭。

f1097

frustrate
['frʌs,tret]
托 雅 學

vt 挫敗，阻撓，使灰心

She was frustrated by another failure of promotion.

她因另一次升遷失敗而感到灰心。

f1098

frustration
[,frʌs'treʃən]
托 雅 學

n 挫折，失敗

He experienced frustration when he voiced his ideas and concerns during last week's meeting.

當他在上週的會議上表達自己的想法與關注時，他遭遇了挫折。

f1099

F

fuel
['fjʊəl]
托 雅 學

n 燃料　　　　　　　　　　　　　　　f1100
Fuels are used in a complex process to release usable energy.
燃料在複雜的程序中被使用，以釋放可用的能源。

fuel
['fjʊəl]
托 雅 學

vt 給……加燃料，刺激　　　　　　　　f1101
The economic boom was fueled by easy credit.
寬鬆的信貸刺激了經濟繁榮。

fulfill
[fʊl'fɪl]
托 雅 學

vt 履行；滿足；完成　　　　　　　　　f1102
Henry is a freshman in college and hopes to fulfill his dream of becoming an interior designer.
亨利是大一新生，他希望能夠實現成為室內設計師的夢想。

function
['fʌŋkʃən]
托 雅 學

n 功能，作用；複數＝職務；函數　　　f1103
The main function of merchant banks is to raise capital for industry.
商業銀行的主要功能是給產業融資。

function
['fʌŋkʃən]
托 雅 學

vi 起作用　　　　　　　　　　　　　　f1104
She functioned as the peacemaker in her family.
她在家起到和事佬的作用。

functional
['fʌŋkʃənl]
托 雅 學

adj 機能的；實用的　　　　　　　　　f1105
I am thankful for functional clothing keeping me dry when it rains.
我感謝實用的衣服使我在下雨的時候身上保持乾燥。

fund
[fʌnd]
托 雅 學

n 資金，基金；存款，現款；（知識等的）累積　f1106
Josh donated all of his savings to the relief fund.
喬希把他所有的存款都捐給了救助基金。

fundamental
[ˌfʌndə'mɛntl]
托 雅 學

adj 基礎的，基本的　　　　　　　　　f1107
They had differences of fundamental opinion about how to raise children.
他們在養育孩子的問題上有不同的基本觀念。

funeral
['fjunərəl]
托 雅 學

n 喪禮，葬禮　　　　　　　　　　　　f1108
The funeral was held at the local Baptist church.
喪禮是在當地的浸信會教堂舉行的。

furious
[ˈfjʊərɪəs]

adj 狂怒的；狂暴的，猛烈的

f1109

He was furious when his favorite team lost the play-off.
當他最喜愛的球隊輸了加時賽時，他感到狂怒。

G

字彙能力檢查表

先自我檢驗是否瞭解以下初階單字，若有不清楚者，請先開啟光碟中的電子書複習。

☐ gang ☐ goal ☐ grab ☐ gradual
☐ glue ☐ gown ☐ grab ☐ ground

---

galaxy
['gæləksɪ]

托 雅 學

g1001

n 一群顯赫的人

A galaxy of performers showed up to attend the charity concert.

一群顯赫的表演者現身參加慈善音樂會。

---

galaxy
['gæləksɪ]

托 雅 學

g1002

n 銀河；星系

We all live in the Milky Way galaxy, but there are billions of others.

我們都住在銀河系裡，但宇宙裡還有數億其他星系。

---

gallery
['gælərɪ]

托 雅 學

g1003

n 長廊，畫廊；美術館

They slowly walked through the gallery of modern art.

他們緩慢地走過現代藝術的畫廊。

---

gamble
['gæmbḷ]

托 雅 學

g1004

n 賭博

Why don't you take a gamble and play roulette?

為什麼不來玩轉盤賭一把呢？

---

gamble
['gæmbḷ]

托 雅 學

g1005

vi/vt 賭博；投機，冒險

The restaurant owner is gambling that the new receipt will be a success.

餐廳老闆在賭新的菜單會取得成功。（英文的賭有兩層意思：一是賭博遊戲，贏家與輸家是對立關係；另一種賭強調的是對成功的不確定性的部分）

garage
['gə'rɑʒ]
托 雅 學

n 車庫，飛機庫；修車廠；加油站
He cleaned out the other side of the garage so they could park their car inside.
他將車庫另一邊清乾淨以便他們將車停進來。

g1006

garbage
['gɑrbɪdʒ]
托 雅 學

n 垃圾，汙物，廢料
She took the garbage out the night before the trashman came.
在垃圾處理人員來的前一天晚上，她將垃圾拿到外面去了。

g1007

gather
['gæðɚ]
托 雅 學

vt 收集；聚集，聚攏；推測，推斷
The police have been gathering evidence against the criminal.
警方一直在收集罪犯的犯罪證據。

g1008

gear
[gɪr]
托 雅 學

n 齒輪，傳動裝置；設備
Our fishing gear is already loaded in the boat.
我們的釣魚設備已經裝載在小船上了。

g1009

gear
[gɪr]
托 雅 學

vi/vt 調整，使適合
Let's gear up the factory to get more orders this month.
讓我們對工廠進行調整，以便這個月有更多的訂單。

g1010

gender
['dʒɛndɚ]
托 雅 學

n （生理上的）性別；詞性
When filling in government forms, you always have to write your name and gender.
當你填政府的表格時，你總是必須填寫你的名字和性別。

g1011

generalization
[,dʒɛnərəlaɪ'zeʃən]
托 雅 學

n 一般化，普遍化；概括性的論述
People tend to form generalizations from specific instances.
人們傾向於從具體的例子中形成概括性的論述。

g1012

generalize
['dʒɛnərəl,aɪz]
托 雅 學

vi/vt 歸納，概括；推廣，普及
He had a tendency to generalize in his writing instead of being specific with the facts.
在他的文章中，他比較傾向於用概括的手法而少在具體的事實上著墨。

g1013

generate
['dʒɛnə,ret]
托 雅 學

vt 產生；生殖；製造出
The President's comments generated a firestorm of criticism from the press.
總統的評論引起一連串的媒體批評。

g1014

generation
[ˌdʒɛnəˈreʃən]

n 一代（人）　　　g1015
Generation X is considered less idealistic than their parents.
X世代人（被遺忘的一代）被認為沒有他們父母親那麼理想化。

generation
[ˌdʒɛnəˈreʃən]

n 產生，發生　　　g1016
The waterfall can be used for the generation of electricity.
瀑布可以用來發電。

generator
[ˈdʒɛnəˌretɚ]

n 發電機，發生器　　　g1017
This industrial park is hosting the world's most advanced power generator.
這個工業園區裡有世界上最先進的發電機。

generosity
[ˌdʒɛnəˈrɑsətɪ]

n 慷慨，寬宏大量　　　g1018
The philanthropist is well-known for his generosity in donating money to good causes.
這個慈善家以為公益事業慷慨捐款而著稱。

generous
[ˈdʒɛnərəs]

adj 寬宏大量的，慷慨的　　　g1019
He was always generous to anyone who came to the church asking for food.
他對來教堂乞討食物的人們向來很慷慨。

gentle
[ˈdʒɛntl̩]

adj 和藹的，文雅的；有禮貌的　　　g1020
Simon is widely regarded as being very gentle and considerate.
大家都認為西蒙很有禮貌，很體貼。

geometry
[dʒɪˈɑmətrɪ]

n 幾何（學）　　　g1021
She loved algebra in school but didn't care much for geometry.
她在學生時代熱愛代數，但不太喜歡幾何學。

germ
[dʒɝm]

n 微生物，細菌，幼芽　　　g1022
Everyone is advised to wash their hands often to guard against germs and prevent the spread of disease.
每個人都被建議多洗手來對抗細菌以預防疾病的傳播。

gesture
[ˈdʒɛstʃɚ]

n 姿勢，姿態，手勢　　　g1023
We shake our hands as a gesture of friendship.
我們以握手作為友好的示意動作。

gesture
['dʒɛstʃə]

托 雅 學

vi/vt 做手勢

"I like that one better," she said as she gestured toward her favorite painting.

「我比較喜歡那幅，」她做手勢指著她最喜愛的畫說。

g1024

gigantic
[dʒaɪˈgæntɪk]

托 雅 學

adj 巨大的，龐大的

He couldn't get his mother to keep the gigantic stray dog they'd found while they were playing.

他們在玩的時候發現了一隻巨大的流浪狗，但他無法說服他的媽媽把它留下。

g1025

giggle
['gɪgl̩]

托 雅 學

vi 癡笑；咯咯地笑；**vt** 咯咯地笑著說

The small girl giggled and then hid in her mother's skirt.

這個女孩咯咯地笑，然後就藏在她媽媽的裙子裡。

g1026

glide
[glaɪd]

托 雅 學

n/vt 溜，滑行；（時間）消逝

It was fun to see all the good skiers just glide down the snow-covered hill.

看見所有的溜冰好手從白雪皚皚的山上滑下來很有趣。

g1027

glimpse
[glɪmps]

托 雅 學

n 一瞥，瞥見

She caught a quick glimpse of the beautiful dress worn by the passing pedestrian.

她快速地瞥了一眼那個穿著漂亮衣服的路人。

g1028

glimpse
[glɪmps]

托 雅 學

vi/vt 一瞥，瞥見

He glimpsed at my new watch and asked where I got it.

他瞥了一眼我的新手錶，問我在哪裡買的。

g1029

global
['globl̩]

托 雅 學

adj 球形的；全球的，全世界的；全面的

Global warming has become cause for worldwide concern.

全球氣候變暖已經成為全世界關注的問題。

g1030

globalize
['globəˌlaɪz]

托 雅 學

vt 使全球化

In this globalized era, each nation is deeply connected with many others.

在這個全球化的時代，每個國家都與其他國家緊密聯繫著。

g1031

globe
[glob]

托 雅 學

n 球體，地球儀；地球，世界

Airplanes can fly us to most places around the globe.

飛機能夠帶我們到地球上大部分地方。

g1032

gloomy
['glumɪ']

`adj` 陰暗的，令人沮喪的，陰鬱的
g1033

She bought some colorful posters to brighten her gloomy room.

她買了一些色彩繽紛的海報來使她陰暗的房間變明亮一點。

glorify
['glorə,faɪ']

`vt` 讚美（上帝）；頌揚；美化
g1034

Goals glorify our lives; indeed, they give us clear directions in life.

目標使生命增色；他們在生命中毋庸置疑帶給我們明確的方向。

glorious
['glorɪəs']

`adj` 壯麗的，輝煌的；光榮的
g1035

G

She was looking forward to a picnic with her children on such a glorious day.

她很期待能在那麼光輝燦爛的一天和她的孩子們野餐。

glow
[glo]

`n` 白熱，灼熱
g1036

He saw a glow of white light coming down from the sky.

他看見白熱的光從天而降。

glow
[glo]

`vi` 發熱，發光，發紅；色彩奪目
g1037

The interior of this café glows with rich colors and reflective lighting.

這家咖啡店的內部裝潢色彩奪目，還會反光發亮。

gorgeous
['gɔrdʒəs']

`adj` 華麗的，燦爛的；宜人的
g1038

She brushed her gorgeous red hair 100 times front to back.

她把自己那美麗的紅頭髮從前面到後面梳了100次。

gossip
['gɑsəp']

`n/vi` （說）閒話，閒聊
g1039

She hated to hear people gossip about her friends.

她討厭聽別人說她朋友的閒話。

govern
['gʌvən']

`vi/vt` 統治；管理；決定；指導；影響
g1040

It is extremely difficult to govern a country during economic recessions.

在經濟衰退期間去管理一個國家是極具困難的。

government
['gʌvənmənt']

`n` 政治學；治理，管理；支配；政府，內閣；政體
g1041

Most of his ministers had no previous experience of government.

他內閣中的大部分成員都沒有管理經驗。

grace
[gres]
托 雅 學

n 優美，文雅　　　　　　　　　　　　　　g1042
The actress captured the audience's attention with her grace and elegance.
這位女演員用她的優美和高貴征服了觀眾的心。

grace
[gres]
托 雅 學

n 恩惠，恩澤；寬限，緩刑；感恩禱告　　　　g1043
By god's grace, the airplane landed safely at last.
靠著神的恩惠，飛機終於安全降落了。

grade
[gred]
托 雅 學

n 等級，級別；年級；分數，成績　　　　　　g1044
My mother is delighted to see that my English grades have improved immensely.
我的媽媽很開心看到我的英文成績突飛猛進。

grade
[gred]
托 雅 學

vi/vt 分等，分級　　　　　　　　　　　　g1045
All students at the school are tested and graded by their abilities.
所有在校的學生都以其能力來測試並分等級。

grant
[grænt]
托 雅 學

n 授予物；vt 同意，准予；授予　　　　　　g1046
If you let your children take everything for granted, they will become spoiled soon.
如果你讓孩子們認為一切都理所當然，他們很快就會被寵壞。

grant
[grænt]
托 雅 學

n 津貼；轉讓證書；授予物　　　　　　　　　g1047
He received a grant from the government for his research.
他從政府那裡得到了研究津貼。

graphic
['græfɪk]
托 雅 學

adj 繪畫似的，圖解的；生動的　　　　　　　g1048
She didn't let her children see the movie because some of the murder scenes were too graphic.
她沒讓小孩看這部電影，因為一些謀殺場景太寫實了。

grasp
[græsp]
托 雅 學

n 抓住，抓緊；掌握，領會　　　　　　　　　g1049
You cannot escape his grasp no matter how hard you try.
你再怎麼努力也逃不過他的控制。

grasp
[græsp]
托 雅 學

vi/vt 抓住，抓緊；掌握，領會　　　　　　　g1050
Some students did not grasp the concept that the teacher was trying to teach them.
有些學生沒有領會老師要教的概念。

grasshopper
['græs,hɑpɚ]

n 蚱蜢，蝗蟲，草蜢 `g1051`

The boys chased grasshoppers in the field by their house.

這些男孩子在家旁邊的草地上追蚱蜢。

grateful
['gretfəl]

adj 感激的，感謝的 `g1052`

She was grateful for the opportunity to audition for such a big role in the production.

她很感激有機會在這部作品中試演主角。

gratitude
['grætə,tjud]

n 感激，感謝 `g1053`

She taught her children the importance of gratitude when dealing with others.

她教導孩子們在與他人相處時感恩的重要性。

G

grave
[grev]

adj 嚴肅的，莊重的；嚴重的 `g1054`

He is in grave condition and he is not going to live through the night.

他的病情很嚴重，活不過今天晚上了。

grave
[grev]

n 墳墓 `g1055`

They selected two grave plots under the tree in the corner of the cemetery.

他們選了墓園角落那棵樹下的兩塊墳墓用地。

greed
[grid]

n 貪婪，渴望 `g1056`

When the hostage said his family would pay anything to get him back, he could see greed in the kidnapper's eyes.

當人質說他的家人願意付出任何代價把他救回去，他看到了綁架者眼中的貪婪。

greedy
['gridɪ]

adj 貪婪的；渴望的 `g1057`

She knew he could be greedy when it came to money.

她知道當事情一扯上金錢，他就會變得貪婪。

grid
[grɪd]

n 格子，網格 `g1058`

The arrangement of streets in our city is a perfect grid.

我們城市的街道排列是完美的網格狀。

grief
[grif]

n 悲傷，悲痛；悲傷的事，悲痛的緣由 `g1059`

The grief over losing both parents at the same time never left her.

同時失去雙親的悲傷從未遠離她。

grill
[grɪl]
托 雅 學

n 烤架，鐵格子；烤肉；vi/vt 燒，烤；嚴加盤問　　g1060
He was grilled because they suspected that he committed the crime.
他被拷問了，因為他們懷疑是他犯的罪。

grin
[grɪn]
托 雅 學

n/vi 露齒而笑，咧嘴一笑　　g1061
She usually grins at people when she's lost for words and doesn't know what to say.
當她不會說話或無話可說時就會朝人家咧嘴一笑。

grind
[graɪnd]
托 雅 學

vi/vt 磨（碎），碾（碎）；磨快　　g1062
The chef grinds the blunt knife skillfully before slicing the meat.
廚師在切肉前很有技巧地把鈍的刀磨鋒利。

grip
[grɪp]
托 雅 學

n 緊握，抓緊；掌握　　g1063
As other climbers slipped, Sally kept a tight grip of the rope.
當其他攀登者打滑時，莎莉緊緊握著繩索。

grip
[grɪp]
托 雅 學

vt 緊握，抓緊；掌握　　g1064
She gripped my hand in fear as she entered the operating room.
在進入手術室時，她害怕地緊握著我的手。

groom
[grum]
托 雅 學

n 馬夫；新郎；男僕　　g1065
The groom gazed at the bride with a contented expression and a smile.
新郎凝視著新娘，帶著滿足的表情與微笑。

groom
[grum]
托 雅 學

vt 照料；打扮，修飾　　g1066
Bill groomed his rabbits carefully as if they were his kids.
比爾精心照料他的兔子，就像自己的孩子一般。

gross
[gros]
托 雅 學

adj 粗魯的，粗俗的；噁心的　　g1067
The princess finds the slimy frog gross and unsightly.
公主覺得又黏又滑的青蛙既噁心又難看。

gross
[gros]
托 雅 學

adj 總的，毛（重）的　　g1068
His gross income is much higher than most recent university graduates.
他的總收入比大多數畢業生高得多。

gross
[gros]

托 雅 學

g1069

n 總額

The gross for last year was thirty-five million dollars.

去年的收入總額是三千五百萬美元。

---

guarantee
[ˌgærənˈti]

托 雅 學

g1070

n 保證，保證書

I cannot give you any guarantee that this antique radio will work.

我不能給你任何保證，說這個古董收音機還能用。

---

guardian
[ˈgɑrdɪən]

托 雅 學

g1071

adj 保護的；n 監護人，保護人

That child needed a guardian because his parents died in a car accident.

那個孩子需要監護人，因為他的雙親都在車禍中喪命了。

---

guideline
[ˈgaɪdˌlaɪn]

托 雅 學

g1072

n 指導方針，指導原則，準則，標準

She laid out the guidelines of the assignment to her students.

她把作業的指導原則解釋給她的學生們聽。

---

guilt
[gɪlt]

托 雅 學

g1073

n 罪過；內疚

I am full of guilt for not making it to my grandfather's funeral.

我對沒能參加祖父的葬禮深感內疚。

---

guilty
[ˈgɪltɪ]

托 雅 學

g1074

adj 有罪的；內疚的

The jury found him guilty of first degree murder.

陪審團判他有罪，犯了一級謀殺罪。

---

gymnasium
[dʒɪmˈnezɪəm]

托 雅 學

g1075

n 體育館，健身房

After work, he headed to the gymnasium for a swim.

下班後，他前往體育館游泳。

---

gymnastics
[dʒɪmˈnæstɪks]

托 雅 學

g1076

n 體育；體操

The gymnastics coach began practice at 7 a.m. every morning.

這位體操教練每天早上都是7點開始訓練的。

G

字彙能力檢查表

先自我檢驗是否瞭解以下初階單字，若有不清楚者，請先開啟光碟中的電子書複習。

☐hail ☐hell ☐hike ☐housing
☐handbook ☐hence ☐hike ☐hum
☐hang ☐herb ☐hike ☐humor
☐hang ☐herd ☐historical ☐humorous
☐harmful ☐herd ☐hobby ☐hunger
☐haste ☐hide ☐honesty ☐hunger
☐hasty ☐hide ☐hop ☐hungry
☐healthcare ☐highly ☐hose

habitat
['hæbə,tæt]

n （動物的）棲息地；（植物的）產地　h1001

The rabbit's habitat was threatened by the new housing development.

兔子的棲息地受到新房屋開發的威脅。

hallmark
['hɔl,mark]

n 特點；品質證明；戳記　h1002

Jason had all the hallmarks of a great language teacher.

傑森具有所有優秀語言教師的特質。

hallmark
['hɔl,mark]

vt 給…蓋上戳記　h1003

The jewelry store hallmarks all their gold and silver items.

這家珠寶店會在所有的金銀製品上打上純度戳記。

handicap
['hændɪ,kæp]

n （身體或智力方面的）缺陷；不利條件　h1004

His physical handicap didn't keep him from playing volleyball.

他身體上的缺陷並沒有阻止他打排球。

handicap
['hændɪ,kæp]

vt 妨礙　h1005

The lack of money seriously handicapped the company's future development.

資金的短缺嚴重地妨礙了這家公司的未來發展。

handle
['hændl]

n 柄，把手，拉手；vi/vt 處理，對待；操縱；觸摸；撫養　h1006

She handled the uncomfortable situation with grace and tact.

她以優雅和機智來處理那不自在的處境。

hands-on
['hændz'ɑn]

adj 親自動手的；實務的　h1007

In our program, students gain hands-on experience in fashion design.

在我們的課程裡，學生會得到時尚設計的實務經驗。

handy
['hændɪ]

adj 手邊的；近便的；方便的；手巧的　h1008

He was handy with a tool box and could fix most things around the house.

他手邊有個工具箱，能夠修理房子裡的大部分東西。

harbor
['harbə]

n 海港；避難所；vt 隱匿，窩藏；懷著　h1009

The old house harbored many refugees, but the police didn't bother them.

那個舊房子裡藏著許多難民，但警方並沒有打擾他們。

hardware
['hard,wɛr]

托 雅 學

n 五金；金屬製品；硬體
She shopped for new drawer pulls at the hardware store.
她在五金器具行裡採購新的抽屜把手。

h1010

hardy
['hardɪ]

托 雅 學

adj 強壯的；耐勞的
The hardy mountain climbers reached their destination in just a few days.
那群強壯的登山者在幾天內就抵達了目的地。

h1011

harsh
[harʃ]

托 雅 學

adj 粗糙的；（聲音）刺耳的；苛刻的，嚴酷的
Though his first novel received harsh criticism, he didn't become discouraged or disappointed in himself.
雖然他的第一本小說受到嚴厲的批評，但他並沒有因此沮喪和對自己失望。

h1012

harshness
['harʃnəs]

托 雅 學

n 嚴厲
The harshness of their grandmother's voice took the naughty children by surprise.
祖母的嚴厲語氣使頑皮的孩子們非常吃驚。

h1013

harvest
['harvɪst]

托 雅 學

n 收穫，收成；成果，後果；vi/vt 收穫，收割
They harvested the winter wheat early to save it from the freeze.
他們早早地收割冬麥，以防止它們被寒冬凍壞。

h1014

hatch
[hætʃ]

托 雅 學

n 艙口，小門
The cargo hatch on the ship was broken.
那船上的貨物艙門壞掉了。

h1015

hatch
[hætʃ]

托 雅 學

vt 孵蛋；策劃，醞釀
Joseph has hatched a plan to surprise his wife for her sixtieth birthday party.
約瑟夫已經為他太太六十歲生日醞釀一個驚喜派對。

h1016

haunt
[hɔnt]

托 雅 學

vi/vt 經常出沒；纏人；使⋯苦惱或擔憂
His relatives haunted him with constant criticism.
他的親戚們接連不斷的批評使他很困擾。

h1017

haunted
['hɔntɪd]

托 雅 學

adj 鬧鬼的；經常被佔據的
The tourists decided to visit the famous haunted house at night.
這些遊客決定晚上造訪那間有名的鬼屋。

h1018

hawk
[hɔk]

n 鷹，隼

h1019

Hawks are a protected bird species that cannot be harmed or endangered.
所有的鷹都是受到保護的鳥類，不能被傷害或危及。

headquarters
['hɛd'kwɔrtəz]

n 司令部；指揮部；總部；總局

h1020

This international company decided to setup their headquarters in Toronto.
這家外資公司決定在多倫多建立總部。

heal
[hil]

vi/vt 治癒，癒合

h1021

I sincerely hope that my sister's emotional scars will heal eventually.
真心希望我姐姐的感情傷疤最終能癒合。

heap
[hip]

n 堆；大量；許多

h1022

His mother was not pleased to see heaps of his dirty clothes on the bedroom floor.
他的媽媽看到兒子的一堆髒衣服堆在臥室地板上，很不高興。

heap
[hip]

vi/vt 堆；堆起

h1023

All of the laundry was heaped in a pile in the corner waiting to be folded.
所有洗好的衣物都堆在一角等待折疊。

hearing
['hɪrɪŋ]

n 聽，傾聽；聽力；審訊

h1024

The hearing outlined the problems leading up to the bridge collapse.
偵訊會概述了導致那座橋坍塌的問題。

hectic
['hɛktɪk]

adj 興奮的；忙亂的；（因患病）發熱的

h1025

Her hectic schedule made it difficult to take time to relax.
她忙亂的日程讓自己很難有時間放鬆。

heir
[ɛr]

n 後嗣；繼承人

h1026

Prince Charles is the rightful heir to the British royal throne.
查理王子是英國皇家王位的合法繼承人。

helicopter
['hɛlɪkɑptə]

n 直升（飛）機

h1027

The rescue helicopter carrying the accident survivors has now landed safely.
載有事故生還者的救援直升機已經安全降落了。

H

helmet
['hɛlmɪt]

托 雅 學

n 頭盔，鋼盔

He always wore a helmet while he was skating.

他溜冰時總是戴著一個頭盔。

h1028

hemisphere
['hɛməs‚fɪr]

托 雅 學

n 半球；半球地圖

The Aurora Borealis can only be seen in the northernmost part of the northern hemisphere.

只有在北半球最北的地區可以看見北極光。

h1029

hesitant
['hɛzətənt]

托 雅 學

adj 遲疑的

She was hesitant to date her husband at first, but he was persistent.

一開始她對與她丈夫的約會還很遲疑，但他很執著。

h1030

hesitate
['hɛzə‚tet]

托 雅 學

vi 不願意，猶豫，躊躇

The team that hesitated in taking the lead at the beginning of the race won in the end.

那支在比賽一開始猶豫帶頭的隊伍最後贏了。

h1031

hierarchy
['haɪə‚rɑrkɪ]

托 雅 學

n 等級制度；統治集團，領導層

The crew followed a strict hierarchy while sailing.

在航行的時候，水手們遵守嚴格的階級制度。

h1032

highlight
['haɪ‚laɪt]

托 雅 學

n 最精彩的部分；**vt** 使顯著，使突出；強調

I must highlight how important education is to the future of our country.

我必須強調教育對我們國家的未來有多重要。

h1033

hinder
['hɪndə]

托 雅 學

adj 後面的；**vi/vt** 阻止，妨礙

His inexperience greatly hindered his team in completing the obstacle course.

他的缺乏經驗大大阻礙了他的團隊完成這個障礙過程。

h1034

hindrance
['hɪndrəns]

托 雅 學

n 障礙，妨礙

The shortage of human resources will be a hindrance to any economic recovery.

人力資源的短缺會成為任何經濟復甦的障礙。

h1035

hint
[hɪnt]

托 雅 學

n 暗示；提示；線索；少量；**vi/vt** 暗示；示意

He hinted that he would be there tonight.

他暗示今晚他會出現在那裡。

h1036

hitherto
[ˌhɪðɚˈtu]

托 **雅** 學

h1037

adv 到目前為止，迄今
He brought back hitherto unknown species of plants from his explorations in the rain forest.
他從熱帶雨林帶回了迄今仍不為人所知的植物物種。

hoe
[ho]

托 雅 學

h1038

vi/vt 鋤地
The farmer was thinking about buying some new tools, since the field was too rocky to hoe.
農夫正在考慮買些新工具，因為農田太多岩石以至於無法鋤地。

hollow
['halo]

托 雅 學

h1039

adj 空的；中空的；空洞的；空虛的
The kids hid inside the old hollow log.
那些小孩子躲進那個古老的中空的圓木裡。

horizon
[həˈraɪzn]

托 雅 學

h1040

n 地平線
They watched the sun set on the horizon as they sat on the back porch.
他們坐在後面的門廊上看著太陽落在地平線上。

horizon
[həˈraɪzn]

托 雅 學

h1041

n 眼界；見識；層位
Traveling around the world can really enrich your life and widen your horizon.
環遊世界真的能豐富你的人生，開拓你的眼界。

horizontally
[ˌharəˈzantlɪ]

托 雅 學

h1042

adv 地平線地；水平地
Lines of latitude encircle the globe horizontally while lines of longitude are vertical.
緯線水平地環繞地球，而經線是垂直的。

horrible
['hɔrəb!]

托 雅 學

h1043

adj 令人恐懼的；可怕的；極討厭的；糟透的
The conductor thought the new band's music was horrible.
指揮家認為那個新樂團的音樂很糟糕。

horrify
['hɔrəˌfaɪ]

托 雅 學

h1044

vt 使恐懼
The citizens were horrified by the invisible toxic chemicals found throughout the neighborhood.
這些在鄰近街區發現的看不見的有毒化學物質使市民感到恐懼。

horror
['hɔrɚ]

托 雅 學

h1045

n 恐怖；戰慄
She looked in horror at the mess that the children had made in the living room.
她恐怖地看著孩子們在客廳裡造成的混亂。

H

host
[host]

托 雅 學

n 主人；旅店老闆；節目主持人；一大群，許多　　h1046

Their host treated them to a tour of the city before they went to a local diner for dinner.

在他們到當地的小餐館吃晚餐前，他們的主人招待他們到城市觀光。

hostage
['hastɪdʒ]

托 雅 學

n 人質；抵押品　　h1047

The terrorists held ten hostages in order to demand a high ransom.

這群恐怖分子劫持了十名人質，以便要求高額的贖金。

hostile
['hastɪl]

托 雅 學

adj 敵對的，敵方的，敵意的　　h1048

The tone of the party grew more and more hostile as the evening progressed.

當傍晚快到時，派對的氣氛變得越來越敵對。

hostility
[has'tɪlətɪ]

托 雅 學

n 敵意　　h1049

The villagers showed hostility to strangers approaching their homes.

村民對靠近他們家園的陌生人表現出敵意。

huddle
['hʌdl]

托 雅 學

n 雜亂；雜亂一團　　h1050

The football team got in a huddle to discuss the next play.

足球隊員們聚成雜亂一團來討論下一場比賽。

huddle
['hʌdl]

托 雅 學

vi/vt 擁擠；聚集；（因寒冷、害怕而）縮成一團　　h1051

We all huddled around the TV to watch the basketball game.

我們大家聚集在電視旁看籃球賽。

humble
['hʌmbl]

托 雅 學

adj 謙卑的；恭順的；地位低下的　　h1052

He was known to be a humble and soft spoken man.

大家都知道他是位謙遜且說話溫和的人。

humble
['hʌmbl]

托 雅 學

vt 降低；貶低　　h1053

He humbled himself at the presence of God.

在神的面前他降低了自己的身份。

humid
['hjumɪd]

托 雅 學

adj 濕的；濕氣重的　　h1054

The nonstop rain has made the air very humid.

連續的降雨讓空氣很濕。

humidity
[hju'mɪdətɪ]

n 濕氣，濕度　h1055
I still haven't gotten used to the humidity in this city.
我仍舊無法適應這個城市的濕度。

hurdle
['hɝdl]

托 雅 學

n 跨欄賽跑；障礙　h1056
The runner fell at the last hurdle and lost the race.
這位運動員因在最後的跨欄跌倒而輸掉比賽。

hurdle
['hɝdl]

vt 跨（欄）；克服（困難）　h1057
The determined young man hurdled over all the obstacles in his path.
這個堅定的年輕人克服了他人生歷程中所有的障礙。

hurl
[hɝl]

托 雅 學

vt 猛投，力擲；大聲叫　h1058
The boy hurled the ball across the street in anger.
那個男孩生氣地將球往街上猛投。

hurricane
['hɝ‚ken]

n 颶風　h1059
The hurricane uprooted the trees and destroyed the whole village.
那場颶風將樹連根拔起，摧毀了整個村落。

hustle
['hʌsl]

托 雅 學

n 忙碌；擁擠　h1060
Some people enjoy the hustle and bustle of New York City.
有些人喜歡紐約市的擁擠和喧囂。

H

字彙能力檢查表

先自我檢驗是否瞭解以下初階單字，若有不清楚者，請先開啟光碟中的電子書複習。

☐icon	☐immigration	☐independent	☐input
☐ideal	☐improve	☐index	☐insight
☐identifiable	☐improvement	☐indicate	☐instruct
☐identification	☐inaccurate	☐indication	☐instruction
☐identify	☐inadequate	☐indicative	☐instructor
☐identify	☐inappropriate	☐indicator	☐international
☐idiot	☐incense	☐infant	☐interview
☐idle	☐incentive	☐influence	☐invitation
☐idle	☐include	☐influence	☐invite
☐immediate	☐income	☐influential	☐item
☐immigrant	☐increase	☐information	☐ivory

identical
[aɪ'dɛntɪkl]

托 雅 學

i1001

adj 同一的，同樣的；同卵的
She and her identical twin sister loved to dress alike on their birthday.
她和她同卵雙胞胎姐姐喜歡在生日那天打扮得一樣。

identity
[aɪ'dɛntətɪ]

托 雅 學

i1002

n 同一（性）；一致；國籍；身份
We must verify his identity before allowing him to get on the plane.
我們必須確認他的身份後才能讓他上飛機。

ignorance
['ɪgnərəns]

托 雅 學

i1003

n 無知，愚昧
There is a saying called "Ignorance is bliss" and at times this statement is so true.
有句諺語叫「無知是福」，有時候這句話說得很對。

ignorant
['ɪgnərənt]

托 雅 學

i1004

adj 無知的，愚昧的；不知道的
He was ignorant of the basic rules of baseball, but picked them up on quickly.
他對棒球的基本規則一無所知，但很快就弄懂了。

ignore
[ɪg'nor]

托 雅 學

i1005

vt 不理，不顧；忽視
He ignored the speed limit and ended up getting a ticket.
他不顧速度限制，最終收到了一張罰單。

illegal
[ɪ'ligl]

托 雅 學

i1006

adj 不合法的，非法的
It is illegal to drive under the influence of alcohol.
酒後駕車是非法的。

illusion
[ɪ'ljuʒən]

托 雅 學

i1007

n 幻想；錯誤的觀念；錯覺，幻覺；假像
The children loved the book on optical illusions that their father brought them.
孩子們很愛父親帶給他們的那本關於光學幻覺的書。

image
['ɪmɪdʒ]

托 雅 學

i1008

n 形象，聲譽；印象；影像；比喻
This political scandal has destroyed the president's image.
這個政治醜聞已經毀壞了總統的形象。

imaginary
[ɪ'mædʒə,nɛrɪ]

托 雅 學

i1009

adj 想像的，虛構的
This poor orphan relies on his imaginary friend for his company.
這個可憐的孤兒靠想像中的朋友跟自己做伴。

imaginative
[ɪ'mædʒəˌnetɪv]

托 雅 學

adj 富有想像力的，愛想像的
i1010
This imaginative story has inspired her interest in reading.
這個富有想像力的故事激發了她的閱讀興趣。

imitate
['ɪməˌtet]

托 雅 學

vt 模仿，仿效；仿製
i1011
Taiwan's drink pearl milk tea is imitated all over the world.
臺灣的飲料珍珠奶茶在全世界都被效仿。

imitation
[ˌɪmə'teʃən]

托 雅 學

n 模仿，仿效，仿製；仿造品
i1012
This pair of gloves is made of imitation leather.
這副手套是用仿造皮革製成的。

immune
[ɪ'mjun]

托 雅 學

adj 免疫的，有免疫力的；未受影響的；豁免的
i1013
She was already immune to chicken pox since she'd had it as a child.
自從小時候得過水痘後，她已經對它免疫了。

impact
[ɪm'pækt]

托 雅 學

n 衝擊，碰撞；影響
i1014
The new paper factory made a huge impact on its environment.
這家新的造紙廠對環境有很大的影響。

impatient
[ɪm'peʃənt]

托 雅 學

adj 不耐煩的，急躁的
i1015
The children grew impatient while waiting for their dinner.
孩子們等待晚餐時變得不耐煩了。

imply
[ɪm'plaɪ]

托 雅 學

vt 意指，含…意思，暗示
i1016
His tone of voice implied that he was expecting bad news.
他聲音的語調暗示了他在等待壞消息的到來。

impractical
[ɪm'præktɪkl]

托 雅 學

adj 不切實際的，沒有實踐能力的；過於昂貴的
i1017
Their vacation plans became impractical after their unexpected medical bills.
在收到未預期的醫療費用帳單後，他們的度假計畫就無法實踐了。

impress
[ɪm'prɛs]

托 雅 學

vt 印，蓋印；留下印象，引人注目，在…上打記號
i1018
He tried hard to impress the interviewer because he really wanted the job.
他努力試著讓面試官留下深刻印象，因為他真的想要這份工作。

impression
[ɪmˈprɛʃən]

托 雅 學

n 印象，感想；蓋印，壓痕
She got the impression that he really liked her.
她印象中他真的很喜歡她。

i1019

impressive
[ɪmˈprɛsɪv]

托 雅 學

adj 給人深刻印象的，感人的
Even though he seemed shy and reserved, his resume was impressive.
雖然他好像很害羞又保守，但他的履歷表的確給人深刻的印象。

i1020

improper
[ɪmˈprɑpɚ]

托 雅 學

adj 不適當的，不合理的
The golfer's improper conduct broke the hearts of his fans, and now they don't support him.
高爾夫球員不恰當的行為讓他的支持者心碎了，現在他們不支持他了。

i1021

impulse
[ˈɪmpʌls]

托 雅 學

n 衝動；推動
Impulse buying is usually triggered by emotions and it may lead to feelings of guilt afterward.
衝動購買通常是被情緒所激發，且也可能在之後產生罪惡感。

i1022

inaccessible
[ˌɪnækˈsɛsəbl]

托 雅 學

adj 達不到的，難接近的
He loved hiking to locations that were inaccessible by vehicle.
他喜愛去交通工具到不了的地方遠足。

i1023

inactivate
[ɪnˈæktəˌvet]

托 雅 學

vt 使無效，使不活動，使停止
When my cell phone was stolen, I requested the company inactivate my service immediately.
我的手機被盜後，我要求公司立即停機。

i1024

inclusive
[ɪnˈklusɪv]

托 雅 學

adj 包括的，包含的；範圍廣的；包圍住的
The total purchase price is $120, inclusive of tax and shipping costs.
購買的總額是120美金，包括稅金和運費。

i1025

incredible
[ɪnˈkrɛdəbl]

托 雅 學

adj 不可相信的；驚人的，不可思議的
Over the course of 30 years she'd taught English to an incredible number of students.
三十年來，她在英語課上教過的學生數量是驚人的。

i1026

indefinite
[ɪnˈdɛfənɪt]

托 雅 學

adj 無限期的；不明確的；不定的
She decided to stay at her beach house to write for an indefinite period of time.
她決定留在她海邊的房子裡寫作，要住多久還不確定。

i1027

individual
[ˌɪndə'vɪdʒʊəl]

托 雅 學

adj 個人的，單獨的；獨特的；**n** 個人，個體　　i1028
Each individual student needs space to exercise.
每個學生都需要運動的空間。

industry
['ɪndəstrɪ]

托 雅 學

n 勤勞，勤奮　　i1029
Her teacher praised her industry and gave her top grades.
她的老師讚賞了她的勤奮並給了她最好的成績。

industry
['ɪndəstrɪ]

托 雅 學

n 工業，產業　　i1030
This country's GDP relies heavily on its IT industry.
這個國家的國內生產毛額高度依賴資訊技術產業。

inevitable
[ɪn'ɛvətəbl]

托 雅 學

adj 不可避免的，必然發生的　　i1031
If you work with children, getting messy is inevitable.
如果你和小孩子一起做事，搞得亂七八糟是不可避免的。

infer
[ɪn'fɝ]

托 雅 學

vi 做出推論　　i1032
The teacher asked again, "What can you infer from the article"?
老師又問了一次：「你們可以從這篇文章推論出什麼？」

inform
[ɪn'fɔrm]

托 雅 學

vi 告發，告密　　i1033
Somebody must have informed the thief last night.
昨晚肯定有人告發了那個竊賊。

inform
[ɪn'fɔrm]

托 雅 學

vt 通知，向…報告　　i1034
The investigator informed his supervisor of the survey and its outcome.
這位調查員將調查及結果報告給他的長官了。

ingredient
[ɪn'gridɪənt]

托 雅 學

n （混合物的）組成部分，配料；成分，要素　　i1035
She realized she was missing a few of the ingredients for her famous pumpkin pie.
她意識到她有名的南瓜派裡少了一些配料。

inherit
[ɪn'hɛrɪt]

托 雅 學

vi/vt 繼承（金錢等），經遺傳而得（性格、特徵）　　i1036
She inherited an antique clock from her uncle.
她從叔叔那裡繼承了一個古董鐘。

inhibit
[ɪnˈhɪbɪt]

托 雅 學

vt 抑制，約束

Her shyness inhibited her from starting conversations very often.

她的羞澀經常讓她跟人開始談話的時候受到約束。

i1037

initial
[ɪˈnɪʃəl]

托 雅 學

adj 創始的；最初的

Their initial contact was pleasant, and over the years, they've become best friends.

他們最初的接觸很愉快，在多年之後，他們成了最好的朋友。

i1038

initially
[ɪˈnɪʃəlɪ]

托 雅 學

adv 最初，開始

He initially refused to respond to comments about his child's misbehavior at school.

他最初拒絕回應他的小孩在校行為不端的評論。

i1039

inject
[ɪnˈdʒɛkt]

托 雅 學

vt 注射（藥液等）；注入

The chef injected broth into the meat to increase the flavor.

廚師將肉湯注入肉裡以便提升風味。

i1040

innocent
[ˈɪnəsn̩t]

托 雅 學

adj 單純的，無知的

At 12, he was no longer an innocent child.

在他十二歲那年，他已不再是個單純的孩子了。

i1041

innocent
[ˈɪnəsn̩t]

托 雅 學

adj 清白的，無罪的；無害的

The jury could tell that the defense attorney did believe his client was innocent.

陪審團能判斷辯護律師真的相信他的當事人是清白的。

i1042

innovation
[ˌɪnəˈveʃən]

托 雅 學

n 改革，革新；新觀念，新方法，新發明

Technology companies pursue technical innovation.

科技公司追求技術革新。

i1043

innovative
[ˈɪnoˌvetɪv]

托 雅 學

adj 創新的

Most critics agree that this mobile phone has the most innovative design in the past 5 years.

大部分評論都認為，這支手機擁有過去五年以來最創新的設計。

i1044

inquire
[ɪnˈkwaɪr]

vi/vt 打聽，詢問；調查

He inquired with the realtor about the price of the house.

他向房地產商打聽到這棟房子的價錢。

i1045

inquiry
[ɪnˈkwaɪrɪ]

托 雅 學

n 詢問，打聽，調查　　i1046

The witness was called to give testimony at the official inquiry.

證人被叫來在正式的調查上提供證詞。

insane
[ɪnˈsen]

托 雅 學

adj 精神錯亂的；瘋狂的；極愚蠢的；荒唐的　　i1047

His mother thought his love of skydiving was insane.

他母親覺得他對跳傘的熱愛太瘋狂了。

insert
[ˈɪnsɚt]

托 雅 學

n 插入物　　i1048

In the movie, a mysterious insert was placed inside his chest cavity by the aliens.

電影中外星人把一件神秘的插入物放置在他的胸腔裡。

insert
[ɪnˈsɚt]

托 雅 學

vt 插入，嵌入　　i1049

He inserted a picture into each of the slides to illustrate his ideas more clearly.

他在每張幻燈片中都插入了一張圖片，以便更清楚地說明自己的想法。

insist
[ɪnˈsɪst]

托 雅 學

vi/vt 堅持要求，堅決主張，堅持　　i1050

She insisted that they stay for dinner.

她堅持要他們留下來吃晚餐。

insistence
[ɪnˈsɪstəns]

托 雅 學

n 堅持　　i1051

The company adjusted my monthly bill at my insistence.

在我的堅持下，公司調整了我的月帳單。

inspect
[ɪnˈspɛkt]

托 雅 學

vi/vt 檢查，調查，視察　　i1052

She inspected the outside of the rental car for dents before she drove it off the lot.

在她把租的車開出停車場之前，她檢查了一下車子外部有無凹痕。

inspection
[ɪnˈspɛkʃən]

托 雅 學

n 檢查，審查；檢閱　　i1053

I am glad our restaurant passed the health inspection.

我很高興我們的餐廳通過了衛生稽查。

inspiration
[ˌɪnspəˈreʃən]

托 雅 學

n 靈感；鼓舞，激勵　　i1054

Her hard work on behalf of the poor was an inspiration to the local community.

她代表窮人家的努力對當地社區來說是一種鼓舞。

inspire
[ɪn'spaɪr]

托 雅 學

vi/**vt** 鼓舞，激起；使產生靈感

i1055

The coach inspired his players to have pride in their game play.

教練鼓舞球員們要為參加比賽而自豪。

inspiring
[ɪn'spaɪrɪŋ]

托 雅 學

adj 鼓舞人心的，啟發靈感的

i1056

Debbie told me that talented actors are very inspiring to young hopefuls.

黛比告訴我，天才演員對年輕的有志者們是非常鼓舞人心的。

install
[ɪn'stɔl]

托 雅 學

vt 安裝，設置，安置；使就職，任命

i1057

She installed her new car stereo herself.

她自己安裝好了新車的音響。

installation
[ˌɪnstə'leʃən]

托 雅 學

n 安裝，設置；裝置，設備

i1058

The installation of the new software caused a few problems in the company's computer system.

新軟體的安裝對公司的電腦系統造成了一些問題。

installment
[ɪn'stɔlmənt]

托 雅 學

n 分期付款；（連載的）一期

i1059

He paid off his car in 10 monthly installments.

他用為期十個月的分期付款去支付他的車貸。

instance
['ɪnstəns]

托 雅 學

n 例子，事例，例證，實例

i1060

In this instance, neither driver was at fault for the crash.

在這個撞車案例裡，兩個駕駛員都不算有錯。

instinct
['ɪnstɪŋkt]

托 雅 學

n 本能，直覺，天性

i1061

Herding dogs have a natural protective instinct.

牧羊犬有天生防護的本能。

institute
['ɪnstətjut]

托 雅 學

n 學會，研究所；學院

i1062

This year, he will start attending the California Institute of the Arts.

今年他將開始就讀於加州藝術學院。

institute
['ɪnstətjut]

托 雅 學

vt 設立，設置，制定

i1063

They instituted a new vaccination program in local schools.

他們在當地學校制定了一個新的接種疫苗計畫。

institution
[ˌɪnstəˈtjuʃən]

托 雅 學

n 公共機構；協會；學校；研究所；制度，慣例　i1064

The Smithsonian Institution is the world's largest museum and research complex.

史密森尼學會是世界上最大的博物館和研究綜合體。

instructive
[ɪnˈstrʌktɪv]

托 雅 學

adj 有教育意義的；提供有用資訊的　i1065

His speech on how to live a healthy life was instructive.

他關於如何過健康生活的演講是有教育意義的。

instrument
[ˈɪnstrəmənt]

托 雅 學

n 工具，儀器，器械；樂器　i1066

Her mother insisted that she take up an instrument, so she decided to play the piano.

她媽媽堅持她開始接觸樂器，所以她決定彈鋼琴。

instrumental
[ˌɪnstrəˈmɛntl̩]

托 雅 學

adj 儀器的；器械的；樂器的；起作用的；有幫助的　i1067

Her input was instrumental in the final design of the new community center.

他對新社區中心最後的設計所給予的投入很有幫助。

instrumentalist
[ˌɪnstrəˈmɛntlɪst]

托 雅 學

n 器樂家　i1068

The professional musician was a very talented instrumentalist.

這個職業音樂家是一個才華橫溢的器樂家。

insult
[ˈɪnsʌlt]/[ɪnˈsʌlt]

托 雅 學

n/vt 侮辱，凌辱　i1069

To show up at your ex-girlfriend's party, you would only insult yourself.

出現在前女友的派對上等於侮辱你自己。

insulting
[ɪnˈsʌltɪŋ]

托 雅 學

adj 侮辱的，有冒犯性的　i1070

The rookie teacher found the principal's condescending attitude insulting.

菜鳥老師認為校長居高臨下的態度是侮辱人的。

insurance
[ɪnˈʃʊrəns]

托 雅 學

n 保險；保險費；保險業　i1071

Home insurance will compensate policy holders if their houses are lost in an accidental fire.

如果在意外火災中失去房子，房屋保險會給予保險契約擁有人補償。

insure
[ɪnˈʃʊr]

托 雅 學

vt 保險，給…保險；保證　i1072

She insured her car against theft and collision.

她給車子買了防盜竊和碰撞的保險。

integrate
['ɪntə,gret]

托 雅 學

vi/vt （使…）成為一體，（使…）結合在一起　　i1073

How can we successfully integrate these refugees into our community?

我們如何才能成功地將這些難民融合進我們的社區呢？

intellectual
[,ɪntl'ɛktʃʊəl]

托 雅 學

adj 智力的，理智的，有理解力的　　i1074

Students with high intellectual abilities are able to respond quickly and confidently.

智力水準高的學生能夠迅速而自信地回答問題。

intelligence
[ɪn'tɛlədʒəns]

托 雅 學

n 情報，消息　　i1075

According to intelligence, North Korea has acquired weapons of mass destruction.

根據情報，北韓已經有了大規模殺傷性武器。

intelligence
[ɪn'tɛlədʒəns]

托 雅 學

n 智力，聰明；理解力　　i1076

She was beautiful, but he loved her intelligence most of all.

她很漂亮，但是他最愛她的聰明才智。

intelligent
[ɪn'tɛlədʒənt]

托 雅 學

adj 聰明的，明智的，理智的　　i1077

Poodles are considered the most intelligent breed of dog.

貴賓犬被認為是最聰明的犬種。

intend
[ɪn'tɛnd]

托 雅 學

vt 想要，打算；企圖　　i1078

She intended to replace the dirty table cloth with a clean one before her husband went back.

在她丈夫回去之前，她打算換一塊乾淨的桌布。

intense
[ɪn'tɛns]

托 雅 學

adj 強烈的，劇烈的；熱烈的，熱情的　　i1079

She decided the sweetness of the batter was too intense, so she added some more milk.

她認為麵糊太甜了，所以她多加了一些牛奶。

intensify
[ɪn'tɛnsə,faɪ]

托 雅 學

vi/vt 加強，增強；（使）變激烈　　i1080

The search party intensified their efforts to find the missing girl before sunset.

搜救團隊在太陽下山之前更加努力尋找那個失蹤的女孩。

intensive
[ɪn'tɛnsɪv]

托 雅 學

adj 加強的，集中的；深入細緻的；精耕細作的　　i1081

She took an intensive Spanish course during the summer.

她在暑期上了集中的西班牙語課程。

intent
[ɪn'tɛnt]

托 雅 學

n 意圖，意思；目的
He had no intent to move back to his hometown after college.
在大學畢業後他並無意圖要搬回他的家鄉。

i1082

intention
[ɪn'tɛnʃən]

托 雅 學

n 意圖，意向；目的
He had no intention of allowing his daughter to take the car that weekend.
他不打算允許他女兒那個週末買下這輛車。

i1083

interact
[ˌɪntə'rækt]

托 雅 學

vi 互相作用，互相影響；互動
My children are outgoing and interact very well with their friends.
我的孩子們很外向並且和他們的朋友們互動地非常好。

i1084

interior
[ɪn'tɪrɪə]

托 雅 學

adj 內部的，裡面的；n 內部；內地
The interior design of this room makes me feel very calm and relaxing.
這個房間的內部設計使我感到平靜和放鬆。

i1085

internal
[ɪn'tɝnl]

托 雅 學

adj 內部的，內的；國內的，內政的
She sent an internal memo to the employees who had missed the meeting.
她給那些沒能開會的員工寄了一個內部備忘錄。

i1086

interrupt
[ˌɪntə'rʌpt]

托 雅 學

vi/vt 中斷，遮斷，阻礙；打斷（話），打擾
The fire drill interrupted his presentation to the financial team.
消防演習中斷了他對財務團隊的報告。

i1087

intersection
[ˌɪntə'sɛkʃən]

托 雅 學

n 相交，交叉；道路交叉口，十字路口
The two long-lost lovers happened to meet at a intersection on their way home from work.
這對失聯已久的戀人在下班回家路上的十字路口偶遇了。

i1088

intimate
['ɪntəmɪt]

托 雅 學

adj 親密的，密切的
They enjoyed a lifelong intimate friendship.
他們很享受這段一生一世親密的友情。

i1089

intimate
['ɪntəmɪt]

托 雅 學

n 熟友，熟人
Our source is from an intimate to the queen.
我們的情報源自皇后的一位熟友。

i1090

intruder
[ɪnˈtrudə]

托 雅 學

n 侵入者；干擾者；闖入者
The intruders started a fire that completely destroyed the historical buildings.
侵入者點起大火，徹底破壞了歷史建築物。

i1091

intuition
[ˌɪntjuˈɪʃən]

托 雅 學

n 直覺，直觀；憑直覺而知的事物
His intuition prompted him to walk through the dark forest.
他的直覺引領他走進黑森林。

i1092

invent
[ɪnˈvɛnt]

托 雅 學

vt 捏造，虛構
He invented colorful stories to cover up his criminal past.
他捏造多姿多彩的故事來掩蓋他的犯罪歷史。

i1093

invent
[ɪnˈvɛnt]

托 雅 學

vt 發明，創造
Thomas Edison invented the first commercially viable light bulb in 1880.
湯馬斯・愛迪生在1880年發明瞭第一個商業上可行的電燈泡。

i1094

invention
[ɪnˈvɛnʃən]

托 雅 學

n 發明，創造；發明物
The invention of the telephone certainly made communication easier and faster.
電話的發明確實讓溝通更加簡易、更加快捷。

i1095

inventory
[ˈɪnvənˌtorɪ]

托 雅 學

n 詳細目錄，存貨，財產清冊，總量
Retailers must manage their inventory properly to reduce unnecessary costs.
零售商必須妥善管理他們的存貨以降低不必要的成本。

i1096

invest
[ɪnˈvɛst]

托 雅 學

vi/vt 投資，投入（精力、時間等）
He invested a large part of his winnings from the lottery in real estate.
他把從彩票中贏得的大部分錢都投資在不動產上了。

i1097

investigate
[ɪnˈvɛstəˌget]

托 雅 學

vi/vt 調查，調查研究
The chief of police selected two of his best detectives to investigate the murder.
警察局長選了兩名最優秀的警探來調查這起兇殺案。

i1098

investigation
[ɪnˌvɛstəˈgeʃən]

托 雅 學

n 調查，調研
The police chief advised there would be a full investigation into Jacob's case.
警察局長提議對雅各的案子展開全面調查。

i1099

investment
[ɪnˈvɛstmənt]

托 雅 學

n 投資，投資額；投入
The investment in our new shop proved very worthwhile.
我們新開店的投資被證明是相當有價值的。

i1100

invisible
[ɪnˈvɪzəbļ]

托 雅 學

adj 看不見的，無形的
Even though electromagnetic waves are invisible, you can still measure their effects.
雖然電磁波是看不見的，但是你還是可以測到它們的效果。

i1101

invoice
[ˈɪnvɔɪs]

托 雅 學

n 發票；發貨清單
I need the commercial invoice before clearing the products through customs.
在將貨物通過海關之前我需要商業發票。

i1102

involve
[ɪnˈvɑlv]

托 雅 學

vt 捲入，陷入，連累；包含，含有，涉及
As a team leader, she tried to make sure everyone was involved in working on the project.
身為隊長，她努力確保每個人都參與到專案的工作中。

i1103

ironically
[aɪˈrɑnɪklɪ]

托 雅 學

adv 說反話地；諷刺地；諷刺的是
Ironically, the local butcher is a vegetarian.
諷刺的是，這個當地的屠夫是位素食主義者。

i1104

irony
[ˈaɪrənɪ]

托 雅 學

n 反話，諷刺；諷刺之事
She smiled at the irony—her father's most popular stories were his least favorite to write.
她父親最受歡迎的故事是他最不喜歡寫的，她對這件諷刺之事報以一笑。

i1105

irritate
[ˈɪrəˌtet]

托 雅 學

vt 激怒，惱火；使…急躁
The tag on the collar of his shirt irritated him, so he cut it out.
他襯衫領口上的標籤讓他很不舒服，所以他把它給剪了。

i1106

isolate
[ˈaɪsļˌet]

托 雅 學

vi/vt 隔離，孤立
The shepherds isolated each sheep from the flock, so they could catch it and brand it.
牧羊人把每隻羊從羊群中隔離出來，好抓住它並烙上印記。

i1107

isolated
[ˈaɪsļˌetɪd]

托 雅 學

adj 孤立的，隔絕的；局部的
Today's weather forecast is calling for isolated thunder storms and showers.
今天的天氣預報預測局部地區將有雷暴雨和陣雨。

i1108

isolation
[ˌaɪsl̩ˈeʃən]

托 雅 學

n 隔離；孤立；絕緣

i1109

If you live alone, you may feel a strong sense of isolation if you don't talk to people every day.

如果你獨自居住而每天又不與人交談，你可能會有強烈的孤立感。

issue
[ˈɪʃju]

托 雅 學

n 問題，爭端；發行（物）；期號

i1110

Let us discuss this issue peacefully without resorting to violence.

讓我們不採取暴力，和平地討論這個問題。

issue
[ˈɪʃju]

托 雅 學

vi/vt 發行；流出

i1111

My favorite band is going to issue a new record this month.

我最喜歡的樂隊本月將發行新的唱片。

itinerary
[aɪˈtɪnəˌrɛrɪ]

托 雅 學

n 旅程，行程

i1112

She drew up an itinerary for their trip through Italy.

她為他們的義大利之行擬定了行程表。

J

jagged
['dʒægɪd]

托 雅 學

adj 鋸齒狀的，參差不齊的
Hilary put the jagged, broken glass in the trash bin.
希拉蕊把鋸齒狀的碎玻璃扔進了垃圾桶。

j1001

janitor
['dʒænɪtɚ]

托 雅 學

n 看門人，門衛
Each evening Jim, the school janitor, works hard to keep the classrooms clean and tidy.
每天晚上學校門衛吉姆都會努力把教室打掃得乾淨整潔。

j1002

jealous
['dʒɛləs]

托 雅 學

adj 妒忌的；猜疑的，警惕的
She was jealous of her sister's natural athletic ability.
她對她妹妹天生的運動能力感到妒忌。

j1003

jerk
[dʒɝk]

托 雅 學

n 猛然一縮，急速一抖
The drowned man started breathing with a jerk in the body.
那個溺水的人身體猛然一抽動，然後就開始呼吸了。

j1004

jerk
[dʒɝk]

托 雅 學

vi/vt 急拉，猛地一動，猛地一跳
She jerked her entire body upon hearing the balloon pop.
一聽到氣球的爆炸聲，她整個身體猛然一縮。

j1005

joint
[dʒɔɪnt]
托 雅 學

adj 聯合的，共同的，連接的　　j1006
Their joint efforts have driven them forward and led them to sweet success.
他們的共同努力驅使他們前進，並最終得以成功。

joint
[dʒɔɪnt]
托 雅 學

n 接合處，接頭；關節　　j1007
He experiences a lot of pain in his joints because he trains too hard at the gym.
由於在健身房過度訓練，他感覺關節十分疼痛。

journal
['dʒɝnl]
托 雅 學

n 定期刊物，雜誌；日報；日誌，日記　　j1008
She kept a daily journal of her time in England.
她在英國期間保持每天寫日記。

journalism
['dʒɝnl,ɪzm]
托 雅 學

n 新聞工作；新聞業；新聞學；（總稱）報章雜誌　　j1009
He majored in English and journalism in college.
他在大學主修英語及新聞學。

J

journalist
['dʒɝnəlɪst]
托 雅 學

n 記者，新聞工作者　　j1010
The politician read a prepared statement to the room full of news cameras and journalists.
那位政客對著滿房間的新聞攝影機鏡頭及記者讀了一個準備好的發言。

journey
['dʒɝnɪ]
托 雅 學

n 旅行，旅程　　j1011
They made their journey to Scotland by train.
他們乘火車去蘇格蘭旅行。

judge
[dʒʌdʒ]
托 雅 學

n 法官；裁判員；鑒定人　　j1012
The judge ruled that the defendant was guilty of trespassing.
那位法官做出裁決，被告因非法侵入私人土地而有罪。

judge
[dʒʌdʒ]
托 雅 學

vi/vt 審判；評論，裁判　　j1013
Without sufficient evidence, the man was judged innocent of the charges against him.
因為缺乏充分的證據，那個人經過審判後被無罪釋放。

judgment
['dʒʌdʒmənt]
托 雅 學

n 審判，判決；判斷（力）；看法，意見　　j1014
Don't let his thoughts and ideas affect your own good judgment.
別讓他的想法和意見左右你良好的判斷力。

judicial
[dʒu'dɪʃəl]

托 雅 學

adj 司法的，與法律體系或程序有關的，法庭的，法定的　j1015

The government has the judicial obligation of helping the poor in case of extreme need.

政府在貧苦人有緊急需求的時候，有協助他們的法定義務。

judiciary
[dʒu'dɪʃɪˌɛrɪ]

托 雅 學

n 司法制度，司法部門；法官（集合名詞）　j1016

Out of caution, the chief procurator carefully selected the judges from the judiciary.

為求謹慎，檢察長小心地從司法部門挑選法官。

jungle
['dʒʌŋgl̩]

托 雅 學

n 生死地帶；生存競爭激烈的地方；叢林　j1017

In his autobiography, he has depicted his childhood in a real jungle.

他在自傳裡描述了童年生活的叢林。

junk
[dʒʌŋk]

托 雅 學

n 廢物，舊貨；舢板　j1018

He has cleaned the house for the New Year and I wonder what he is going to do with the junk.

他打掃了房子以迎接新年，我想知道他準備如何處理那些廢物。

jury
['dʒʊrɪ]

托 雅 學

n 陪審團；全體評審員　j1019

The jury deliberated over the case for 12 hours before returning a verdict of not guilty.

陪審團仔細考慮那件案子達十二小時後，回庭判決被告無罪。

justice
['dʒʌstɪs]

托 雅 學

n 公正，公平；審判，司法　j1020

The prosecutor agreed that justice could be served by sentencing the defendant to 60 hours of community service.

那位原告贊同為了維護正義，應當判處被告60小時的社區服務。

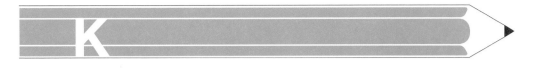

字彙能力檢查表

先自我檢驗是否瞭解以下初階單字，若有不清楚者，請先開啟光碟中的電子書複習。

□key　　　　□kit　　　　□kneel

keen
[kin]
托 雅 學

k1001

adj 鋒利的，敏銳的，敏捷的；熱心的，渴望的
Having a keen desire for success, he makes an all-out effort to learn whatever is new to him.
因為渴望成功，所以他盡全力學習新知識。

kidnap
['kɪdnæp]
托 雅 學

k1002

vt 誘拐；綁架，劫持
The opposing team kidnapped their mascot the night before the big game.
對方在大賽的前一天晚上綁架了他們的吉祥物。

kidney
['kɪdnɪ]
托 雅 學

k1003

n 腎，腎臟
He had a serious car accident and was badly in need of a kidney transplant.
他遇上了嚴重車禍，急需腎臟移植。

kindle
['kɪnd]
托 雅 學

k1004

vi 著火；**vt** 點燃
The boy scouts learned how to kindle a fire using dry sticks and friction.
這些男童子軍學會了怎麼用乾樹枝和摩擦來點燃起火。

knit
[nɪt]
托 雅 學

k1005

vi/vt 編織，編結；接合，黏合
During the war, the two parties were knit together by shared goals.
戰爭期間，共同的目標使那兩個政黨團結起來。

knob
[nɑb]

托 雅 學

k1006

n 門把，（球形）把手，旋鈕
I turned the door knob and pushed the door open.
我轉動把手，把門打開。

knot
[nɑt]

托 雅 學

k1007

vi/vt 打結；纏繞；
n （繩）結；（樹）節；節（＝海浬/小時）
He carefully knotted the ropes together to ensure safety.
他仔細地將繩子打結以確保安全。

knowledge
['nɑlɪdʒ]

托 雅 學

k1008

n 知識，學識；知道，瞭解
The job requires a lot of specialized knowledge on this particular subject.
這份工作需要對這個特定主題有許多專業知識。

knowledgeable
['nɑlɪdʒəb]

托 雅 學

k1009

adj 博學的；有見識的
My husband is very knowledgeable about the mechanics of most vehicles.
我先生在多數車輛的機械構造方面非常博學。

字彙能力檢查表

先自我檢驗是否瞭解以下初階單字，若有不清楚者，請先開啟光碟中的電子書複習。

☐ label	☐ lawn	☐ lie	☐ loaf
☐ label	☐ lay	☐ light bulb	☐ local
☐ lace	☐ layer	☐ likelihood	☐ lock
☐ lace	☐ lead	☐ likewise	☐ lock
☐ lack	☐ leader	☐ limestone	☐ locker
☐ lack	☐ leadership	☐ limited	☐ log
☐ lamb	☐ leading	☐ line	☐ log
☐ land	☐ lean	☐ linen	☐ long-range
☐ landlord	☐ lean	☐ liner	☐ lose
☐ lane	☐ lecture	☐ link	☐ lose
☐ lap	☐ lecture	☐ link	☐ loss
☐ lap	☐ legume	☐ liquor	☐ lottery
☐ laptop	☐ lend	☐ livelihood	☐ luggage
☐ laundry	☐ level	☐ livestock	☐ lumber
☐ law	☐ level		

L

labor
['lebɚ]
托 雅 學

n 工作，勞動；勞力
The company is going to hold a meeting between the management and labor groups.
公司即將召開一個關於勞資雙方的會議。

I1001

labor
['lebɚ]
托 雅 學

vi/vt 勞動，苦幹
They labored all through the day to finish the fence.
為了完成柵欄的建造，他們勞動了一整天。

I1002

lag
[læg]
托 雅 學

n 落後，滯後
I felt sleepy all day long yesterday because of the jet lag.
因為時差的關係，昨天一整天我都覺得很睏。

I1003

lag
[læg]
托 雅 學

vi/vt 落後，滯後
Compared with other companies, we lag behind in the development of our stocking system.
跟其他公司相比，我們在庫存管理系統上的發展落後了。

I1004

lame
[lem]
托 雅 學

adj 跛的；（辯解、論據等）無說服力的
It is not advisable to give lame excuses to cover your stupid mistakes.
為遮蓋自己愚蠢的錯誤而編個無說服力的理由是不可取的。

I1005

lame
[lem]
托 雅 學

vt 使跛腳；使變得無力
The street dog was lamed from the car accident.
這隻流浪狗的腳因為車禍跛了。

I1006

landscape
['lænd,skep]
托 雅 學

n 風景，景色，景致
She spent several hours a day painting the landscape outside her house.
她一天花數個小時描繪房子外的風景。

I1007

landslide
['lænd,slaɪd]
托 雅 學

n 山崩；滑坡
The landslide destroyed part of the beachhouse.
山崩摧毀了部分海濱別墅。

I1008

layout
['le,aʊt]
托 雅 學

n 安排，佈局，設計；規劃圖，佈局圖
The layout of the community was entirely based on the designer's idea.
社區的佈置完全是遵照設計師的想法。

I1009

leaflet
['liflɪt]

托 雅 學

n 嫩葉；傳單，活頁；廣告；vt 發傳單給（人）　I1010

He found many leaflets for the restaurant in the hotel lobby.
他在旅館的大廳發現了很多餐廳的傳單。

---

leak
[lik]

托 雅 學

n 漏洞，漏隙；洩漏，漏出　I1011

There is a leak in my bedroom ceiling, and I'm planning to fix it myself.
我臥室的天花板上有個漏洞，我正計畫自己修理。

---

leak
[lik]

托 雅 學

vi/vt 漏，洩漏　I1012

The traitor leaked a list of special agents operating overseas.
這個賣國賊洩漏了一份海外工作的特工名單。

---

leakage
['likɪdʒ]

托 雅 學

n 漏，洩漏；漏損物　I1013

The leakage of gas caused the fire downtown.
市區大火是瓦斯漏氣造成的。

L

---

leap
[lip]

托 雅 學

n 跳躍，飛躍　I1014

The lion took a long leap from one side of the river to the other.
這頭獅子做了一個長長的跳躍，從河的這頭跳到那頭。

---

leap
[lip]

托 雅 學

vi/vt 跳，跳躍　I1015

At the end of the game, the gymnast leapt high in the air with his last ounce of strength.
在比賽的最後，這個體操選手用盡了最後的力氣在高空中奮力一跳。

---

lease
[lis]

托 雅 學

n 租借，租期，租賃物　I1016

Brian signed a three-year lease on his new car at 0% interest.
布萊恩的新汽車簽了一個三年零利率的租約。

---

lease
[lis]

托 雅 學

vt 租賃　I1017

I was able to lease the apartment for a full 12 months under the new terms of the housing contract.
根據新的住房合約中的條款，我能夠租賃那棟公寓整整12個月。

---

leisure
['liʒɚ]

托 雅 學

n 閒置時間；悠閒　I1018

Lily loved to read mystery novels for leisure.
莉莉喜歡在空閒時間讀推理小說。

lever
['lɛvɚ]

托 雅 學

n 杆，杠桿；控制杆；途徑，工具，手段
The extended handle is a lever used to operate the machine.
這根延伸出來的把手是用來操作機器的控制杆。

I1019

---

lever
['lɛvɚ]

托 雅 學

vt （用杠桿）移動，撬；用控制杆操縱
Mom levered the lid off the cookware with a chopstick.
媽媽拿一根筷子把炊具的蓋子撬開了。

I1020

---

liberal
['lɪbərəl]

托 雅 學

adj 大量的，豐富的，充足的，充裕的
She added a liberal amount of spice to the pumpkin pie to intensify the flavor.
為了加重味道，她在南瓜派裡加了大量的香料。

I1021

---

liberal
['lɪbərəl]

托 雅 學

adj 慷慨的，大方的；心胸寬大的；自由的，思想開放的
My family is very liberal about the decision I make.
我的家人對我的決定持相當開明的態度。

I1022

---

license
['laɪsns]

托 雅 學

n 許可證，執照
She got her driving license at the age of 16 after passing her 1st driving test.
她在十六歲時通過第一次路考後拿到了駕駛執照。

I1023

---

license
['laɪsns]

托 雅 學

vt 准許，認可
The beauty salon was not licensed to practice surgical treatment.
這家美容院並未獲得實施手術治療的許可。

I1024

---

lick
[lɪk]

托 雅 學

n 舔；少量；vt 舔；（火焰或浪）掠過，吞沒
The flames are licking the furniture in the room.
火舌正在吞噬房間裡的傢俱。

I1025

---

limb
[lɪm]

托 雅 學

n 分支，枝幹；突出物；延伸部分
After trimming the dead limbs off the trees, the garden looks green again.
在修剪掉很多枯死的枝幹後，這個花園看起來又很綠了。

I1026

---

limb
[lɪm]

托 雅 學

n 肢，臂；翼
The woman got a cramp in her limbs and could not move for a while.
那個女人四肢抽筋，好一陣子動彈不得。

I1027

limb
[lɪm]
托 雅 學

I1028
vt 肢解；截去樹枝
We limb the old oak tree in the backyard every year before winter.
我們每年冬季前都會修剪後院的老橡樹。

limousine
[ˈlɪməˌzin]
托 雅 學

I1029
n 大型豪華轎車；大轎車；加長轎車
He picked up his date in a limousine hoping to impress her.
為了使約會對象印象深刻，他用禮車來接她。

limp
[lɪmp]
托 雅 學

I1030
adj 鬆塌的，軟的；無精神的
Rachel's leg went limp and she fell to the ground upon hearing the bad news.
一聽到這個壞消息，瑞秋的腿一軟就跌倒在地上了。

limp
[lɪmp]
托 雅 學

I1031
adj 柔軟的，易曲的
The pants in the pile are limp and shapeless.
這堆衣服裡的長褲非常柔軟，不成形。

limp
[lɪmp]
托 雅 學

I1032
n 蹣跚，跛行；**vi/vt** 跛行；緩慢費力地前進
The cruise ship lost engine power at sea and could only limp slowly back to the port.
遊艇在海上失去了引擎動力，只能費勁慢慢駛回港口。

linear
[ˈlɪnɪə]
托 雅 學

I1033
adj 線的，直線的；線狀的；長度的；線性的
There is no linear relationship between how tall people grow and how strong they are.
人們長多高和他們有多壯沒有線性關係。

linger
[ˈlɪŋgə]
托 雅 學

I1034
vi/vt 逗留，徘徊；拖延；浪費光陰，消磨；苟延殘喘
The gangsters lingered about near the bar for several days.
這群匪徒在酒吧附近逗留了幾天。

liter
[ˈlitə]
托 雅 學

I1035
n 公升（容量單位）
This car's fuel tank takes approximately 60 liters of petrol gas.
這輛車的油箱可裝大約60公升的汽油。

literacy
[ˈlɪtərəsɪ]
托 雅 學

I1036
n 有文化，有教養；有讀寫能力
The young students quickly learned computer literacy before the end of their first semester.
在第一學期結束前，年輕學子們很快就學會了電腦知識。

L

literal
['lɪtərəl]

托 雅 學

adj 照字面的；不誇張的；刻板的；字母的

I1037

Many stories have allegorical meaning in addition to the literal sense of the words.

很多故事除了字面意義外，還包含了諷喻的意義。

literally
['lɪtərəlɪ]

托 雅 學

adv 照字面意義地，逐字地；確實

I1038

She had literally read over 1,000 applications for the job.

她確實讀了一千多份應徵這份工作的申請表。

literature
['lɪtərətʃə]

托 雅 學

n 文學，文學作品；文獻，圖書資料；印刷品

I1039

William Shakespeare is considered one of the great writers of English literature.

威廉·莎士比亞被視為英國文學最偉大的作家之一。

litter
['lɪtə]

托 雅 學

n 垃圾，（雜亂的）廢物

I1040

The beach was covered with litter from all the vacationers.

這個海灘被來度假的遊客所丟的垃圾給覆蓋了。

litter
['lɪtə]

托 雅 學

vi/vt 亂丟（雜物）；產仔

I1041

The tourist got a ticket for littering the park.

這個觀光客因為在公園亂丟垃圾被罰款。

loan
[lon]

托 雅 學

n 貸款；出借，借出

I1042

She is going to request a loan from the bank for the down payment.

她打算要求銀行貸款以便支付房子的頭期款。

loan
[lon]

托 雅 學

vt 借出

I1043

My mother loaned Mona 5,000 dollars for her tuition.

我媽媽借給夢娜五千美金繳學費。

lobby
['labɪ]

托 雅 學

n 門廊，門廳；（會議）休息廳

I1044

It's not safe to leave your belongings in the lobby.

把你的東西留在門廳是很不安全的。

lobby
['labɪ]

托 雅 學

vi/vt 對（議員）進行遊說；從事幕後活動

I1045

She lobbied Congress to cut taxes on middle class families.

她遊說國會對中產階級家庭進行減稅。

locate
[lo'ket]

托 雅 學

vi/vt 查出，探出；查找⋯地點；使⋯坐落於，位於

I1046

She quickly located the Band-Aids and put one on her child's cut.

她迅速地找到了OK繃並把它貼在孩子的傷口上。

location
[lo'keʃən]

托 雅 學

n 位置，場所；定位，測位

I1047

The newly opened hotel is recognized for its contemporary design and convenient location.

新開的飯店以現代的設計和便利的位置而聲名大噪。

lodge
[ladʒ]

托 雅 學

n 傳達室；小旅館；門房

I1048

Jack is searching the web for the nearest ski lodge in this area.

傑克正在網路上搜尋這個地區最近的滑雪小旅館。

lodge
[ladʒ]

托 雅 學

vi/vt 臨時住宿，寄宿；寄存；容納

I1049

The orphans were lodged in an old farm.

孤兒們被安排在一個舊農場寄宿。

L

logic
['ladʒɪk]

托 雅 學

n 邏輯，邏輯學

I1050

Logic dictates that something can't be true and untrue at the same time.

邏輯學認為，某件事情不能同時為真又為假。

longitude
['landʒə'tjud]

托 雅 學

n 經度

I1051

All lines of longitude are measured from Greenwich, England.

地球上的經度都是以英格蘭的格林威治為基準畫出的。

loop
[lup]

托 雅 學

n 圈，環；電子郵件的聯絡群組

I1052

Please keep me in the loop on this project and inform me of up-to-date development.

請把我加入這個項目的聯絡群組並告知我最新進展。

loose
[lus]

托 雅 學

adj 寬鬆的；不精確的；自由的，散漫的

I1053

She lost so much weight over the summer that her pants became loose on her.

今年夏天她瘦了太多，以至於她的褲子穿在身上都變寬鬆了。

lounge
[laʊndʒ]

托 雅 學

n 閒蕩；（飯店）會客廳，候機室；躺椅

I1054

The General Manager waited for his flight in the first class lounge at the airport.

總經理在機場的頭等艙候機室等飛機。

lounge
['laʊndʒ]

托 雅 學

vi/vt 閒蕩；懶散地混時間

He liked to lounge around in pajamas at home all day in weekends.

在週末的時候，他喜歡整天穿著睡衣在家閒蕩。

I1055

loyal
['lɔɪəl]

托 雅 學

adj 忠誠的，忠貞的

He was a loyal friend to those he really trusted.

他是個對自己真正信任的人很忠誠的朋友。

I1056

loyalty
['lɔɪəltɪ]

托 雅 學

n 忠誠，忠心

The company worked hard to gain the loyalty of more than ten thousand customers.

公司努力贏得一萬多個顧客的忠心。

I1057

lump
[lʌmp]

托 雅 學

n 團，塊；腫塊

The sculptor can always work on a lump of clay to make it come to life.

雕塑家總是可以讓一團黏土變得有生命。

I1058

lump
[lʌmp]

托 雅 學

vi 結塊；**vt** 使成團

Please don't lump all these different things together.

請不要將不同的東西混成一團。

I1059

lunar
['lunɚ]

托 雅 學

adj 月亮的

Ancient Chinese believed that the lunar eclipse was a bad sign for the emporor.

古代中國人相信月蝕是帝王厄運的徵兆。

I1060

lyric
['lɪrɪk]

托 雅 學

n 歌詞；抒情詩

She wrote the lyrics to the song and her partner wrote the music.

她替歌曲寫歌詞，而她的搭檔譜曲。

I1061

M

字彙能力檢查表

先自我檢驗是否瞭解以下初階單字，若有不清楚者，請先開啟光碟中的電子書複習。

□maize
□majesty
□major
□major
□majority
□mall
□mammal
□manage
□management
□mansion
□manual
□manual
□marble
□march
□markedly
□market
□marrow
□marsh
□mask
□mask
□massive

□masterpiece
□match
□match
□material
□material
□mathematics
□mature
□mature
□mature
□maximum
□maximum
□mayor
□meadow
□mean
□mean
□means
□mechanic
□mechanical
□mechanical
□medal
□medical

□medicine
□medium
□medium
□membership
□memo
□mention
□mention
□mess
□mess
□metallic
□metallic
□method
□mighty
□mighty
□millionaire
□miniature
□minimal
□minimize
□minimum
□minimum

□minor
□minor
□minus
□minus
□minute
□minute
□minute
□miscarriage
□misguided
□mist
□misuse
□mixture
□mobile
□monitor
□monitor
□motel
□moustache
□mushroom
□myth
□mythology

magnetic
[mæg'nɛtɪk]
托 雅 學

adj 磁的，有磁性的；有吸引力的
Chalk is not magnetic because unlike metals, it is unable to conduct any type of electrical field.
粉筆是沒有磁性的，因為它不像金屬一樣可以傳導出任何一種電場。

m1001

---

magnificent
[mæg'nɪfəsənt]
托 雅 學

adj 華麗的；高尚的；宏偉的
He stood in awe of the artwork in the magnificent cathedral.
他懷著對藝術作品敬畏的心站在那座宏偉的教堂裡。

m1002

---

maintain
[men'ten]
托 雅 學

vt 主張，支持
Many vegetarians maintain that eating animals is cruel.
許多素食者主張吃動物是殘忍的。

m1003

---

maintain
[men'ten]
托 雅 學

vt 維修；維持；供養
She maintained good relations with her in-laws.
她和她的姻親們維持良好關係。

m1004

---

maintenance
['mentənəns]
托 雅 學

n 維修，保養，維持，保持；生活費用
She took her car in for its scheduled maintenance at the garage.
她把車送到修車廠來進行定期保養。

m1005

---

majestic
[mə'dʒɛstɪk]
托 雅 學

adj 雄偉的，壯麗的；威嚴的
They had a majestic view of the Grand Canyon outside their window.
他們在窗外看到了大峽谷的雄偉景色。

m1006

---

malnutrition
[ˌmælnju'trɪʃən]
托 雅 學

n 營養不良
The released hostages were fed mild, nutritious foods at first to help treat their extreme malnutrition.
被釋放的人質一開始被餵食較溫和及有營養的食物，以便幫助他們治療極度營養不良的情況。

m1007

---

managerial
[ˌmænə'dʒɪrɪəl]
托 雅 學

adj 管理（層級）的
John's managerial experience will help cut the red tape for the company.
約翰過去的管理經驗一定有助於減少公司的繁文縟節。

m1008

---

mantle
['mæntl]
托 雅 學

n 壁爐
For their anniversary, Dee and Dave lit candles on the fireplace mantle.
迪億和黛夫在結婚紀念日裡點亮了壁爐上的蠟燭。

m1009

manufacture
[ˌmænjəˈfæktʃɚ]

n 產品；製造
Japan is famous for exporting high-tech manufactures.
日本以出口高科技產品而聞名。

m1010

manufacture
[ˌmænjəˈfæktʃɚ]

vi/vt 製造，加工
The new factory will manufacture car parts.
這家新的工廠將製造汽車零件。

m1011

manuscript
['mænjəˌskrɪpt]

n 手稿，原稿
The historian handled the ancient medieval manuscript with gloves on to avoid staining it.
歷史學家戴著手套拿中世紀的原稿，以免弄髒它。

m1012

margin
['mɑrdʒɪn]

n 頁邊空白；邊緣；餘地；幅度
Please make notes in the left margin of the book.
請在書本左側邊緣的空白處做筆記。

m1013

M

marginal
['mɑrdʒɪnl]

adj 頁邊的；邊緣的；低水準的，勉強通過的
The author only had a marginal success with his new book sales, so the publisher is disappointed.
這位作者的新書銷售只能勉強算成功，因此出版商很失望。

m1014

marine
[məˈrin]

adj 海的，海生的；船舶的，航海的
The third grade class loved seeing all the marine life at the aquarium.
三年級的學生們喜愛觀賞水族館裡的所有海洋生物。

m1015

marital
['mærətl]

adj 婚姻的，夫妻之間的
Strong friendship was the key to their marital happiness.
牢固的友誼是他們婚姻幸福的關鍵。

m1016

marshal
['mɑrʃəl]

n 元帥；陸軍元帥
General Douglass MacArthur was field marshal of the Philippines Army in 1937.
道格拉斯·麥克阿瑟將軍是1937年時菲律賓軍隊的陸軍元帥。

m1017

martial
['mɑrʃəl]

adj 軍隊的；軍事的；戰爭的
The general declared martial law in the city until the legitimate authorities could be reinstated.
將軍宣佈對城市實行軍事管制，直到政府恢復行使權力為止。

m1018

marvel
['mɑrvl]
托 雅 學

n 奇蹟；驚奇
The pyramids in Egypt are considered ancient engineering marvels.
埃及金字塔是公認的古代工程奇蹟。

m1019

marvel
['mɑrvl]
托 雅 學

vi/vt 驚奇；驚歎
The children lay on the grass and marveled at the stars in the sky.
小朋友躺在草地上為天上的星星驚歎。

m1020

marvelous
['mɑrvələs]
托 雅 學

adj 驚人的，奇蹟般的；妙極的
The weather was marvelous for a picnic.
這天氣對野餐而言實在妙極了。

m1021

maternal
[mə'tɜnl]
托 雅 學

adj 母親的，母親般的
She had a strong maternal feeling for her students.
她對她的學生們有強烈的母親般的情感。

m1022

measure
['mɛʒɚ]
托 雅 學

n 尺寸；量度器；措施，辦法
A weight scale is a measure for calculating kilograms or pounds.
體重計是一種以公斤或磅為單位的量度計。

m1023

measure
['mɛʒɚ]
托 雅 學

vi/vt 測量；分派；權衡
They measured the distance between the two bridges very carefully and precisely.
他們仔細而精確地測量了這兩座橋之間的距離。

m1024

mechanism
['mɛkə,nɪzəm]
托 雅 學

n 機械裝置，機構；機制
The locking mechanism in the car door was broken.
車門的上鎖機械裝置壞了。

m1025

media
['midiə]
托 雅 學

n 媒介物，媒體；傳導體
The story of the murder was all over the news media the next day.
這個兇殺案的故事第二天已刊登在各大新聞媒體。

m1026

medieval
[,mɪdɪ'ivəl]
托 雅 學

adj 中世紀的，中古（時代）的；老式的，原始的
Medieval castles were designed to defend against long sieges.
中古城堡是設計用來抵禦長期圍困的。

m1027

melody
['mɛlədɪ]
托 雅 學

m1028
n 旋律，曲調；悅耳的音樂
He whistled a cheerful melody on his way to the souvenir store.
他一路吹著愉悅的曲調到紀念品店去。

memorable
['mɛmərəbl]
托 雅 學

m1029
adj 值得紀念的
The play was memorable for the excellent performance of the lead actress.
舞臺劇由於領銜女主角的出色表演而讓人難以忘記。

mend
[mɛnd]
托 雅 學

m1030
n 改進；修補處；vi/vt 修理，縫補；改正，改善
Two years after the financial meltdown, the world economy is finally on the mend.
金融風暴後的兩年，世界經濟才終於開始改善。

mental
['mɛntl]
托 雅 學

m1031
adj 精神的，思想的，心理的；智力的，腦力的
He did a few quick mental calculations and realized he could afford to take the trip.
他進行了幾個快速的心理推算，發現自己是能夠負擔該次旅行的。

M

mentality
[mɛn'tæləti]
托 雅 學

m1032
n 心態
Fearing further attacks from the enemy, all the troops have developed a bunker mentality.
由於擔心敵軍進一步攻擊，部隊士兵都有了背水一戰的心態。

merchandise
['mɝtʃən,daɪz]
托 雅 學

m1033
n 商品，貨物
The manager straightened up the merchandise before he closed up the shop for the night.
這個經理在晚上關店之前把商品收拾整齊。

mercy
['mɝsɪ]
托 雅 學

m1034
n 仁慈，憐憫，寬恕
The convicted murderer asked the judge for mercy before his sentencing.
已定罪的兇手在執刑前向法官請求寬恕。

mere
[mɪr]
托 雅 學

m1035
adj 純粹的；僅僅的，只不過的
Please don't scold him, he is but a mere child and just doesn't know any better.
請不要責怪他，他僅僅是個還不懂事的孩子。

migrate
['maɪ,gret]
托 雅 學

m1036
vi 遷移，移居（國外）
Sparrows migrate south every winter.
麻雀每年冬天都遷往南方。

mileage
['maɪlɪdʒ]
托 雅 學

n 里程
The odometer will record the mileage of the car.
里程計會將車輛的里程記錄下來。

m1037

militant
['mɪlətənt]
托 雅 學

adj 好戰的，富於戰鬥性的；激進的；**n** 鬥士
He was known for his militant views on immigration policy.
他因為對移民政策持有激進的觀點而著名。

m1038

military
['mɪlə,tɛrɪ]
托 雅 學

adj 軍事的，軍用的，軍隊的
He joined the military after high school.
高中畢業後他加入了軍隊。

m1039

mingle
['mɪŋɡl]
托 雅 學

vi/vt （使）混合
She mingled with some new friends at the party before she went home.
她在回家前和宴會上一些新朋友混在一起。

m1040

minister
['mɪnɪstə]
托 雅 學

n 部長；大臣
Mr. Black will be the new Minister of Education.
布萊克先生將是新任的教育部長。

m1041

ministry
['mɪnɪstrɪ]
托 雅 學

n 部門
She started a ministry to help educate homeless children.
她成立了一個部門來教育無家可歸的孩子。

m1042

minority
[maɪ'nɔrətɪ]
托 雅 學

n 少數，少數派；少數民族
She voted for the third-party candidate even though she knew she was in the minority.
即使知道自己是少數派，她還是把票投給了第三黨派的候選人。

m1043

miracle
['mɪrəkl]
托 雅 學

n 奇蹟，令人驚奇的人（或事）
When her daughter became ill, she began to pray for a miracle.
當她女兒生病時，她開始祈禱有奇蹟發生。

m1044

miraculous
[mɪ'rækjələs]
托 雅 學

adj 神奇的
It was miraculous that most people weren't injured in the train crash.
神奇的是，火車撞車事故中大半乘客沒有受傷。

m1045

miserable
['mɪzərəbl]

m1046

adj 痛苦的，悲慘的
Being cold and wet made it a miserable day.
又冷又濕使那天變得很慘。

misery
['mɪzərɪ]

m1047

n 痛苦，悲慘，不幸
Her friends tried to ease her misery by taking her out to a movie.
她的朋友試著帶她去看電影減輕她的痛苦。

misfortune
[mɪs'fɔrtʃən]

m1048

n 不幸，災禍，災難
She didn't let the misfortune of the car accident get her down.
她沒讓車禍的不幸把她擊倒。

misrepresent
[,mɪsrɛprɪ'zɛnt]

m1049

vt 歪曲，誤傳
The judge cautioned the lawyer not to misrepresent the facts of the case.
法官警告那個律師不要歪曲本案的事實。

M

missile
['mɪsl]

m1050

n 導彈；發射物
A nuclear missile was launched this morning.
一枚核導彈今天早上發射升空了。

mission
['mɪʃən]

m1051

n 使命，任務；使團，代表團
The unit was sent on a special rescue mission behind enemy lines.
該部隊被送往敵營執行一項特殊的營救任務。

mobilize
['mobl,aɪz]

m1052

vi/vt 動員，調動
The leader of the party mobilized all the members to participate in the campaign.
黨的領導人動員所有黨員參加活動。

mock
[mɑk]

m1053

adj 假的；模擬的
The teacher nodded her head in mock approval.
這位老師點點頭，假裝贊同。

mock
[mɑk]

m1054

n 複數＝模擬考試
Students take mocks before the entrance exam to familiarize themselves with the test format.
學生在入學考試前會參加模擬考試，以熟悉考試題型。

mock
[mak]
托 雅 學

vi/vt 嘲笑
People who enjoy mocking others sometimes have inferiority complex.
喜歡嘲笑別人的人有時有自卑情結。

m1055

mode
[mod]
托 雅 學

n 方式，式樣
Bicycle was her usual mode of transportation.
腳踏車是她常用的交通方式。

m1056

moderate
['madərɪt]
托 雅 學

adj 溫和的；有節制的；中等的
I grew up in a family of moderate income.
我在一個中等收入家庭長大。

m1057

moderate
['madə,ret]
托 雅 學

vt 節制；調解；使和緩；主持
He volunteered to moderate the debate team practices.
他自願主持辯論隊練習。

m1058

modest
['madɪst]
托 雅 學

adj 謙虛的；有節制的；適度的；端莊的
She selected a modest black dress for the funeral.
為了那場喪禮，她挑選了一條莊重的黑色裙子。

m1059

modification
[,madəfə'keʃən]
托 雅 學

n 緩和；修改；修飾
The project needs modifications or it will not work well.
這項計畫需要修改，否則無法順利運行。

m1060

modify
['madə,faɪ]
托 雅 學

vi/vt 更改，修改，修飾
She modified her speech to make it longer since the next speaker was late.
她把講稿修改得長了一些，因為下一個演講者遲到了。

m1061

module
['madʒul]
托 雅 學

n 元件，模組，模件；（航天器的）艙
This key module has to be joined together with others to complete the structure.
這個重要模件得和其他部分結合起來，以使結構完整。

m1062

moist
[mɔɪst]
托 雅 學

adj 潮濕的，濕潤的，多雨的
The baker's cakes are famous for their moist texture.
這位糕點師傅的蛋糕有名就有名在吃起來有濕潤的質感。

m1063

moisture
['mɔɪstʃə]

m1064

n 潮濕，濕氣，濕度，水分，水氣

The moisture in her breath condensed quickly in the cold air.

她呼出的水氣在冷空氣中很快凝結了。

monarchy
['manəkɪ]

m1065

n 君主國；君主政體，君主制

Queen Elizabeth is the current sovereign ruling in the British monarchy.

伊莉莎白女皇是英國的君主政體下在位的君王。

monster
['manstə]

m1066

n 怪物，妖怪；畸形的動植物

When she was little, she was scared of monsters under her bed.

當她還小時，她害怕床下的怪物。

monstrous
['manstrəs]

m1067

adj 可怕的；極大的

There is no shortage of monstrous being in Greek mythology.

希臘神話中不乏可怕的生物。

monument
['manjəmənt]

m1068

n 紀念碑；紀念館

The town erected a monument to their veterans of foreign wars.

鎮上設立了一座紀念碑以紀念參與對外戰爭的老兵。

M

morality
[mə'rælətɪ]

m1069

n 道德，美德

Many people are concerned that our standards of morality seem to be dropping nowadays.

很多人擔憂我們現在的道德標準似乎在下降。

mortal
['mɔrtḷ]

m1070

adj 致命的；終有一死的；人世間的

The fallen soldier was awarded a medal because he sustained a mortal wound in the process of rescuing his friend from the ambush.

陣亡士兵被授予勳章，因為他在受伏擊時為營救朋友而遭受了致命的傷害。

mortal
['mɔrtḷ]

m1071

n 凡人

We are only mortals, so it is inevitable that one day we will all die.

我們只是凡人，總有一天會死，這是不可避免的。

mortar
['mɔrtə]

m1072

n 迫擊炮

The Army reports that there are constant mortar attacks on the front lines.

軍隊報告稱前線經常受到迫擊炮的襲擊。

mortgage
['mɔrgɪdʒ]
托 雅 學

n/vt 抵押（借款）　　　　　　　　　　m1073
They agreed to mortgage their house to help their daughter attend music school.
他們同意抵押他們的房子，讓女兒讀音樂學校。

motion
['moʃən]
托 雅 學

n 運動；手勢；提議　　　　　　　　　m1074
The lights in this room are connected to motion detectors to save energy.
這個房間的燈光和運動探測器相連，以便節省能源。

motivate
['motə,vet]
托 雅 學

vt 促動；激勵，激發　　　　　　　　　m1075
The teacher offered extra credit assignments to motivate her students to study.
老師提供了額外的加分作業以激勵學生學習。

motivation
[,motə'veʃən]
托 雅 學

n 動機　　　　　　　　　　　　　　　m1076
She questioned her boss's motivation for replacing his secretary.
她問老闆換秘書的動機是什麼。

motive
['motɪv]
托 雅 學

adj 發動的；運動的　　　　　　　　　m1077
The fuel provides the motive power for the car to run.
燃油給車提供了發動的動力。

mount
[maʊnt]
托 雅 學

n 支架，底板；山峰　　　　　　　　　m1078
Mount Ali is one of the most popular tourist attractions in Taiwan.
阿里山是臺灣地區最著名的旅遊景點之一。

mount
[maʊnt]
托 雅 學

vi/vt 騎上；登上；安裝　　　　　　　　m1079
She slowly mounted the steps to the Lincoln Memorial.
她緩慢地登上通往林肯紀念堂的階梯。

multicultural
[,mʌltɪ'kʌltʃərəl]
托 雅 學

adj 多元文化的　　　　　　　　　　　m1080
Camp goers will be immersed in multicultural programs for ten days.
營隊學員十天都會沉浸在多元文化課程之中。

multiply
['mʌltəplaɪ]
托 雅 學

vi/vt 乘，（使）相乘；倍增，增加；繁殖　m1081
The students watched the cell colony multiply under the microscope.
學生們在顯微鏡下觀察細胞群繁殖。

multitude
['mʌltə,tjud]

m1082

n 大批，大群；大量

Pay a visit to that gallery, and you'll find that multitudes of cultural events were held there.

你去參觀那間藝廊就會發現，那裡舉辦過大量藝文活動。

---

municipal
[mju'nɪsəpl]

m1083

adj 市（立、政）的；地方性的，地方自治的

He went to the municipal court to pay his traffic ticket.

他到地方法院繳他的交通罰單。

---

murmur
['mɝmə]

m1084

n/vi/vt 小聲說（話），呢喃；小聲抱怨，咕噥；潺潺聲

She lay on the grass and listened to the murmur of the creek.

她躺在草地上聽小溪潺潺的流水聲。

---

muscular
['mʌskjələ]

m1085

adj 肌肉的；肌肉發達的，強健的

Adam has improved his muscular strength after eight-week intense workouts.

亞當經過八週高強度健身後，提升了肌肉的耐力。

---

mutual
['mjutʃʊəl]

m1086

adj 相互的，彼此的；共同的，共有的

Their affection for each other was strong and mutual.

他們對彼此有著強烈的愛意。

M

N

字彙能力檢查表

先自我檢驗是否瞭解以下初階單字，若有不清楚者，請先開啟光碟中的電子書複習。

- [ ] naked
- [ ] nap
- [ ] napkin
- [ ] narrative
- [ ] narrative
- [ ] narrator

- [ ] narrow
- [ ] nasty
- [ ] native
- [ ] native
- [ ] natural
- [ ] natural

- [ ] navigation
- [ ] neat
- [ ] nevertheless
- [ ] nickel
- [ ] nightmare

- [ ] nonetheless
- [ ] notwithstanding
- [ ] nowadays
- [ ] nowhere
- [ ] numerous

namely
['nemlɪ']

托 雅 學

adv 即，也就是　　　　　　　　　　n1001
We need to focus on our target market, namely teenagers aged between 13 and 18.
我們需要專注於目標市場，也就是十三歲到十八歲的青少年。

naval
['nevl̩]

托 雅 學

n 海軍的，軍艦的　　　　　　　　　n1002
Our math teacher is a retired naval officer.
我們的數學老師是一個退休的海軍軍官。

navigate
['nævə,get]

托 雅 學

n 航行；航海術；導航　　　　　　　n1003
The old captain taught the new crew how to navigate across the oceans.
老船長教新水手們如何航行於海洋。

negative
['nɛɡətɪv]

托 雅 學

adj 否定的，消極的；陰性的；負面的　　n1004
The frequent snow storms had a negative impact on the local economy.
經常性的暴風雪給當地經濟造成了負面的影響。

negative
['nɛɡətɪv]

托 雅 學

n 負數；（攝影）底片　　　　　　　n1005
I want to have the negatives developed into large, colorful pictures to share with everyone.
我想要將底片沖洗成大張彩色照片跟大家一起分享。

N

neglect
[nɪɡ'lɛkt]

托 雅 學

n 忽視；疏忽，漏做，忽略　　　　　n1006
The weedy garden was suffering from neglect.
雜草叢生的花園被忽略了。

neglect
[nɪɡ'lɛkt]

托 雅 學

vt 忽視；疏忽，漏做，忽略　　　　　n1007
He has been busying working and has neglected his health.
他一直忙於工作，忽略了身體健康。

negotiable
[nɪ'ɡoʃɪəbl̩]

托 雅 學

adj 可談判的，可協商的，可商量的　　n1008
Zoë was advised that her first modeling gigs were not negotiable.
柔伊被告知，她的第一次造型演出沒什麼可商量的餘地。

nobility
[no'bɪlətɪ]

托 雅 學

n 貴族身份　　　　　　　　　　　n1009
The nobility of Philip's family stretches back generations.
菲力浦家族的貴族身份能往前追溯好幾代人。

nominee
[ˌnɑməˈni]
托 雅 學

n 被提名人
Every year actors are proud to be an Oscar nominee.
每年演員們都以成為奧斯卡獎被提名人而感到自豪。

n1010

nonsense
[ˈnɑnsɛns]
托 雅 學

n 胡說，廢話；無法懂的話
Since he missed the lecture, the math homework seemed like nonsense to him.
由於他逃了課，數學作業在他看來像是看不懂的天書。

n1011

normally
[ˈnɔrmlɪ]
托 雅 學

adv 正常地
I checked all the function keys to make sure they are operating normally.
我檢查了鍵盤上所有的功能鍵，以確保它們都能正常地運作。

n1012

notable
[ˈnotəbl]
托 雅 學

n 值得注意的；顯著的，著名的
His skill at chess was notable for his age.
相對他的年紀而言，他下西洋棋的技巧相當值得關注。

n1013

notice
[ˈnotɪs]
托 雅 學

n 通知，通告，佈告；注意，認識
Upon receiving the notice of an approaching typhoon, all ships went back to the harbor.
一收到颱風即將來襲的通知，所有船隻都返回港口。

n1014

notice
[ˈnotɪs]
托 雅 學

vt 注意到，注意
She noticed that he seemed happier today.
她注意到他今天似乎高興一些了。

n1015

notify
[ˈnotəˌfaɪ]
托 雅 學

vt 通知，告知；報告
The court notified her to appear for jury duty the next week.
法院通知她下週出席陪審團。

n1016

notion
[ˈnoʃən]
托 雅 學

n 概念，想法，意念；看法，觀點
She had a notion that her father would enjoy the novel she was reading.
她的看法是，爸爸會喜歡她正在讀的這本小說。

n1017

nourish
[ˈnɝɪʃ]
托 雅 學

vt 提供養分；養育；懷有（希望、仇恨等）
She was nourished by her mother's affectionate attention.
她在媽媽充滿愛的照料中長大。

n1018

novel
['nɑvl̩]

托 雅 學

adj 新奇的，新穎的；**n** 小說

n1019

After hours of brainstorming, they finally came up with a novel solution to the problem.

幾小時的腦力激盪後，他們終於想出解決問題的新奇辦法。

---

novelty
['nɑvl̩tɪ]

托 雅 學

n 新奇，新穎；新奇的事物

n1020

She enjoyed the novelty of her new smart phone.

她喜歡新智慧型手機的新穎。

---

nuclear
['njuklɪə]

托 雅 學

adj 核心的，中心的；原子核的，核能的

n1021

The United Nations would allow any country to make nuclear weapons.

聯合國同意任何國家製造核武器。

---

nucleus
['njuklɪəs]

托 雅 學

n 核，核心，原子核；複數＝nuclei

n1022

DNA is stored in the nucleus of a living cell.

DNA是貯存在活細胞核中的。

---

numb
[nʌm]

托 雅 學

adj 麻木的，失去感覺的；**v** 使麻木

n1023

The freezing temperature makes my fingers numb very quickly.

寒冷的氣溫讓我的手指很快地麻掉了

N

nursery
['nɝsərɪ]

托 雅 學

n 托兒所

n1024

Many children go to nursery school before five years old.

許多孩子在五歲之前都上托兒所。

O

字彙能力檢查表

先自我檢驗是否瞭解以下初階單字，若有不清楚者，請先開啟光碟中的電子書複習。

□oasis   □offence   □organically   □oval
□obedient   □officer   □organize   □overall
□obey   □offshore   □ounce   □overall
□obligation   □oil   □outcome   □overflow
□observe   □ongoing   □outfit   □overlap
□obtain   □onward   □outgoing   □overlap
□obvious   □operate   □outline   □overseas
□occasion   □operation   □outline   □overtime
□occasional   □opinion   □outlook   □overturn
□occupant   □oral   □outright   □overturn
□occupation   □orderly   □outstanding   □owe
□occupation   □orderly   □outward   □owe
□occupy   □organ   □outward   □own
□occupy   □organ   □oval   □ownership
□occur

oath
[oθ]

n 誓言，誓約；詛咒　o1001

After the car accident, Amy took an oath to give up drinking.

車禍過後，艾米立下誓言絕對不再喝酒。

object
['ɑbdʒɪkt]

n 物體；對象；目標　o1002

After his stroke, Sam was trained to squeeze soft objects to strengthen his hand.

山姆中風後被訓練擠捏柔軟的物品以增強手勁。

object
[əb'dʒɛkt]

vi/vt 反對　o1003

We all strongly objected to the mayor's proposal for new civic center.

我們堅決反對市長的新市政中心提議。

objection
[əb'dʒɛkʃən]

n 反對，異議，不喜歡　o1004

The opposition party raised a loud objection concerning the abortion laws.

反對黨對人工流產的法律提出強烈的反對意見。

objective
[əb'dʒɛktɪv]

adj 客觀的，真實的　o1005

The professor asked us to take an objective point of view on this assignment.

教授要求我們採用一個客觀的觀點來做這份作業。

objective
[əb'dʒɛktɪv]

n 目標，目的　o1006

The objective of the meeting today is to decide when we should finish the project.

今天會議的目標是要決定我們何時應該要完成這個項目。

oblige
[ə'blaɪdʒ]

vi 幫忙；施恩惠　o1007

He asked her to look up his patient's medical record and she was happy to oblige.

他請她查詢病人的病例，她很樂意幫忙。

oblige
[ə'blaɪdʒ]

vt 強迫，迫使　o1008

That scandal obliged the movie star to resign from the role of the Hollywood movie.

那個醜聞迫使這位電影明星辭演那部好萊塢電影。

obscure
[əb'skjʊr]

adj 暗的；模糊的；無名的　o1009

He liked to listen to obscure rock bands that no one had heard of.

他喜歡聽那種沒人聽說過的無名搖滾樂團的歌曲。

occupational
[ˌɑkjəˈpeʃən]]
托 雅 學

adj 職業的
The father forced his son to quit the well-paying job because it has high occupational risks.
這位父親強迫他的兒子辭掉待遇豐厚的工作，因為它的職業風險很高。
o1010

odd
[ɑd]
托 雅 學

adj 奇怪的，古怪的
Kenny is an odd boy and many of his classmates find it hard to get along with him.
肯尼是一個古怪的男孩，很多同學覺得跟他很難相處。
o1011

odd
[ɑd]
托 雅 學

adj 奇數的，單數的
How will you divide the class equally into two groups with an odd number of students?
你要怎麼把奇數學生人數的班級分成完全相等的兩組呢？
o1012

odds
[ɑds]
托 雅 學

n 機會；可能性；不和；優勢
Even though the odds are against them, they still want to give it a try.
雖然成功的機會很小，他們仍想要一試。
o1013

offend
[əˈfɛnd]
托 雅 學

vi 違反；犯罪；vt 冒犯，觸犯
The clerk was offended by the customer's rude joke.
這位店員因為客人講的粗俗笑話而感到被冒犯。
o1014

offensive
[əˈfɛnsɪv]
托 雅 學

adj 冒犯的，攻擊的
The author's remarks were highly offensive to gays.
這位作者的言論是相當冒犯同性戀者的。
o1015

offensive
[əˈfɛnsɪv]
托 雅 學

n 攻勢，進攻
Our team is taking the offensive now.
我們的球隊現在正採取攻勢。
o1016

offer
[ˈɔfɚ]
托 雅 學

n 提供，提議；提案；出價
I appreciate your kind offer of support for this project.
我很感謝你在這個項目中所提供的支援。
o1017

offer
[ˈɔfɚ]
托 雅 學

vt 提供；提議；出現
I was offered a well-paid job as an English teacher at a local high school.
當地的中學向我提供英文老師的高薪工作。
o1018

official
[əˈfɪʃəl]

托 雅 學

adj 官方的，正式的 o1019
The official report included a commendation for the soldier's bravery.
此份正式的報告對士兵的勇敢提出了讚揚。

official
[əˈfɪʃəl]

托 雅 學

n 官員，行政官員 o1020
The school officials will discuss the building of the swimming pool in the meeting.
學校官員將會在會議上討論游泳池的建設問題。

offspring
[ˈɔfˌsprɪŋ]

托 雅 學

n 子孫，後代；結果，產物 o1021
Mother birds feed and warm their offspring until they are old enough to fly.
母鳥給牠的後代餵食取暖，一直到牠們長大會飛為止。

opponent
[əˈponənt]

托 雅 學

adj 對立的，敵對的，對抗的 o1022
To avoid encountering the opponent army, the general decided to take a detour.
為了避免遇到敵軍，將軍決定繞道而行。

opponent
[əˈponənt]

托 雅 學

n 對手，反對者，敵手 o1023
The opponents of the policy are going to have a demonstration on Sunday morning.
此項政策的反對者將在星期天早上舉行示威活動。

opportunity
[ˌɑpəˈtjunətɪ]

托 雅 學

n 機會 o1024
This time don't miss your promotion opportunity!
這次不要錯失升遷的機會喔！

oppose
[əˈpoz]

托 雅 學

vi/vt 反對；反抗 o1025
The child is strongly opposed to celebrating Christmas with her stepmother.
這個孩子強烈反對與她的繼母一起慶祝耶誕節。

opposite
[ˈɑpəzɪt]

托 雅 學

adj 相反的，對立的 o1026
The couple had an argument because their views on the political issue were opposite.
這對夫妻發生了口角，因為他們對政治事件的看法是相反的。

opposite
[ˈɑpəzɪt]

托 雅 學

n 對立面；相反 o1027
Jack is considerate; his wife is just the opposite.
傑克能體貼人，而他妻子恰恰相反。

optimism
['ɑptəmɪzəm]

托 雅 學

n 樂觀，樂觀主義

o1028

He had boundless optimism and good humor.

他非常樂觀，也很有幽默感。

optimistic
[ˌɑptə'mɪstɪk]

托 雅 學

adj 樂觀主義的

o1029

The economists are optimistic about next year's GDP growth.

經濟學家們對明年的國內生產毛額增長持樂觀態度。

option
['ɑpʃən]

托 雅 學

n 選擇（權），（商）選擇買賣的特權

o1030

She considered her options carefully before selecting her college.

在挑選大學前她仔細地考慮她的選擇。

optional
['ɑpʃənl]

托 雅 學

adj 可以任選的，隨意的，非強制的

o1031

Ties are optional in the club lounge, but please remember you do have to wear a club jacket in the dining room.

領帶在俱樂部的休息室裡可以選擇戴或不戴，但是請記得在餐廳要穿俱樂部的外套。

orbit
['ɔrbɪt]

托 雅 學

n （天體等的）運行軌道

o1032

Earth's orbit is like a road in space for our planet to travel around the sun.

地球的運行軌道像太空中的一條路，它就沿著這條路繞行太陽。

orbit
['ɔrbɪt]

托 雅 學

vt 使…沿軌道繞行

o1033

Many people don't know that it takes our Earth a year to complete orbiting the sun.

很多人不知道要我們的地球沿軌道繞行太陽需要一年的時間。

orchestra
['ɔrkɪstrə]

托 雅 學

n 管弦樂隊；管弦樂隊的全部樂器

o1034

The orchestra tuned up before the performance.

管弦樂隊在表演前調音熱身。

organic
[ɔr'gænɪk]

托 雅 學

adj 有機的，有機體的；器官的

o1035

Organic produce has now become a very popular but expensive choice.

有機農產品現已成為一種流行但昂貴的選擇。

organism
['ɔrgən,ɪzəm]

托 雅 學

n 生物體；有機體

o1036

Many tests have been run to try to identify the organism that caused the infection.

目前為止已經做了很多測試來辨別造成這次感染的生物體。

organization
[ˌɔrgənəˈzeʃən]

托 雅 學

n 組織，團體，機構　　　　　　　　o1037
We run a non-profit organization and rely on the charity of our community.
我們經營一個非營利組織，依賴我們社區的捐助。

orient
[ˈorɪənt]

托 雅 學

n 東方，亞洲　　　　　　　　　　o1038
She loved the history and culture of the Orient.
她喜歡東方的歷史與文化。

orient
[ˈorɪɛnt]

托 雅 學

vt 使朝東；為⋯定位；使適應　　　o1039
The lost boy oriented himself by searching the North Star in the forest at night.
迷路的小男孩在夜晚的森林裡通過尋找北極星來為自己定位。

oriental
[ˌorɪˈɛntl̩]

托 雅 學

adj 東方的，東方諸國的　　　　　　o1040
In Oriental languages, Chinese has the most learners.
在所有的東方語言中，中文的學習者最多。

oriental
[ˌorɪˈɛntl̩]

托 雅 學

n 東方人　　　　　　　　　　　　o1041
Even though she has blue eyes, she is truly an Oriental.
雖然她有雙藍色的眼睛，她的確是個東方人。

orientation
[ˌorɪɛnˈteʃən]

托 雅 學

n 方向，傾向性，向東方；新生訓練　o1042
They attended the orientation at their new school later that day.
他們在當天參加了新學校的新生訓練。

origin
[ˈɔrədʒɪn]

托 雅 學

n 起源，由來；出身，來歷　　　　　o1043
Can anyone tell me something about the origin of the game of rugby?
有人可以告訴我橄欖球運動的起源嗎？

original
[əˈrɪdʒən̩l]

托 雅 學

adj 最初的，原文的；新穎的　　　　o1044
She owned an original copy of his writings.
她有他著作的原版。

original
[əˈrɪdʒən̩l]

托 雅 學

n 原物，原作，原文　　　　　　　o1045
The original of that oil painting is said to have been missing for a hundred years.
那幅油畫的原作據說已遺失一百年了。

ornament
['ɔrnəmənt]

托 雅 學

n 裝飾物；裝飾

o1046

She bought new ornaments for their Christmas tree.
她為他們的聖誕樹買了新的裝飾品。

ornament
['ɔrnəmənt]

托 雅 學

vt 裝修

o1047

The lavish king ornamented his parlor with gold and rubies.
這個極度浪費的國王用金子和紅寶石裝飾他的起居室。

outbreak
['aʊtˌbrek]

托 雅 學

n （戰爭、憤怒、火災等的）爆發；（疾病的）發作

o1048

We should try our best to prevent an outbreak of violence in our region.
我們應該盡最大努力防止暴亂在本地區發生。

outcast
['aʊtˌkæst]

托 雅 學

n 被拋棄者；被排斥者

o1049

She felt like an outcast in her school.
她感覺自己在學校裡像個棄兒。

outlet
['aʊtˌlɛt]

托 雅 學

n 出路，出口；銷路，市場；發洩方法

o1050

The mother hopes that the basketball camp can be an outlet for her super-energetic twin boys.
這位媽媽希望籃球營可以成為她那兩個雙胞胎男孩發洩過人精力的地方。

outlet
['aʊtˌlɛt]

托 雅 學

n 電源插座

o1051

She plugged the lamp into a nearby electrical outlet.
她把檯燈的插頭插入就近的電源插座。

outlying
['aʊtˌlaɪɪŋ]

托 雅 學

adj 遠離中心的，偏僻的

o1052

Please go with Kayla on the ferry to see the outlying islands.
請和凱拉一起登上渡船去瞧瞧那片偏僻的小島。

overdue
['ovɚ'dju]

托 雅 學

adj 過期的，未兌的；遲到的，早該發生的

o1053

The region was overdue for a good rain.
這個地方早就該好好下一場雨了。

overhear
[ˌovɚ'hɪr]

托 雅 學

vt 無意中聽到，從旁聽到

o1054

Don't talk loudly on your cell phone in public if you don't want anyone to overhear your conversation.
如果你在公共場所大聲用手機打電話，旁人可能會無意中聽到你的談話。

overlook
[ˌovəˈlʊk]

vt 看漏，忽略；俯瞰；寬容　　o1055
We overlook the lake in our new house on the hill.
我們在山坡上的新房子裡俯瞰湖面。

overwhelm
[ˌovəˈhwɛlm]

vt 覆沒，壓倒；制服；使不知所措　　o1056
If I think about all the work I have to do, it will overwhelm me.
一想要做的事情有那麼多，我就不知所措。

oxide
[ˈɑksaɪd]

n 氧化物　　o1057
After examination, Will thought the oxide was a flammable substance.
測試之後，威爾相信氧化物是一種易燃物質。

O

P

☐ pace	☐ pave	☐ pole	☐ pride
☐ pace	☐ pavement	☐ polite	☐ privacy
☐ pack	☐ peak	☐ pollute	☐ private
☐ pack	☐ peak	☐ porch	☐ probably
☐ pad	☐ pedal	☐ pore	☐ process
☐ paddle	☐ pedal	☐ port	☐ process
☐ paddle	☐ peg	☐ portable	☐ profile
☐ palm	☐ personal	☐ portion	☐ profit
☐ palm	☐ personality	☐ position	☐ profit
☐ pamphlet	☐ personnel	☐ positive	☐ profitable
☐ panel	☐ persuade	☐ postage	☐ promise
☐ pants	☐ phase	☐ postal	☐ promise
☐ parade	☐ picnic	☐ poster	☐ promising
☐ parade	☐ pillow	☐ potential	☐ proof
☐ paradise	☐ pilot	☐ pottery	☐ property
☐ paragraph	☐ pimple	☐ pound	☐ proposal
☐ parcel	☐ pin	☐ pour	☐ propose
☐ partial	☐ pinch	☐ poverty	☐ protect
☐ particularly	☐ pine	☐ precious	☐ protection
☐ partner	☐ pitch	☐ pregnant	☐ protein
☐ partnership	☐ pitch	☐ preparation	☐ proud
☐ passenger	☐ plague	☐ present	☐ provide
☐ passive	☐ plot	☐ present	☐ publish
☐ passport	☐ plot	☐ present	☐ pumpkin

☐pastime	☐plow	☐preserve	☐purpose
☐patch	☐plow	☐prevent	☐pursue
☐patch	☐plug	☐prevention	☐pursuit
☐patience	☐plug	☐previous	☐puzzle
☐patient	☐plumber	☐price	☐puzzle
☐patio	☐plus	☐pride	

psychology
[saɪˈkɑlədʒɪ]

托 雅 學

n 心理學，心理狀態　p1001

The writer enjoyed creating characters with a unique psychology that allowed him to explore strange ideas about the human mind.

那位作家喜愛創造有獨特心理狀態的角色，使他可以去探索這個人的奇思妙想。

painstaking
[penz,tekɪŋ]

托 雅 學

adj 需細心的；辛苦的　p1002

She was a careful seamstress and the dress was finished with painstaking detail just in time for the wedding.

她是個細心的裁縫，而這件禮服就是在她細心辛苦的手工下，趕在婚禮前完成的。

pane
[pen]

托 雅 學

n 窗格玻璃　p1003

The boys hit the baseball against the front door and broke the window pane.

在外頭打棒球的男孩們把球打到了前門，還打碎了門上的窗格玻璃。

panic
[ˈpænɪk]

托 雅 學

adj/n 恐慌（的），驚慌（的）　p1004

There is a panic spreading among businessmen because the stock market may crash.

因為股市可能會崩潰，因此生意人之間傳播著一陣恐慌。

panic
[ˈpænɪk]

托 雅 學

vi/vt 使驚慌，使害怕　p1005

The fireman did not panic when the fire got out of control.

當火勢失去控制時消防隊員並沒有很恐慌。

parachute
[ˈpærəˌʃut]

托 雅 學

n 降落傘　p1006

When the plane went down, three of the crew jumped to safety with parachutes.

當飛機墜落時，其中三名機務人員利用降落傘到達了安全的地方。

parachute
[ˈpærəˌʃut]

托 雅 學

vi 跳傘；**vt** 空投　p1007

The supplies were parachuted to the victims to relieve their urgent needs of water and food.

供應物資空投給了受難者，以緩解他們對於水和食物的迫切需求。

parallel
['pærə,lɛl]

托 雅 學

adj 平行的;n 平行線;類似;對比 p1008
The boy drew two parallel lines on the board.
男孩在板子上畫了兩條平行線。

paralysis
[pə'ræləsɪs]

托 雅 學

n 麻痺,癱瘓 p1009
After the accident she suffered some paralysis in her legs and could not walk.
在這個意外之後,她的腳就癱瘓了沒辦法走路。

paralyze
['pærə,laɪz]

托 雅 學

vt 使麻痺,使癱瘓 p1010
His grandfather suffered from a terrible disease, which paralyzed him.
他的祖父患上了可怕的疾病,使他癱瘓了。

paraphrase
['pærə,frez]

托 雅 學

vt 重述,轉述 p1011
I can't remember exactly what the article said word for word, but I can paraphrase it for you.
我沒有辦法把那篇文章逐字逐句地說給你聽,但是它的意義我倒是可以轉述。

parasite
['pærə,saɪt]

托 雅 學

n 寄生蟲;食客 p1012
A tapeworm is a type of parasite that lives in the intestines of some animals.
條蟲是一種生活在動物腸子裡的寄生蟲。

parliament
['parləmənt]

托 雅 學

n 國會,議會 p1013
A session of parliament was called to investigate the allegations against the prime minister.
為了調查針對首相的控訴,在國會中專門成立了一個小組。

participant
[par'tɪsəpənt]

托 雅 學

n 參加者,參與者 p1014
I refuse to be a participant in this stupid argument.
我拒絕成為這場愚蠢爭論的參與者。

participate
[par'tɪsə,pet]

托 雅 學

vi/vt 參與 p1015
I want to participate in the charity fundraiser this year.
今年我想參與慈善募款。

particle
['partɪkl]

托 雅 學

n 粒子;極小量;小品詞 p1016
I can still see particles of dust and dirt on the surface of the desk.
我仍然可以看到桌子表面的塵粒。

partition
[par'tɪʃən]

托 雅 學

n 分開；隔牆；分隔物；分隔間
p1017
Folding partitions separated the living and dining areas.
折疊式的隔板將起居和吃飯的地方分開。

passionate
['pæʃənɪt]

托 雅 學

adj 熱情的，有激情的
p1018
After thirty years of marriage, the couple was still very passionate to each other.
即使已結婚三十年，那對夫妻對彼此仍非常有激情。

pasture
['pæstʃə]

托 雅 學

n 牧草地，牧場；牲畜飼養；vi/vt 放牧，吃草
p1019
The cows pasture on the hillside during the day and go back to the barn at night.
牛在白天的時候在山坡上的牧場上吃草，到了晚上就回牛棚裡。

patent
['pætənt]

托 雅 學

n 專利權
p1020
The inventor received many patents on the inventions he designed.
那位發明家擁有他設計的許多發明專利。

patent
['pætənt]

托 雅 學

vt 批准專利；獲得專利
p1021
The steam elevator was patented by Elisha Otis in 1861.
以利沙‧奧堤斯於1861年獲得了蒸氣電梯專利。

pathetic
[pə'θɛtɪk]

托 雅 學

adj 可憐的，悲慘的
p1022
Our team lost by so many points that after a while it became pathetic.
我們這一隊輸了好多分，沒過多久結局就變得很悲慘了。

patrol
[pə'trol]

托 雅 學

n 巡邏，巡查；巡邏隊
p1023
Policemen were on patrol at night on the streets when the violence occurred.
警方晚上會在暴力常發生的街道巡邏。

payment
['pemənt]

托 雅 學

n 付款，（將付）款額
p1024
It's important that you make the required minimum monthly payment to avoid accruing purchase interest.
你必須每個月支付最低償還金額以避免被收取應計利息。

payroll
['pe,rol]

托 雅 學

n 薪水帳冊；（應付）薪資總額
p1025
A big company has a large number of employees on its payroll.
大公司的薪水帳冊上有一大批員工等著發工資。

P

pebble
['pɛbl]
托 雅 學

n 卵石

Because it rains so little here, we can line the front walk with small gray pebbles.

這裡很少下雨，因此我們可以用灰色的鵝卵石標示出前院步道。

p1026

peculiar
[pɪ'kjuljə]
托 雅 學

adj 怪異的；特殊的，特有的

The man across the street was very peculiar and few of the neighbors had ever spoken to him.

那個對街的男人非常怪異，幾乎沒有鄰居跟他說過話。

p1027

peculiarity
[pɪ,kjulɪ'ærətɪ]
托 雅 學

n 特性，獨特性；怪癖

There is a certain peculiarity about American politics that allows it to be polite and vicious at the same time.

美國政治的獨特性就是它可以既紳士又邪惡。

p1028

pedestrian
[pə'dɛstrɪən]
托 雅 學

adj 徒步的；呆板的；通俗的；n 行人

In this city you have to watch out for pedestrian traffic because most people walk everywhere.

在這做城市裡，要留心徒步的交通狀況，因為大部分的人去哪兒都是用走的。

p1029

peel
[pil]
托 雅 學

n 果皮，蔬菜皮

You are not supposed to eat the banana peel, but just the fruit inside when it's been peeled.

你不能吃香蕉的果皮，而是吃剝皮後的果肉。

p1030

peel
[pil]
托 雅 學

vt 剝皮，削皮

Every morning Lydia peels potatoes at the restaurant.

每天早晨，莉蒂亞都會在餐廳削馬鈴薯。

p1031

peer
[pɪr]
托 雅 學

n 同輩，同等地位的人；貴族

Parents need to know how to help their teens resist pressure from other peers.

父母親需要知道如何幫助他們青春期的孩子抵禦來自同輩人的壓力。

p1032

peer
[pɪr]
托 雅 學

vi 凝視；隱約出現

The sailors on the ship were peering into the fog, looking for the shore.

船上的水手們凝視著霧，尋找著海岸。

p1033

penalty
['pɛnltɪ]
托 雅 學

n 懲罰；害處；（對犯規者的）判罰

The player tripped his opponent during the game and received a penalty from the referee.

那個選手在比賽期間絆倒了他的對手，因此受到了裁判員的處罰。

p1034

pendulum
['pɛndʒələm]

n 擺，鐘擺 p1035

In labor and management relations, the pendulum has always swung toward the employers.

在勞資關係方面，鐘擺幾乎都偏向雇主這方。

penetrate
['pɛnəˌtret]

vi/vt 穿過；滲入；看穿 p1036

It was impossible to penetrate the concrete wall without explosives.

這面由混凝土築成的牆，不用炸藥不可能穿過。

penetrating
['pɛnəˌtretɪŋ]

托 雅 學

adj 犀利的；響亮的；精闢的；滲透的 p1037

The oil is penetrating and lubricating the engine parts.

這種油可以滲透和潤滑引擎零件。

pension
['pɛnʃən]

托 雅 學

n 養老金，年金 p1038

My grandfather retired from the army and lived on his pension for the rest of his life.

我的祖父從軍中退伍了，靠著養老金度過餘生。

perceive
[pə'siv]

托 雅 學

vt 注意到；將…理解為；察覺，感知；理解，領悟 p1039

There are different ways that people perceive an article in a newspaper however objectively it is written.

無論報紙的文章寫得多客觀，人們還是會用各種不同方式去領會（詮釋）。

perception
[pə'sɛpʃən]

托 雅 學

n 知覺，感知能力；洞察力；看法 p1040

My son had no perception of distance when he learned to drive for the first time.

我的兒子第一次學習開車時沒有距離感。

P

perfection
[pə'fɛkʃən]

托 雅 學

n 盡善盡美，完美 p1041

That piece of Beethoven Symphony is absolute perfection.

那首貝多芬交響曲絕對完美。

perform
[pə'fɔrm]

托 雅 學

vi/vt 執行；表演；完成（事業） p1042

I was asked to perform a piano concerto for an audience of 300 students.

我被要求為三百名學生表演一首鋼琴協奏曲。

performance
[pə'fɔrməns]

n 執行；表演；性能；成績 p1043

The singer gave a memorable performance on Saturday night.

那位歌手星期六晚上進行了一場值得紀念的表演。

perfume
[pəˈfjum]
托 雅 學

n 香味；香料；香水
I remember the smell of my grandmother's perfume sprayed liberally on all of her clothes.
我記得祖母大量噴灑在她衣服上的香水的味道。

p1044

perimeter
[pəˈrɪmətə]
托 雅 學

n 周（邊），周長
The perimeter of the castle was always guarded by twenty soldiers.
城堡周邊一直被二十個士兵駐守。

p1045

periodic
[ˌpɪrɪˈɑdɪk]
托 雅 學

n 週期的；一定時期的
The students are into observing the periodic motion of the planets.
學生們喜愛觀察星球的週期運動。

p1046

periodical
[ˌpɪrɪˈɑdɪkl]
托 雅 學

adj 週期的，定期的；n 期刊，雜誌
Sally's aunt really enjoys reading the periodical that her church mails out.
莎麗的阿姨真的很喜歡閱讀教會寄給她的期刊。

p1047

permanent
[ˈpɝmənənt]
托 雅 學

adj 永久的，持久的
This is not a permanent solution to your problem but for now it will have to suffice.
這不是一個永久解決你的問題的方法，但目前應該足夠應付。

p1048

permissible
[pəˈmɪsəbl]
托 雅 學

adj 可允許的
It is not permissible for students to smoke on the campus.
校園內是不允許學生抽煙的。

p1049

permission
[pəˈmɪʃən]
托 雅 學

n 允許，同意
A visa provides a person with the official permission required to enter a foreign country.
簽證是進入外國必要的官方許可證。

p1050

permit
[ˈpɝmɪt]
托 雅 學

n 許可證，執照
You are required to apply for a hunting permit before going hunting in the mountains.
你需要申請狩獵許可證才能上山去打獵。

p1051

permit
[pəˈmɪt]
托 雅 學

vi/vt 許可，允許
The glass windows permit the light to brighten the room.
玻璃窗讓陽光照亮房間。

p1052

perpetual
[pɚ'pɛtʃʊəl]

adj 永久的，永恆的；長期的；四季開花的　　p1053

Work has been so busy that it seems like a perpetual cycle of deadlines and overtime.

工作一直很忙，好像最後期限和加班成了一個永久的迴圈。

persistent
[pɚ'sɪstənt]

adj 堅持不懈的；持續的；反復不斷的　　p1054

My grandmother cannot get rid of her persistent cough, so she went to see a doctor.

我的祖母無法擺脫持續的咳嗽，於是她去看了醫生。

perspective
[pɚ'spɛktɪv]

n 觀點，看法；客觀判斷力；透視畫法；景觀　　p1055

I need your perspective on this dress because it seems fine to me but my husband says it is ugly.

我需要你對於這條裙子的看法，因為我覺得還好，但我先生說很醜。

pervert
[pɚ'vɝt]

vt 使墮落變壞；濫用；歪曲，曲解；顛倒　　p1056

Simon explained the legal charges for trying to pervert the course of court justice.

西蒙解釋了法律指控，試圖歪曲司法公正的法庭。

pessimistic
[ˌpɛsə'mɪstɪk]

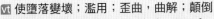

adj 悲觀主義的　　p1057

Stop being so pessimistic all the time and this time look on the bright side of life.

別再這麼悲觀，這一次樂觀地看待生命吧。

P

pest
[pɛst]

n 害蟲；害人蟲　　p1058

Most of the pests cannot be killed entirely, even with the newest pesticides.

即使最新的農藥也不能完全殺死大多數害蟲。

petition
[pə'tɪʃən]

n 請願書，申請書　　p1059

Hundreds of people signed the petition asking the mayor and city council to change the law.

數以百計的人簽了請願書，要求市長和市議會修改法律。

petition
[pə'tɪʃən]

vt 向…請願；正式請求　　p1060

The young suspect's parents have petitioned the court for a retrial.

年輕嫌犯的父母親已經正式請求法院進行二審。

petroleum
[pə'trolɪəm]

n 石油　　p1061

There are many consumer products made from petroleum, such as plastics.

很多日用消費品是由石油製造而成的，例如塑膠。

petty
['pɛtɪ]
托 雅 學

adj 器量小的；小規模的；細微的 p1062
The manager was being very petty about losing his promotion and was often rude to his employees without any reason.
經理對於沒有升遷這件事表現出器量小的態度，並且常常無緣無故對他的下屬發脾氣。

pharmaceutical
[ˌfɑrmə'sjutɪkl̩]
托 雅 學

adj 製藥的 p1063
The pharmaceutical industry is a billion dollar enterprise marketing medical drugs.
製藥業是一個億萬美元規模的行業，主營醫藥。

pharmacy
['fɑrməsɪ]
托 雅 學

n 藥房；藥劑學；製藥業；配藥業；一批備用藥品 p1064
This brand of ointment is available from many pharmacies without a doctor's prescription.
沒有醫生的處方，這個牌子的藥膏還是可以從許多藥店買到。

phenomenon
[fə'namə,nan]
托 雅 學

n 現象；傑出人才；複數＝phenomena p1065
Tsunamis, hurricanes, tornadoes are all examples of natural phenomena.
海嘯、颶風和龍捲風都是自然現象的實例。

philosophy
[fə'lasəfɪ]
托 雅 學

n 哲學；思想體系；人生觀，價值觀 p1066
I studied philosophy for a time in college but I decided engineering was more practical.
我在大學時讀過一陣子的哲學，但我決定念更實際的機械工程。

physical
['fɪzɪkl̩]
托 雅 學

adj 物質的；身體的；動作激烈的；自然科學的；物理學的 p1067
He has great physical strength, moving about the entire stage with energy.
他體能很好，帶著能量在整個舞臺移動。

physician
[fɪ'zɪʃən]
托 雅 學

n 內科醫生 p1068
My physician insisted at my last appointment that all my problems could be resolved with diet and exercise.
我的內科醫生在最後一次會面中堅持我所有的問題都可以靠節食和運動來解決。

physiological
[ˌfɪzɪə'ladʒɪkl̩]
托 雅 學

adj 生理學的，生理學上的 p1069
Seeing one's idols in person gives people a physiological rush and increases heart rate and body temperature.
親眼看到自己的偶像給人一種生理上的衝動，增加心臟速率，體溫也會上升。

pier
[pɪr]
托 雅 學

n 橋墩；碼頭 p1070
A couple was taking a walk along the wooden pier and watching the sun going down.
一對夫婦正沿著木頭碼頭散步，看著日落。

pierce
[pɪrs]

托 雅 學

vt 刺穿，刺破

p1071

The cautious mother finally allowed her young daughter to get her ears pierced.

這位謹慎的媽媽最後同意她年幼的女兒去打耳洞了。

pilgrim
['pɪlgrɪm]

托 雅 學

n 旅遊者；朝聖者，香客；最初的移民

p1072

I went to see the pilgrims walking toward the great cathedral praying with every step.

我去看朝聖者們邊走邊祈禱著朝大教堂走去。

plague
[pleg]

托 雅 學

vt 折磨；糾纏

p1073

For decades, the country has been plagued by the war caused by its aggressive emperor.

幾十年來，由於國王好戰，這個國家一直被戰爭折磨著。

plantation
[plæn'teʃən]

托 雅 學

n 種植園

p1074

The old antebellum house sat on a large plantation with vast cotton fields.

這座南北戰爭之前就建起來的老房子坐落在一片大的種植園中，那裡有著大片的棉花地。

platform
['plæt͵fɔrm]

托 雅 學

n 月臺；講台；平臺

p1075

The platform at the front of the room can be used as a kind of stage during the ceremony.

典禮期間房間前面的平臺可以被當作舞臺使用。

P

pleasant
['plɛzənt]

托 雅 學

adj 令人愉快的；友好的

p1076

A massage is often considered a very pleasant way to relax.

按摩往往是一種令人愉悅的放鬆方式。

pleasure
['plɛʒɚ]

托 雅 學

n 快樂，開心；玩樂；樂事

p1077

It is my pleasure and privilege to be invited to your 30th birthday party.

我很開心也很榮幸能受邀參加你的30歲生日聚會。

poke
[pok]

托 雅 學

n 刺，戳；懶漢；袋子

p1078

My daughter suddenly gave me a poke on the back, and I got scared.

我的女兒突然向我背部一戳，使我受驚了。

poke
[pok]

托 雅 學

vt 戳，刺；伸（頭等）；刺探；閒蕩

p1079

Stray dogs poke their noses into loose garbage looking for food.

流浪狗將它們的鼻子伸進散放的垃圾堆裡尋找食物。

179

polar
['polə]
托 雅 學

adj 兩極的，極地的；南轅北轍的　　p1080
There are no easy ways to communicate in the Polar regions.
在極地地區通訊相當不容易。

polarize
['polə,raɪz]
托 雅 學

vt 使兩極化，使形成對立兩派　　p1081
Controversial subjects tend to polarize the posted comments in forums.
爭議性的話題常讓留言板上的評論兩極化。

policy
['pɑləsɪ]
托 雅 學

n 政策，方針　　p1082
Our store has a strict return policy and we cannot accept items without a receipt.
我們的商店有嚴格的退貨政策，不接受無收據貨物。

polish
['pɑlɪʃ]
托 雅 學

n 擦光劑，上光蠟；**vi/vt** 磨光，擦亮；（使）優美（潤飾）　　p1083
My mother and I polish my grandmother's amazing silvers every year to use it for Christmas dinner.
母親與我每年都會擦亮祖母的了不起的銀器，以用於聖誕晚餐。

politician
[,pɑlə'tɪʃən]
托 雅 學

n 政治家；政客　　p1084
Bill Clinton was a respected politician until his sex scandal became public knowledge.
性醜聞曝光之前，比爾‧柯林頓一直是一位受人尊敬的政治家。

politics
['pɑlətɪks]
托 雅 學

n 政治；權術；政見　　p1085
Residents should always pay close attention to politics as it impacts their everyday life.
民眾應該密切關心政治，因為這對他們的日常生活有影響。

poll
[pol]
托 雅 學

n 民意測驗；投票；複數＝政治選舉　　p1086
The election poll is going to be a very tight race indeed.
選舉的投票將會是很勢均力敵的競爭。

poll
[pol]
托 雅 學

vi/vt 獲得…選票　　p1087
Bill Clinton polled more of the votes than his competitor and was elected the President of the United States in 1993.
1993年，比爾‧柯林頓比他的競爭者獲得更多選票，因此被選為美國總統。

pollutant
[pə'lutənt]
托 雅 學

n 污染物，污染源　　p1088
Cigarette smoke is a pollutant in many households.
香煙的煙霧在很多家庭中都是污染物。

ponder
['pɑndɚ]

托 雅 學

vi/vt 沉思，考慮

p1089

I need time to ponder over that question before I can give you an answer.

在回答你之前，我需要考慮一下這個問題。

popularity
[ˌpɑpjə'lærətɪ]

托 雅 學

n 受歡迎程度；通俗性；普及

p1090

His popularity was a curse because he could never go anywhere without being recognized.

他的受歡迎程度對他而言是詛咒，因為他走到哪兒都會被認出來。

populate
['pɑpju,let]

托 雅 學

vt 居住於；殖民於

p1091

The settlers have populated the west side of the city.

新移民已經入住城西地區。

population
[ˌpɑpju'leʃən]

托 雅 學

n 人口，（全體）居民

p1092

The Italian population is declining very rapidly.

義大利人口正迅速下降。

porcelain
['pɔrslɪn]

托 雅 學

adj 像瓷器般精製的；瓷器的；**n** 瓷器

p1093

Spencer stood with his hands braced on the porcelain sink and his muscles twitching.

斯賓賽站著，雙手環抱瓷器的洗手台，肌肉抽搐著。

pose
[poz]

托 雅 學

n 姿勢，姿態

p1094

Adopting a graceful pose, he pretended to be a lady.

擺了一個優雅的姿勢，他假裝自己是一位女士。

pose
[poz]

托 雅 學

vi/vt 提出；擺姿勢；佯裝

p1095

All the family members posed around grandmother in the photograph.

相片裡所有的家族成員都在外婆的身旁擺姿勢。

possession
[pə'zɛʃən]

托 雅 學

n 擁有；所有權；所有物；複數＝財產

p1096

He is in possession of many valuable paintings and other interesting works of art.

他擁有許多貴重的畫及其他有趣的工藝品。

postgraduate
[post'grædʒuɪt]

托 雅 學

n 研究生的

p1097

He was finishing postgraduate work at Harvard and decided to apply for a job in the private sector.

他即將在哈佛大學完成研究生階段的學業，決定到私人企業申請一份工作。

P

posture
['pastʃə]
托 雅 學

n 姿勢，姿態；心態，態度　　p1098
Her posture revealed that she was exhausted.
她的姿態顯露出她筋疲力盡了。

posture
['pastʃə]
托 雅 學

vi/vt 做出某種姿勢　　p1099
A good photographer knows how to posture the models elegantly.
好的攝影師知道如何讓模特兒擺出優美的姿勢。

practicable
['præktɪkəbl]
托 雅 學

adj 能實行的；適用的　　p1100
The board meeting resulted in at least one practicable solution to their budget problems.
這次的董事會會議至少為預算問題提出了一項能實行的解決方案。

practical
['præktɪkl]
托 雅 學

adj 實際的，實務的；實用的　　p1101
Many graduates choose to gain practical work experience in other countries.
許多畢業生選擇去另外一個國家累積實際的工作經驗。

practically
['præktɪklɪ]
托 雅 學

adv 幾乎；實際上地　　p1102
I had heard so many stories about Janet that I felt like I practically knew her already.
我聽過太多珍妮特的故事，以至於我覺得我實際上已經認識她了。

preach
[pritʃ]
托 雅 學

vi/vt 說教，佈道；鼓吹　　p1103
Father Anderson preached tolerance to the assembly of people in the church.
安德森神父對教堂集會的人群佈道，要大家包容。

precaution
[prɪ'kɔʃən]
托 雅 學

n 預防措施；謹慎，警惕　　p1104
The scientist took every precaution before beginning his dangerous experiment.
那個科學家在開始危險的實驗前採取了所有的預防措施。

precise
[prɪ'saɪs]
托 雅 學

adj 精確的，準確的　　p1105
She was not very precise in her calculations, so the curtains were far too short for the window.
她的計算不是非常精確，結果窗簾對窗戶而言太短了。

predict
[prɪ'dɪkt]
托 雅 學

vi/vt 預言，預測　　p1106
I cannot predict the weather, but chances are it will be hot in August and cold in February.
我雖無法預測天氣，但有可能八月會很熱，而二月會很冷。

predictable
[prɪˈdɪktəbḷ]

托 雅 學

`adj` 可預言的，可預見的
The summer weather has become so predictable now - always hot all the time.
夏日的天氣現在已經是可預見的了——總是這麼熱。

p1107

prefer
[prɪˈfɝ]

托 雅 學

`vt` 更喜歡，寧願
I prefer coffee to tea though I like tea very much.
雖然我很喜歡茶，但我更喜歡咖啡。

p1108

preferable
[ˈprɛfərəbḷ]

托 雅 學

`adj` 較適合的；更可取的
It would be preferable to take my vacation in fall but I can wait until winter.
在秋天休假更為適合，但我也可以等到冬天。

p1109

preference
[ˈprɛfərəns]

托 雅 學

`n` 偏愛；優惠；優先選擇
My preference for beer always annoyed my friends who were wine experts.
我對啤酒的偏愛總是惹惱我酒類專家的朋友們。

p1110

prejudice
[ˈprɛdʒədɪs]

托 雅 學

`n` 偏見，成見
Many people have prejudice against strange cultures and religions without realizing it.
很多人對陌生的文化與信仰抱有偏見，而且自己都不清楚偏見的存在。

p1111

prejudice
[ˈprɛdʒədɪs]

托 雅 學

`vt` 使抱偏見；損害
Getting bitten by a stray dog led to Cathy's being prejudiced against all dogs.
因為被流浪狗咬過，導致凱西對所有狗都抱有偏見。

p1112

premature
[ˌpriməˈtjʊr]

托 雅 學

`adj` 不成熟的；早產的；草率的
Any speculation about the scandal before the investigation is complete would be premature.
在調查完之前，任何針對這起醜聞的猜測都很草率。

p1113

premiere
[prɪˈmjɛr]

托 雅 學

`vi/vt` 首次上演
The movie will premiere at the film festival.
這部電影會在電影節的時候首映。

p1114

prescription
[prɪˈskrɪpʃən]

托 雅 學

`n` 藥方，處方
I had a bad cough, so my doctor wrote me a prescription for the proper medicine.
我嚴重咳嗽，所以我的醫生給我開了一張適當的藥方。

p1115

P

presence
['prɛzns]

托 雅 學

n 出席，到場；存在
`p1116`

The movie star noticed the presence of the paparazzi, so she put on her best behavior for them.

這位明星注意到有許多狗仔隊出席，因此向他們表現出自己最佳的行為舉止。

presentation
[,prizɛn'teʃən]

托 雅 學

n 介紹；贈送；呈現，展示
`p1117`

The sales manager gave an impressive presentation at the conference.

銷售經理在會議上做了一場令人印象深刻的展示。

press
[prɛs]

托 雅 學

n 報刊，通訊社，媒體
`p1118`

The press was present in large numbers at the new product launch, and asked the electronics company some awkward questions.

大量媒體出席了新產品的發佈會，並且問了這家電子公司一些奇怪的問題。

press
[prɛs]

托 雅 學

vi/vt 壓；壓榨；緊迫，催促
`p1119`

He will be hard pressed to explain his actions.

他被人緊緊催促著解釋自己的行為。

pressure
['prɛʃə]

托 雅 學

n 壓力；大氣壓力；壓迫
`p1120`

Derek is the type of person who performs particularly well under pressure.

德雷克是那種在壓力下表現得特別好的人。

prestige
[prɛs'tiʒ]

托 雅 學

n 聲望，威望
`p1121`

This trading company has gained international prestige because of its quality service.

這家貿易公司因為優質的服務而獲得了國際性的聲望。

prestigious
[prɛs'tɪdʒɪəs]

托 雅 學

adj 有名望的，著名的；受人尊敬的
`p1122`

Kevin thanked his peers for his prestigious award as they cheered loudly.

凱文感謝了他的同行們，他們為他獲得這一著名的獎項而大聲歡呼。

primal
['praɪml]

托 雅 學

adj 第一的，主要的
`p1123`

I believe that there is a primal and unconscious instinct in a mother to protect her children.

我相信每個母親都有份第一本能要保護他的孩子們，儘管自己不會察覺。

primary
['praɪ,mɛrɪ]

托 雅 學

adj 最初的；主要的，基本的
`p1124`

Her primary goal is to get a good education.

她主要的目標是得到良好的教育。

prime
[praɪm]
托 雅 學

adj 首要的；最好的，第一流的　p1125
Thanks to a rebuilding effort by the city, this neighborhood has become prime real estate.
多虧了市政府重建的努力，這個街區已經成為首要的地產。

prime
[praɪm]
托 雅 學

n 青春，全盛期　p1126
It is estimated that most athletes pass their prime around the age of thirty.
據估計，大多數運動員在三十歲左右就過了他們的全盛期。

principal
['prɪnsəpl]
托 雅 學

adj 最重要的，主要的　p1127
He was the principal dancer for the ballet company and a highly respected artist.
他是這個芭蕾舞團的主要舞者，也是一位非常受尊重的藝術家。

principal
['prɪnsəpl]
托 雅 學

n 資本，本金；負責人；校長　p1128
The interest on a principal of $1,000,000 is increased because of the unstable market.
因為市場的不穩定，一百萬元本金的利息增加了。

principle
['prɪnsəpl]
托 雅 學

n 原理，原則；主義　p1129
My first principle in art is to always strive for humility.
我對藝術的第一原則是永遠奮力保持謙卑。

prior
['praɪɚ]
托 雅 學

adj 優先的；在前的　p1130
Prior to my arrival at the party, I went to have dinner with a client.
在我抵達派對之前，我去跟一個客戶吃了晚餐。

priority
[praɪ'ɔrətɪ]
托 雅 學

n 優先，重點，優先權　p1131
Because of the economic crises, the issue of civil rights wasn't a priority for most people.
由於經濟危機，人權的議題已經不再是大多數人優先討論的問題了。

privilege
['prɪvlɪdʒ]
托 雅 學

n 特殊利益；特權，優惠；榮幸；vt 給予優惠，給予特權　p1132
His background and social status have privileged him to secret information.
他的背景與社會地位給予他獲取秘密資訊的特權。

probability
[ˌprɑbə'bɪlətɪ]
托 雅 學

n 可能性，或然性；概率　p1133
The probability is very low that you will win the lottery.
你彩券中獎的可能性非常低。

P

probation
[pro'beʃən]

托 雅 學

n 檢驗，鑒定；見習；緩刑

p1134

This celebrity was under a probation order after attacking the paparazzi.

在攻擊狗仔隊之後，這位名人被判緩刑。

---

probe
[prob]

托 雅 學

n 探針，探測器；調查

p1135

The FBI launched a serious probe into the illegal gambling ring.

聯邦調查局針對這個非法賭場進行了一場重大調查。

---

probe
[prob]

托 雅 學

vi/vt （以探針等）探查；穿刺；查究

p1136

The witty detective questioned this suspect for hours, probing for any inconsistency in his story.

機智的偵探訊問了嫌疑犯數小時，以刺探他故事裡任何不一致之處。

---

proceed
[prə'sid]

托 雅 學

vi 進行，繼續下去；發生

p1137

You may proceed with your closing remarks.

你可以繼續進行你的總結陳詞了。

---

proceeding
[prə'sidɪŋ]

托 雅 學

n 進行；行動；複數＝事項；訴訟；訴訟程序；會議紀錄

p1138

The lawyer started legal proceedings to have the child permanently taken away from his cruel parents.

律師開始法律訴訟程序，讓小孩永遠脫離殘忍的雙親。

---

proclaim
[prə'klem]

托 雅 學

vt 宣告，聲明

p1139

The referee wanted to proclaim him the new champion, but he did not have the judges' final scores yet.

裁判員想要宣告他是新的優勝者，但是他尚未得到裁判最後的分數。

---

prod
[prad]

托 雅 學

n 針刺，籤子；vt 戳，頂

p1140

I told him to stop prodding me with his elbow.

我叫他停止用手肘頂我。

---

produce
['pradjus]

托 雅 學

n 農產品

p1141

Fresh produce such as apples and lettuces are a necessary part of a healthy diet.

新鮮農產品，比方說蘋果以及萵苣，是健康飲食中不可或缺的一部分。

---

produce
[prə'djus]

托 雅 學

vi/vt 生產，製造；生長；顯示

p1142

These cows produced more milk this season than they did last season.

這些乳牛本季產奶比上一季多。

producer
[prəˈdjusɚ]

n 生產者；製片人

p1143

The largest producer of wheat has encountered some problems following the severe drought.

最大的小麥生產者在嚴峻的乾旱後遭遇了一些問題。

product
[ˈprɑdəkt]

托 雅 學

n 產品，產物；乘積

p1144

A computer was the first product the company sold in stores.

電腦是這家公司上架賣的第一個產品。

production
[prəˈdʌkʃən]

托 雅 學

n 產品；作品；總產量

p1145

The price of our production cannot be lowered because of our expensive labor costs.

產品的價格不能降低，因為我們的勞動力成本很高。

productive
[prəˈdʌktɪv]

adj 生產（性）的；多產的

p1146

Just listening to soft music makes me more productive than I normally am.

只聆聽輕音樂讓我比平常更多產。

productivity
[ˌprodʌkˈtɪvətɪ]

n 生產率

p1147

The productivity has certainly declined at the factory under new management.

工廠的生產率在新管理團隊的領導下無疑下降了。

profession
[prəˈfɛʃən]

n 職業；專業；表白

p1148

He wanted to find a new profession because he was bored being an accountant.

他想要找一個新的職業，因為他已經厭倦做一個會計了。

P

professional
[prəˈfɛʃən!]

adj 職業的，專門的

p1149

She was a professional teacher with over thirty years of teaching experience.

她是一位有著三十多年教學經驗的專業老師。

proficient
[prəˈfɪʃənt]

托 雅 學

adj 精通的；熟練的

p1150

I am not proficient in Italian.

我的義大利語不夠熟練。

profound
[prəˈfaʊnd]

托 雅 學

adj 深刻的，意義深遠的；淵博的，造詣深的

p1151

I found the Beethoven concertos to be very profound.

我認為貝多芬的協奏曲意義深遠。

progress
['prɑgrɛs]

托 雅 學

n 進步，進展；前進

p1152

I've made some progress on this project and will finish it by Friday.

我在這個專案上已取得一些進展，星期五將完成。

progress
[prə'grɛs]

托 雅 學

vi 進步；前進

p1153

Construction on the new shopping center progressed at an amazing rapid rate.

購物中心的建築工程以令人驚異的速度進行著。

progression
[prə'grɛʃən]

托 雅 學

n 發展；系列

p1154

There is a progression of events in the novel that lead to a surprising end.

小說中的事件不斷發展，最終導致一個令人意外的結局。

progressive
[prə'grɛsɪv]

托 雅 學

adj 進步的，先進的；前進的；逐漸的

p1155

There's a continuously progressive decline in the standard of living in this country.

這個國家的生活水準正持續下降。

prohibit
[prə'hɪbɪt]

托 雅 學

vt 禁止；阻止

p1156

The city will vote today on whether to prohibit smoking inside public buildings.

那個城市今天將會投票決定是否禁止在公共建築物裡面吸煙。

prohibitive
[prə'hɪbɪtɪv]

托 雅 學

adj 禁止的；價格過高的

p1157

I found the expensive enrollment fees prohibitive to my taking the program.

我發現參加此專案的報名費用過高，使我無法負擔。

project
['prɑdʒɛkt]

托 雅 學

n 方案，工程，專案

p1158

I am working on a new project for my firm to design a marketing campaign.

我正在為公司設計一個新的行銷活動方案。

project
[prə'dʒɛkt]

托 雅 學

vi/vt 投射，放映；設計，規劃

p1159

The violent images of the riots were projected onto a screen, but no one could keep looking at them.

動亂的暴力景象被投射在螢幕上，但沒人能夠一直看下去。

promote
[prə'mot]

托 雅 學

vt 促進，提升，助長

p1160

My boss promised to promote me if the new products sold well.

我的老闆答應，如果新產品銷售成功的話就晉升我。

promotion
[prə'moʃən]
托 雅 學

n 促進，提升；創立 `p1161`
My promotion at work includes a higher salary.
我工作上的晉升包括更高的薪資。

---

prompt
[prampt]
托 雅 學

adj 敏捷的，迅速的，即刻的 `p1162`
As an employee she is very prompt and has never been late.
身為一個員工，她工作非常迅速，從來不曾有延誤。

---

prompt
[prampt]
托 雅 學

vt 激起，促使，促進，推動 `p1163`
The birth of my daughter prompted me to quit smoking.
我女兒的出生促使我戒煙。

---

promptly
[pramptlɪ]
托 雅 學

adv 敏捷地，迅速地 `p1164`
After she got the pocket money from her father, the girl promptly put it in her backpack.
在拿到她爸爸給的零用錢之後，那個女孩迅速地把它放進背包裡。

---

proportion
[prə'porʃən]
托 雅 學

n 部分；比例；均衡 `p1165`
The furniture was so big and completely out of proportion to the tiny room.
那傢俱太大了，和小房間不成比例。

P

---

proposition
[‚prapə'zɪʃən]
托 雅 學

n 主張，建議；陳述；命題 `p1166`
My brother is a good entrepreneur and often listens to many propositions from salesmen for new ideas.
我的弟弟是個優秀的企業家，他常常聽取業務員的許多建議以尋求新點子。

---

prose
[proz]
托 雅 學

n 散文 `p1167`
Many news articles are written in prose.
很多新聞文章是用散文體寫成的。

---

prosecute
['prasɪ‚kjut]
托 雅 學

vi/vt 實行，從事；起訴，告發；做檢察官 `p1168`
The police said the boy stole several small items, but the store owner decided not to prosecute him because he was so young.
員警說那個男孩偷了幾樣小東西，但店主決定不告發那個孩子，因為他還太小。

---

prospect
['praspɛkt]
托 雅 學

n 景色；前途，展望 `p1169`
The prospect for promotion at this office is limited.
在這個辦公室的升遷前景是非常有限的。

prospective
[prə'spɛktɪv]

托 雅 學

adj 預期的

p1170

There are three prospective buyers wanting to buy my house.

有三個預期的買家想要買我的房子。

prospectus
[prə'spɛktəs]

托 雅 學

n 章程，簡章，簡介

p1171

I've written a prospectus for my new book but I am not certain how the story will end.

我的新書已經寫出了簡單的輪廓，但是還不確定最後故事該怎麼結尾。

prosperous
['prɑspərəs]

托 雅 學

adj 繁榮的，興旺的；成功的

p1172

Some people in the world of finance seem very prosperous, but they can easily lose everything with one mistake.

某些人在金融界似乎非常成功，但他們可能因為一個錯誤而輕易地失去所有的東西。

protest
['protɛst]

托 雅 學

n 抗議

p1173

Recently, many protests have been staged to support the needs of under-privileged citizens.

最近，人們發動了很多抗議來支持貧困市民的需求。

protest
[prə'tɛst]

托 雅 學

vi/vt 抗議，反對；主張，斷言

p1174

People began to protest against the government's new policies.

人們開始抗議政府的新政策。

provocative
[prə'vɑkətɪv]

托 雅 學

adj 挑撥的，刺激的

p1175

The party candidate is intentionally provocative with the questions he's asking.

那個政黨候選人故意提出刺激性的問題。

provoke
[prə'vok]

托 雅 學

vt 挑動；激發；招惹

p1176

It is very dangerous to provoke another driver on the road.

在路上招惹另外一個司機是非常危險的事情。

psychiatry
[saɪ'kaɪətrɪ]

托 雅 學

n 精神病學，精神病療法

p1177

He has a Ph.D.in psychiatry but never practiced as a licensed therapist.

他有精神醫療學的博士學位，但從未做為一位有執照的治療家來行醫。

publication
[ˌpʌblɪ'keʃən]

托 雅 學

n 出版物；出版；發表

p1178

The New York Times is an internationally respected publication.

《紐約時報》是一份在國際上受到重視的出版物。

publicity
[pʌbˈlɪsətɪ]

托 雅 學

n 公開;宣傳,廣告;推銷 `p1179`

Talk show appearances have been good publicity for the actor and his new movie.

出現在脫口秀節目對該演員及他的新電影而言都是很好的宣傳。

---

publicize
[ˈpʌblɪˌsaɪz]

托 雅 學

vt 宣傳;公佈;廣告 `p1180`

The charity will publicize their annual lottery for 3 months using a media blitz.

這個慈善機構接下來三個月將要用媒體閃電戰的方式公佈他們的年度抽彩。

---

puddle
[ˈpʌdl]

托 雅 學

n 水坑;膠土 `p1181`

Be careful not to step in the puddle on the road.

小心不要踩在路上的水坑裡。

---

puddle
[ˈpʌdl]

托 雅 學

vi 攪泥漿;**vt** 使泥濘;把……搗製成膠土 `p1182`

After a heavy rain, the naughty children puddled about in the park.

傾盆大雨後,頑皮的孩子們在公園裡攪和泥漿。

---

pump
[pʌmp]

托 雅 學

n 泵 `p1183`

The water is forced into the boiler by the feed pump.

水是用水泵壓入鍋爐中的。

---

pump
[pʌmp]

托 雅 學

vi/vt 用(泵)抽(水);打氣,泵送 `p1184`

Morgan pumped air in the flat tire to see whether there was a hole in it.

摩根給漏氣的輪胎打氣,看看那裡是否有個破洞。

---

punctual
[ˈpʌŋktʃʊəl]

托 雅 學

adj 嚴守時刻的,準時的 `p1185`

I can be punctual when I am going to a movie or dinner, but I am often late for work.

看電影或者是吃晚餐的時候我可以很準時,但是工作時我常遲到。

---

purchase
[ˈpɝtʃəs]

托 雅 學

n 購買;購買的物品 `p1186`

The lawyer rewarded herself on winning her court case with the purchase of a jacket from one of her favorite stores.

作為對自己打贏官司的犒賞,這位律師從自己最喜愛的商店之一購買了一件外套。

---

purchase
[ˈpɝtʃəs]

托 雅 學

vi/vt 購買 `p1187`

Her parents were happy when she decided to purchase a house in their neighborhood.

當她決定要購買與父母鄰近的房子時,她的父母都非常開心。

P

purify
['pjʊrəˌfaɪ]

托 雅 學

vt 淨化，使純淨；提純，精煉（金屬） p1188

A main water line burst in the middle of the city and the residents were told to boil all drinking water in order to purify it.

一條主要的水管在市中心炸開了，所以本市的居民都被告知要把水煮沸淨化後才能喝。

purity
['pjʊrətɪ]

托 雅 學

n 純淨；純潔；純度 p1189

The number of visitors allowed to the fresh water areas is strictly controlled to maintain the purity of the water.

許多泉水區的遊客被嚴格控管人數是為了維持水的純淨。

Q

字彙能力檢查表

先自我檢驗是否瞭解以下初階單字，若有不清楚者，請先開啟光碟中的電子書複習。

□quartz   □questionable

---

qualification
[ˌkwaləfəˈkeʃən]

n 資格，條件；合格；合格證   q1001
He applied for the job in spite of the fact that his only qualification was a summer course he took in college.
儘管他唯一符合的條件是在大學裡修過暑期課程，他還是去應徵了這份工作。

---

qualify
[ˈkwaləˌfaɪ]

vi/vt （使）具有資格，證明合格；限定   q1002
All of the athletes have to compete for years to qualify for the Olympic Games.
所有的運動員都必須經過幾年的競爭才具有參加奧運會的資格。

Q

---

qualitative
[ˈkwaləˌtetɪv]

adj 性質上的，定性的   q1003
There are striking differences between qualitative and quantitative research.
定性研究與定量研究有顯著的差異。

---

quality
[ˈkwalətɪ]

n 品質；品質；特性   q1004
It is a little expensive, but the quality is guaranteed.
這個東西有些昂貴，不過品質具有保證。

---

quantity
[ˈkwantətɪ]

n 量，數量，分量   q1005
In most cases quality matters more than quantity.
大部分情況下，品質比數量更重要。

193

quarry
['kwɔrɪ]
托 雅 學

n 採石場；露天礦場；岩石開鑿
The quarry crushes boulders and rocks into stone chips.
在採石場，大石頭和石塊會被碾壓成碎石。

q1006

quarterly
['kwɔrtəlɪ]
托 雅 學

adv 每季一次
The company's board decides to meet quarterly.
公司董事會決議每一季度開會一次。

q1007

quarterly
['kwɔrtəlɪ]
托 雅 學

n 季刊
The science fiction quarterly has became popular among the youth.
那本科幻季刊在青少年中迅速流行起來。

q1008

quest
[kwɛst]
托 雅 學

n/vi 探尋，探求；追求
The pirates were impatient to quest for hidden treasure.
這群海盜迫不及待探尋秘密寶藏。

q1009

questionnaire
[ˌkwɛstʃən'ɛr]
托 雅 學

n 調查表，問卷
I filled out the questionnaire on the website and received a coupon for a free drink!
我填了網路上的問卷，並得到一張免費飲料的優惠券。

q1010

quit
[kwɪt]
托 雅 學

vi/vt 離開；放棄；辭職
I despise my job and I may quit today.
我看不起我的工作，我今天可能會辭職。

q1011

quotation
[kwo'teʃən]
托 雅 學

n 引用；引文；報價單
The interesting article in the paper today featured a lengthy quotation from Shakespeare's *Hamlet*.
今天報紙上那篇有趣的文章特色在於引用了一長段莎士比亞的《哈姆雷特》。

q1012

quote
[kwot]
托 雅 學

vt 引用，引證；報價
The man quoted Shakespeare's sonnet and won the woman's heart.
這位男士引用了莎士比亞的十四行詩來贏得她的芳心。

q1013

R

字彙能力檢查表

先自我檢驗是否瞭解以下初階單字，若有不清楚者，請先開啟光碟中的電子書複習。

☐rack	☐reduce	☐remedy	☐reward
☐racket	☐reduction	☐remind	☐ribbon
☐radar	☐reflect	☐remove	☐ridiculous
☐radiation	☐reflection	☐rent	☐rifle
☐raft	☐refrigerator	☐replace	☐rise
☐rail	☐refugee	☐replacement	☐roar
☐raise	☐refuse	☐reputation	☐roast
☐range	☐refuse	☐request	☐rod
☐range	☐regarding	☐require	☐role
☐rare	☐regardless	☐requirement	☐rough
☐rarely	☐region	☐rescue	☐roughly
☐rate	☐related	☐resist	☐rub
☐rate	☐relax	☐resistant	☐rug
☐react	☐relaxation	☐resource	☐ruin
☐readily	☐reliable	☐retire	☐rule
☐recipe	☐rely	☐retirement	☐rush
☐recognize	☐remain	☐review	☐rust
☐rectangular	☐remarkable	☐review	☐rust
☐recycle			

R

rack
[ræk]

托 雅 學

vt 使痛苦，折磨 `r1001`

The old man had been racked by diabetes for almost ten years before his death.

那位老人去世前被糖尿病折磨了將近十年的時間。

radical
['rædɪkl]

托 雅 學

adj 基本的，根本的；重要的；激進的，極端的 `r1002`

The conventional treatments for her cancer were not working, so the doctor suggested trying some radical new therapies.

對於她的癌症，傳統療法並未起作用，因此醫生建議嘗試一些更激進的新療法。

rage
[redʒ]

托 雅 學

n 憤怒 `r1003`

When the young girl told her father that she was pregnant, he fought hard to hold back his rage.

當這個未成年的女孩告訴父親她懷孕了時，他使勁忍住憤怒。

ragged
['rægɪd]

托 雅 學

adj 破舊的，破衣爛衫的；不流暢的；精疲力竭的 `r1004`

The ragged little girl has begged for money on the cold street for many nights.

這個破衣爛衫的小女孩已經在寒冷的街道上乞討錢很多個晚上了。

random
['rændəm]

托 雅 學

adj 隨機的，隨意的 `r1005`

The computer selected a random security code and I am having trouble memorizing it.

這台電腦隨機挑選了一個安全密碼，所以現在我無法牢記這個密碼。

random
['rændəm]

托 雅 學

n 隨機，隨手 `r1006`

Before I got on the train, I bought a magazine at the stall at random.

在我上火車之前，我在小攤上隨手買了一本雜誌。

ratio
['reʃo]

托 雅 學

n 比，比率 `r1007`

When I make rice, I use a ratio of two parts water to one part rice.

當我煮飯時，水與米的比例是2比1。

ration
['ræʃən]

托 雅 學

vt 定量供應，配給 `r1008`

During World War II, many nations would ration certain foods like butter and cream.

在第二次世界大戰期間，很多國家對黃油和奶油類食物實施配給。

rational
['ræʃənl]

托 雅 學

adj 理性的，出於理性的；推理的；適度的 `r1009`

When my emotions are strong, it is very hard for me to be rational.

當我情感強烈時，很難保持理性。

rave
[rev]

托 雅 學

n （英國）狂歡晚會　　　　r1010

The graduates held an all-night rave at the beach last night.

大學畢業生昨晚在沙灘上舉辦了通宵狂歡晚會。

rave
[rev]

托 雅 學

vi/vt 熱烈討論（或書寫）；咆哮；胡說八道　　　r1011

After declaring bankruptcy, the man commonly wandered on the street, raving at the passers-by.

在宣佈破產之後，這個男人總是游走街頭，並且對路人咆哮。

raw
[rɔ]

托 雅 學

adj 未煮過的，生的；未加工過的；未經訓練的　　　r1012

Doctors suggest that we should not eat raw meat because it may carry lots of bacteria.

醫生建議我們不該吃生肉，因為它可能帶有很多細菌。

realize
['rɪə,laɪz]

托 雅 學

vi/vt 認識到，體會到；實現　　　r1013

The car accident made Andy realize that he should drive more carefully in the future.

這場車禍讓安迪意識到他日後開車應當更加小心。

reap
[rip]

托 雅 學

vi/vt 收割，收穫　　　r1014

My sister reaped the benefits of her hard work during high school, and now she's been accepted into a top university.

我妹妹獲益於高中時期的認真努力，現在她被一流的大學錄取了。

rear
[rɪr]

托 雅 學

n 後面，背後，後方　　　r1015

I can see a car following too fast behind me in my rear view mirror.

我從後視鏡看到有一輛開得飛快的車子跟著我。

rear
[rɪr]

托 雅 學

vi/vt 飼養，撫養，栽培；舉起　　　r1016

That kind-hearted woman not only rears stray dogs but also helps them find new homes.

那位仁慈的婦女不但飼養流浪狗，而且還協助牠們找到新的家。

reasonable
['riznəbl]

托 雅 學

adj 合情合理的；公道的　　　r1017

In fact, it is reasonable that you didn't accept his insincere apology.

事實上，你不接受他沒有誠意的道歉是合情合理的。

reassure
[,riə'ʃʊr]

托 雅 學

vt 使安心，使放心，使消除疑慮　　　r1018

The doctor reassured me that my mother would recover soon.

這位醫生要我放心，說我母親很快就會痊癒。

R

rebuke
[rɪˈbjuk]

托 雅 學

vt 指責，非難，斥責

r1019

His behavior had become so volatile that she had to rebuke him and take the consequences.

他的行為變得非常反復無常，她只好將他斥責一頓，然後承擔一切後果。

recall
[rɪˈkɔl]

托 雅 學

n 召回；回憶；**vt** 回想；叫回，收回

r1020

The toys had a serious defect, so the company issued a recall and lost millions of dollars.

這批玩具有嚴重的缺陷，因此公司宣佈全面回收，損失了數百萬元。

receipt
[rɪˈsit]

托 雅 學

n 收據；接收

r1021

Please don't forget to get the receipt for reimbursement.

請不要忘記拿收據來報帳。

reception
[rɪˈsɛpʃən]

托 雅 學

n 接待，招待會；接受

r1022

The family gave their guests a warm reception and everyone felt comfortable at once.

這個家庭給客人熱情的招待，所有人立刻感到很輕鬆自在。

receptionist
[rɪˈsɛpʃənɪst]

托 雅 學

n 接待員

r1023

The receptionists in that hotel provide best service.

那家飯店的接待員提供最好的服務。

receptive
[rɪˈsɛptɪv]

托 雅 學

adj （對新觀點、建議等）願意傾聽的

r1024

My parents are receptive to my own long-term plan for my life.

我的父母願意傾聽我對人生的長遠規劃。

recital
[rɪˈsaɪtl]

托 雅 學

n 獨唱會；獨奏會；小型音樂會、舞蹈表演會等

r1025

The piano teacher insisted that all of her students perform in the spring recital.

鋼琴教師堅持讓所有學生都在春季的小型音樂會上表演。

recite
[rɪˈsaɪt]

托 雅 學

vi/vt 背誦，朗誦

r1026

I like to recite poetry but many people find it pompous or silly.

我喜歡背誦詩，但很多人覺得這樣太自命不凡或是愚蠢。

reckless
[ˈrɛklɪs]

托 雅 學

adj 粗心大意的；魯莽的

r1027

She is so reckless to ride on top of the handlebars of that bicycle.

她騎在自行車的車把上，太魯莽了。

recommend
[ˌrɛkə'mɛnd]

托 雅 學

vt 推薦；建議；使受歡迎　　　　r1028

My thesis advisor recommended that I read Dr. Brown's studies in order to get more ideas.

我的論文指導老師建議我閱讀布朗博士的研究以獲得更多想法。

recommendation
[ˌrɛkəmɛn'deʃən]

托 雅 學

n 推薦，介紹；勸告；建議　　　　r1029

They are asking for a cost-efficient recommendation to help support the implementation of this ambitious project.

他們要求一個節省成本的方案來實施這個有雄心的計畫。

reconstruct
[ˌrɪkən'strʌkt]

托 雅 學

vt 重建，再建；改組；修復　　　　r1030

The witness then began to reconstruct for the jury the events of her day just before the attack.

目擊者接著開始為陪審團重建攻擊前的那一天她的生活。

recover
[rɪ'kʌvə]

托 雅 學

vi/vt 康復，恢復常態；全數追回　　　　r1031

Jenny spent a lot of time recovering from her parents' divorce.

珍妮花了很長時間才從父母離婚的陰影中走出來。

recovery
[rɪ'kʌvərɪ]

托 雅 學

n 痊癒；改善；取回　　　　r1032

I heard that my tutor had a speedy recovery after he broke his leg.

我聽說我的家庭教師腿骨折後痊癒得很快。

recreation
[ˌrɛkrɪ'eʃən]

托 雅 學

n 娛樂，消遣　　　　r1033

Some people go to the park on Saturday for recreation.

有些人星期六去公園消遣。

R

recruit
[rɪ'krut]

托 雅 學

n 新兵；新成員　　　　r1034

After graduating from the college, John becomes a new recruit in the workplace.

大學畢業之後，約翰成為職場新成員。

recruit
[rɪ'krut]

托 雅 學

vt 徵募（新兵）；動員…（提供幫助）　　　　r1035

The army intends to recruit 3,000 soldiers in two years.

軍隊計畫在兩年內徵募三千名士兵。

rectify
['rɛktəˌfaɪ]

托 雅 學

vt 糾正；調整；精餾　　　　r1036

I know that I hurt your feelings and I hope to rectify the situation in time.

我知道我傷害了你的感情，我希望可以及時糾正這個情況。

redundant
[rɪ'dʌndənt]

托 雅 學

adj 多餘的，過剩的；（食物）豐富的；被解雇的

r1037

The previously redundant employee revealed our product's secret formula to our opponent.

這位被解雇的職員向我們的對手公司洩漏了我們產品的獨家秘方。

reed
[rid]

托 雅 學

n 蘆葦，葦叢；蘆笛，牧笛

r1038

Dried reeds were used extensively in Europe to build the cottage roofs.

乾的蘆葦在歐洲被廣泛的使用來建蓋農舍屋頂。

refer
[rɪ'fɝ]

托 雅 學

vi 談到

r1039

Teacher Karen is a devoted Christian; she always refers to the Bible in her class.

凱倫老師是一位虔誠的基督教徒，她常常在課堂上談到《聖經》。

refer
[rɪ'fɝ]

托 雅 學

vt 使求助於；歸因於…

r1040

Lance referred to the fengshui of his ancestral grave when he tried to figure out what caused all of his recent problems.

蘭斯想著他最近所發生的所有麻煩事情時，把原因都歸於他祖先墓地的風水。

reference
['rɛfərəns]

托 雅 學

n 提及，涉及；參考，參考書目；證明書（人）

r1041

I saw a reference to an old silent film in the new movie that just came out.

我覺得新上映的那部電影中提及了舊時的一部默片。

refine
[rɪ'faɪn]

托 雅 學

vi/vt 精煉，提純

r1042

He wants to refine his taste, so he started taking classes on wine tasting.

為了提升品味，他開始上品酒的課。

refresh
[rɪ'frɛʃ]

托 雅 學

vi 恢復精神；**vt** 使清新

r1043

Let me refresh your memory: we were married on the nineteenth and not the thirtieth.

讓我來提醒你一下：我們是19日結婚的，不是13日。

refreshing
[rɪ'frɛʃɪŋ]

托 雅 學

adj 使人恢復活力的；提神的

r1044

The little boy drank a refreshing glass of orange juice after his playtime.

小男孩遊戲時間過後喝了一杯柳橙汁提神。

refreshment
[rɪ'frɛʃmənt]

托 雅 學

n 複數＝點心，飲料；精力恢復，爽快

r1045

She asked them to come in and take some refreshment before the meeting began.

在會議開始前，她邀請他們進來用一些茶點。

refusal
[rɪˈfjuzḷ]

托 雅 學

n 拒絕

r1046

Jimmy's cold refusal toward Amy's confession of love broke her heart.

吉米冷酷拒絕艾米愛的告白傷透了她的心。

---

register
[ˈrɛdʒɪstə]

托 雅 學

n/vt 登記，註冊

r1047

You have to register to vote in the presidential election.

你必須註冊才能參與總統選舉投票。

---

registrar
[ˈrɛdʒɪˌstrar]

托 雅 學

n 主管註冊者；記錄者；登記員

r1048

The University had an excellent registrar office to keep accurate academic records.

大學裡有非常棒的主管註冊的辦公室，那裡各種學業記錄都精準地保留下來。

---

registration
[ˌrɛdʒɪˈstreʃən]

托 雅 學

n 登記，掛號，註冊

r1049

If you want to attend the conference, you have to complete your registration by tomorrow.

如果你想參加研討會的話，你必須在明天之前完成註冊手續。

---

regret
[rɪˈgrɛt]

托 雅 學

n/vt 遺憾，懊悔，抱歉

r1050

I regret yelling at you this morning and I hope you can forgive me.

我很後悔今天早上對你大吼，我希望你可以原諒我。

---

regular
[ˈrɛgjələ]

托 雅 學

adj 有規律的；普通的；正規的

r1051

Regular exercise and taking medicine are important for patients' rehabilitation after surgery.

有規律性的運動和吃藥對患者手術後的康復來說很重要。

R

---

regularity
[ˌrɛgjəˈlærəti]

托 雅 學

n 規則性；整齊

r1052

The police had observed regularities in the behavior of the thieves.

員警已經觀察到了這些竊賊行為的規律性。

---

regulate
[ˈrɛgjəˌlet]

托 雅 學

vt 管理，控制；調整，調節；對準

r1053

The federal government regulates all business conducted in the stock exchange, mostly for monitoring illegal insider trades.

聯邦政府管理所有證券交易所的交易，主要是監控違法的內線交易。

---

regulation
[ˌrɛgjəˈleʃən]

托 雅 學

n 規則，規章；調節，校準；調整

r1054

Contestants are advised to study the rules and regulations carefully.

參賽者需要仔細地閱讀參賽的規章制度。

regulatory
['rɛgjələ,torɪ]

托 雅 學

adj 管理的，控制的，監控的

r1055

Tax payers are always dissatisfied with the regulatory laws of government.

納稅人往往對政府的監管法律表示不滿。

rehearse
[rɪ'hɝs]

托 雅 學

vi/vt 排練；背誦；重複

r1056

The students rehearsed for the play until very late last night.

學生們昨天晚上排練話劇到很晚。

reinforce
[,riɪn'fɔrs]

托 雅 學

vt 增援，支援；加強

r1057

The walls of the old church had begun to buckle under the weight of the roof, so the architect added buttresses to reinforce them.

那座古老教堂的外牆因屋頂的重量而開始彎曲變形，因此建築師增加扶壁來加強結構。

reject
['rɪdʒɛkt]

托 雅 學

n 落選者

r1058

The expressions on the faces of the rejects clearly showed how disappointed they were.

那些落選者臉上的表情明顯地顯示出他們有多麼失望。

reject
[rɪ'dʒɛkt]

托 雅 學

vt 拒絕，抵制；丟棄，排斥；退掉

r1059

He is such a snob and will reject any food brought to his table that isn't absolutely perfect.

他是一個很勢利的人，任何送到他桌上的食物如果不夠完美就會被他退掉。

relay
[rɪ'le]

托 雅 學

n 分程傳遞；傳達；替班；繼電器

r1060

It is time to fix the relay antenna so our signal can reach its destination.

是該修理轉接天線的時候了，這樣我們的信號才能傳到目的地。

relay
[rɪ'le]

托 雅 學

vt 中繼；轉播；接力；轉達

r1061

I can relay a message for you if you want to make an appointment to see him.

如果你想跟他約時間見面的話，我可以幫你轉達訊息。

release
[rɪ'lis]

托 雅 學

n 釋放，豁免，鬆開，公開

r1062

A release date for his upcoming novel has not yet been announced.

他下一本小說新書發表日期尚未公佈。

release
[rɪ'lis]

托 雅 學

vt 釋放；放鬆；發表

r1063

You must remember to release the brake before you put the car in gear.

車子排擋開動前記得放開剎車。

relentless
[rɪˈlɛntlɪs]

托 雅 學

r1064

adj 不停的，不放棄的
The audience was moved by the athlete's relentless spirits.
觀眾被這位運動選手不放棄的精神感動了。

relevant
[ˈrɛləvənt]

托 雅 學

r1065

adj 有關的，貼切的
Our boss only hires people who have the relevant working experience.
我們老闆只雇用有相關工作經驗的員工。

reliance
[rɪˈlaɪəns]

托 雅 學

r1066

n 信任，信心；依靠，依靠的人或物
He had reliance upon his friend's honesty and looked to him for constructive criticisms.
他很依賴他朋友的誠實，並向他尋求有建設性的批評意見。

relief
[rɪˈlif]

托 雅 學

r1067

n 減輕；救濟，援救
It was such a relief to hear that his plane had landed safely in spite of the terrible weather.
在這種極壞的天氣下，聽到他的飛機安全著陸的消息真是令人寬心。

relieve
[rɪˈliv]

托 雅 學

r1068

vt 減輕，解除；救濟
The midnight crew came to relieve the workers who had been there for twelve straight hours.
夜班工作人員的到來減輕了已經連續工作了十二個小時的工作人員的壓力。

religion
[rɪˈlɪdʒən]

托 雅 學

r1069

n 宗教；宗教信仰；信念，信條
Politics and religion are popular topics of conversation.
政治和宗教是對話中常見的話題。

R

reluctant
[rɪˈlʌktənt]

托 雅 學

r1070

adj 不願意的，勉強的
They were reluctant to begin the meal before their father got home from work.
在爸爸下班回家前，他們不願意開始吃晚餐。

remainder
[rɪˈmendɚ]

托 雅 學

r1071

n 剩餘物，剩下的；餘數，餘項
After the tycoon died, his son only kept 1 % of his inheritance and donated the remainder to charities.
在這位大亨去世後，他的兒子只保留他百分之一的遺產，而將剩下的都捐給了慈善機構。

renew
[rɪˈnju]

托 雅 學

r1072

vi/vt 恢復；（使）更新
Before she applies for the U.S. visa, Mia needs to renew her passport beforehand.
在申請美國簽證之前，蜜亞必須事先更新她的護照。

renown
[rɪ'naʊn]

托 雅 學

n 名譽;聲望

r1073

The speaker is a professor of great renown from Harvard University.

這位演講者是哈佛大學極有聲望的一位教授。

renowned
[rɪ'naʊnd]

托 雅 學

adj 有名的;受尊敬的

r1074

As a renowned person, Lily cares about public issues very much.

作為一位名人,莉莉非常關心公眾問題。

reorient
[ri'orɪɛnt]

托 雅 學

vt 復位方向;再調整;使適應

r1075

Oh dear, I think I'm lost so could you please give me a moment to reorient myself?

噢親愛的,我想我是迷路了,請給我點時間讓我重新確定方向好嗎?

represent
[ˌrɛprɪ'zɛnt]

托 雅 學

vt 描繪;代表,象徵

r1076

Symbols represent various meaning; for instance, a dove means peace.

符號代表各式各樣的含義,比如鴿子意指和平。

representation
[ˌrɛprɪzɛn'teʃən]

托 雅 學

n 描寫,陳述;代表

r1077

The artist's painting is a representation of her simplistic lifestyle.

這位藝術家的畫是她簡單化生活方式的代表。

reptile
['rɛptl]

托 雅 學

n 爬行動物;兩棲動物

r1078

When I was young, I used to think a frog was a type of reptile, like a turtle without a shell.

當我年紀還小時,經常認為青蛙是爬行動物的一種,就像沒有殼的烏龜。

resemblance
[rɪ'zɛmbləns]

托 雅 學

n 相似,相似性

r1079

I was surprised by the strong family resemblance between the mother and the daughter.

我對那對母女極強的家族相似感到驚訝。

resemble
[rɪ'zɛmbl]

托 雅 學

vt 像,類似

r1080

Your sister looks exactly like your mother but you resemble your father.

你妹妹和你媽媽長得幾乎一模一樣,你則像你爸爸。

resent
[rɪ'zɛnt]

托 雅 學

vt 對…不滿,怨恨

r1081

Even though my book did not sell well, I do not resent having it published.

即使我的書賣得不好,我也不會怨恨出版了它。

resentment
[rɪˈzɛntmənt]

r1082

n 憤恨，不滿
After their bitter argument, the friends continued to feel resentment towards each other.
經過激烈的爭執，朋友們相互間依然充滿憤恨。

reservation
[ˌrɛzɚˈveʃən]

r1083

n 保留，保留意見；預定，預訂
My husband made a hotel reservation for his overnight business trip.
我丈夫為他出差過夜預訂了賓館房間。

reserve
[rɪˈzɝv]

r1084

n 緘默，自我克制，拘謹
It's better to be a person who speaks with reserve in the workplace.
在工作場所做一個說話謹慎的人是比較好的。

reserve
[rɪˈzɝv]

r1085

vt 儲備，保留；預定
I have reserved a table at the restaurant on our chosen date of January 30th.
我已經為我們在一月三十號的約會預訂了一個餐廳位置。

reservoir
[ˈrɛzɚˌvɔr]

r1086

n 水庫，蓄水池
Our country relies on several reservoirs to supply water.
我們國家依靠幾座水庫來供水。

reside
[rɪˈzaɪd]

r1087

vi 居住，駐紮；屬於
He lives in New York City now but he will soon reside in California.
他現居紐約市，但是他即將定居加州。

R

residence
[ˈrɛzədəns]

r1088

n 住所；居住
Mike has welcomed us to visit his residence in New York.
邁克歡迎我們去拜訪他在紐約的住所。

residential
[ˌrɛzəˈdɛnʃəl]

r1089

adj 適合居住的；住宅的；提供住宿的
Farmland in Taiwan cannot be used for residential purposes.
臺灣的農田不能用作居住用途。

residual
[rɪˈzɪdʒʊəl]

r1090

adj 剩餘的；殘數的
I have a small residual amount of money in my bank account after the Christmas holiday.
聖誕假期結束後，我的銀行帳戶裡只剩一些剩餘的錢了。

residue
['rɛzə,dju]
托 雅 學

n 殘留物
The dishwasher is broken and leaving a greasy residue on all of the dishes.
洗碗機壞了,在所有盤子上留下油膩的殘留物。

r1091

resign
[rɪ'zaɪn]
托 雅 學

vi/vt 辭去,辭職;(使)聽從(於),(使)順從
He will resign from his job as president of the company on the first day of the next year.
他明年第一天就會辭去公司董事長的職務。

r1092

resignation
[,rɛzɪg'neʃən]
托 雅 學

n 放棄;辭職;反抗;聽從;屈從
I plan to send a letter of resignation next month.
我打算下個月遞交辭職信。

r1093

resolution
[,rɛzə'luʃən]
托 雅 學

n 堅決,堅定;決定
Many people make resolutions on New Year's Eve to start exercising more.
很多人會在除夕夜下決心增加運動量。

r1094

resolve
[rɪ'zɑlv]
托 雅 學

n 決心
I made a resolve to leave my family and depend on myself in the future.
我下定決心離開家人並且未來靠我自己。

r1095

resolve
[rɪ'zɑlv]
托 雅 學

vt 解決;決心
You and your sister need to resolve your problems and stop fighting all the time.
你和你妹妹需要解決自己的問題,不要總是吵來吵去的。

r1096

resort
[rɪ'zɔrt]
托 雅 學

n/vi 求助,憑藉
She tried everything to stop the baby from crying and finally resorted to driving her around in the car to calm her.
她嘗試各種方法讓嬰兒停止哭泣,最後借助開車兜風讓她平靜下來。

r1097

respect
[rɪ'spɛkt]
托 雅 學

n/vt 尊敬,尊重
The priest earned people's respect for his devotion to helping the needy.
這位牧師因為他對需要幫助的人的奉獻而贏得了人們的尊敬。

r1098

respectable
[rɪ'spɛktəbl]
托 雅 學

adj 可敬的;人格高尚的
Sir Goodman has been recognized as a respectable gentleman in their village.
古德曼爵士是村子裡被認為值得尊敬的紳士。

r1099

respectful
[rɪˈspɛktfəl]

托 雅 學

adj 尊敬的，表示敬意的 　　　　　　r1100
She greets everyone in the house with a respectful attitude.
她用尊敬的態度迎接屋子裡的每個人。

respective
[rɪˈspɛktɪv]

托 雅 學

adj 各自的，各個的 　　　　　　r1101
After we arrived at the library, we split up to look for books in our respective fields.
我們到達圖書館之後，就分頭去找各自領域的書。

respectively
[rɪˈspɛktɪvlɪ]

托 雅 學

adv 分別；依次為 　　　　　　r1102
My husband and I have to pay income tax of $1,000 and $2,000 respectively.
我先生跟我分別需要繳1000美金及2000美金的所得稅。

respond
[rɪˈspɑnd]

托 雅 學

vi 作答，回應 　　　　　　r1103
He waited a very long time to respond to the question.
他等了好長一段時間才回答這個問題。

respondent
[rɪˈspɑndənt]

托 雅 學

n 回答問題的人；被告 　　　　　　r1104
In court, it is the responsibility of a respondent to provide as detailed information as possible.
在法庭上，被告有責任提供盡可能詳實的資訊。

responsibility
[rɪˌspɑnsəˈbɪlətɪ]

托 雅 學

n 責任，責任心；職責 　　　　　　r1105
It takes a lot of responsibilities and patience to raise a dog.
養狗需要很強的責任心和耐心。

R

responsible
[rɪˈspɑnsəbl̩]

托 雅 學

adj 應負責的；可靠的；責任重大的 　　　　　　r1106
My son is now responsible enough to stay at home without an adult.
我兒子現在已經可靠到可以不用大人陪，自己留在家裡了。

restless
[ˈrɛstlɪs]

托 雅 學

adj 不安定的，焦慮的 　　　　　　r1107
The child's mother couldn't help but feel restless until she knew that her son was safe.
這位母親無法控制自己的焦慮情緒，直到確知她的兒子安全。

restoration
[ˌrɛstəˈreʃən]

托 雅 學

n 修復，整修 　　　　　　r1108
The museum restoration is now complete and is once again open to the public.
博物館的修葺工作現在已經完成，博物館又可以向公眾開放了。

restrain
[rɪ'stren]
托 雅 學

vt 抑制，遏制，制止，限制　　r1109

The children found it hard to restrain themselves from talking in the class.

小孩們上課克制自己不說話是很困難的事。

resume
[ˌrɛzjʊ'me]
托 雅 學

n 個人簡歷　　r1110

Make sure to bring along your resume when you go to a job interview.

去面試的時候一定要記得帶個人簡歷。

resume
[rɪ'zjum]
托 雅 學

vi/vt 再繼續，重新開始；再用；恢復　　r1111

I hope you will resume the program you are watching soon after we repair the sound system.

希望在我們修理音響系統後你們可以繼續看原來的節目。

retail
['ritel]
托 雅 學

adj 零售的；**n** 零售　　r1112

She worked in retail stores for many years and understood marketing well.

她在零售業工作很多年，而且對行銷很在行。

retrospect
['rɛtrəˌspɛkt]
托 雅 學

n/vt 回顧，回想，追溯　　r1113

In retrospect, I should never have fired him because of his scheduling conflicts.

回想起來，我真不該因為他的行程安排有衝突而解雇他的。

reveal
[rɪ'vil]
托 雅 學

n/vi 展現，顯示，揭示，揭露，告訴，洩露　　r1114

The teacher accidentally revealed some answers to the test before our final exam.

老師無意間在期末考試前透漏了一些考題的答案。

revenge
[rɪ'vɛndʒ]
托 雅 學

n 報仇　　r1115

Studies show that seeking revenge can have an adverse effect on your health.

研究顯示，尋求報復對健康有不良的影響。

revenge
[rɪ'vɛndʒ]
托 雅 學

vt 替…報仇　　r1116

The people will find a way to revenge themselves on the governor's constant rash behaviors.

人民將會找到方法對時常做出輕率行為的政府進行報復。

revenue
['rɛvəˌnju]
托 雅 學

n 財政收入；稅收　　r1117

The company had multiple streams of revenue and was well protected against any economic crises.

這家公司有很多收入來源，因此能很好地抵抗任何經濟危機。

reverse
[rɪ'vɝs]

托 雅 學

r1118

adj 相反的

The student came to school from a reverse direction from his home today.

這個學生今天從與家相反的方向來上學。

reverse
[rɪ'vɝs]

托 雅 學

r1119

n 相反；挫折

Amy suffered a great reverse when she divorced her husband last year.

愛米去年跟她老公離婚時遭受了相當大的挫折。

revise
[rɪ'vaɪz]

托 雅 學

r1120

vt 修訂，校訂，修改

She needed to revise her paper before she turned it in to the teacher.

在她交論文給老師前，需要先修改。

revision
[rɪ'vɪʒən]

托 雅 學

r1121

n 修訂，修改；溫習

I need to hand in the revision version of my thesis by next Friday.

在下星期五之前我必須提交論文的修訂稿。

revolution
[ˌrɛvə'luʃən]

托 雅 學

r1122

n 革命；旋轉，繞轉

There was a revolution in France in 1789.

1789年發生了法國大革命。

revolve
[rɪ'valv]

托 雅 學

r1123

vi/vt （使……）旋轉；考慮；公轉，迴圈

The earth revolves in an orbit around the sun.

地球繞著太陽在軌道上公轉。

R

rhythm
['rɪðəm]

托 雅 學

r1124

n 韻律，格律；節奏

African music has more complex rhythms than western music.

非洲音樂比西方音樂的韻律更複雜。

ridge
[rɪdʒ]

托 雅 學

r1125

n 脊，嶺，山脈；壟

Not until he reached the mountain ridge did he realize that he forgot to bring the tent.

到了山脊他才想到自己忘了帶帳篷。

rig
[rɪg]

托 雅 學

r1126

n 鑽井設備；帆裝；大卡車

With a telescope, the captain saw a gas rig drifting in the North Sea.

船長用望遠鏡看到北海上漂移著一台氣體燃料鑽機。

rig
[rɪg]
托 雅 學

vt （以不正當手段）操控；（秘密地）安裝
Losing the votes, the candidate accused his opponent of rigging the election.
因為失去選票，候選人控訴對手操控選舉。

r1127

righteous
['raɪtʃəs]
托 雅 學

adj 公正的，正當的
In Bible stories, Abraham is characterized with righteous personality.
在《聖經》故事中，亞伯拉罕擁有正直的品格。

r1128

rigid
['rɪdʒɪd]
托 雅 學

adj 剛硬的；僵硬的
She went rigid as she nervously waited to hear the results of her exam.
當她緊張地等著考試結果的時候，她的身體變得僵硬。

r1129

rigidity
[rɪ'dʒɪdəti]
托 雅 學

n 堅硬；嚴格；死板
Some parents have unwavering rigidity regarding discipline.
有些父母對於紀律要求嚴格，不容質疑。

r1130

rigorous
['rɪgərəs]
托 雅 學

adj 嚴格的，嚴酷的，嚴謹的
Soldiers who want to join the SWAT team must pass a rigorous test.
想加入霹靂小組的軍人必須通過嚴峻的考驗。

r1131

rim
[rɪm]
托 雅 學

n （圓物的）邊，邊緣；（眼鏡）框
The huge mirror has a rim made of pure gold.
這面巨大的鏡子有著純金的邊緣。

r1132

riot
['raɪət]
托 雅 學

n 暴亂，騷亂；彩色繽紛
The verdict of the trial caused a riot in nearby districts.
那件審判案件的判決結果引起了鄰近行政地區的暴動。

r1133

riot
['raɪət]
托 雅 學

vi 騷亂，暴動
Students are rioting in front of the main building of the university.
學生們在大學主樓前暴動。

r1134

rip
[rɪp]
托 雅 學

n 裂口，裂縫；搶劫
Such an expensive dinner was a total rip because both the food and service were terrible.
我認為那頓昂貴的晚餐完全就是搶劫，因為食物和服務兩方面都糟透了。

r1135

rip
[rɪp]
托 雅 學

vi/vt 撕，剝；劈，鋸；裂開，撕裂

r1136

Unable to open a plastic bag, the kid ripped the whole bag apart.
打不開塑膠袋，這個小孩索性把整個袋子都扯開了。

ripple
['rɪpl̩]
托 雅 學

n 漣漪，細浪，波紋

r1137

There was a ripple in the water where he had skipped a stone.
他扔石頭的地方出現了漣漪。

rival
['raɪvl̩]
托 雅 學

adj 競爭的

r1138

After careful consideration, the CEO chose to sign a contract with a rival company.
仔細考慮之後，執行長選擇與競爭對手簽訂合約。

rival
['raɪvl̩]
托 雅 學

n 競爭者

r1139

They were rivals at school and competed against each other in sports and academics.
他們是校內競爭對手，不論運動或學業方面都彼此競爭。

roam
[rom]
托 雅 學

vi/vt 在…漫步，漫遊

r1140

Sally enjoys roaming around the empty streets at midnight.
莎莉喜歡半夜在空蕩蕩的街上漫遊。

rot
[rɑt]
托 雅 學

vi/vt （使）腐爛；（使）腐敗，腐朽

r1141

The food that she cooked two days ago has now gone rotten.
她兩天前煮的食物現在已經腐爛。

rotate
['rotet]
托 雅 學

vi/vt （使…）旋轉

r1142

I always rotate the cookies about half way through baking so they are evenly browned.
我總是在餅乾烤到一半的時候轉動一下，這樣他們會有差不多的焦色。

route
[rut]
托 雅 學

n 路，路線，路程

r1143

Trail number 9 and 10 are the most popular routes for hikers.
九號及十號步道是最受登山者歡迎的路徑。

routine
[ru'tin]
托 雅 學

adj 常規的，例行的

r1144

In his routine chores, he doesn't need for any fancy equipment.
在他的日常事務中，他不需要任何花稍的儀器設備。

R

routine
[ruˈtin]

托 雅 學

n 日常工作；例行公事 r1145

The family had a morning routine that began with a warm breakfast together in the kitchen.

這個家庭早上有一個常規，即在廚房裡一起吃熱的早餐。

royalty
[ˈrɔɪəltɪ]

托 雅 學

n 皇家，皇族，皇族成員 r1146

The doctor has suspected that becoming royalty deteriorated her health.

醫生懷疑當皇族使她的健康惡化。

rustproof
[ˈrʌstˌpruf]

托 雅 學

adj 防銹的 r1147

The patio furniture is rustproof so it can be left outdoors in the rain.

露臺上的傢俱是防銹的，所以下雨時可以放在室外。

ruthless
[ˈruθlɪs]

托 雅 學

adj 殘酷的，無情的 r1148

He is a ruthless boss and will fire anyone whom he feels has become unproductive.

他是一個無情的老闆，隨時會把他覺得無生產力的員工開除。

S

字彙能力檢查表

先自我檢驗是否瞭解以下初階單字，若有不清楚者，請先開啟光碟中的電子書複習。

☐sack	☐seminar	☐source	☐stress
☐sack	☐separate	☐spacecraft	☐stretch
☐sacred	☐series	☐span	☐stretch
☐saddle	☐service	☐spare	☐strict
☐safeguard	☐shallow	☐spare	☐string
☐safeguard	☐shareholder	☐spark	☐strip
☐saline	☐shave	☐spark	☐stripe
☐satisfactory	☐shed	☐spill	☐stroke
☐satisfy	☐shield	☐split	☐stroke
☐sauce	☐shock	☐split	☐structure
☐scale	☐short	☐sponge	☐stubborn
☐scan	☐shout	☐spotlight	☐studio
☐scan	☐shovel	☐spouse	☐stuff
☐scandal	☐shrink	☐spray	☐stuffing
☐scar	☐shrug	☐spring	☐suggest
☐scent	☐shutter	☐spring	☐suggestion
☐scent	☐shy	☐square	☐suitable
☐schedule	☐sincere	☐stack	☐suitcase
☐schedule	☐skip	☐stadium	☐suite
☐scholarship	☐skyscraper	☐staff	☐sum
☐seaport	☐slender	☐staff	☐support
☐secondary	☐slim	☐stage	☐supportive
☐secret	☐slim	☐stalk	☐suppress

S

□secretary	□slope	□standard	□surroundings
□section	□smooth	□standby	□swallow
□sector	□snail	□starch	□swear
□seedling	□soil	□state	□swing
□seek	□solar	□state	□swing
□seemingly	□sole	□steam	□switch
□segment	□solo	□stiffen	□switch
□select	□sound	□sting	□systematic
□selection	□sour	□stink	□systematically

sacrifice
['sækrə,faɪs]
托 雅 學

n 犧牲，犧牲品；祭品　　　　s1001
Like many cultures from antiquity, some Polynesian cultures practice human sacrifice to appease their gods.
就像許多古文化一樣，某些玻里尼西亞文化實施真人獻祭以平息神的怒氣。

sacrifice
['sækrə,faɪs]
托 雅 學

vi/vt 犧牲，獻出　　　　s1002
There is nothing Bill would not sacrifice for his family.
比爾願意為家人犧牲一切。

sake
[sek]
托 雅 學

n 緣故，理由　　　　s1003
Oh for heaven's sake, I said I would pay for our lunch today so just hand me the bill, please.
喔！看在老天的緣故上，我說過今天由我付午餐的錢，所以請把帳單遞給我吧。

salary
['sæləri]
托 雅 學

n 薪金，薪水　　　　s1004
The interview went well but he declined the job offer because the annual salary was too low.
面試進行得很順利，但他因年薪太低而婉拒了工作機會。

salute
[sə'lut]
托 雅 學

n （軍人）敬禮（姿勢）；vt 敬禮；鳴禮炮；迎接，歡迎　　s1005
Cadets at the military academy gave their instructor a salute as a sign of respect every time he addressed them.
每當指導員與軍校學生交談時，學生們都對他敬禮以示尊重。

sample
['sæmpl]
托 雅 學

n 樣品，實例，標本；抽樣檢查　　　　s1006
The company sent me a sample of their new product to see if I like it.
那家公司寄給我一份新產品的樣品，讓我看是否喜歡。

sample
['sæmpl]
托 雅 學

vt 取樣，採樣 s1007
The food products sampled last month have been found to contain illegal plasticizers.
上個月採樣的食品已被發現含有非法的塑化劑。

savage
['sævɪdʒ]
托 雅 學

adj 野蠻的；兇惡的，殘暴的 s1008
The rebels launched a savage attack against the coalition forces.
叛軍對聯軍發動了相當殘暴的攻擊。

savage
['sævɪdʒ]
托 雅 學

n 野人，未開化的人 s1009
The early settlers thought the Native Americans were savages.
早期拓荒者認為美洲印第安人是野人。

scapegoat
['skep,got]
托 雅 學

n 代罪羔羊 s1010
Tyler said how unfair of his coach to make him the scapegoat for his team's loss.
泰勒說他的教練把全隊的失利都怪罪到他一個人頭上是非常不公平的。

scatter
['skætə]
托 雅 學

vi/vt 使消散；撒；散播 s1011
The gardener likes to scatter coffee grinds and used tea leaves on the roses.
園丁喜歡將咖啡渣和沖泡過的茶葉灑在玫瑰上。

scenery
['sinərɪ]
托 雅 學

n 風景，舞臺佈景 s1012
I thought the scenery in the Canadian Rockies was breathtaking.
我認為加拿大洛磯山脈的風景美到令人屏息。

scenic
['sinɪk]
托 雅 學

adj 風景優美的；舞臺的，戲劇的 s1013
The Pacific Coast Highway in California is the most scenic route I have ever traveled.
加利福尼亞州的太平洋海岸公路是我旅行過的風景最優美的路線。

scheme
[skim]
托 雅 學

n 計畫，方案；詭計；陰謀 s1014
They thought of a scheme for robbing a local bank on Friday.
他們想了一個在星期五搶當地銀行的計畫。

scheme
[skim]
托 雅 學

vi/vt 計畫，策劃；搞陰謀 s1015
The concubine was scheming against the queen in secret.
那位妃嬪正秘密策劃如何對抗皇后。

S

scoop
[skup]
托 雅 學

n 勺子，匙；鏟斗
The cook added three scoops of salt to the soup.
廚師在湯裡加了三匙鹽。

s1016

scoop
[skup]
托 雅 學

vi/vt 挖空；舀取
The cook scooped ice cream out of a can.
廚師從桶子挖空了霜淇淋。

s1017

scope
[skop]
托 雅 學

n （活動）範圍；機會，餘地
On the first day of class the teacher outlined the scope of the entire semester for the students.
在上課第一天，老師為學生概述整個學期的授課範圍。

s1018

scope
[skop]
托 雅 學

vt 端詳；評估
Gary announced he wanted to scope out the competition.
蓋瑞宣佈他想拈一拈他競爭對手的分量。

s1019

scout
[skaʊt]
托 雅 學

n 偵察員；偵察工具；vi/vt 搜索，偵察
Three soldiers were sent out to scout the hostile forces outside the perimeter of the town.
三名士兵被送出鄉鎮週邊偵查敵軍。

s1020

scramble
['skræmbl]
托 雅 學

n/vi （快速地）爬，攀登；互相爭奪，爭先
I paid the fair and watched the children scramble to find empty seats on the crowded bus.
我付了車費，然後看著孩子們登上擁擠的巴士尋找空座位。

s1021

scrap
[skræp]
托 雅 學

n 碎片；廢料
I did not find any paper scraps in the room.
我在房間內找不到任何碎紙片。

s1022

scrap
[skræp]
托 雅 學

vi/vt 廢棄，報廢；拋棄
Before the Chinese New Year, we will scrap all the waste.
我們會在過年前把所有的廢物丟掉。

s1023

scrape
[skrep]
托 雅 學

n 刮，擦痕，刮擦聲；vi/vt 刮（掉），擦過；勉強度日
The long scrape on my car door wasn't there when I parked it earlier today.
我今天稍早把車停好的時候，我的車門上沒有這條長刮痕。

s1024

scratch
[skrætʃ]

托 雅 學

n 抓，搔；抓痕；起跑線　　　　　　s1025

Let's start from scratch this time because the old design had some problems.

咱們這次從零開始，因為舊的設計有些問題。

scratch
[skrætʃ]

托 雅 學

vi/vt 抓；扒；劃傷　　　　　　s1026

The mother monkey helped the baby monkey scratch its back.

母猴幫著幼猴撓背。

screen
[skrin]

托 雅 學

n 螢幕；屏風；簾；**vi/vt** 掩蔽，包庇；篩選；裝簾　　s1027

The exam was held to screen new teachers for the school.

舉辦這場考試是為學校篩選新老師的。

screw
[skru]

托 雅 學

n 螺旋，螺絲（釘）　　　　　　s1028

I hung the heavy mirror on the wall by using a metal screw and strong hook.

我用金屬螺絲和堅固的鉤子把這個很重的鏡子掛在牆上。

screw
[skru]

托 雅 學

vi/vt 擰，擰緊　　　　　　s1029

The interior designer decided to screw the cupboard directly into the wall.

室內設計師決定將櫥櫃直接擰在牆上。

script
[skrɪpt]

托 雅 學

n 劇本（原稿）；手稿，原稿；筆跡，手跡　　s1030

The film director asked the actor to read in character from the movie script.

這個電影導演要求演員照電影劇本的角色讀劇本。

S

scroll
[skrol]

托 雅 學

n （寫字或作畫用的）一卷（羊皮）紙，卷軸　　s1031

Isabelle unrolled the ancient scroll and began to slowly read it.

伊莎貝拉打開古老的羊皮紙卷，開始慢慢地讀起來。

scum
[skʌm]

托 雅 學

n 浮垢，浮渣；泡沫　　　　　　s1032

Scarlett used a cloth to wipe the scum off the bath tub.

斯佳麗用一塊布擦去粘在浴盆上的浮垢。

seal
[sil]

托 雅 學

n 封鉛，封條；印，圖章；海豹；**vt** 封，密封　　s1033

The official sealed the confidential file before sending it to the president.

官員在將密件寄給總統前進行了密封。

sect
[sɛkt]

托 雅 學

n 派別；黨派；教派；學派

The scrolls were found in the desert, hidden in jars by a lesser known sect of Christians for thousands of years.

那個卷軸在沙漠中被人發現，它已經被一支鮮為人知的基督教宗派藏在罐子裡長達數千年。

s1034

secure
[sɪ'kjʊr]

托 雅 學

adj 安全的，放心的

He personally checked every window and door at night to be certain the house was secure.

他晚上親自檢查每扇門窗以確認房子是安全的。

s1035

secure
[sɪ'kjʊr]

托 雅 學

vi/vt 獲得安全；防護

After the meeting, the border of the two countries was secured.

兩國之間的邊界在會議後得到了防護。

s1036

security
[sɪ'kjʊrətɪ]

托 雅 學

n 安全（感）；防禦（物）；保證（人）；複數＝證券

Great efforts are made to ensure the security of the President because of his special status.

因為總統的特殊身份，所以大家努力確保總統的安全。

s1037

segregate
['sɛgrɪ,get]

托 雅 學

vt 使…分開，隔離（病患等）

During the early 20th century, black children were often segregated from the whites in shabby public schools that were poorly funded.

二十世紀初，黑人孩童常與白人隔離，就讀破舊且資金不足的公立學校。

s1038

senior
['sinjə]

托 雅 學

adj 年長的；地位較高的；**n**（大學）四年級學生

Most movie theaters offer a discount to senior citizens.

大部分電影院都給年長者提供折扣。

s1039

sensation
[sɛn'seʃən]

托 雅 學

n 感覺，知覺；激動，轟動，轟動一時的事情

She felt the sharp and cold sensation of the rain falling on the back of her neck.

她感覺到雨滴滴在脖子後的寒冷刺骨的感覺。

s1040

sensational
[sɛn'seʃənəl]

托 雅 學

adj 引起轟動的，轟動社會的

The story of the movie is based on a sensational bank robbery in 1998.

這部電影的情節是改編自1998年那件轟動社會的銀行搶劫案。

s1041

sensible
['sɛnsəbl̩]

托 雅 學

adj 明智的，達理的；可覺察的，明顯的

He was a sensible person and rarely did anything rash or foolish.

他是一個明智的人，很少做草率或愚蠢的事。

s1042

sensitive
['sɛnsətɪv]

adj 敏感的，易受傷害的；靈敏的   s1043

My teeth are sensitive and hurt when I drink ice water or hot coffee.

我的牙齒很敏感，當我喝冰水或是熱咖啡時就會痛。

sensitivity
[‚sɛnsə'tɪvətɪ]

n 敏感（性）；靈敏性   s1044

This machine has become the company's most popular product because of its high sensitivity.

由於它的高度靈敏性，這台機器已成為這家公司最熱賣的產品。

sentiment
['sɛntəmənt]

n 感情，柔情；看法；感覺   s1045

Whenever I see the book I read often as a child, I am overcome with sentiment of nostalgia.

每當我看到這本小時候常讀的書，一股懷舊的感情油然而生。

sequence
['sikwəns]

n 先後，次序；連續，數列   s1046

The police asked her to give an account of the sequence of events before the accident.

警方要求她詳細敘述意外發生前所發生事件的順序。

session
['sɛʃən]

n （一屆）會議，一段（時間），一次   s1047

She went to her first physical therapy session after the surgery today.

她在今天接受手術後的第一次物理治療。

setback
['sɛt‚bæk]

n 挫折；失效；復發；倒退   s1048

Although there have been a few setbacks in your career, that does not mean you are a loser.

儘管你的職業生涯中有些挫折，但這不代表你就是個失敗者。

S

settle
['sɛtl̩]

vi/vt 安定，安頓；停息；定居；解決，調停   s1049

My sister is not ready to settle down in a relationship until she is financially stable.

我的姐姐在經濟穩定之前是不準備安家的。

settlement
['sɛtl̩mənt]

n 解決，決定，調停；居留區，住宅區   s1050

The settlement lies in the valley and has no more than 100 residents.

這個住宅區坐落於山谷間，居民不超過一百人。

severe
[sə'vɪr]

adj 嚴厲的；劇烈的，嚴重的，嚴峻的，艱難的   s1051

Her son's punishment for lying should be severe for he had done it before without much consequence.

她兒子說謊的懲罰應該要嚴厲，因為他之前說過謊卻沒有承擔什麼後果。

sewer
['suɚ]

托 雅 學

n 下水道，污水管，陰溝；裁縫師，縫紉工具　　s1052

The sewer on our street backed up and caused a sanitation problem.

我們這條街上的下水道堵塞了，引起了衛生問題。

shatter
['ʃætɚ]

托 雅 學

n 碎片；粉碎；**vi/vt** 粉碎；（使）疲憊；（使）震駭　　s1053

The glass fell on the marble floor but amazingly it did not shatter.

這個玻璃杯掉落在大理石地板上，但令人驚奇的是它沒有粉碎。

shed
[ʃɛd]

托 雅 學

vi/vt 流出；發散，散發；脫落，脫去　　s1054

Do you know any quick way to shed unwanted pounds?

你知不知道有何快速減肥的方法？

sheer
[ʃɪr]

托 雅 學

adj 純粹的，十足的，全然的；陡峭的，險峻的　　s1055

It was sheer luck that my lottery ticket was picked out of thousands.

我的彩券在幾千張中被抽中純屬運氣。

shelter
['ʃɛltɚ]

托 雅 學

n 掩蔽處；掩蔽；保護；**vi/vt** 掩蔽，躲避，庇護　　s1056

Although the house is small, at least it can shelter us from the wind and rain.

這房子雖小，但它至少可以為我們遮蔽風雨。

shepherd
['ʃɛpɚd]

托 雅 學

n 牧羊人，羊倌　　s1057

He lived in the northwestern part of Texas and worked as a shepherd on one of the many sheep farms.

他住在德州西北邊，是一個綿羊牧場的牧羊人。

shift
[ʃɪft]

托 雅 學

n 轉換；（輪）班；**vi/vt** 替換，轉移；推卸，轉嫁　　s1058

The magician pointed his finger at the ceiling of the auditorium to shift the audience's attention.

魔術師把手指指向表演廳的天花板以轉移觀眾的注意力。

shiver
['ʃɪvɚ]

托 雅 學

n/vi/vt 戰慄，發抖　　s1059

The temperature was dropping quickly outside and I began to shiver.

室外溫度快速下降讓我開始發抖。

shortage
['ʃɔrtɪdʒ]

托 雅 學

n 不足，缺少　　s1060

If there is not enough rain in summer, we will have a water shortage in winter.

如果夏天雨下得不夠，我們冬天就會水資源短缺。

shred
[ʃrɛd]
托 雅 學

n 碎片，碎條，破布；最少量，少量剩餘　s1061
Michelle made use of shreds of newspapers to create a collage.
蜜雪兒利用報紙碎片來製作拼貼畫。

shred
[ʃrɛd]
托 雅 學

vi/vt 撕碎，切碎　s1062
Julie helped to shred old documents at work.
朱莉上班時幫著粉碎舊檔。

shuttle
['ʃʌtl]
托 雅 學

n 往返的交通工具；vi/vt 往返穿梭　s1063
The businessman shuttled between the two cities to hammer out a multi-million-dollar deal.
這名商人在這兩座城市間往返穿梭，以敲定一筆數百萬美元的生意。

signal
['sɪgnl]
托 雅 學

n 信號，暗號；vi/vt 發信號，用信號通知　s1064
The militants signaled to their chief by flashing the torches.
好戰分子運用閃手電筒的方式向他們的首領發信號。

signature
['sɪgnətʃɚ]
托 雅 學

n 簽名，署名，簽字　s1065
The signature does not match the one on file, so we are probably dealing with a case of stolen identity.
這個簽名和檔案上的不相符，所以我們有可能正在處理一個盜用身份的案子。

significant
[sɪg'nɪfəkənt]
托 雅 學

adj 有意義的；重大的，重要的　s1066
Some writers believe that every detail of a short story should be significant.
有些作家認為短篇故事的每個細節都應該是有意義的。

simplify
['sɪmplə,faɪ]
托 雅 學

vt 簡化，使單純　s1067
I really think I need to simplify my life because I am always too busy.
我真的認為我需要簡化生活，因為我總是太忙。

simultaneous
[,saɪml'tenɪəs]
托 雅 學

adj 同時的，同時存在的　s1068
The longer you live, the more likely you will have to deal with simultaneous health problems.
你活得越久，你就越有可能必須面對同時發生的健康問題。

simultaneously
[saɪməl'tenɪəslɪ]
托 雅 學

adv 同時地，同時存在地　s1069
The potatoes can be cooked simultaneously with the rib roast so long as you keep the oven temperature high enough.
只要烤箱保持夠高溫度的話，這些馬鈴薯可以與肋排同時烹烤。

S

situate
['sɪtʃʊ,et]
托 雅 學

vt 使位於，使處於；建於，建在
The Disney company once considered situating a theme park in Taiwan.
迪士尼公司曾考慮在臺灣建一個主題公園。

s1070

situation
[,sɪtʃʊ'eʃən]
托 雅 學

n 形勢；位置；職位
The situation got even worse after the new policy was implemented.
在新政策執行後，整個形勢變得更糟了。

s1071

skeleton
['skɛlətn]
托 雅 學

n 骨骼，骨架；框架；梗概，提要
There was a skeleton in the anatomy and physiology class that they used and was nicknamed "Slim."
他們在解剖學和生理學課上使用的骷髏被暱稱為「斯利姆」。

s1072

skeptical
['skɛptɪkl]
托 雅 學

adj 懷疑的
The coupon said I could get the TV for half the price but I was skeptical.
折價券上說可用半價買到電視機，但我很懷疑。

s1073

sketch
[skɛtʃ]
托 雅 學

n 草圖；梗概；**vi/vt** 繪略圖，速寫，寫生
He sketched the coal miner in a few minutes.
他幾分鐘就畫了一幅那位煤礦工人的素描。

s1074

skim
[skɪm]
托 雅 學

vi 輕輕掠過；瀏覽，略讀
My father skimmed through the newspapers before he went to work.
我爸爸上班前瀏覽了一下報紙。

s1075

skim
[skɪm]
托 雅 學

vt 撇去（液體表面之）漂浮物
She skimmed the soup to remove most of the fat.
她撇去了湯上的大部分浮油。

s1076

slack
[slæk]
托 雅 學

adj 懈怠的，鬆弛的；蕭條的
Don't become too slack in class or you will fail the course.
課堂上不要過於鬆懈，不然你這堂課會當掉。

s1077

slack
[slæk]
托 雅 學

n 閒置或富餘的部分；複數＝便褲
The manager wants to know how to create a little more slack in the budget.
經理想知道如何才能在預算中再找出一點閒置的款項。

s1078

slam
[slæm]

托 雅 學

n 猛然關閉的聲音；**vi/vt** （門、窗等）砰地關上
s1079
His neighbor slammed the door in his face.
他的鄰居當著他的面把門砰然關閉。

slip
[slɪp]

托 雅 學

n 疏忽，小錯，口誤，筆誤；**vi/vt** 滑，滑倒；滑掉；溜走
s1080
After the meeting, I'm going to slip away unnoticed.
會議之後我打算悄悄地溜走。

slippery
['slɪpərɪ]

托 雅 學

adj 滑的，滑溜的
s1081
There was ice on the front steps and the porch itself was very slippery.
前面的階梯有冰塊，所以走廊很滑。

slit
[slɪt]

托 雅 學

n 細長裂縫，狹長切口；**vi/vt** 切開，截開，縱割
s1082
The pirates slit the box and found no treasure inside.
海盜切開箱子發現裡面沒有寶藏。

slogan
['slogən]

托 雅 學

n 標語，口號
s1083
The new ad slogan for the company sounded a lot like their competitor's.
該公司的新廣告標語聽起來就像競爭對手的標語。

slot
[slɑt]

托 雅 學

n 狹縫；空位；**vt** 放入狹縫中，把…納入
s1084
The teacher slotted a CD into a CD player before the listening test began.
老師在聽力考試前，先把CD放入播放機的狹縫中。

slum
[slʌm]

托 雅 學

n 貧民窟，貧民區，陋巷
s1085
The life of the slum is clearly depicted by a novelist.
貧民窟的生活被那位小說家描繪得很清楚。

smash
[smæʃ]

托 雅 學

n/vi/vt 打碎，粉碎；用力擊球
s1086
The tennis player wanted to smash the ball over the net.
這位網球選手想用力擊球，把它打過網。

smother
['smʌðɚ]

托 雅 學

vt 使窒息；（用灰等）悶熄
s1087
He shoveled dirt onto the camp fire to smother it so it could not relight and start a forest fire.
他把土鏟進營火上好把火悶熄，這樣才不會復燃而引起森林大火。

S

snap
[snæp]

托 雅 學

vi/vt 啪地移動；（使）突然斷開，斷開（成兩截）；打響指　s1088
The singer started to snap his fingers in tune with the song.
這位歌手開始跟著歌曲節拍打響指。

snapshot
['snæp,ʃɑt]

托 雅 學

n 快相，快照；vi/vt （給…）拍快照　s1089
The application for a passport requires that you include two
snapshots when you submit it.
提交護照申請表時需要同時交兩張快照。

snatch
[snætʃ]

托 雅 學

vi/vt 一把抓起，一下奪過；搶走，偷竊　s1090
The robber tried to snatch the gun from the security guard.
搶匪試著搶走保全人員的槍。

soak
[sok]

托 雅 學

vi/vt 浸泡，浸濕，浸透　s1091
The lady had been standing up all day and she only wanted
to go home and soak her feet.
這位女士已經站了一整天了，她只想回家泡腳。

soar
[sor]

托 雅 學

vi （指鳥等）高飛，翱翔；飛漲；高聳　s1092
Eagles soar in the sky.
老鷹在天空翱翔。

society
[sə'saɪətɪ]

托 雅 學

n 社會；社團，協會，社；社交界，上流社會　s1093
Good education is a way of becoming more competitive in
modern societies.
良好的教育是在現代社會中提升競爭力的方法。

sociologist
[,soʃɪ'alədʒɪst]

托 雅 學

n 社會學家　s1094
The sociologist conducted a study to investigate the lives of
several immigrants.
那名社會學家進行了一項關於幾個移民生活的研究。

sociology
[,soʃɪ'alədʒɪ]

托 雅 學

n 社會學　s1095
Sociology is the scientific analysis of society, social
institutions, and social relationships.
社會學是社會、社會制度和社會關係的科學分析。

sole
[sol]

托 雅 學

adj 單獨的，唯一的　s1096
My son is the sole heir of my estate and will inherit my house
and all of my assets.
我兒子是我財產的唯一繼承人，他將會繼承我的房子及我所有的資產。

solo
['solo]

托 雅 學

adj/adv 單獨的（地）；獨唱的（地）；**n** 獨唱曲

s1097

After the superstar performed solo, the audience stood up and applauded him.

那位超級巨星獨唱後，觀眾站起來為他喝彩。

solution
[sə'luʃən]

托 雅 學

n 解答，解決辦法；溶解，溶液

s1098

My students were willing to spend hours to find the solution to the math problem.

我的學生願意花幾小時的時間找出數學題的解決辦法。

solve
[salv]

托 雅 學

vi/vt 解決，解答

s1099

We can easily solve this problem for you.

我們可以輕易地為你解決這個問題。

sophisticate
[sə'fɪstɪ,ket]

托 雅 學

vt 使變得世故，使矯揉造作；使更高級，使精緻；使迷惑，曲解；篡改，摻入

s1100

So much is lost when folks feel the need to sophisticate something naturally beautiful.

當人們感覺到需要把自然美的東西變得矯揉造作時，許多韻味就喪失了。

sophisticated
[sə'fɪstɪ,ketɪd]

托 雅 學

adj 老於世故的；高級的，考究的

s1101

The magazine editor was impeccably dressed and sophisticated.

雜誌編輯穿著十分得體且考究。

sore
[sor]

托 雅 學

adj 疼痛的；痛心的；**n** 痛處，瘡口

s1102

After my sister fell down the stairs and twisted her foot, she had a swollen sore ankle for a week.

我妹妹從樓梯上摔下來扭傷腳以後，她的腳踝腫痛了一個禮拜。

S

sort
[sort]

托 雅 學

vi/vt 分類，整理

s1103

Every household is encouraged to sort their rubbish in an environmentally friendly way.

家家戶戶都被鼓勵用一個環保的方式來對垃圾進行分類。

souvenir
['suvə,nɪr]

托 雅 學

n 紀念品

s1104

She brought home a small reproduction of her favorite painting as a souvenir from her trip to Paris.

她從巴黎的旅行中帶回一小幅她最喜歡畫作的複製品作為紀念品。

sow
[so]

托 雅 學

vi/vt 播種

s1105

He plowed the land and then sowed the seeds.

他先翻土，然後播種。

span
[spæn]

托 雅 學

s1106

n 跨度，跨距；全長，全幅；時間段，持續時間

The attention spans of kids are said to be shorter than those of adults.

小孩的注意力跨度據說比成人的短。

sparkle
['sparkl]

托 雅 學

s1107

n 閃光

Megan had a warm smile and sparkle in her eyes because today's her birthday.

梅根臉上掛著微笑，眼裡放著亮光，因為今天是她的生日。

specialize
['spɛʃəl,aɪz]

托 雅 學

s1108

vi/vt 專攻，專門研究；專業化

The professor specialized in the study of Chinese history.

那位教授專門研究中國歷史。

specialty
['spɛʃəltɪ]

托 雅 學

s1109

n 專業，專長；特產，名產

The professor's specialty was Chinese history, especially the study in the Qing Dynasty.

那位教授的專業是中國史，尤其是清代的研究。

species
['spiʃiz]

托 雅 學

s1110

n （物）種，種類

The oceanographer was happy to find an unknown species of marine life on the remote coral reef.

海洋學家很高興在遙遠的珊瑚礁中發現一種未知的海洋物種。

specific
[spɪ'sɪfɪk]

托 雅 學

s1111

adj 明確的，具體的；特定的，特有的

The trouble with Bill was that he never had a specific aim in life.

比爾的問題是他從未有過明確的人生目標。

specification
[,spɛsəfə'keʃən]

托 雅 學

s1112

n 詳述；複數＝規格；說明書；規範

Before using the machine, please read the specifications carefully.

在使用這台機器前，請詳讀說明書。

specify
['spɛsə,faɪ]

托 雅 學

s1113

vt 指定，詳細說明

Our contract will specify what kind of wood to use for the floor.

我們的合約中會規定地板要用哪種木材。

spectacle
['spɛktəkl]

托 雅 學

s1114

n 場面；景象；奇觀，壯觀；複數＝眼鏡

He made a spectacle of himself at the grocery store when he knocked over a large stack of bean cans.

他撞倒了一大堆豆類罐頭，在雜貨店裡大出洋相。

spectacular
[spɛk'tækjələ]

托 雅 學

adj 壯觀的，引人注目的　s1115

The fireworks show on the National day was spectacular.

國慶當天的煙火秀十分壯觀。

spectator
[spɛk'tetə]

托 雅 學

n 觀眾，旁觀者　s1116

The shy little girl lived by the park, but she was only a spectator, content to watch other children play.

這個害羞的小女孩就住在公園旁，然而她只是個旁觀者，她看著其他小孩玩耍就滿足了。

speculate
['spɛkjə,let]

托 雅 學

vi/vt 思索；推測　s1117

It was tempting to speculate about the outcome of the election, but journalists were careful to not announce a winner until the vote was fully counted.

推測選舉的結果是很吸引人的，但是選票最後完全數完後，記者們才小心宣佈當選者。

sphere
[sfɪr]

托 雅 學

n 球，球體；範圍，領域　s1118

Young as he is, Kerry has become famous in many spheres.

克里雖然年輕，卻已在許多領域出了名。

spin
[spɪn]

托 雅 學

n 旋轉，自轉；驚慌失措　s1119

He has been in a spin since the defeat.

他被擊敗以後一直驚慌失措。

spin
[spɪn]

托 雅 學

vi/vt 旋轉；紡紗；織網，吐絲　s1120

If you click the red heart on the screen, you can spin the Wheel of Fortune.

如果你點擊螢幕上的那個紅心，就可以旋轉幸運之輪。

spiral
['spaɪrəl]

托 雅 學

n 螺旋，螺線　s1121

The staircase rose in a spiral up to the lofted bedroom saving much needed space in the living room.

這個螺旋形樓梯上升到閣樓中的臥室，節省了許多客廳的空間。

spiral
['spaɪrəl]

托 雅 學

vi/vt 螺旋上升；盤旋；連續上升　s1122

The educational budget is expected to spiral upward but no official ever listens.

有人希望教育預算連續上升，但是沒有任何官員聽得進去。

spiritual
['spɪrɪtʃʊəl]

托 雅 學

adj 精神（上）的，心靈的　s1123

I found the story to be quite spiritual because of the character's discussions about life and death and the possibility of a resurrection.

我發現那個故事是有關心靈層面的，因為主角談論生死及復活的可能性。

S

227

spit
[spɪt]

托 雅 學

s1124

n 唾液；vt 吐，吐痰；飄落

Bring an umbrella along because the dark clouds are about to spit rain.

隨身帶把傘，因為烏雲就要飄落雨點了。

splash
[splæʃ]

托 雅 學

s1125

n 濺，飛濺聲；vi/vt 濺；潑

The girl splashed the milk and then ran away.

女孩濺出牛奶後逃跑了。

splendid
['splɛndɪd]

托 雅 學

s1126

adj 壯麗的，輝煌的；極好的

They sat down at a splendid table covered in the most amazing feast.

他們坐在極好的餐桌前，桌上擺滿了最美味的佳餚。

spontaneous
[spɑn'tɛnɪəs]

托 雅 學

s1127

adj 自發的，自然產生的

During the Christmas season in the United States, there can be spontaneous outbursts of singing in public places.

在美國耶誕節期間，公共場合裡有大量自發的歌唱活動。

squeeze
[skwiz]

托 雅 學

s1128

n 榨取，勒索；愛人，交往物件

He told me his main squeeze is a pretty blonde.

他告訴我他最要好的交往對象是個漂亮的金髮碧眼女孩。

squeeze
[skwiz]

托 雅 學

s1129

vi/vt 壓榨，擠，捏

Take hold of my hand, but don't squeeze too hard because I hurt my finger.

握住我的手，但請不要用力捏，因為我手指受傷了。

stabilize
['stebḷˌaɪz]

托 雅 學

s1130

vi/vt 穩定，安定，保持恆定

The hospital patient's condition began to stabilize after treatment.

經過治療後，醫院病人的情況開始穩定下來。

stain
[sten]

托 雅 學

s1131

vi/vt 沾汙；染色

Although these carpets are expensive, they won't stain easily.

雖然這些地毯很貴，卻不易沾汙。

stake
[stek]

托 雅 學

s1132

n 樁，標樁；賭注，利害關係

Each of us has a stake in the future of our country.

國家的未來對我們每個人都有利害關係。

stalk
[stɔk]

托 雅 學

s1133

n 莖，梗；**vi** 昂首闊步地走
The speaker proudly stalked out of the room after his presentation.
演講者在演說後很驕傲地昂首闊步走出房間。

stalk
[stɔk]

托 雅 學

s1134

vt 悄悄地跟蹤
The police officer stalked the suspect in secret.
員警悄悄跟蹤那名嫌疑犯。

staple
['stepl]

托 雅 學

s1135

n 主要產品；名產；主要成分，主食
Dry cereal is a staple in our family because everyone eats it for breakfast.
乾麥片是家中主食，因為所有人早餐時都會吃。

stare
[stɛr]

托 雅 學

s1136

vi/vt 盯，凝視
Much to my embarrassment, I found him staring at me with a smile.
令人很尷尬的是，我發現他帶著笑容凝視著我。

startle
['startl]

托 雅 學

s1137

vi/vt 驚嚇，（使）吃驚
I did not mean to startle you; I just wanted to ask you a question.
我無意嚇你，我只是想問你一個問題。

starve
[starv]

托 雅 學

s1138

vi/vt （使）餓死；挨餓
The poor orphan was starving to death and couldn't find any help.
孤兒即將餓死，求助無門。

statement
['stetmənt]

托 雅 學

s1139

n 聲明，陳述；帳單
The man's credit card statement showed a zero balance.
這位男士的信用卡帳單顯示餘額是零元。

static
['stætɪk]

托 雅 學

s1140

adj 靜態的，靜止的，靜力的
Despite the static population of the city, the local economy still prospered.
縱使城市人口變化趨於靜止，地方經濟依舊蓬勃發展。

statistics
[stə'tɪstɪks]

托 雅 學

s1141

n 統計；統計資料；統計學
There were a lot of statistics in the article about employment rates and inflation.
這篇文章裡有很多關於就業率和通貨膨脹的統計資料。

S

statue
['stætʃʊ]
托 雅 學

n 塑像，雕像

The statue of the founder of the university was cast in bronze and set in the middle of the campus.

大學創辦人的雕像以青銅鑄成，佇立在校園中央。

s1142

status
['stetəs]
托 雅 學

n 地位，身份；情形，狀況，狀態

Her Facebook status was updated, saying she was in a new relationship.

她把臉書狀態更新為與他人交往中。

s1143

steady
['stɛdɪ]
托 雅 學

adj 穩定的，不變的；堅定的

I need a steady ladder to stand on while I fix the ceiling fan.

我需要一個穩固的梯子以便我修理天花板上的電扇時可以站在上面。

s1144

steep
[stip]
托 雅 學

adj 陡峭的，險峻的；急劇升降的

The steep hill made the trip to the village extremely tough.

陡峭的山坡使得到村落的旅途格外艱辛。

s1145

steep
[stip]
托 雅 學

vi/vt 浸泡，沉浸

The cherries were steeped in salty water for two months.

這些櫻桃被浸泡在鹽水中兩個月了。

s1146

stem
[stɛm]
托 雅 學

vi 起源於，由…造成；堵（擋）住

The history of Singapore stemmed from different ethnic groups.

新加坡的歷史起源於不同的族群。

s1147

stereo
['stɛrɪo]
托 雅 學

adj 立體聲的；n 立體聲；立體音響裝置

The stereo in this theater was the best in town.

這家戲院的立體音響裝置是全鎮最棒的。

s1148

stereotype
['stɛrɪə,taɪp]
托 雅 學

n 陳規，老套，模式化；刻板印象；vt 使定型，使模式化

I don't think it's fair to stereotype a whole group of people because of one person you don't like.

我認為你因為一個你不喜歡的人就對整個團體有成見是不公平的。

s1149

sticky
['stɪkɪ]
托 雅 學

adj 黏的，黏性的；棘手的；（道路）泥濘的

The rice cake is quite sticky and sweet.

那塊米糕又黏又甜。

s1150

stimulate
['stɪmjə,let]

vi/vt 刺激，（使）興奮；激勵，鼓舞　s1151

The special soil is supposed to stimulate the growth of the roses.

這種特殊土壤應該可以刺激玫瑰的生長。

stimulus
['stɪmjələs]

托 雅 學

n 刺激（物），激勵（物）；促進因素　s1152

The government is always talking about an economic stimulus plan to boost the country's recovery.

政府總是在談論一個經濟刺激計畫，以促進這個國家的經濟復蘇。

stitch
[stɪtʃ]

托 雅 學

n 一針；肋部劇痛；**vi/vt** 縫（合）　s1153

The vet stitched the cut on the dog's head.

獸醫縫合那隻狗頭上的傷口。

stock
[stak]

托 雅 學

n 備料；庫存；股票；湯的原汁，湯頭　s1154

The recipe requires to add a cup of chicken stock to the soup.

這份食譜要求把一杯雞湯原汁加到湯裡。

stock
[stak]

托 雅 學

vi/vt 儲存　s1155

The goods are stocked in a big warehouse.

貨物被儲存在一個大的倉庫裡。

storage
['storɪdʒ]

托 雅 學

n 貯藏（量），保管；庫房　s1156

All the goods are kept in the storage before delivery.

所有的貨物在寄送前都存放在庫房。

strain
[stren]

托 雅 學

n 壓力；負擔，焦慮；**vi/vt** 拉緊；扭傷；竭盡全力　s1157

Relations between these two countries have been strained over some territorial disputes.

由於一些領土爭端，兩國關係已經很緊張了。

strained
['strend]

托 雅 學

adj 緊張的；勉強的，不自然的　s1158

The sisters had always had a strained relationship, which their mother attributed to jealousy and sibling rivalry.

這對姐妹關係總是很緊張，她們的母親將其歸咎於相互嫉妒和手足之爭。

strap
[stræp]

托 雅 學

n 皮帶，帶子　s1159

The strap is now detached from the bag and has to be stitched back.

這個包的帶子脫落了，得縫上去才行。

S

strap
[stræp]

托 雅 學

vt 用帶扣住，束牢；用繃帶包紮

Helen's baggage was so bulky that she decided to strap it down.

海倫的行李太大箱了，所以她決定用帶子束牢。

s1160

strategic
[strə'tidʒɪk]

托 雅 學

adj 戰略的，（戰略上）重要的

The bridge is located in a strategic position for military vehicles.

為了軍方車輛的運載，這座橋坐落在戰略上重要的位置。

s1161

strategy
['strætədʒɪ]

托 雅 學

n 戰略，策略；對策，政策

I consider it a sound strategy when a country makes a plan of action to defeat their enemy.

我認為一個國家採取行動計畫擊敗敵人是一個很好的策略。

s1162

stride
[straɪd]

托 雅 學

n 一大步；複數＝長足進步；**vi/vt** 大踏步走；跨越

The smooth stride of the racehorse was fascinating to watch.

這匹賽馬平穩的步伐讓人看得好著迷。

s1163

strike
[straɪk]

托 雅 學

n 罷工；**vt** 打，擊；攻擊；給……深刻印象

He struck me as being the best quarterback.

他是最好的四分衛，給我留下了很深刻的印象。

s1164

striking
['straɪkɪŋ]

托 雅 學

adj 顯著的；惹人注目的，容貌出眾的

The fashion model has a striking appearance; she is so tall and her features are perfect.

這個時尚模特兒的外表真惹人注目，她長得很高，又有非常完美的五官。

s1165

strive
[straɪv]

托 雅 學

vi 奮鬥，努力

Black people suffered a lot from discrimination in the past and had to strive for their human rights.

黑人以前飽受歧視之苦，他們只能努力爭取人權。

s1166

stumble
['stʌmbl]

托 雅 學

n/vi 絆（摔）倒；結結巴巴說

He ran across the yard, careful not to stumble on the large root of the oak tree.

他小心穿過庭院，以防被大橡樹根絆倒。

s1167

stun
[stʌn]

托 雅 學

vt 使…失去知覺；使目瞪口呆，使吃驚

The explosion in the parking lot stunned all the moviegoers.

看電影的民眾全都被停車場的爆炸嚇呆了。

s1168

subject
['sʌbdʒɪkt]

托 雅 學

s1169

adj 隸屬的；**vt** 受制於；使經歷，經受

Oil prices these days are subject to many factors, including energy policies.

時下油價受許多因素影響，包括能源政策。

subject
['sʌbdʒɪkt]

托 雅 學

s1170

n 主題；學科

Math was my brother's favorite subject at school.

數學是我弟弟在學校最喜歡的科目。

subject
[ˌsəb'dʒɛkt]

托 雅 學

s1171

vt 使隸屬；受制於

Marsha wasn't going to subject herself to being made a fool of.

瑪莎不會使自己成為被愚弄的對象。

submarine
['sʌbmə,rin]

托 雅 學

s1172

adj 水底的，海底的；**n** 潛水艇

Submarines became increasingly important strategic weapons during the 20th century.

潛水艇在二十世紀變成日益重要的戰略武器。

submit
[səb'mɪt]

托 雅 學

s1173

vi/vt （使）服從，屈服；呈送，提交

He was asked to submit a written request to the office to take his vacation.

他必須向辦公室提交書面申請才能休假。

subscribe
[səb'skraɪb]

托 雅 學

s1174

vi 訂閱，訂購；同意；**vt** 捐助，贊助

I want to subscribe to some magazines but I never have time to read them.

我想要訂閱雜誌，但是卻從來沒有時間去閱讀。

subscription
[səb'skrɪpʃən]

托 雅 學

s1175

n 捐獻；簽署；訂閱

The subscription fee for the monthly magazine has already gone up, discouraging its readers to renew subsequently.

這本月刊的訂閱費已上漲，讓讀者望而卻步不再續訂。

substitute
['sʌbstə,tjut]

托 雅 學

s1176

n 代替者；替身；代用品；**vi/vt** 代替，替換

You can substitute brown sugar for white in the recipe but the cookies will taste slightly different.

你可以將食譜裡的紅糖以白糖代替，但餅乾嘗起來會有一些不同。

subtract
[səb'trækt]

托 雅 學

s1177

vi/vt 減（去）

I forgot to subtract a bill from my budget this month and I may have spent too much.

這個月我忘記從預算中減去一筆帳單，我可能花太多錢了。

S

succession
[sək'sɛʃən]

托 雅 學

n 連續，系列；繼任，繼承

The family suffered through a succession of bad years.

這個家庭多年來連續遭受厄運。

s1178

successive
[sək'sɛsɪv]

托 雅 學

adj 接連的，連續的

Germany has seen robust economic growth for two successive years.

德國連續兩年經濟增長強勁。

s1179

successor
[sək'sɛsə]

托 雅 學

n 接替的人或事物；繼任者

The coach picked one of his assistants to be his successor at the end of the year.

那個教練在年終時挑選他其中一個助理當繼任者。

s1180

summarize
['sʌmə,raɪz]

托 雅 學

vt 概括，總結

Mary tried to summarize her essay as clearly as she could to her class.

瑪莉盡力試著對全班清晰地總結她的文章。

s1181

summary
['sʌmərɪ]

托 雅 學

adj 概括的；速決的；n 摘要，概要；一覽

The general wrote a summary report of life in the army in the letter to his wife.

這名將軍在寫給妻子的信中，概括報告了軍中生活。

s1182

superb
[sʊ'pɝb]

托 雅 學

adj 極好的，傑出的；華麗的

The violinist performing the new concerto was superb.

演奏這首新協奏曲的小提琴家非常出色。

s1183

superficial
['supə'fɪʃəl]

托 雅 學

adj 表面的；膚淺的，淺薄的

The cut on her arm was superficial, but her mother panicked and began to scream with alarm.

她手臂上的傷口是表面傷口，但她媽媽慌了手腳並開始驚慌大喊。

s1184

supersonic
[,supə'sanɪk]

托 雅 學

adj 超音速的，超聲波的；n 超聲波，超聲頻

Supersonic aircrafts first came into being in the 1960s, mostly for military purposes.

超音速飛機於1960年代出現，主要用於軍事目的。

s1185

superstition
[,supə'stɪʃən]

托 雅 學

n 迷信，迷信的觀念習俗

There is an old superstition that says if you break a mirror, you will have years of bad luck.

古老的迷信說打破鏡子會帶來許多年的壞運氣。

s1186

supervise
['supəˌvaɪz]

vt 管理，監督，指導 s1187

Could you please supervise the group and show them around?

可以請你指導這個團體並帶他們四處瞧瞧嗎？

supplement
['sʌpləmənt]

n 補遺；增刊；附錄 s1188

The literary supplement of the local newspapers is very popular with citizens.

這份當地報紙的文學增刊很受市民歡迎。

supplement
['sʌpləˌmɛnt]

vt 增刊，補充 s1189

The doctor suggested I supplement my diet with vitamin C pills during cold and flu season.

醫生建議我在寒冷季節及流感季節時用維生素C補充我的日常飲食。

supplementary
[ˌsʌpləˈmɛntəri]

adj 增補的，追加的，補充的 s1190

At the end of the meeting, he raised a supplementary question regarding the trend towards the falling value of storage.

在會議結束時，他提了個補充問題，是關於庫存價值下降趨勢的。

supply
[səˈplaɪ]

n 供應，供應量；**vi/vt** 供給，供應，補足 s1191

This big warehouse can supply canned corn to all of the stores in the city.

這間倉庫很大，能供應玉米罐頭給這個城市的所有商店。

supreme
[səˈprim]

adj 極度的，最重要的；至高的，最高的 s1192

The firefighter who rescued the little girl was a man of supreme courage.

營救小女孩的消防員是一位具有極度勇氣的人。

S

surgeon
['sɝˌdʒən]

n 外科醫生 s1193

The surgeon had a reputation for performing the most difficult operations with ease.

這位外科醫生以輕易完成高難度手術而聞名。

surgery
['sɝˌdʒərɪ]

n 外科，外科學；手術室，診療室；手術 s1194

The doctor suggested to the patient that he should undergo heart surgery.

醫生建議該病人接受心臟手術。

surpass
[səˈpæs]

vt 超過，勝過 s1195

The violin instructor was thrilled to see her student surpass her own artistic abilities and hoped he would do well.

這個小提琴老師很興奮地看到學生的藝術能力勝過她，並期望學生能表現得很好。

surrender
[sə'rɛndə]
托 雅 學

n 投降，認輸
The surrender of Japan marked the end of World War Ⅱ.
日本投降標誌著第二次世界大戰的結束。

s1196

surrender
[sə'rɛndə]
托 雅 學

vi/vt 投降，屈服；放棄，交出
The general came out in uniform to surrender to the opposing army.
將軍身著軍服向敵軍投降。

s1197

survey
[sə've]
托 雅 學

n/vi/vt 全面審視，調查；俯瞰，眺望
The city took a survey of the grounds to decide if they were appropriate for development.
市政府對土地進行了調查，以便決定它們是否適合開發。

s1198

survival
[sə'vaɪvl]
托 雅 學

n 倖存，生存；倖存者，殘存物
The survival of many endangered animals now depends on animal protection activists.
很多瀕臨絕種的動物現在都依賴動物保護者才能倖存。

s1199

survive
[sə'vaɪv]
托 雅 學

vi/vt 倖免於，倖存；存活；比…長命
This cancer is one of the treatable ones and she is likely to survive for many years.
這種癌症是可治療的癌症之一，她很可能會再多活許多年。

s1200

suspect
['səspɛkt]
托 雅 學

n 嫌疑犯；可疑物
The detective had a suspect in the case but needed more evidence to arrest him.
偵探在此案中鎖定了一位嫌疑人，但需要更多證據來逮捕他。

s1201

suspect
[sə'spɛkt]
托 雅 學

vi/vt 猜想；懷疑；察覺
The detective suspected that there might be a mastermind behind this robbery.
這名偵探懷疑，此起搶劫案背後可能有一個策劃者。

s1202

suspicious
[sə'spɪʃəs]
托 雅 學

adj 可疑的，多疑的，疑心的
His wife was suspicious that he had forgotten their anniversary, but then a bouquet of roses was delivered to her office that afternoon.
他的太太疑心他忘記結婚週年紀念日了，但是下午時就有一束玫瑰花送到她的辦公室。

s1203

sustain
[sə'sten]
托 雅 學

vt 撐住；維持；經受；供養，贍養；支援
The talk show host can sustain everyone's interest till the end.
這個脫口秀主持人能夠維持每個人的興趣直到節目尾聲。

s1204

236

swell
[swɛl]

托 雅 學

n/vi/vt 腫脹，膨脹；增大，增加

s1205

Her leg began to swell where the snake had bitten.

她腿上被蛇咬的地方開始腫起來了。

swift
[swɪft]

托 雅 學

adj/adv 快的（地）；敏捷的（地）；立刻的（地）

s1206

The professor did not expect such a swift response from the usually quiet student.

這位教授怎麼也沒料到，平時安靜的學生這回反應竟然如此敏捷。

swift
[swɪft]

托 雅 學

n 雨燕

s1207

The bird watcher caught a glimpse of a swift flying across the night sky.

這名賞鳥人士瞥見一隻雨燕掠過夜空。

symbol
['sɪmbl̩]

托 雅 學

n 符號，標誌；象徵

s1208

The Christmas tree, the wreath, and garland made from evergreen trees and shrubs are symbols of eternal life.

由常綠樹木和灌木叢做成的聖誕樹、花環和花冠都是永生的象徵。

symbolic
[sɪm'bɑlɪk]

托 雅 學

adj 作為象徵的，象徵性的

s1209

The lighting of candles during a wedding ceremony is symbolic of two people uniting as one.

在婚禮上點燃蠟燭象徵著兩個人合為一體。

symbolize
['sɪmbl̩ˌaɪz]

托 雅 學

vt 象徵

s1210

The sign of the cross is used to symbolize Christianity.

十字架的標誌是用來象徵基督教的。

sympathetic
[ˌsɪmpə'θɛtɪk]

托 雅 學

adj 有同情心的；贊同的

s1211

The teacher was sympathetic to the boy's struggles and offered to tutor him after school.

老師對這個男孩的困境深感同情，並給他提供課後輔導。

sympathetic
[ˌsɪmpə'θɛtɪk]

托 雅 學

n 交感神經

s1212

Our sympathetic basically controls how we respond to emergencies, such as the increase of breathing rates.

我們的交感神經控制我們對緊急情況的應變方式，呼吸加速便是一例。

sympathy
['sɪmpəθɪ]

托 雅 學

n 同情；同情心；贊同；慰問

s1213

I have deep sympathy for the people who lost their homes and all of their possessions in the fire.

我對那些在火災中失去家園及財產的人們深表同情。

S

symphony
['sɪmfənɪ]

s1214

n 交響樂，交響曲

The city symphony band was playing a concert of Beethoven in spring.

這個城市交響樂團春天時會舉辦貝多芬的演奏會。

symptom
['sɪmptəm]

s1215

n （疾病的）症狀；（不好事情的）徵兆，表徵

His only symptom in the first week of his illness was a persistent cough.

他第一週生病的唯一症狀是持續咳嗽。

synonym
['sɪnə,nɪm]

s1216

n 同義字，近義詞

"Tremendous" and "enormous" are synonyms and are often used interchangeably.

Tremendous 和 enormous 是同義字，使用時常常可以互換。

字彙能力檢查表

先自我檢驗是否瞭解以下初階單字，若有不清楚者，請先開啟光碟中的電子書複習。

☐tablet	☐thoughtful	☐tonic	☐treat
☐tackle	☐throat	☐topic	☐treatment
☐tag	☐thumb	☐torch	☐trial
☐tag	☐thunder	☐toss	☐triple
☐talent	☐thunderstorm	☐total	☐triple
☐talented	☐tick	☐total	☐trunk
☐tap	☐tide	☐touchy	☐trust
☐tap	☐tighten	☐tough	☐tube
☐tar	☐tile	☐tour	☐tuition
☐team	☐time-consuming	☐tour	☐tunnel
☐tear	☐timetable	☐towel	☐turkey
☐tense	☐tip	☐tower	☐tutor
☐term	☐tip	☐trade	☐twig
☐terrible	☐title	☐traffic	☐twilight
☐terrific	☐toast	☐training	☐twinkle
☐thigh	☐toast	☐translation	☐typical
☐thirst	☐tongue	☐treat	

tame
[tem]

托 雅 學

adj 馴服的，溫順的；沉悶的，乏味的 `t1001`

Most house cats are very tame and enjoy the companionship of humans.

大多數家裡養的貓都是非常溫馴的，並且喜歡跟人類做伴。

tame
[tem]

托 雅 學

vi/vt 馴服 `t1002`

It is incredible how the man can tame the fierce lion.

真是令人難以置信，這個人這麼會馴服兇猛的獅子。

target
['tɑrgət]

托 雅 學

n 目標，物件，靶子 `t1003`

He aimed at a point just above the target and shot the arrow right into the center.

他瞄準靶子上方的一個點並將箭射中靶心。

tariff
['tærɪf]

托 雅 學

n 關稅，稅率；（旅館、飯店等的）價目表，收費表 `t1004`

The Chinese government is expected to increase the tariff on imported luxury items.

中國政府估計要提高進口奢侈品的關稅。

task
[tæsk]

托 雅 學

n 任務，作業；工作 `t1005`

He was unable to finish the assigned tasks within the given time.

他無法在給定的時間內完成被安排的工作。

tax
[tæks]

托 雅 學

n 稅；**vt** 對…徵稅，使負重擔 `t1006`

This new government is empowered by the Congress to tax its citizens.

這個新政府被國會授權對人民進行征稅。

tease
[tiz]

托 雅 學

n （愛）戲弄他人者；戲弄；**vt** 戲弄，取笑，挑逗 `t1007`

Stop teasing that cat; it might scratch you!

不要再戲弄那隻貓了。它可能會抓你！

technical
['tɛknɪkl]

托 雅 學

adj 技術（性）的，工藝的；專門性的；專業性的 `t1008`

The description of the book is very technical, but you can read it just as a story.

這本書的描述非常專業，但是你可以把它當故事來閱讀。

technician
[tɛk'nɪʃən]

托 雅 學

n 技術員，技師，技工 `t1009`

The technician will be here shortly to repair the machine.

那個技術人員很快會到這裡來修理那台機器。

technique
[tɛk'nik]

n 技巧，手藝，技能；技術，工藝

t1010

The chef studied French cooking techniques in Paris before opening his own restaurant.

這個主廚開自己的餐廳之前在巴黎學了法式烹飪技巧。

technology
[tɛk'nɑlədʒɪ]

n 科學技術，工業技術；應用科學

t1011

The technology used in cellular phones was originally developed for portable video game players.

運用於手機的技術原本是為了電子遊戲玩家而研發的。

tedious
['tidɪəs]

adj 乏味的，單調的，冗長的

t1012

The introduction to the novel was tedious.

這本小說的簡介很乏味。

temperature
['tɛmprətʃə]

n 溫度，體溫；熱度，發燒

t1013

The temperature outside was well below freezing and was not likely to rise.

外頭的溫度遠低於冰點，而且也不太可能升溫。

temporary
['tɛmpə,rɛrɪ]

adj 暫時的，臨時的

t1014

She moved into a temporary apartment when she looked for a house to buy in the area.

當她在這個區域找要買的房子的時候，她搬進了一間臨時公寓。

tenant
['tɛnənt]

n 承租人，房客，佃戶；**vt** 租借，承租

t1015

The tenant in the upstairs apartment is very noisy.

樓上公寓的房客非常吵。

tendency
['tɛndənsɪ]

n 趨勢，趨向，傾向

t1016

He has a tendency to lower the volume of his voice when he becomes nervous.

當他變得緊張時，他傾向於降低音量。

tender
['tɛndə]

adj 嫩的；敏感的；溫柔的

t1017

The meat on the barbecued ribs was so tender that it fell off the bone.

燒烤肋排上的肉嫩到骨肉分離了。

tender
['tɛndə]

vi/vt 提出，提供；投標

t1018

Jack has tendered his resignation through the governmental agency.

傑克已經透過政府機構提出辭呈。

T

tense
[tɛns]
托 雅 學

adj 繃緊的；緊張的；**vi/vt** 拉緊；（使）緊張
It is hard for me to act naturally when I am tense.
當我緊張的時候，我很難表現自如。

t1019

tension
['tɛnʃən]
托 雅 學

n 緊張（狀態）；拉緊，繃緊；張力，拉力
The tension in the room was very high while they waited to see if he has won the election.
當他們等著看他是否贏得選舉的時候，房間內的氣氛非常緊張。

t1020

terminal
['tɝmɪnl]
托 雅 學

adj 晚期的；終點的；期末的
The bus is driving toward the terminal station.
這輛巴士正駛往終點站。

t1021

terminal
['tɝmɪnl]
托 雅 學

n 終點（站）；航空站
He ran to the airport terminal and hoped he would not miss his flight home.
他趕到機場航空站，希望不會錯過回家的班機。

t1022

terminate
['tɝməˌnet]
托 雅 學

vi/vt （使）結束，（使）停止
He received a letter from the company informing him that they would terminate his employment on the first day of the month.
他收到公司的信，通知他公司將於這個月第一天停止雇用他。

t1023

terminology
[ˌtɝməˈnɑlədʒɪ]
托 雅 學

n 術語學，術語
Ordinary people are not familiar with medical terminology.
一般人對醫學術語都不熟悉。

t1024

terrify
['tɛrəˌfaɪ]
托 雅 學

vt 使害怕，使驚恐
The sound of the tornado sirens always terrifies me.
龍捲風警報器的聲響總是讓我感到害怕。

t1025

terror
['tɛrə]
托 雅 學

n 恐怖；可怕的人（事）
She felt a paralyzing terror as she realized that there was someone else in her house.
當她察覺屋子裡有其他人時，她感到一陣無力的恐懼。

t1026

text
[tɛkst]
托 雅 學

n 正文，文本；原文；教科書
You may refer to the additional text of the report for more concise details.
要知道更多精確的細節，你可以參考報導的附加文本。

t1027

242

theft
[θɛft]
托 雅 學

n 偷竊（行為），偷竊罪
t1028
The store owner reported the theft to the police and claimed it on his insurance.
店主將盜竊案報告給員警，並向保險公司索賠。

theme
[θim]
托 雅 學

n 題目；詞幹；主旋律
t1029
We are told that this Saturday's party has a Hawaiian theme, so please dress appropriately.
我們被告知這週六的派對是夏威夷主題的，所以請穿著適當。

theoretical
[ˌθiəˈrɛtɪk]
托 雅 學

adj 理論（上）的
t1030
The course will focus on the theoretical aspect, so we will not be doing experiments.
這堂課將會著重於理論的方面，所以我們不會做實驗。

theory
[ˈθiərɪ]
托 雅 學

n 理論；見解，看法
t1031
The detective had a theory that the murderer was a friend of the victim's, but he needed more evidence to make sure.
偵探推測兇手是被害者的朋友，但是他需要更多的證據來確認。

thesis
[ˈθisɪs]
托 雅 學

n 論文；論題，論點
t1032
Bill is conducting an empirical experiment for his thesis.
比爾正在為他的論文做一個實證實驗。

thorough
[ˈθɝo]
托 雅 學

adj 徹底的，完全的；精心的
t1033
Her investigation report was very thorough and she was praised for accuracy and fairness.
她的調查報告非常徹底，她也因準確性和公正性備受讚揚。

thrill
[θrɪl]
托 雅 學

n 一陣激動或恐懼
t1034
It was a real thrill to personally meet my idol.
遇見我的偶像真是太令人激動了。

T

thrill
[θrɪl]
托 雅 學

vi/vt 激動；（使）毛骨悚然
t1035
I was thrilled by simply being able to stand on the stage.
單單因為能站上這個舞臺，我就很激動。

thrive
[θraɪv]
托 雅 學

vi 興旺，繁榮
t1036
I am glad to see that your bakery business is finally starting to thrive.
我很高興看到你的麵包店生意終於開始興旺了。

throughout
[θru'aʊt]

托 雅 學

adv/prep 到處，自始至終，遍及，貫穿　t1037

Since the speaker was an important presenter, everyone paid full attention throughout his entire lecture.

因為這個演講者是一位很重要的人，每個人自始至終都在專心聽課。

thump
[θʌmp]

托 雅 學

vi/vt 重擊；強有力地跳動　t1038

The kidnapper thumped the rich man on the head.

綁匪往富人的頭上重重一擊。

tidy
['taɪdɪ]

托 雅 學

adj 整潔的，整齊的　t1039

Even though her house was tiny, it was always very tidy and well-organized.

即便她的房子很小，它總是非常整齊又井然有序。

tidy
['taɪdɪ]

托 雅 學

vi/vt 整理，收拾　t1040

Mandy, please tidy your room as soon as possible!

曼蒂，請儘快整理你的房間！

tilt
[tɪlt]

托 雅 學

n 傾側，傾斜　t1041

The second shelf of the bookcase has a tilt to the back.

書櫥的第二層有一點向後傾斜。

tilt
[tɪlt]

托 雅 學

vi/vt （使）傾側，（使）傾斜　t1042

Compared to your opinions, I'm tilted more toward Maggie's.

相較於你的意見，我傾向於同意瑪姬的。

timid
['tɪmɪd]

托 雅 學

adj 膽怯的，怯懦的　t1043

She was a timid child, but she grew up to be an assertive adult.

她小時候個性膽怯，長大後卻充滿自信。

tissue
['tɪʃʊ]

托 雅 學

n 織物，薄絹，紙巾；（動植物的）組織　t1044

She wiped the sweat on her forehead with a soft facial tissue.

她用柔軟的面紙擦掉額頭上的汗水。

token
['tokən]

托 雅 學

adj 象徵性的　t1045

Winners of the game will just get some token prizes.

這項比賽的獲勝者只會得到一些象徵性的獎品。

token
['tokən]

托 雅 學

t1046

n 表示，標誌，記號；代用硬幣
He gave the operator his token and boarded the train.
他付給駕駛員代幣並上了火車。

tolerance
['talərəns]

托 雅 學

t1047

n 寬容，容忍，忍受；耐藥力；公差
Children usually have a low tolerance to pain.
小孩子通常不太能忍受疼痛。

tolerant
['talərənt]

托 雅 學

t1048

adj 容忍的，寬容的；有耐藥力的
Teachers should be tolerant of different types of students.
老師應該寬容不同類型的學生。

toll
[tol]

托 雅 學

t1049

n （道路、橋等的）通行費；犧牲，死傷人數
It's illegal to refuse to pay tolls on an expressway.
在高速公路上拒絕支付通行費是不合法的。

tornado
[tɔr'nedo]

托 雅 學

t1050

n 龍捲風
To be caught in a tornado is an extremely dangerous situation.
被困在龍捲風裡是一種極其危險的情況。

torture
['tɔrtʃə]

托 雅 學

t1051

n 拷問；折磨，痛苦
It is shocking to realize that torture is only recently considered a crime against human rights.
拷問直到最近才被視為違反人權的罪行，著實令人震驚。

torture
['tɔrtʃə]

托 雅 學

t1052

vt 拷問，拷打；折磨，磨難
The gangsters tortured the man until he signed the unfair contract.
那些流氓折磨那個男人，直到他簽下那紙不公平的契約。

tourism
['turɪzəm]

托 雅 學

t1053

n 旅遊業，觀光業
The local government should find better ways to promote tourism.
地方政府須找到更好的方法來促進旅遊業。

tourist
['turɪst]

托 雅 學

t1054

n 旅遊者，觀光客；巡迴比賽的運動員
After the little town appeared in a movie, it began to attract tourists from all over the world.
這個小城鎮在電影中出現後，開始吸引來自全世界的遊客。

T

toxic
['taksɪk]

托 雅 學

adj 有毒的;中毒的　　　　　t1055

The fumes from the factory were toxic and the government decided to close it down.

工廠排出來的刺鼻氣體是有毒的,政府已決定關閉這家工廠。

trace
[tres]

托 雅 學

n 痕跡,蹤跡;極少量　　　　t1056

He secretly moved from town without leaving any trace of himself.

他秘密地搬出了城鎮,不留任何痕跡。

trace
[tres]

托 雅 學

vi/vt 描繪;跟蹤,追蹤　　　　t1057

The history of that painting can be traced back to the 1950s.

那幅畫作的歷史可追溯到20世紀50年代。

track
[træk]

托 雅 學

n 跑道;軌跡,足跡,腳步　　　t1058

The hunter followed the rabbit tracks into the woods.

獵人跟隨著兔子的蹤跡進入了森林。

track
[træk]

托 雅 學

vi/vt 追蹤,跟蹤　　　　　　t1059

The police used electronic devices to track down the gangsters.

員警用電子設備追蹤歹徒。

tract
[trækt]

托 雅 學

n (身體器官的)道;一大片土地;傳單　t1060

This large tract of land is owned by a famous politician.

這一大片土地為一個有名的政治家所有。

tradition
[trə'dɪʃən]

托 雅 學

n 傳統,慣例;傳說　　　　　t1061

My family has a strange tradition of singing Christmas carols very badly after we finish decorating the Christmas tree.

我們家有個奇怪的傳統,就是在裝飾完聖誕樹後五音不全地唱聖誕歌。

traditional
[trə'dɪʃənl]

托 雅 學

adj 傳統的,慣例的　　　　　t1062

Some patients turn to traditional Chinese medicine only after Western medicine is ineffective for them.

一些病人在使用西藥沒效果後才轉用傳統的中藥。

tragedy
['trædʒədɪ]

托 雅 學

n 悲劇;慘事,災難　　　　　t1063

The play was a tragedy and five characters died in the last scene.

這齣戲是個悲劇,最後一幕中五位角色死了。

tragic
['trædʒɪk]

托 雅 學

t1064

adj 悲劇的，悲慘的

Her marriage with that abusive man led to her tragic death not long afterwards.

她和那個會虐待人的男人的婚姻讓她不久後悲慘地離世了。

trail
[trel]

托 雅 學

t1065

n 痕跡；小路；線索

The thief did not leave any trail, which made the police investigation particularly difficult.

那個小偷沒有留下任何痕跡，這使得員警的調查非常困難。

trail
[trel]

托 雅 學

t1066

vi/vt 跟蹤，追蹤；拖，拖曳

The dog trailed the smells on streets in order to find its master.

為了找到主人，這隻狗追蹤著街道上的氣味。

tramp
[træmp]

托 雅 學

t1067

n/vi/vt 步行，沉重的腳步聲（走）；流浪；踩

Before entering this inn, the traveler has tramped around the countryside for three days.

進入這家小旅館之前，這名旅客已經在鄉村周圍遊走三天了。

tramp
[træmp]

托 雅 學

t1068

n 流浪者

The kind man gave a blanket to the shivering tramp.

那個好心的男人給了顫抖的流浪者一條毯子。

transcript
['træn,skrɪpt]

托 雅 學

t1069

n 抄本，謄本

The drama provides its transcript to viewers on its official website.

那齣戲在官方網站上向觀眾提供文字稿。

transfer
[træns'fɝ]

托 雅 學

t1070

n/vi/vt 轉移，轉換，轉讓，過戶，遷移；改乘

He transferred money from his savings account in order to pay his bills.

他從存款帳戶將錢轉出以支付帳單。

T

transform
[træns'fɔrm]

托 雅 學

t1071

vi/vt 改變，轉化，改造

She was able to transform the old run-down shack into a beautiful little two room cottage.

她成功地把破舊的棚屋改造成一個漂亮的兩室小木屋。

transformation
[,trænsfɚ'meʃən]

托 雅 學

t1072

n 變化；改造；轉變

After a dramatic transformation, the mall successfully reopened and attracted many more customers than before.

經過了一個戲劇性的改造，這個百貨公司成功地重新開張並且吸引比以前更多的顧客。

transit
['trænsɪt]

托 雅 學

n 運送；過境；交通運輸系統　　t1073

She likes using the public transit system because she does not like to drive.

她喜歡搭乘公共交通工具，因為她不喜歡開車。

transport
['træns,pɔrt]

托 雅 學

vt 運輸，運送，搬運　　t1074

The ship will transport the cargo all the way to Chile and return with a load of imported goods.

這艘船會將貨物一路運送到智利，並且帶著一整船的進口貨回航。

transportation
[,trænspə'teʃən]

托 雅 學

n 運輸，運輸系統；運載工具　　t1075

Have you decided whether to use public transportation or drive to work?

你決定要搭乘公共交通運輸工具或開車上班了沒？

trap
[træp]

托 雅 學

n 陷阱，圈套　　t1076

Before civilization, humans set up traps in the woods to help them catch their prey.

人類文明開始之前，人類常在森林裡設下陷阱來幫助他們狩獵。

trap
[træp]

托 雅 學

vi/vt 設圈套誘捕；（使）中圈套　　t1077

The prisoner was trapped by the police as he tried to escape.

犯人試圖逃跑時中了警方的圈套。

tremble
['trɛmbl̩]

托 雅 學

n 戰慄，顫抖　　t1078

There was a slight tremble in the reporter's voice when he talked about the earthquake.

當記者談論地震的時候，他的聲音有點兒顫抖。

tremble
['trɛmbl̩]

托 雅 學

vi/vt 發抖，顫抖；撼動　　t1079

Her lip began to tremble from the cold and she hurried inside to drink hot tea.

她的嘴唇因為寒冷開始顫抖，於是她急忙進屋喝熱茶。

tremendous
[trɪ'mɛndəs]

托 雅 學

adj 巨大的，極大的　　t1080

The doctors and paramedics made a tremendous effort to save the man's life.

醫生和醫務人員做出了非常大的努力來救這個男子的生命。

trend
[trɛnd]

托 雅 學

n 傾向，趨勢　　t1081

Economists constantly analyze data to help predict the future trend of the economy.

經濟學家不斷地分析資料，以便推測未來的經濟趨勢。

trend
[trɛnd]
托 雅 學

vi 伸向，傾向   t1082
Teenagers have recently trended more toward Korean dramas than Japanese dramas.
青少年近來更傾向於韓劇而不是日劇。

tribe
[traɪb]
托 雅 學

n 種族，部落；（植物、動物）族，類   t1083
The cultures of the Native American tribes are vastly different from one another.
印第安部落的文化彼此間大相徑庭。

trick
[trɪk]
托 雅 學

n 詭計，騙局；惡作劇；竅門   t1084
The naughty boy played a trick on his classmate.
調皮的男孩對他的同班同學惡作劇。

trick
[trɪk]
托 雅 學

vt 欺騙，哄騙   t1085
I tricked my father into giving me some pocket money.
我騙我父親給我一些零用錢。

trifle
['traɪf!]
托 雅 學

n 少量；小事，瑣事；小玩意兒   t1086
He bought his daughter a trifle at the gift shop, but she thought it was a special treasure.
他在禮品店給女兒買了一個小玩意兒，但她以為是特別貴重的物品。

trifle
['traɪf!]
托 雅 學

vi/vt 玩弄，嬉耍；浪費，虛度   t1087
Tom usually trifles with his younger sister and makes her cry.
湯姆經常戲弄他妹妹，惹得她哭。

trigger
['trɪgə]
托 雅 學

n 扳機；觸發，引起   t1088
Don't pull the trigger if you are not ready.
在你還沒準備好之前，不要扣下扳機。

T

trigger
['trɪgə]
托 雅 學

vt 觸發，引起   t1089
His hatred for his ex-girlfriend triggered this tragedy.
他對前女友的憎恨引起了這場悲劇。

trim
[trɪm]
托 雅 學

n 修剪，整理；妝點，佈置   t1090
The bush in my backyard needs a trim.
我家後院的灌木叢需要修剪一下。

trim
[trɪm]

托 雅 學

vt 修剪，整理；妝點，佈置
The hairdresser carefully trims the groom's hair for his wedding.
髮型師小心翼翼地替新郎整理頭髮以參加婚禮。

t1091

trivial
['trɪvɪəl]

托 雅 學

adj 瑣碎的，無足輕重的
The professor politely answered all of his student's questions although he felt that they were trivial.
教授客氣地回答了學生所有的問題，雖然他覺得學生的問題很瑣碎。

t1092

tropical
['trɑpɪkl̩]

托 雅 學

adj 熱帶的
I want to go to a tropical island for my next vacation.
下次我希望去一個熱帶島嶼度假。

t1093

trustworthy
['trʌst,wɝði]

托 雅 學

adj 值得信賴的，可靠的
Paula is very trustworthy especially when it comes to opening the store on time.
寶拉是個可靠的人，尤其是開店營業特別準時。

t1094

tug
[tʌg]

托 雅 學

n 拖；苦幹；拖船
The government used several tugs to remove the airplane's wreckage from the harbor.
政府動用許多拖船來移動那架飛機的殘骸。

t1095

tug
[tʌg]

托 雅 學

vi/vt 用力拖（或拉）；苦幹
The skinny girl tugged on the door, but it still didn't open.
那個瘦弱的女孩用力拉門，但門依舊沒開。

t1096

turbulence
['tɝbjələns]

托 雅 學

n 混亂，動亂，騷亂，騷動；大氣湍流，亂流
When the plane started hitting turbulence, the passengers experienced a bumpy ride.
當飛機開始遭遇亂流後，乘客們經歷了一段顛簸的旅程。

t1097

turbulent
['tɝbjələnt]

托 雅 學

adj 狂暴的；無秩序的
It has been a turbulent year for the world's economy.
今年是世界經濟動盪的一年。

t1098

turnover
['tɝn,ovɚ]

托 雅 學

n 翻倒；人員調整；（資金等）周轉；營業額
My grandmother owns a food stand and it has a turnover of $100 a day.
我祖母擁有一個小吃攤，每日營業額達一百美金。

t1099

twist
[twɪst]

托 雅 學

t1100

n 擰;歪曲,曲折
The mountain is famous for its numerous twists.
這座山因其數不清的轉彎而聞名。

twist
[twɪst]

托 雅 學

t1101

vi/vt 撚,擰,扭曲;蜿蜒曲折而行
The criminal twisted the truth to his own advantage, not truthful in his statement to the police.
犯人為了對自己有利扭曲了事實,並且對警方做了不真實的陳述。

T

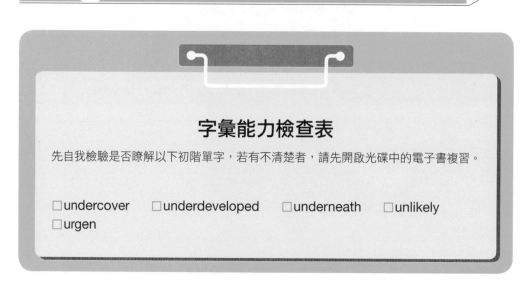

U

字彙能力檢查表

先自我檢驗是否瞭解以下初階單字，若有不清楚者，請先開啟光碟中的電子書複習。

☐undercover ☐underdeveloped ☐underneath ☐unlikely
☐urgen

---

ultimate
['ʌltəmɪt]
托 雅 學

adj 最後的，最終的；根本的；最好的　　　　u1001
My grandmother has the ultimate recipe for apple pie and she won't tell anyone how to make it.
我奶奶有做蘋果派最好的食譜，而她不會告訴任何人怎麼做。

---

ultimately
['ʌltəmɪtlɪ]
托 雅 學

adv 最終，最後　　　　u1002
After 10 weeks of intense training, he ultimately won the competition.
在十個星期的密集訓練之後他終於贏得了比賽。

---

unbearable
[ʌn'bɛrəbl̩]
托 雅 學

adj 難堪的，忍受不了的　　　　u1003
The wait for summer vacation can be unbearable for school children.
對上學的孩子來說，等待暑假是難以忍受的。

---

unconditional
[ˌʌnkən'dɪʃənəl]
托 雅 學

adj 無條件的　　　　u1004
Lily's parents gave her unconditional love and support throughout her childhood.
莉莉的父母在她童年時一直給她無條件的愛和支持。

---

unconscious
[ʌn'kɑnʃəs]
托 雅 學

adj 失去知覺的，不省人事的　　　　u1005
He fell down unconscious after being out in the heat all day and had to be taken to the hospital.
他在戶外炎熱的天氣裡待了一整天後中暑暈倒，只能被送往醫院。

uncover
[ʌnˈkʌvɚ]

托 雅 學

vi/vt 揭開，揭露，發現　　　　　　u1006

The archaeological exploration was to uncover how the dinosaurs died millions of years ago.

考古學的探索是要發現恐龍數百萬年前是怎麼死的。

underestimate
[ˈʌndɚˈɛstəˌmet]

托 雅 學

vt 低估，看輕　　　　　　u1007

Do not underestimate the ability of a child to understand some adult issues.

不要低估小孩理解大人問題的能力。

undergraduate
[ˌʌndɚˈgrædʒuət]

托 雅 學

n 大學生；大學肄業生　　　　　　u1008

She was an undergraduate at the university studying biology.

她曾是這所大學生物系的學生。

underground
[ˈʌndɚˌgraʊnd]

托 雅 學

adj/adv 地面下的；秘密的　　　　　　u1009

The rail system is underground in New York but elevated above ground in Chicago.

這條鐵路在紐約是地下的，但在芝加哥又變成地上的了。

underlie
[ˌʌndɚˈlaɪ]

托 雅 學

vt 引起；成為⋯的基礎　　　　　　u1010

Her concern for her child's safety is the reason that underlies her controlling behavior.

她對孩子安全的擔心是導致她操控行為的直接原因。

underlying
[ˌʌndɚˈlaɪɪŋ]

托 雅 學

adj 含蓄的，潛在的；在下面的　　　　　　u1011

Has anyone identified the underlying causes of these problems?

有人看到這些問題的潛在原因了嗎？

undermine
[ˌʌndɚˈmaɪn]

托 雅 學

vt 暗中破壞，逐漸削弱，侵蝕⋯⋯的基礎　　　　　　u1012

The supervisor tried to undermine him, fearing he would be promoted to her position.

主管試圖暗中損害他（的聲譽威信），因為害怕他升職到她的位置。

undertake
[ˌʌndɚˈmaɪn]

托 雅 學

vi/vt 承擔，擔任；許諾，保證；著手，從事　　　　　　u1013

I would like to undertake the project and I think I can finish it before the deadline.

我想要著手開始此計畫，而且我認為我可以在截止日前完成。

undertaking
[ˌʌndɚˈtekɪŋ]

托 雅 學

n 任務，事業；許諾；承擔　　　　　　u1014

Although travelling alone has been the most challenging undertaking for me, it has helped me to become a more independent person.

雖然一個人旅行對我來說是一個很有挑戰性的任務，它卻讓我成為更加獨立的人。

undo
[ʌn'du]
托 雅 學

vi/vt 取消，消除；破壞
I wish I could undo all my mistakes, but I can't.
我希望我可以消除所有的過錯，但我不能。

u1015

undoubtedly
[ʌn'daʊtɪdlɪ]
托 雅 學

adv 無疑，必定
Professor Wang is undoubtedly one of the most influential people in this field.
王教授無疑是這個領域中最具影響力的人物之一。

u1016

uneasy
[ʌn'izɪ]
托 雅 學

adj 不安的，焦慮的
She felt uneasy about the project and thought it might need to change the concept.
她對此專案感到不安，認為它可能需要更換概念。

u1017

unemployment
[ˌʌnɪm'plɔɪmənt]
托 雅 學

n 失業，失業人數
It is good to have a job with the current unemployment caused by the factory closure.
就目前由工廠關閉所造成的失業率來看，找到工作是件好事。

u1018

unexpected
[ˌʌnɪk'spɛktɪd]
托 雅 學

adj 想不到的，意外的，未預料到的
The new job offer was unexpected, but she decided to take it anyway and start a new career.
新的工作機會令人料想不到，但她還是決定接受它並開始新的事業。

u1019

unfold
[ʌn'fold]
托 雅 學

vi 呈現，顯示，展示；**vt** 打開，顯露，展示
As the story began to unfold, I hoped that the author would write six more books just like it.
隨著情節開始展開，我期盼作者會多寫六本像這樣的書。

u1020

unfortunately
[ʌn'fɔrtʃənətlɪ]
托 雅 學

adv 不幸地
We were astounded when the judge announced that unfortunately only five contestants out of fifty registrants remained in the grueling competition.
當聽到裁判宣佈很不幸五十位參賽者中只有五位可以繼續留在這場殘酷的比賽中時，我們覺得很震驚。

u1021

uniform
['junɪˌfɔrm]
托 雅 學

adj 相同的，一律的；**n** 制服，軍服
The job was successfully done owing to their uniform beliefs and joint efforts.
工作之所以順利完成是由於他們相同的信念和共同的努力。

u1022

unique
[ju'nik]
托 雅 學

adj 唯一的，獨一無二的
The artist has unique perspectives on photography and uses the camera in surprising ways.
這位藝術家對攝影有獨到的觀點，並用出乎意料的方式使用相機。

u1023

universal
[ˌjunəˈvɝsl̩]

托 雅 學

adj 普遍的，全體的，通用的；宇宙的，世界的　u1024

Birth and death are universal experiences for all human beings.

生與死是全人類共通的經歷。

---

unload
[ʌnˈlod]

托 雅 學

vt 卸貨；退子彈　u1025

Unloading the appliances from the truck is his routine job.

從卡車上卸下設備是他的日常工作。

---

update
[ʌpˈdet]

托 雅 學

v 更新，使現代化　u1026

Please keep me updated with the latest information.

請持續讓我知道最新的訊息。

---

upgrade
[ˈʌpˈgred]

托 雅 學

vt 提升，使升級　u1027

I was surprised to be upgraded to first class as compensation for the delayed flight.

作為班機延誤的補償，我被升到了頭等艙，這讓我感到驚訝。

---

uphold
[ʌpˈhold]

托 雅 學

vt 支持，贊成；舉起；堅持　u1028

A doctor promises to uphold the pledge to first do no harm.

一位醫生保證堅守誓言，首先不傷害病人。

---

upright
[ˈʌpˌraɪt]

托 雅 學

adj 垂直的，直立的；正直的，誠實的；豎立的　u1029

The little girls sat perfectly upright at the dinner table, aware of the presence of guests.

這些小女孩意識到有客人在，直挺挺地坐在餐桌旁。

---

upset
[ʌpˈsɛt]

托 雅 學

vi/vt （使……）心煩意亂；打翻，推翻　u1030

He was upset by the news of his grandmother's death and decided to take some time off from work.

他因祖母的死訊感到難過不安，便決定向公司請假一段時間。

---

usage
[ˈjusɪdʒ]

托 雅 學

n 使用，用法；習慣，習俗；慣用法　u1031

Some words have their usage changed over time until they become almost unrecognizable.

有些字隨著時間改變習慣用法，直到它們變成幾乎認不出來。

---

utility
[juˈtɪlətɪ]

托 雅 學

n 效用，有用，實用　u1032

I can't see much utility of a tablet computer, but some people swear they can't live without it.

我看不出平板電腦有多實用，但有些人卻發誓說沒有它不行。

U

utilization
[ˌjutɪlaɪˈzeʃən]
托 雅 學

n 利用，效用
The locals developed the utilization of wind energy to save power for decades to come.
這些當地人開發了風力，為以後的數十年省電。

u1033

utmost
[ˈʌtˌmost]
托 雅 學

adj 最遠的；極度的
I will try my utmost effort to see to it that you are rewarded for your hard work this year.
我會盡最大努力保證你今年會因為努力而獲得獎勵。

u1034

utmost
[ˈʌtˌmost]
托 雅 學

n 極限，極度，最大可能
Michael did his utmost to save his business, but unfortunately, he failed in the end.
麥可盡全力挽救他的生意，但不幸的是，他最後失敗了。

u1035

V

字彙能力檢查表

先自我檢驗是否瞭解以下初階單字，若有不清楚者，請先開啟光碟中的電子書複習。

☐vacancy ☐victory ☐violence ☐vomit
☐vacant ☐view ☐violent ☐vote
☐vacation ☐view ☐virus ☐vowel
☐valley ☐vine ☐vomit ☐vulnerable

V

vacuum
['vækjʊəm]

托 雅 學

n 真空；真空吸塵器
The final experiment was conducted in a vacuum.
最後一個實驗是在真空中實施的。

v1001

vain
[ven]

托 雅 學

adj 徒勞的，徒然的；愛虛榮的
She was a vain girl and worried too much about her hair.
她是個愛虛榮的女生，非常擔憂她的頭髮。

v1002

valid
['vælɪd]

托 雅 學

adj 有效的；有根據的；正當的
Her teenage son was making a valid reason for getting a new car.
她十幾歲的兒子為了得到一輛新車提出了正當理由。

v1003

validity
[və'lɪdətɪ]

托 雅 學

n 有效，效力；正確
The term of validity for my credit card has expired.
我的信用卡有效期限過了。

v1004

vanish
['vænɪʃ]

托 雅 學

vi/vt 突然不見，消失
Her husband would vanish every time she had to discipline the children.
每次要教訓孩子的時候，老公就消失了。

v1005

varied
['vɛrɪd]

托 雅 學

adj 各種各樣的
There was a varied selection of wines at the restaurant, but she never knew which to choose.
飯店裡紅酒品種繁多，她永遠不知道該選哪種。

v1006

variety
[və'raɪətɪ]

托 雅 學

n 種類；多樣化，品種
Red Silks Restaurant in Melbourne serves a variety of Asian dishes.
墨爾本的新潮樓餐廳提供多樣的亞洲食物。

v1007

various
['vɛrɪəs]

托 雅 學

adj 各種各樣的，不同的
There will be various entrees at my sister's wedding.
我姐姐的婚宴上會有各種各樣的菜肴。

v1008

vast
[væst]

托 雅 學

adj 巨大的；遼闊的；大量的
A vast amount of ice cream is sold whenever the weather is hot.
在高溫的天氣裡總是能賣出大量霜淇淋。

v1009

vegetarian
[ˌvɛdʒəˈtɛrɪən]

v1010

n 素食主義者

Many Buddhists are also vegetarians, who abide by religious principles.

許多佛教徒遵守教義，是素食主義者。

vehicle
[ˈviɪkl̩]

v1011

n 車輛，交通工具；媒介

I drive an old vehicle and I have to maintain it well to avoid breaking down.

我開的是輛舊車，因此我必須好好保養它，防止故障。

veil
[vel]

v1012

n 面紗，面罩；托詞

Carrie wore a large hat with a black veil across her face.

卡麗戴了一頂大禮帽，並用黑色的面紗遮住臉龐。

vein
[ven]

托 雅 學

v1013

n 血管；靜脈；葉脈；紋理；情緒

The nurse took a long time to find a vein in my forearm for an injection.

護士打針時花了好久才找到我手臂上的血管。

vein
[ven]

托 雅 學

v1014

vt 使成脈絡，像脈絡一樣分佈

After a little rock hit the window of the car at high speed, it appeared to be veined with cracks.

高速行駛中的車窗被一顆小石子擊中後，道道裂痕像脈絡一樣分佈其上。

vendor
[ˈvɛndɚ]

托 雅 學

v1015

n 小販；（某產品的）銷售公司

They have been our long-term cooperating vendor who offered us reasonable prices for years.

他們是我們多年來提供合理價格的合作銷售公司。

vent
[vɛnt]

托 雅 學

v1016

n 風孔；排放；發洩，表達；火山口

The service technician cleans the air vent every six months.

那位服務技術員每六個月清理一次通風孔。

venue
[ˈvɛnju]

托 雅 學

v1017

n 聚會地點（如音樂廳，會場）

We are on the waiting list to reserve the hotel's main dining hall as the venue for our wedding party.

我們在飯店的申請人名單上，預約飯店大廳做婚禮派對場地。

version
[ˈvɝˈʒən]

托 雅 學

v1018

n 版本，翻譯

Amy wondered if there was another version to the story she'd heard.

艾米在想她聽到的故事是否還有另一個版本。

V

vertical
['vɝtɪkl̩]

托 雅 學

adj 垂直的，豎的；**n** 垂線 `v1019`

She drew a vertical line down the page and began to list the pros and cons of each college.

她在這頁紙上畫上一條垂直線，然後開始列出每所大學的優缺點。

via
['vaɪə]

托 雅 學

prep 經由，通過，憑藉 `v1020`

He became a chef via law school where he used to cook for his study group but fail all of his tests.

他是在法學院時成為廚師的，那時他曾為了煮食物給學習小組吃而沒有通過所有考試。

violate
['vaɪə,let]

托 雅 學

vt 違反，冒犯，褻瀆 `v1021`

Daniel did not want to violate the rules of his contract.

丹尼爾不想違反合約規定。

visible
['vɪzəbl̩]

托 雅 學

adj 看得見的；明顯的，顯著的 `v1022`

There were no visible scars after her surgery because the incisions were so small.

她手術後沒有留下明顯的疤痕，因為切口都很小。

vision
['vɪʒən]

托 雅 學

n 憧憬；想像；幻覺；視力；視野 `v1023`

Harsh, glaring sunlight beating down on a vehicle's windshield can affect a driver's vision especially when driving.

刺目耀眼的陽光打在汽車的擋風玻璃上會影響司機的視野，特別是在駕駛時。

visual
['vɪʒuəl]

托 雅 學

adj 看的，看得見的；視覺的 `v1024`

The visual segments of the presentation—the videos and power point—were not as good as the written sales pitch.

展示中視覺的部分——影片及簡報——不如書面的商品銷售話語。

visualize
['vɪʒʊə,laɪz]

托 雅 學

vi/vt 使形象化；想像；構思 `v1025`

It is hard to visualize the situation you are describing.

你所形容的狀況是很難視覺化的。

vital
['vaɪtl̩]

托 雅 學

adj 至關重要的，生死攸關的；有活力的 `v1026`

Even at 80 years of age, their grandmother was still very spry and vital and could run rings around them.

即使在80歲的高齡，他們的祖母仍然是非常敏捷和有活力的，各方面都很厲害。

vivid
['vɪvɪd]

托 雅 學

adj 鮮豔的；生動的，栩栩如生的 `v1027`

I had a vivid dream last night, but the harder I try, the less I can remember about it.

我昨晚做了一個生動的夢，但我越努力去想就越想不起來。

vocal
['vok!]

托 雅 學

adj 聲音的；有聲的；歌唱的；**n** 母音；聲樂作品　　v1028

The singer experienced great vocal fatigue because she was performing too often.

這歌手遭遇到聲音疲乏，因為她太常表演了。

vocational
[vo'keʃən!]

托 雅 學

adj 職業的　　v1029

Kevin is a well-trained mechanic, who graduated from the local vocational school.

凱文畢業於當地職業學校，是一個訓練有素的機械工。

volcanic
[val'kænɪk]

托 雅 學

adj 火山的；暴烈的，猛烈的；易突然發作的　　v1030

Volcanic rock showered down on the mountain.

山上的火山岩紛紛滾落下來。

volcano
[val'keno]

托 雅 學

n 火山　　v1031

She took a helicopter ride over the active volcano in Hawaii and was amazed watching the lava steam and glow as it flowed into the ocean.

她在夏威夷活火山的上空搭乘直升機，看著岩漿冒煙發熱流進大海，覺得不可思議。

volume
['valjəm]

托 雅 學

n 容積，體積；卷，冊；音量　　v1032

He turned down the volume on the television and everyone breathed a sigh of relief.

他把電視的音量調小，每個人都鬆了口氣。

voluntary
['valən,tɛrɪ]

托 雅 學

adj 自願的，志願的　　v1033

The military is a voluntary service now, but it used to be mandatory.

兵役目前是自願服役，但過去曾是義務性的。

vow
[vaʊ]

托 雅 學

n 誓言，誓約，許願　　v1034

The groom made a touching vow and it brought tears to the bride's eyes.

新郎說的誓言十分感人，新娘感動得哭了。

V

W

字彙能力檢查表

先自我檢驗是否瞭解以下初階單字,若有不清楚者,請先開啟光碟中的電子書複習。

☐walnut	☐wax	☐weigh	☐worldwide
☐warning	☐web	☐weight	☐worth
☐waste	☐website	☐well-known	☐worth
☐waste	☐weed	☐whistle	☐worthless
☐wax	☐weed	☐whistle	☐worthwhile

wage
[wedʒ]

托 雅 學

n 工資，報酬

w1001

His teacher's salary was much higher than his waiter's hourly wage.

他當老師的薪水比他當服務員的時薪要高多了。

wage
[wedʒ]

托 雅 學

vt 進行，開展

w1002

They waged a hunger strike against the government.

他們展開一場絕食抗議來反對政府。

walkout
['wɔk,aʊt]

托 雅 學

n 罷工；退出會場，退席

w1003

This morning the union workers were set to walkout over a pay dispute with management.

因與管理階層的工資爭議，今天上午工會工人們決定罷工。

wander
['wɑndə]

托 雅 學

vi/vt 漫步，徘徊；迷路，迷失方向；離題

w1004

He wandered around the building looking at the architecture and decor with mild interest.

他在大樓周圍閒逛，帶著淡淡的興趣看此建築物和它的裝潢。

ward
[wɔrd]

托 雅 學

n 病房；行政區；監護；被監護人

w1005

Upon the death of both of his parents, the orphan became a ward of the state by court order.

父母雙亡後，法院判定這個孤兒受到本州監護。

ward
[wɔrd]

托 雅 學

vt 擋開，擋住；避開，防止；擊潰，消除

w1006

To ward off crazy fans, the bodyguards stood arm-in-arm around the movie star.

為了擋開瘋狂的影迷，保鏢臂挽著臂圍著這位巨星。

warden
['wɔrdn]

托 雅 學

n 看守人；典獄官

w1007

The prison warden is responsible for all the cell blocks and has to account for every prisoner in each one.

監獄看守人負責所有的牢房分區，並且必須對每個分區內的每一位囚犯負責。

wardrobe
['wɔrd,rob]

托 雅 學

n 衣櫃；衣服；行頭，劇裝

w1008

He had a tall old wooden wardrobe in his bedroom like something out of a story or a movie.

他的臥室裡有一個像故事書裡或電影裡描繪的又高又舊的木製衣櫥。

warehouse
['wɛr,haʊs]

托 雅 學

n 倉庫，貨棧

w1009

The warehouse that supplied the store was completely out of several essential items.

給這家店供貨的倉庫缺少了好幾樣必要的商品。

W

warfare
['wɔr,fɛr]

托 雅 學

n. 戰爭（狀態），鬥爭，衝突

w1010

The two largest car manufacturers seem to be in a state of economic warfare.

這兩家最大的汽車製造商似乎處於經濟上的交戰狀態。

warrior
['wɔrɪə]

托 雅 學

n. 武士

w1011

The temple was built as a memorial to those brave warriors killed in the war.

這座廟是為紀念戰爭中犧牲的英勇戰士所建造的。

wasp
[wɑsp]

托 雅 學

n. 黃蜂，馬蜂

w1012

There were a few wasps buzzing and flying around the flowers in the garden.

花園裡有一些黃蜂在花叢中嗡嗡地飛舞著。

waterproof
['wɔtə,pruf]

托 雅 學

adj. 防水的，耐水的

w1013

My mother bought me a waterproof watch as a special birthday gift.

我媽媽給我買了一塊防水手錶作為特別的生日禮物。

wealth
[wɛlθ]

托 雅 學

n. 財富，財產；大量

w1014

My boss lost most of his wealth by gambling it away.

我的老闆因為賭博而散盡了他大部分財富。

wealthy
['wɛlθɪ]

托 雅 學

adj. 富有的，豐裕的；充分的

w1015

The wealthy businessman constantly devotes his time to charity events.

這個富商不斷地投入時間從事慈善活動。

weave
[wiv]

托 雅 學

n. 編織法，編織式樣

w1016

The weave of their tribal cloth failed to be passed on to the next generation.

他們部落布料的織法沒有傳給下一代。

weave
[wiv]

托 雅 學

vi./vt. 編（織）

w1017

Spiders can weave intricate webs that are almost invisible to the naked eye.

蜘蛛可以編織出肉眼幾乎看不見的複雜的網。

welfare
['wɛl,fɛr]

托 雅 學

n. 福利；幸福；福利事業

w1018

I was concerned about the welfare of my dog because I was away from home for long periods.

因為我要離開家很長一段時間，所以我很擔心狗狗的福祉。

well-being
['wɛl'biɪŋ]

w1019

🔳 健康快樂，幸福，福利
The mother made her son's well-being her priority.
這位母親把她兒子的健康快樂放在第一位。

whereas
[hwɛr'æz]

w1020

conj 而，卻，反之
I wanted to talk to my daughter immediately whereas my husband thought we should leave her alone until she was ready to talk.
我想要即刻跟我女兒談談，而我老公卻認為我們應該避免打擾她，直到她準備好要聊為止。

whereby
[hwɛr'baɪ]

w1021

adv 靠什麼；靠那個
They did not have a clue whereby they could make a million dollars within a month.
他們不曉得怎樣才能在一個月內賺一百萬美元。

whilst
[waɪlst]

w1022

conj / 🔳 當…的時候；同…同時；然而
I can't believe he fell asleep whilst watching such an exciting movie.
我不敢相信他竟然在看這刺激的影片時睡著。

whip
[hwɪp]

w1023

🔳 鞭子；車夫
They used a whip on the slaves to control them.
他們用鞭子抽打奴隸來控制他們。

whip
[hwɪp]

w1024

vi / vt 鞭打，抽打；突然移動
If necessary, we can whip the horses to go faster so that we arrive on time.
必要的話，我們可以鞭打馬兒讓牠們跑快點，以確保我們可以按時到達。

whirl
[hwɝl]

w1025

🔳 旋轉；連串快速的活動
The professional ice skater performed a remarkable whirl as a perfect ending.
那位專業的溜冰選手以一個很棒的旋轉完美地結束了表演。

whirl
[hwɝl]

w1026

vi / vt （使）旋轉，打轉
The strong medication made my head whirl and my knees go weak.
這個強效藥讓我頭暈目眩，膝蓋發軟。

W

wholesale
['hol,sel]

w1027

adj / 🔳 批發（的），批發店
She always bought a lot of food wholesale in large quantities.
她總是在食物批發商店大量地採購。

wholesome
['holsəm]

托 雅 學

adj 衛生的，有益的，健康的，有益健康的
w1028

The wholesome meal included salad, fruit and whole grain bread.

養生餐包含了沙拉、水果及全麥麵包。

wicked
['wɪkɪd]

托 雅 學

adj 壞的，邪惡的，不道德的，惡劣的；淘氣的
w1029

The man was thoroughly wicked and the police were determined to arrest him.

這個男人十惡不赦，警方下定決心逮捕他。

wilderness
['wɪldənəs]

托 雅 學

n 荒野；沙漠
w1030

He loved to camp in the wilderness and enjoy the quiet loneliness of being far away from the city.

他喜歡在荒野裡宿營，可以享受遠離城市的靜謐和獨處時光。

wildlife
['waɪld,laɪf]

托 雅 學

n 野生動物
w1031

There are always lots of wildlife in rural country areas.

鄉下總是能發現很多野生動物。

willow
['wɪlo]

托 雅 學

n 柳樹，柳木
w1032

The willow tree by the lake had been there since I was a child.

自從我小時候起湖旁的柳樹就已存在了。

wisdom
['wɪzdəm]

托 雅 學

n 智慧，明智；名言，格言
w1033

Meditation is a relaxation technique that can help you facilitate peace, calm and wisdom in your everyday life.

冥想是一個日常生活中可以增長內心平和、冷靜及智慧的放鬆方法。

wit
[wɪt]

托 雅 學

n 智力，才智，智慧
w1034

I was completely dazzled by his incredible bravery and fun-loving wit.

我完全被他無比的英勇與風趣的才智迷住了。

witness
['wɪtnɪs]

托 雅 學

n 目擊者，證人；證據，證明
w1035

The witness for the defense told us that the defendant was a good man.

辯方的證人告訴我們被告是個好人。

witness
['wɪtnɪs]

托 雅 學

vi/vt 目擊，目睹；作證
w1036

We were lucky to witness the historic moment.

我們很幸運見證了歷史性的一刻。

workforce
['wɝkfɔrs]

w1037

n 全體員工，勞動人口，勞動力
Ben's mother rejoined the workforce when he was old enough to go to school.
當班到了學齡後，他媽媽就又重新開始工作了。

workplace
['wɝk,ples]

w1038

n 工作場所
Insurance companies reward their employees with an enviable workplace environment.
保險公司用一個令人羨慕的工作環境獎賞他們的員工。

workshop
['wɝk,ʃɑp]

w1039

n 車間，工廠，修理廠；研討會，講習班
The carpenters are unemployed because their workshop shut down without warning.
工匠們因為工廠無預警的關閉而失業了。

wrap
[ræp]

w1040

n 披肩，圍巾；包裝
The plastic wrap on the meat is recyclable.
肉的塑膠外包裝是可回收材料。

wrap
[ræp]

w1041

vi/vt 裹，纏，捲，包
Remember to wrap all of your glass in newspaper when you pack and move.
記得你在打包和移動玻璃的時候要用報紙包裹好。

wreck
[rɛk]

w1042

n 失事船（或飛機）
Unfortunately no survivors were found after the plane wreck.
不幸的是，飛機失事後沒有生還者被發現。

wreck
[rɛk]

w1043

vi/vt （船等）失事，遇難；破壞
The explosion wrecked three buildings on the street.
爆炸毀掉了這條街上的三棟建築物。

wrench
[rɛntʃ]

w1044

n 扳手；痛苦，難受
I can't tighten the bolt without a wrench.
沒有扳手我沒法旋緊螺栓。

W

wrench
[rɛntʃ]

w1045

vi/vt 猛擰；掙脫；（使）扭傷
She wrenched her back while lifting her baby up, and now she is in pain.
當她把孩子抱起來的時候扭傷了背，現在痛得要命。

wrestle

['rɛsl]

托 雅 學

n/vi/vt 摔角；鬥爭，搏鬥

w1046

The boys would wrestle in the yard and someone always got hurt.

這些男孩們喜歡在後院玩摔角，並且總是有人會受傷。

wretched

['rɛtʃɪd]

托 雅 學

adj 可憐的，悲慘的；骯髒的；惡劣的

w1047

It was a wretched day at the office so she brought donuts to help cheer everyone up.

今天對辦公室的人來說是悲慘的一天，所以她買了甜甜圈來讓大家開心。

wrinkle

['rɪŋkl]

托 雅 學

n 皺紋；vi/vt 起皺；皺眉

w1048

She had sat for so long at the doctor's office that her skirt had begun to wrinkle.

她在醫生的辦公室坐了很久，以至於她的裙子都開始皺了。

X・Y・Z

X-ray
['ɛks're']
托 雅 學

n X射線，X光
X-ray examination offers valuable health information.
X光檢查提供了寶貴的健康資訊。

x1001

yacht
[jɑt]
托 雅 學

n 遊艇，快艇
The billionaire bought a yacht and named it after his beloved wife.
這個億萬富翁買了一艘遊艇，還用他心愛的妻子命名。

y1001

yard
[jɑrd]
托 雅 學

n 院子，場地；碼
The weeds grow very quickly when the yard is neglected.
在無人照顧的院子裡的雜草長得非常快。

y1002

yarn
[jɑrn]
托 雅 學

n 紗線，粗纖維；奇談，故事
The lady wound the yarn into a ball and put it in her knitting basket.
那位女士把紗線捲成了一個球，然後放進她的編織籃裡。

y1003

yawn
[jɔn]
托 雅 學

n 呵欠；vi/vt 打呵欠
Jack tries his best not to yawn in boring classes.
傑克儘量不在無聊的課上打呵欠。

y1004

yield
[jild]
托 雅 學

n 產量，收穫
The yield of our latest product was beyond our expectation.
我們最新產品的產量超出了我們的預期。

y1005

yoke
[jok]
托 雅 學

n 軛，牛軛；枷鎖
The divorce seemed to be like a yoke on their necks for a long time.
離婚似乎是他們長久以來戴在脖子上的枷鎖。

y1006

youngster
['jʌŋstɚ]
托 雅 學

n 小夥子，年輕人；少年，兒童
The youngster sped down the path on his tricycle, peddling as fast as his legs could go.
這個孩子沿著小徑快速騎著三輪車，以他的腿能負荷的最快速度踩著踏板。

y1007

X
Y
Z

zero
['zɪro]
托 雅 學

vt 瞄準；將…調到零　　z1001
Before you shoot a gun, be sure to zero in on the target.
在你開槍之前，要確定瞄準目標。

zest
[zɛst]
托 雅 學

n 風味；熱心；強烈的興趣　　z1002
In order to enhance the flavor of his fruitcake, the baker
included the grated zest of a fresh lemon.
為了提升水果蛋糕的口感，烘焙師加入了鮮檸檬碾碎的風味。

zigzag
['zɪgzæg]
托 雅 學

n 鋸齒型線條，之字形　　z1003
I like the pattern of blue zigzags on the dress.
我喜歡這條裙子上藍色鋸齒狀的花樣。

zigzag
['zɪgzæg]
托 雅 學

vi 曲折前進　　z1004
The snake zigzagged very fast to catch its prey.
這條蛇很快地彎曲前進捕捉獵物。

zone
[zon]
托 雅 學

n 地區，區域　　z1005
Generally speaking, most people are not permitted in the
military zone.
一般說來，大部分人都不允許進入軍事區域。

zone
[zon]
托 雅 學

vi/vt 分區，劃分地帶　　z1006
The forest was zoned for endangered animals' protection.
這片森林被劃出來保護瀕臨絕種的動物。

PART 2　進階字彙

abort
[ə'bɔrt]
托 雅 學

vt 放棄，中斷（計畫、任務） `a2001`

The headquarters called to abort the mission because of a potential hazard.

總部打來電話終止任務，因為有潛在危險。

abortion
[ə'bɔrʃən]
托 雅 學

n 流產，墮胎；放棄 `a2002`

Although she has always been against abortion, it is the only choice she has now.

雖然她一直很反對墮胎，但現在這是她唯一的選擇。

abrasion
[ə'breʒən]
托 雅 學

n 磨損，摩擦；擦傷 `a2003`

I think the scratches and abrasion on your knee need to be cleaned with antiseptic lotion to avoid infection.

我認為你膝蓋上的割痕和擦傷需要用消炎液清潔一下以免感染。

abrasive
[ə'bresɪv]
托 雅 學

adj 研磨的，磨蝕的；傷感情的；**n** 研磨料 `a2004`

Everyone agrees that John is the biggest jerk they have ever met; not only is he abrasive, he is annoying as well.

大家都認為約翰是他們見過最蠢的人，他既粗魯又討厭。

accommodate
[ə'kamə,det]
托 雅 學

vt 提供住處；容納；供應，供給 `a2005`

The room had several features designed to accommodate guests in wheelchairs.

這個房間有多處為坐輪椅的客人提供的專門設計。

accommodation
[ə,kamə'deʃən]
托 雅 學

n 住宿；複數＝膳宿供應 `a2006`

Please fill out the form if you want to request an accommodation.

如果您需要申請食宿，請填寫這張表格。

activate
['æktə,vet]
托 雅 學

vt 啟動，啟動；驅動，驅使；使開始起作用 `a2007`

Sunlight and water can activate a plant's growth.

陽光與水分可刺激植物的成長。

acupuncture
[,ækjʊ'pʌŋktʃɚ]
托 雅 學

n 針灸（療法） `a2008`

Acupuncture can be used to treat headaches.

針灸可用來治療頭痛。

acute
[ə'kjut]

托 雅 學

adj 劇烈的；敏銳的；尖銳的；高音的   a2009

The pain in his knee after the injury was acute.

他膝蓋受傷後劇烈疼痛。

A

addict
['ædɪkt]

托 雅 學

n 沉溺於不良嗜好的人   a2010

He became an alcohol addict because he wanted to escape from the cruel reality.

因為想要逃避殘酷的現實，他成了酒鬼。

addict
[æ'dɪkt]

托 雅 學

vi/vt （使）沉溺；（使）上癮   a2011

Michael was addicted to football and never missed watching a game on television.

麥克沉溺於足球賽事，從未錯過電視上任何一場比賽。

adhere
[əd'hɪr]

托 雅 學

vi 粘著；堅持，遵守；依附，追隨   a2012

The ranger warned them all sternly to adhere to the park rules for their own protection.

國家公園管理員嚴格告誡他們必須遵守公園規範以保護自身安全。

adhesive
[əd'hisɪv]

托 雅 學

n 黏合劑   a2013

He used a powerful, clear adhesive to fix his mother's broken vase.

他用透明的強力黏合劑為母親修補破碎的花瓶。

adolescent
[ˌædḷ'ɛsnt]

托 雅 學

adj 青春期的，青少年的；n 青少年   a2014

As a high school teacher, she had a lot of experience dealing with adolescents.

身為一個高中老師，她有許多和青少年相處的經驗。

adverse
[æd'vɝs]

托 雅 學

adj 逆的，相反的；敵對的；不利的，有害的   a2015

The flight was cancelled because of adverse weather conditions.

由於天候不佳，此航班被取消了。

adversity
[əd'vɝsətɪ]

托 雅 學

n 逆境，厄運，災難   a2016

Paula's grandparents told her stories of the adversities they had faced when growing up.

寶拉的祖父母給她講了他們成長過程中遭受的災難。

aesthetic
[ɛs'θɛtɪk]

托 雅 學

adj 美學的，藝術的；審美的   a2017

I liked walking in the landscaped park for its pleasing aesthetic look.

我喜歡在景觀公園散步，因為它有令人賞心悅目的景緻。

affiliate
[ə'fɪlɪˌet]

托 雅 學

n 附屬機構，分公司；vi/vt （使）隸屬（或附屬）於

a2018

Affiliate marketing is an emerging marketing technique used in the online retail.

聯盟行銷是網路零售新興的行銷手法。

afflict
[ə'flɪkt]

托 雅 學

vt 使受痛苦；折磨

a2019

She was afflicted with measles that summer, but she recovered by autumn.

那個夏天她受到了麻疹的折磨，但秋天就康復了。

aggravate
['æɡrəˌvet]

托 雅 學

vt 加重（劇），使惡化；激怒，使惱火

a2020

The alternative treatment has aggravated the health condition of the patient.

替代療法使病人的健康狀況惡化了。

aggregate
['æɡrəˌvet]

托 雅 學

vi/vt 總計，合計

a2021

Even with three different jobs, Henry's monthly earnings did not aggregate $30,000.

即使幹三份工作，亨利的月總收入也未曾達到三萬美元。

aggressive
[ə'ɡrɛsɪv]

托 雅 學

adj 侵略的，好鬥的；有進取心的

a2022

The dog was too aggressive for the young family to adopt him safely.

這隻狗太好鬥了，以至於那個年輕的家庭不能安全地收養它。

agitation
[ˌædʒə'teʃən]

托 雅 學

n 鼓動，煽動；攪動；焦慮，不安

a2023

People with depression often experience irritability, agitation, and negative thinking.

憂鬱症患者常會感到易怒、焦慮並有負面想法。

agony
['æɡənɪ]

托 雅 學

n （精神或肉體的）極大痛苦，創傷

a2024

The mother cried in agony when she got the news about the death of her son.

母親聽見兒子死去的消息後極痛苦地哭泣著。

ailment
['elmənt]

托 雅 學

n 小病，微恙

a2025

An ailment can quickly develop in people who don't stay healthy.

小病在不健康的人身上會發展得很快。

allegation
[ˌælə'ɡeʃən]

托 雅 學

n （未經證實的）指控，指責

a2026

The police officer made note of the robbery victim's allegation.

警官記下搶劫案受害者的指控。

allegiance
[əˈlidʒəns]

托 雅 學

n 擁護；忠誠

a2027

Military students start their day by reciting the Pledge of Allegiance.

軍校生每天第一件事就是背誦效忠誓言。

alleviate
[əˈlivɪˌet]

托 雅 學

vt 減輕，緩和，緩解（痛苦等）

a2028

Two aspirins seemed to alleviate the pain of the headache.

兩片阿斯匹靈似乎緩解了頭痛的症狀。

alliance
[əˈlaɪəns]

托 雅 學

n 同盟（國），結盟；聯姻

a2029

The alliance among the nations was formed to fortify their military forces for protection against the enemy states.

國與國之間結盟是為了加強軍事力量以防禦敵國。

alliteration
[əˌlɪtəˈreʃən]

托 雅 學

n 頭韻，頭韻法

a2030

Alliteration is a common way for writers to make their prose more interesting.

頭韻是作者為散文增色的常見方法之一。

allocate
[ˈæləˌket]

托 雅 學

vi/vt 分配，分派；撥給；劃歸

a2031

The father planned to allocate sufficient money for his children's education.

父親計畫要給孩子們的教育分配足夠的錢。

ally
[əˈlaɪ]

托 雅 學

n 盟國，同盟者；夥伴

a2032

My wife is always my biggest fan and my best ally.

我的妻子永遠是我最大的粉絲以及最好的夥伴。

ally
[əˈlaɪ]

托 雅 學

vt 使結盟；與…有關聯

a2033

In World War II, the Soviet Union allied itself with England and France.

第二次世界大戰時，蘇聯與英國和法國結盟。

alter
[ˈɔltə]

托 雅 學

vi/vt 改變，變化

a2034

Greg took his suit to the tailor to have it altered.

葛列格把他的西服帶給裁縫修改了一下。

alteration
[ˌɔltəˈreʃən]

托 雅 學

n 變更，改變

a2035

The designer made some alterations to the dress to better fit his client.

設計師對服飾進行了一些修改，好讓顧客穿了更為合身。

alternate
['ɔltɚnət]

托 雅 學

adj 交替的；替補的；n 替換物

a2036

Jenifer auditioned for the lead role, but she was only offered a part as the alternate.

珍妮佛試鏡了主角，但結果只給了她替補的小角色。

alternate
['ɔltɚˌnet]

托 雅 學

vt 交替，輪流

a2037

For exercise, I alternate swimming and jogging.

對於運動，我游泳和慢跑輪著做。

alternative
[ɔl'tɝnətɪv]

托 雅 學

adj 可供選擇的；另類的

a2038

Some local scientists offer an alternative explanation for the volcano eruption.

一些當地的科學家對火山爆發提出了另類解釋。

alternative
[ɔl'tɝnətɪv]

托 雅 學

n 供選擇的項目；替代性事物，另類的形態

a2039

The doctor informed her that there were alternatives to surgery.

醫生告訴她有替代手術的治療方案。

ambivalence
[æm'bɪvələns]

托 雅 學

n 矛盾心理，舉棋不定

a2040

Kieran wanted to join the football team and that's why he showed rebellious ambivalence towards his perfect choir boy image.

奎倫想加入足球隊，那就是為什麼他有時會對自己完美的唱詩班男孩形象表現出叛逆的矛盾心理。

amenable
[ə'minəbḷ]

托 雅 學

adj 願意服從的，順從的；有責任的，有義務的

a2041

Joy's mother knew that she raised well-behaved, polite and amenable children.

喬伊的母親知道自己養育了幾個舉止得體、禮貌乖巧的小孩。

amend
[ə'mɛnd]

托 雅 學

vt 修改，修訂；改進

a2042

He amended his previous statement to include the new information.

他修改了之前的聲明，以加入新的訊息。

ammunition
[ˌæmjə'nɪʃən]

托 雅 學

n 彈藥

a2043

The hunter brought enough ammunition with him for the entire weekend.

獵人帶了充足的彈藥，以備整個週末所需。

analogy
[ə'nælədʒɪ]

托 雅 學

n 類似，相似，類比，類推

a2044

The teacher preferred to use analogies when she introduced a new concept.

老師較喜歡運用類比方式介紹新概念。

A

anecdote
[ˈænɪkˌdot]

n 軼事，趣聞；短故事
Darrel was famous for his humorous anecdotes.
達洛以他幽默的趣聞而知名。

a2045

anesthetic
[ˌænəsˈθɛtɪk]

n 麻醉劑，麻醉藥
The dentist administered several shots of anesthetic before he began the root canal.
牙醫在進行根管手術之前打了幾針麻醉劑。

a2046

anonymous
[əˈnɑnəməs]

adj 匿名的，無名的，姓氏不明的
Although her writing was quite popular, she preferred to publish it anonymously.
雖然她的作品非常受歡迎，她寧願匿名出版。

a2047

anthropology
[ˌænθrəˈpɑlədʒɪ]

n 人類學，人類社會學
Anthropology concerns the study of ancient human remains.
人類學關注的是對古代的人類遺跡的研究。

a2048

antiquate
[ˈæntəˌkwet]

vt 使具有古式的外表，使古色古香；廢棄，使過時
Juliana decided to antiquate her picture frames with gold leaf.
朱莉安娜決定用金葉把相框裝飾得古色古香。

a2049

antiquity
[ænˈtɪkwətɪ]

n 古代；古物；古董；古跡
My aunt said the magnificent stately houses she toured reflected the essence of antiquity.
我舅媽說她參觀的壯觀豪華的住宅反映了古蹟的精髓。

a2050

antiseptic
[ˌæntəˈsɛptɪk]

adj 抗菌的，防腐的，冷淡的；n 抗菌劑
The nurse sponged the wound with an antiseptic to treat the patient.
護士用紗布蘸了消毒水為病患擦傷口。

a2051

appealing
[əˈpilɪŋ]

adj 上訴的；哀求的；有魅力的
Spending holidays in big cities does not seem appealing to me.
在大城市度假對我而言似乎並沒有吸引力。

a2052

appraisal
[əˈprezl̩]

n 對…做出的評價；評價，鑒定，評估
The appraisal report of the stolen items took the insurance agent hours to complete.
保險代理人花了數小時來完成失竊物品的評估報告。

a2053

apprentice
[ə'prɛntɪs]

托 雅 學

n 學徒，徒弟

The apprentice had been working in the shop for five days.

那個學徒已經在店裡工作五天了。

a2054

aptitude
['æptə,tjud]

托 雅 學

n 天資，資質；才能

Candidates have to pass an aptitude test before their first interview.

應徵者在第一次會談之前都須通過能力測驗。

a2055

arbitration
[,ɑrbə'treʃən]

托 雅 學

n 仲裁

The union leaders and management have agreed on arbitration to try to settle their issues.

工會領導者跟管理階層同意提請仲裁以解決爭議。

a2056

archive
['ɑrkaɪv]

托 雅 學

n 檔案保管處；資料庫；檔，記錄

There was no mention of his family in the archives of the town.

政府記錄中沒有提到他們家族。

a2057

armor
['ɑrmə]

托 雅 學

n 裝甲；盔甲

Knights in medieval Europe often wore full armor into battle.

中世紀歐洲的騎士都全身披著鎧甲戰鬥。

a2058

arrogant
['ærəgənt]

托 雅 學

adj 傲慢的；狂妄自大的；趾高氣揚的

Don't you think that man was arrogant when he spoke to you?

你不覺得那個男人跟你說話的時候很傲慢嗎？

a2059

arsenal
['ɑrsnəl]

托 雅 學

n 武器庫；軍械庫；（一大批）儲藏的武器

The accused had a complete arsenal of illegal weapons.

被告有一個非法的武器彈藥庫。

a2060

artery
['ɑrtərɪ]

托 雅 學

n 動脈；幹線，要道

Bill had a surgery on his heart to unclog one of his arteries.

比爾做了心臟手術以疏通一條動脈。

a2061

articulate
[ɑr'tɪkjə,let]

托 雅 學

adj 善於表達的；有關節相連的；**vi/vt** 清楚地講話

During the investigation, the police officer had to articulate his thoughts to his superiors.

在調查過程中，警官必須向主管闡述自己的想法。

a2062

A

artillery
[ɑr'tɪlərɪ]

a2063

n 炮，大炮；炮兵（部隊）

The family woke up when they heard the loud sound of artillery and shell explosions.

這家人被大炮跟彈殼的巨大爆炸聲吵醒了。

---

ascent
[ə'sɛnt]

a2064

n 上升，攀登

His ascent up the mountain was dangerous, but the views were beautiful.

他登山的過程非常艱險，但是風景很美。

---

ascertain
[ˌæsə'ten]

a2065

vt 確定，查明，弄清

The detective preferred to delay forming a judgment until he had ascertained all the facts.

在查明所有事實之前，那位偵探寧可延後做判斷。

---

ascribe
[ə'skraɪb]

a2066

vt 把⋯歸於

Because he was always sharply dressed, people ascribed him a certain level of success.

他總是一身幹練的穿著，大家都認為他事業有成。

---

assassin
[ə'sæsɪn]

a2067

n 暗殺者，行刺者，刺客

In history, there has been more than one assassin stalking the President.

在歷史上有過不只一個刺客跟蹤那位總統。

---

assassinate
[ə'sæsɪnˌet]

a2068

vt 暗殺，行刺；中傷

In the world of dirty politics, it is always easy to assassinate your opponents' character through lies, exaggeration and misinterpretation of the facts.

在污穢的政治世界裡，通過謊言、誇大其詞與扭曲事實來中傷對手的人格一直是很容易的事。

---

assassination
[əˌsæsə'neʃən]

a2069

n 刺殺，暗殺

Most of the evidence disappeared after President John F.Kennedy's assassination.

在約翰・甘迺迪總統被刺殺之後，大部分的證據都消失了。

---

assault
[ə'sɔlt]

a2070

n 暴力事件，攻擊；vt 猛攻，襲擊

The mayor announced that the number of sexually assaulted women is decreasing every year.

市長宣佈，被性侵犯的婦女人數每年都在下降。

---

assemble
[ə'sɛmbl̩]

a2071

vi 聚集；vt 集合；裝配；收集

She assembled the parts of her new toy without even reading the instructions.

她還沒看說明就把新玩具組裝好了。

assert
[ə'sɝt]

托 雅 學

vt 斷言；宣稱；堅持；主張（權利、權威等）
Tony never had difficulty asserting himself.
托尼從來都堅決地堅持自己的主張。

a2072

assertive
[ə'sɝtɪv]

托 雅 學

adj （性格）果敢的；有衝勁的；堅定而自信的
Studies show that more assertive children are given more responsibilities at home.
研究表明，性格更果斷的孩子在家裡承擔更多責任。

a2073

assess
[ə'sɛs]

托 雅 學

vt 評估（財富）；徵稅；評價
It is never easy to precisely assess the damage caused by a storm.
要準確評估風暴造成的損失向來不是一件容易的事。

a2074

assessment
[ə'sɛsmənt]

托 雅 學

n 估定；查定；估計數
He made a very perceptive assessment of the situation before taking any action.
他在採取任何行動之前，已經對局勢作了非常敏銳的評估。

a2075

asset
['æsɛt]

托 雅 學

n 有價值的物品；天賦；複數＝資產
His assets totaled in the millions.
他的財產總額達數百萬。

a2076

assimilate
[ə'sɪmḷˌet]

托 雅 學

vi/vt 吸收；消化；（使）同化
Most families assimilate to their new countries after living there for three generations.
大多數家庭在新的國家住了三代之後都會被同化。

a2077

astonish
[ə'stɑnɪʃ]

托 雅 學

vt 使驚訝，使吃驚
The acrobats astonished the crowd with their aerial performance.
雜技演員的空中表演震驚四座。

a2078

astound
[ə'staʊnd]

托 雅 學

vt 使震驚，使大吃一驚
They were astounded by her beautiful singing voice.
她那美妙的聲音使他們為之震撼。

a2079

astute
[ə'stjut]

托 雅 學

adj 精明的，敏銳的；狡猾的，詭計多端的
Bill Gates is a very astute businessman who made Microsoft a billion dollar company.
比爾·蓋茨是一個非常精明的生意人，他把微軟做成了一個10億美元的公司。

a2080

A

asylum
[ə'saɪləm]
托 雅 學

n 避難所；精神病院
a2081
After his psychotic episode, he was sent to an asylum.
精神病發作之後，他被送進了精神病院。

atheist
['eθɪɪst]
托 雅 學

n 無神論者，不信神的人
a2082
Although he had gone to church as a child, he became an atheist later in life.
儘管兒時他去教堂做禮拜，後來卻成了無神論者。

atomization
[ˌætəmə'zeʃən]
托 雅 學

n 霧化，原子化
a2083
Electrothermal atomization is the release of an atom cloud with a small volume of gas.
電熱霧化是指用一小團氣體把一個原子雲釋放出來。

attorney
[ə't3·nɪ]
托 雅 學

n （業務或法律事務上的）代理人；辯護律師
a2084
The attorney recommended settling the lawsuit.
律師建議和解。

auction
['ɔkʃən]
托 雅 學

vt 拍賣
a2085
Some of the farmer's land will be auctioned to pay his debts.
這個農夫的一些土地會被拍賣來支付他的債務。

audit
['ɔdɪt]
托 雅 學

n 審計；查帳；vt 審計；查帳；核對
a2086
The accountant has now completed his financial audit for this month.
會計師現在已經完成了這個月的財務審計。

audit
['ɔdɪt]
托 雅 學

vt 旁聽
a2087
Would it be possible for the hospital surgeon to audit the medical lecture?
有可能讓醫院的外科醫生來旁聽醫療講座嗎？

augment
[ɔg'mɛnt]
托 雅 學

vt 使…增大，增加，增長；擴張
a2088
The garlic augmented the lemon flavor in the dish beautifully.
在那道菜裡，大蒜出色地增加了檸檬的風味。

autonomous
['ɔ'tɑnəməs]
托 雅 學

adj 自治的，有自治權的；自主的，有自主權的
a2089
Although it is a small nation in comparison with others, it remains fully autonomous.
雖然跟其他國家比起來很小，這個國家還是完全自治的。

avail
[ə'vel]

托 雅 學

vt 有益於，使對某人有利

a2090

The visiting professors are encouraged to avail themselves to all the research facilities.

訪問教授被鼓勵利用各種研究設備讓自己受益。

avalanche
['ævl̩ˌæntʃ]

托 雅 學

n 雪崩

a2091

An avalanche of heavy snow careened down the mountainside.

大雪的雪崩沿著山坡傾塌下來。

averse
[ə'vɝs]

托 雅 學

adj 討厭的，反對的

a2092

The citizens of the town were averse to legalizing the sale of alcohol within city limits.

市民們反對在城區範圍內使酒品銷售合法化。

avert
[ə'vɝt]

托 雅 學

vt 防止，避免；轉移（目光、注意力等）

a2093

The new levees installed last year averted disasters when the rainy season came.

去年新建造的堤岸是用於防止雨季所帶來的災害。

aviator
['evɪˌetɚ]

托 雅 學

n 飛行員；男飛行員

a2094

Amelia Earhart was one of the first female aviators.

阿米莉亞·伊爾哈特是最早的女飛行員之一。

axis
['æksɪs]

托 雅 學

n 軸線；坐標軸，基準線

a2095

The Earth's axis is tilted at a 23 degree angle away from perpendicular to the solar plane.

地軸傾斜成約23度角，偏離太陽的垂直面。

B

baffle
['bæfl]
托 雅 學

n 阻礙;隔板　　　　　　　　　　　　　　　b2001
The wall baffle is extra thick to deflect any loud noises from next door neighbors.
牆上的隔板是加厚的,以轉移隔壁鄰居發出的噪音。

baffle
['bæfl]
托 雅 學

vt 使困惑;使受挫　　　　　　　　　　　　　b2002
You can easily baffle people if you talk about a topic they don't understand.
如果你談論人們不明白的話題,就可以輕易地使他們感到困惑。

ballot
['bælət]
托 雅 學

n (不記名)投票;投票總數;投票權;vi 投票　b2003
They cast their ballots for mayor after hearing a lengthy debate.
在聽過了長時間的辯論後,他們投票選市長。

banish
['bænɪʃ]
托 雅 學

vt 放逐,驅逐　　　　　　　　　　　　　　　b2004
Napoleon was banished to the island of St.Helena in 1815.
1815年,拿破崙被放逐到聖海倫娜島上。

barb
[bɑrb]
托 雅 學

n (魚鉤、魚叉、箭頭等的)倒刺;諷刺;鋒利,鋒芒　b2005
Be careful when you are casting a fishing line not to catch the barb of the hook in your or someone else's clothing.
當你把釣魚竿拋出去的時候,小心不要掛到你自己或者別人衣服掛鉤上的倒鉤。

barren
['bærən]
托 雅 學

adj 貧瘠的;無益的;不能孕育的　　　　　　b2006
During the cold winter, the farmer's field was totally barren of crops.
在寒冷的冬天,農民的田地無法栽種農作物。

barter
['bɑrtə]
托 雅 學

vi/vt 以(等價物或勞務)作為交換　　　　　b2007
Tom bartered a roof repair in exchange for doing the contractor's taxes.
湯姆以修補屋頂作為交換,頂替為承包商計算稅務的工作。

batter
['bætə]

n 麵粉,麵糊;vt 塗上麵糊　　　　　　　　　b2008
Ginger battered the catfish before she fried them.
金格在煎鯰魚之前先裹上一層麵糊。

bearing
['bɛrɪŋ]
托 雅 學

n 軸承；忍受；關係，影響；舉止；方向
b2009
The bearing I have to put up with because of the disease is excruciating.
我因為這個疾病必須承受的一切是極其痛苦的。

besiege
[bɪ'sidʒ]
托 雅 學

vt 包圍，圍困；糾纏
b2010
She has been besieged by her financial problems in the past years.
過去幾年來她被財務問題所糾纏。

betray
[bɪ'tre]
托 雅 學

vt 背叛，出賣；流露
b2011
Her tears betrayed her true feelings about the news.
她的眼淚出賣了她對於這個消息的真實情感。

bias
['baɪəs]
托 雅 學

n 偏見；偏愛
b2012
The politician defended himself by blaming the media for bias against his party.
這個政客為自己辯護，批評媒體對他政黨的偏見。

bilateral
[baɪ'lætərəl]
托 雅 學

adj 雙邊的
b2013
Territorial disputes between the two countries will be discussed on a bilateral basis.
這兩個國家間的領土問題將會在雙邊基礎上討論。

bizarre
[bɪ'zar]
托 雅 學

adj 異乎尋常的，稀奇古怪的
b2014
It was such a bizarre story because it seemed so incredulous.
那是個非常奇異的故事，因為實在是讓人很難相信。

bleach
[blitʃ]
托 雅 學

vi 變白；vt 漂白
b2015
You can bleach these jeans if you want to make them look torn.
如果你想讓牛仔褲更顯舊，可以漂白它。

bleak
[blik]
托 雅 學

adj 荒涼的，光禿禿的；陰冷的；淒涼的，蕭瑟的；暗淡無光的
b2016
I looked out the window this morning and it looked so bleak with the cold wind blowing and winter's snow.
這天早上，我望著窗外，外面看起來是那麼的陰冷，寒風呼嘯，冬雪飄飛。

blizzard
['blɪzəd]
托 雅 學

n 暴風雪
b2017
The air traffic controller cancelled all the flights out of Chicago because of the blizzard.
由於暴風雪，空中管制人員取消了所有從芝加哥出發的航班。

B

blunder
['blʌndə]

托 雅 學

n （因無知等而犯）大錯；跌跌蹌蹌地走 · b2018

The CEO of the company had to step down owing to a series of administrative blunders.

由於一連串的行政錯誤，這家公司的執行長必須下臺。

blunder
['blʌndə]

托 雅 學

vi （因無知等而）犯大錯；跌跌蹌蹌地走 · b2019

They blundered through the forest scaring off most of the wildlife.

他們跌跌撞撞地走進森林，嚇跑了許多野生動物。

blunt
[blʌnt]

托 雅 學

adj 率直的；生硬的；鈍的 · b2020

The politician gave a blunt reply to avoid answering the journalist's question.

政治家用一個生硬的回答回避了記者的問題。

boast
[bost]

托 雅 學

n 自誇，大話；vt 自誇，誇耀 · b2021

Melbourne boasts a very diversified cultural background.

墨爾本以擁有多元文化背景為豪。

bolster
['bolstə]

托 雅 學

n 靠枕，靠墊；墊木，軟墊 · b2022

When I sit up and read in bed, I need to prop myself up comfortably with my bolster pillow.

當我坐起來，在床上看書時，我需要用靠枕把自己舒服地支撐起來。

bolster
['bolstə]

托 雅 學

vt 鞏固；援助 · b2023

The best way to bolster confidence is to become successful.

鞏固信心最好的方法是成功。

bolster
['bolstə]

托 雅 學

vt 支持，支撐；提高，鼓舞 · b2024

Kevin's lighthearted attempts to bolster his friend's spirits usually worked.

凱文用以鼓舞朋友士氣的那些輕鬆的嘗試，通常都很有效。

bolt
[bolt]

托 雅 學

n 螺栓，插銷；vi 閂門，關窗，拴住；衝出 · b2025

The runners quickly bolted towards the finish line.

跑步運動員迅速地衝往終點線。

bounty
['baʊntɪ]

托 雅 學

n 大量，豐富；賞金，慷慨 · b2026

Mark's family enjoys a bounty of fruit crops every summer.

每年夏季，馬克一家都會收穫大量水果作物。

boutique
[bu'tik]

托 雅 學

n 流行女裝商店，精品店

b2027

Alice finally achieved her dream of opening a boutique that summer.

那個夏天愛麗絲終於實現了開精品店的夢想。

---

breach
[britʃ]

托 雅 學

n 違反，不履行；破裂

b2028

Her comment was a major breach of etiquette, and everyone at the table fell silent.

她的評論嚴重違背禮節，桌上的所有人都陷入了沉默。

---

brink
[brɪŋk]

托 雅 學

n 邊緣，離某事物不遠

b2029

John thought he was on the brink of success after writing his book.

寫完這本書之後，約翰覺得他已經站在了成功的邊緣。

---

briny
['braɪnɪ]

托 雅 學

adj 很鹹的，（像）海水的

b2030

Scandinavians enjoy eating fish, such as herrings, from a jar filled with a briny liquid.

北歐人喜歡吃魚，例如鹹汁醃製的鯡魚。

---

brood
[brud]

托 雅 學

n 同窩幼鳥；窩；一夥；**vt** 孵（蛋）

b2031

I can see a brood of birds resting on the tree from the window.

我從視窗可以看見樹上有一群小鳥在休息。

---

brood
[brud]

托 雅 學

vi 沉思

b2032

He is brooding on the materials for his next novel.

他正在為下一本小說的題材而沉思。

---

buggy
['bʌgɪ]

托 雅 學

n 馬車；童車；小貨車

b2033

Ranchers ride into town on their horse-drawn buggy for fresh supplies at the general store.

牧場主們坐著他們的馬拉小貨車進城，去雜貨店買一些新貨。

---

burrow
['bɝo]

托 雅 學

n 地洞，穴窟；藏身處，躲避處

b2034

The rabbit darted across the field and disappeared underground into a burrow.

那隻兔子急速竄過田野，鑽進一個地洞，消失了。

---

bust
[bʌst]

托 雅 學

n 突襲搜捕，逮捕；破產，經濟蕭條；爆裂，破裂

b2035

There was a police bust last night at a downtown nightclub and many drug dealers were arrested.

昨天晚上，在市中心夜總會，員警突襲搜捕，很多毒販落網。

bypass
['baɪˌpæs]

托 雅 學

n 旁道；**vt** 繞過

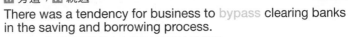

There was a tendency for business to bypass clearing banks in the saving and borrowing process.
企業在存款或借款過程中有繞過清算銀行的趨勢。

B

C

cabal
[kə'bæl]
托 雅 學

n 陰謀，密謀；陰謀集團
c2001

It would be quite dangerous to have a cabal in a country such as Cuba plotting to overthrow the government.

一個國家，例如古巴，有一個政變集團密謀推翻政府，是非常危險的。

cadence
['kedns]
托 雅 學

vt 使有節奏，抑揚頓挫
c2002

The singer could easily cadence his voice to reach high notes and project them over his audience.

這名歌手能輕鬆地使他的聲音抑揚頓挫達到高音，並呈現在觀眾面前。

candid
['kændɪd]
托 雅 學

adj 公正的,公平的
c2003

Carlos was famous for his candid way of speaking.

卡洛斯以講話公正而出名。

caricature
['kærɪkətʃɚ]
托 雅 學

n （人物）漫畫；諷刺畫
c2004

Isabelle made money during the summer by drawing caricatures of people at the park.

在夏季，伊莎貝拉靠給公園的遊客畫漫畫賺錢。

catastrophe
[kə'tæstrəfɪ]
托 雅 學

n 大災難；（悲劇）結局
c2005

The tsunami was the largest catastrophe that had ever hit the small fishing village.

這次海嘯是這個小漁村有史以來最大的一場災難。

census
['sɛnsəs]
托 雅 學

n 人口普查
c2006

A full census of the United States is taken every 10 years.

美國每十年進行一次全面的人口普查。

chafe
[tʃef]
托 雅 學

vi 擦，蹭；磨損，擦傷；變得煩惱，焦躁；流水沖刷
c2007

I just rubbed lotion on my hands because the cold weather is making them chafe and crack.

我剛剛抹了些乳液在我的手上，因為這寒冷的天氣讓手擦傷和皸裂得很厲害。

charter
['tʃɑrtɚ]
托 雅 學

n 憲章；特許狀；綱領
c2008

The company's charter laid out the leadership structure recommended by the board of directors.

公司的綱領中列出了董事會推薦的領導層格局。

C

charter
['tʃartə]

vt 租（船、車、飛機）

`c2009`

My husband wants to charter a boat to go fishing when we go on vacation.

我丈夫想要在我們度假時租一艘小船去釣魚。

chronic
['kranɪk]

adj （病）慢性的

`c2010`

Her chronic illnesses forced them to move south to a warmer climate.

她的慢性病迫使他們遷到氣候溫暖的南部。

chronic
['kranɪk]

adj 積習難改的；嚴重的；長期的；慣常的

`c2011`

My friend is really a great and loyal friend except for her chronic lateness.

除了她習慣性的遲到之外，我的朋友實在是一個偉大和忠實的朋友。

chronology
[krə'naləd31]

n 大事記；年代學；年表

`c2012`

Tina's group was assigned the project of making a chronology of the Civil War.

蒂娜組的工作是做出內戰的大事記。

cipher
['saɪfə]

n 密碼；暗號

`c2013`

During World War II, intelligence officers devised secret codes in cipher language to outsmart their enemy.

二戰期間，情報官員們用暗號語言設計了密碼來打敗他們的敵人。

civilian
[sɪ'vɪljən]

adj 平民的；民用的；**n** 平民

`c2014`

The military leader prohibited the intentional harming of civilians by uniformed soldiers in a conflict.

軍事領袖禁止武裝士兵在衝突中故意傷害民眾。

clan
[klæn]

n 氏族；家族；幫派

`c2015`

The Scottish clan played the bagpipes dressed in their tartan kilts.

那個蘇格蘭部落穿著他們的格子呢裙表演風笛。

cliché
[kli'ʃe]

n 陳詞濫調

`c2016`

The set-up of the film was a cliché, but the ending added a surprise twist.

電影的編排非常老套，但是結局卻是個意外的轉折。

clutch
[klʌtʃ]

n 抓住，攫住；掌握；離合器

`c2017`

The baby held the toy firmly in her clutches while she examined it.

當小嬰兒檢查玩具時，她用手緊抓住玩具不放。

coalescence
[ˌkoəˈlɛsns]

托 雅 學

n 合併；聯合；接合

c2018

The coalescence of the tibia and fibula form into a major leg bone.

脛骨和腓骨的接合組成一塊主要的腿骨。

coalition
[ˌkoəˈlɪʃən]

托 雅 學

n 結合體，同盟；結合，聯合

c2019

There is a worldwide coalition of countries hoping to bring about peace.

全世界的國家正聯合起來，希望帶來和平。

coincide
[ˌkoɪnˈsaɪd]

托 雅 學

vi 相符合，相巧合

c2020

Her birthday coincided with the weekend, so she invited all of her friends out to dinner.

她的生日剛好是週末，所以就請了所有的朋友到外面聚餐。

coincidence
[koˈɪnsɪdəns]

托 雅 學

n 巧合；共同存在；符合

c2021

It's no coincidence that my arch rival is at the event today.

我的主要對手今天也在賽事現場，這絕不是一種巧合。

collaborate
[kəˈlæbəˌret]

托 雅 學

vi 協作，合作；協調

c2022

They collaborated frequently on design projects as professionals.

作為專業人員，他們在設計專案上經常合作。

collaboration
[kəˌlæbəˈreʃən]

托 雅 學

n （指在科學、藝術等方面的）合作，協作

c2023

George Lucas and his team often join in for the collaboration of special effects for sci-fi movies.

喬治‧盧卡斯和他的團隊經常為科幻電影特效的合作而加入。

collide
[kəˈlaɪd]

托 雅 學

vi 碰撞；衝突，抵觸

c2024

The car ran into a stop sign and collided with anther car.

一輛車跑出了停車標誌，撞上了另一輛車。

collision
[kəˈlɪʒən]

托 雅 學

n 碰撞；（利益、意見等的）衝突

c2025

The collision only caused minor damages to her car.

碰撞只給她的車造成了輕微的損壞。

collusion
[kəˈluʒən]

托 雅 學

n 共謀，同謀，勾結，串通

c2026

The brother and sister worked in collusion to defraud their insurance company regarding a vehicle damage claim.

關於一個汽車損傷索賠，這兄妹倆彼此串通，合夥詐騙他們的保險公司。

C

colossal
[kə'lɑsl̩]

adj 巨大的，龐大的   c2027
The green office design has reduced a colossal expense for the company.
環保辦公室設計為這家公司省下了巨大的開銷。

combat
['kɑmbæt]

n/vt 戰鬥，搏鬥   c2028
We always try to recycle plastics to combat the expense of our city.
我們總是試著回收塑膠來減少城市的消費。

commence
[kə'mɛns]

vi 開始   c2029
The Olympic games will commence soon and a winner will receive a gold medal.
奧運比賽很快就會開始，而冠軍會得到一個金牌獎章。

commentary
['kɑmən,tɛrɪ]

n 評論，注釋   c2030
The fans enjoyed the running TV commentary throughout the baseball game.
在棒球比賽過程中，粉絲們很喜歡連續不斷的電視評論。

commentator
['kɑmən,tetɚ]

n 時事評論者；實況播音；注釋者，評注者   c2031
Sports events are often broadcasted with a commentator explaining the rules of the games.
體育節目播報時通常都有一位評論員解釋運動專案的規則。

commiserate
[kə'mɪzə,ret]

vi 表示同情，憐憫；慰問   c2032
The friends decided to commiserate over their recent loss.
朋友們決定對他們最近的損失表示同情。

commotion
[kə'moʃən]

n 騷動，喧鬧   c2033
The commotion in the barn woke the farmer and his wife in the middle of night.
半夜裡牲畜棚的騷動驚醒了農民和妻子。

compact
[kəm'pækt]

adj 緊密的，結實的；緊湊的；小巧的   c2034
The latest trend for mobile devices is to become more and more compact.
移動設備有越來越迷你的趨勢。

compact
[kəm'pækt]

vt 使緊密；壓緊   c2035
She compacted all her personal items neatly in her suitcase to fit more souvenirs from her trip.
她把所有個人用品整齊地塞入行李箱，以便裝入更多這次旅程所買的紀念品。

compartment
[kəm'partmənt]

托 雅 學

n 車廂，艙；分隔間
The train compartment was cozy and relatively quiet.
火車的包廂裡非常舒適，也相對安靜多了。

c2036

compatible
[kəm'pætəbl]

托 雅 學

adj 能共處的；可並立的；與…相容的
I am looking for a compatible hard disk for my existing computer.
我在找一個和我現在的電腦相容的硬碟。

c2037

competence
['kampətəns]

托 雅 學

n 能力，勝任，稱職
She freely admitted that the job was currently beyond her level of competence.
她坦然承認這項工作目前超出了她的能力範圍。

c2038

competent
['kampətənt]

托 雅 學

adj 有能力的，能勝任的；足夠的
Ann was a competent piano player for the choir.
安可以勝任合唱團的鋼琴演奏者。

c2039

compile
[kəm'paɪl]

托 雅 學

vt 編輯，編制；搜集
Hannah compiled a list of the students who still needed to pay their fees.
漢娜把仍需要繳納學費的學生名單彙編出來了。

c2040

comply
[kəm'plaɪ]

托 雅 學

vi 應允；遵照，照做
The students were quick to comply with their teacher's instructions.
學生們很快就遵照老師的指令去做了。

c2041

concede
[kən'sid]

托 雅 學

vt 承認；容許；（比賽結束前）認輸；退讓
He conceded that he didn't know how to get to the next town and asked for directions.
他承認自己不知道怎麼去下一個城鎮，並問了路。

c2042

conceive
[kən'siv]

托 雅 學

vt 設想，以為；懷孕
After years of trying to conceive, Debra and Paul finally welcomed their first child.
黛布拉和保羅幾年來一直在計畫懷孕，現在終於迎來了他們的第一個孩子。

c2043

concession
[kən'sɛʃən]

托 雅 學

n 讓步；特許（權）
Both the management and the union made concessions in order to reach an agreement.
管理方和工會都做出了讓步，以達成協議。

c2044

C

concourse
['kankors]

托 雅 學

n 匯合；集合；廣場；（車站/機場）中央大廳　c2045

Her next flight was located all the way at the end of the next concourse.

她的下一班飛機在下一個大廳一直走到盡頭的位置。

concurrent
[kən'kɜrənt]

托 雅 學

adj 同時存在或發生的　c2046

The judge demanded that the criminal serve four concurrent sentences.

法官要求對罪犯四項罪名併罰。

conductivity
[ˌkandʌk'tɪvəti]

托 雅 學

n 導電率；傳導性　c2047

The physics teacher planned an electrical conductivity experiment for his class.

這名物理老師計畫在任教班級進行一項電力傳導性的實驗。

confer
[kən'fɜ]

托 雅 學

vt 商討；授予，頒給（勳銜，學位等）　c2048

The siblings conferred about how best to care for their aging parents.

兄弟姊妹（手足）們商討如何能夠給年老的雙親最好的照顧。

configuration
[kən,fɪgjə'reʃən]

托 雅 學

n 構造，結構；佈局　c2049

The configuration of the planets in the sky changes as they rotate around the Sun.

行星在繞太陽公轉的過程中在天空中的方位會發生變化。

confine
[kən'faɪn]

托 雅 學

vt 限制；使不外出，禁閉　c2050

Nathan was confined to his bed until his broken leg healed.

南森被困在床上，直到骨折的腿痊癒。

confines
[kən'faɪnz]

托 雅 學

n 界限，範圍　c2051

The confines of my job make it difficult to visit my relatives.

我工作上的限制讓我很難去拜訪親戚。

conform
[kən'fɔrm]

托 雅 學

vi/vt （使）遵守；（使）一致　c2052

Her work conformed to the highest standards of interior decorating.

她的工作遵照室內裝潢的最高標準。

conformity
[kən'fɔrməti]

托 雅 學

n 一致，符合（公認準則的行為）；遵守　c2053

Conformity to rules and regulations is necessary in the military.

對各種規則與規定的服從在部隊裡是必須的。

congress
['kɑŋgrəs]

托 雅 學

n （代表）大會；（美國等國的）國會，議會　　c2054
The Congress passed the budget after a long debate.
經過了長時間的爭論，國會通過了預算。

conjunction
[kən'dʒʌŋkʃən]

托 雅 學

n 接合，聯合；連（接）詞　　c2055
She planned her wedding in conjunction with Christmas holidays so that more family members would be able to come.
她計畫在聖誕節假日舉辦婚禮，這樣更多的家人可以來參加。

connoisseur
[ˌkɑnə'sɝ]

托 雅 學

n 鑑賞家，鑑定家　　c2056
The wine connoisseur exported fine wines worldwide to the rich and famous direct from his own vineyard.
這位葡萄酒鑒賞家直接從自家葡萄園向全世界的富人和名人們出口美酒。

conscience
['kɑnʃəns]

托 雅 學

n 良心，良知　　c2057
His conscience prevented him from speaking ill of others.
他的良知使他不會說別人的壞話。

consecutive
[kən'sɛkjʊtɪv]

托 雅 學

adj 連續不斷的　　c2058
My son's football team won the championship for three consecutive years.
我兒子的足球隊連續三年都贏得了冠軍。

consensus
[kən'sɛnsəs]

托 雅 學

n 共識　　c2059
The board quickly reached a consensus on the new direction for the company.
董事會很快就公司的新方向達成了共識。

consequence
['kɑnsəˌkwɛns]

托 雅 學

n 結果，後果，影響；重要性　　c2060
The consequences of his recklessness taught him to be more careful behind the wheel.
他莽撞造成的後果教會他在開車時要更加謹慎。

consign
[kən'saɪn]

托 雅 學

vt 把…委託給，寄託　　c2061
She consigned herself to reading her new book in the long boring flight.
在漫長的無聊的航程中，她完全寄託於讀她的新書。

consignee
[ˌkɑnsaɪ'ni]

托 雅 學

n 收貨人　　c2062
The consignee was delighted when his mail parcel arrived on schedule.
收貨人看到包裹如期送達，非常開心。

console
[kən'sol]

vt 安慰，慰問　　　　　　　　　　c2063

Jack did his best to console his sister after her dog died.
在妹妹的狗死後，傑克盡最大可能安慰她。

C

conspicuous
[kən'spɪkjʊəs]

adj 顯眼的，明顯的　　　　　　　　c2064

The daisies were conspicuous in the green field.
雛菊在綠地看起來格外顯眼。

conspiracy
[kən'spɪrəsɪ]

n 陰謀，密謀，共謀　　　　　　　　c2065

Fortunately, the police discovered the conspiracy before the president was shot.
幸運的是，暗殺總統的陰謀在實施之前被員警識破了。

constituent
[kən'stɪtʃʊənt]

n 成分，組成的要素；選民　　　　　c2066

The senator frequently returned to his home state to consult with his constituents.
議員經常回到自己生長的州徵求選民的意見。

contaminate
[kən'tæmə,net]

vt 弄汙；毒害；傳染　　　　　　　c2067

Tourists are more likely to get sick when swimming in contaminated beach water.
在受到污染的海水中游泳，遊客更容易得病。

contemplate
['kɑntɛm,plet]

vt 盤算，計議；周密考慮；注視，凝視　c2068

She contemplated the painting for several minutes before moving on.
她駐足在這幅畫作前，凝視了好幾分鐘，才繼續往前走。

contempt
[kən'tɛmpt]

n 輕蔑，藐視，受辱　　　　　　　c2069

Martin couldn't hide his contempt for his opponent's arguments.
馬丁忍不住對他對手的論點表現出鄙視。

contiguous
[kən'tɪgjʊəs]

adj 邊界的，鄰近的　　　　　　　c2070

The U.S. and Mexico are contiguous countries and not without their problems associated with border control.
美國和墨西哥是鄰近的國家，在邊界管理上雙方存在很多問題。

contingency
[kən'tɪndʒənsɪ]

n 可能性；偶然性　　　　　　　　c2071

Your contingency for success lies in good team work.
你們成功的可能性在於良好的團隊合作。

continuum
[kən'tɪnjʊəm]

n 連續的一系列；統一體，連續體　　　c2072

There seems to be a continuum of temperatures that range very hot to very cold.

似乎有連續的一系列氣溫，範圍從非常熱到非常冷。

contradict
[ˌkɑntrə'dɪkt]

vt 反駁，否認；與…相矛盾　　　c2073

The evidence contradicted the testimony of the policeman.

證據與員警提供的證詞相左。

contrive
[kən'traɪv]

vt 謀劃，策劃；設法做到；設計，想出　　　c2074

She contrived to be in the right place at the right time.

她精心策劃，把握恰當的時機出現在恰當的地方。

converge
[kən'vɝdʒ]

vi 聚集，靠攏；收斂　　　c2075

All the collector lanes converge on to the major highway, which always results in a traffic jam.

所有的進出車道都聚集在那條主要的公路上，總是會造成交通擁堵。

convict
['kɑnvɪkt]

n 囚犯　　　c2076

Convicts frequently have difficulty finding a job after their incarceration.

罪犯服刑期滿後常常難以找到工作。

convict
[kən'vɪkt]

vt 定罪，判罪　　　c2077

The district attorney swayed the jury and convicted the repeat offender.

地方檢察官動搖了陪審團並將該慣犯定罪。

conviction
[kən'vɪkʃən]

n 罪行判決　　　c2078

The appeals court upheld his previous conviction.

上訴法庭維持了對他先前的判決。

cordial
['kɔrdʒəl]

adj 真誠的，誠懇的　　　c2079

Dana's relationship with her mother was cordial but not close.

達娜和母親的關係很真誠，但是並不親密。

corrode
[kə'rod]

vi/vt （受）腐蝕，侵蝕　　　c2080

Acid leaked from old batteries can corrode other parts of the engine.

從電池裡漏出來的酸性物質會腐蝕引擎的其他零件。

C

cosmic
['kazmık]

adj 宇宙的；廣大無邊的 　　　　c2081

Light years are used to measure distances on the cosmic scale.

光年用以測量宇宙中天體間的距離。

cosmopolitan
[ˌkazmə'palətn]

adj 世界性的；國際的 　　　　c2082

Her taste in clothing was quite cosmopolitan.

她的衣著品味很有國際風範。

counsel
['kaʊnsl̩]

n 勸告，忠告 　　　　c2083

Amanda sought out the counsels of her parents before choosing a college.

艾曼達在選擇上哪所大學之前先聽取了父母的忠告。

counsel
['kaʊnsl̩]

n 法律顧問；辯護人 　　　　c2084

Following her car accident, my aunt sought a legal counsel for her injuries.

在發生車禍之後，我姑姑就她的傷勢諮詢了法律顧問。

counterfeit
['kaʊntɚˌfɪt]

adj 仿製品的，偽造物的 　　　　c2085

Many cashiers use special highlighters to check for counterfeit bills.

許多收銀員使用特殊的檢測儀來鑒別偽鈔。

credential
[krɪ'dɛnʃəl]

n 憑證；複數＝國書，證明書 　　　　c2086

Her credentials were superior to most of the other candidates.

她的證書與大多數的候選人相比要強很多。

crude
[krud]

adj 天然的，未加工的；未熟的；粗魯的；粗糙的 　　　　c2087

The boy's letters were still crude, but his mother noticed a definite improvement.

男孩的信寫得還是很粗糙，但他母親看到了明顯的進步。

crumble
['krʌmbl̩]

vi 破碎；崩潰；**vt** 粉碎；摧毀 　　　　c2088

Every summer the farmer repaired the places where his rock wall had crumbled.

每年夏天農民都會修補石牆坍塌的地方。

crumple
['krʌmpl̩]

vt 弄皺；使一蹶不振 　　　　c2089

The bride did not want to wear a satin dress because she knew it would crumple easily on the way to her wedding.

那位新娘不想穿緞緞婚紗，因為她知道緞緞婚紗很容易在去婚禮的路上就變皺了。

culminate
['kʌlmə,net]

托 雅 學

vi 達到頂點，達到極點；告終

I think those grey clouds looming overhead are about to culminate into a thunder and lightning storm.

我認為那些在頭頂若隱若現的灰色雲層即將以一場電閃雷鳴的暴風雨而告終。

c2090

cumulative
['kjʊmjʊ,letɪv]

托 雅 學

adj 累積的，蓄積的

Hopefully this week will bring some cumulative rainfall.

希望這週能帶來一些累積的降雨。

c2091

cunning
['kʌnɪŋ]

托 雅 學

adj 狡猾的，狡詐的

Wolves are cunning pack hunters.

狼是狡猾的群體獵食動物。

c2092

curt
[kɝt]

托 雅 學

adj 唐突草率的；簡明的，簡要的

I think our waitress was a little curt with us so maybe she's having a bad day.

我覺得我們的女服務生對我們有點兒簡慢無禮，也許是她今天不開心。

c2093

cyclone
['saɪklon]

托 雅 學

n 氣旋；暴風；龍捲風

Fortunately, the cyclone lost most of its energy before making landfall.

值得慶幸的是，龍捲風在登陸之前已經喪失了大部分能量。

c2094

D

---

dazzle
['dæzl̩]
托 雅 學

d2001

n 耀眼的光；vt 使目眩；使驚歎
The brilliant sunset dazzled the tourists who looked to the west across the calm sea.
輝煌的日落景觀使望向西方平靜海面的遊客們驚歎。

---

dazzling
['dæzlɪŋ]
托 雅 學

d2002

adj 令人印象深刻的，迷人的；刺眼的，眼花繚亂的
The beautiful actress had a dazzling smile and she looked radiant.
那位漂亮的女演員擁有迷人的笑容，她看上去光彩照人。

---

dearth
[dɝθ]
托 雅 學

d2003

n 缺乏，不足；饑饉
The dearth of jobs in farming forced the father to move to the city to find work.
農業中工作機會的缺乏迫使這位父親移居到城裡去找工作。

---

debris
[də'bri]
托 雅 學

d2004

n 殘骸，破瓦殘礫；垃圾，殘渣，廢棄物
The volunteers helped clear the beach of debris.
志願者幫助清除了海灘上的垃圾。

---

decadent
['dɛkədnt]
托 雅 學

d2005

adj 頹廢的，放縱的，墮落的
She didn't serve wine because she considered it decadent.
她沒有提供酒，因為她感覺喝酒是墮落的表現。

---

decay
[dɪ'ke]
托 雅 學

d2006

n/vi/vt 腐朽，腐爛；衰退
He threw away the pumpkin before it decayed on the front porch.
他在南瓜腐爛在前廊之前就扔掉了它。

---

decipher
[dɪ'saɪfɚ]
托 雅 學

d2007

vt 破譯；辨認；解釋
Let's hope we're able to decipher the writings and their meanings on the monastery wall.
讓我們希望我們能夠破譯修道院牆上的那些字跡和它們的含義。

---

defect
[dɪ'fɛkt]
托 雅 學

d2008

n 過失，缺點，不足，缺陷
She inspected the fruit for any defects before she paid.
付款前，她檢查了水果是否有任何缺陷。

defection
[dɪˈfɛkʃən]

托 雅 學

n 背叛；脫黨；不履行義務

d2009

The defection of the leader shocked the whole party.

領導者的背叛震驚了整個政黨。

defective
[dɪˈfɛktɪv]

托 雅 學

adj 有缺陷的，不完美的

d2010

Mary returned her new blender and got a refund from the store because it was clearly defective.

瑪莉退還了她新買的攪拌機並得到了商店的退款，因為那明顯是有缺陷的。

deference
[ˈdɛfərəns]

托 雅 學

n 遵從，服從；敬意，尊重，敬重

d2011

Out of deference to the victims' families, the police chief would not reveal names until next of kin had been notified.

出於對受害者家人的尊重，警察局長不會在受害者親屬得到通知前公佈受害者的名字。

deficiency
[dɪˈfɪʃənsɪ]

托 雅 學

n 不足，缺點，缺陷

d2012

The tutor worked hard to help Emma correct the deficiencies in her spelling.

老師努力地幫愛瑪糾正她拼寫中的不足之處。

deficit
[ˈdɛfɪsɪt]

托 雅 學

n 赤字，逆差，虧損，虧空；缺乏

d2013

The size of the budget deficit indicates potential problems for a company.

預算赤字的大小暗示了一家公司的潛在問題。

defy
[dɪˈfaɪ]

托 雅 學

vt （公然）違抗；蔑視；經受住；傲視

d2014

His next movie defied critical opinion and became a box office success.

他的下一部電影經受住了批評意見，取得了很好的票房成績。

degenerate
[dɪˈdʒɛnəˌrɪt]

托 雅 學

adj 墮落的；退化的，衰退的

d2015

She felt that the culture she admired has become degenerate since embracing television.

她覺得自從電視流行之後，她欽佩的文化就淪為次等了。

degenerate
[dɪˈdʒɛnəˌret]

托 雅 學

vi 衰退；墮落

d2016

The man's nervous system is not degenerating as quickly as the doctors had expected.

那個男人的神經系統並未像醫生預期的速度衰退。

dehydrate
[diˈhaɪˌdret]

托 雅 學

vt 脫水，使乾燥

d2017

You can dehydrate your own fruit using a fine wire mesh and a fan.

你可以使用一個細網篩子和電扇，來為你自己的水果脫水。

delegate
['dɛlə,gɪt]

n 代表　　　　　　　　　　d2018
I visited many countries all over the world as a delegate.
我作為一個代表訪問了世界許多國家。

delegate
['dɛlə,get]

vt 委派……為代表；授權，委託　　　d2019
Nancy delegated the work to the members of her operations team secretly.
南茜秘密地把工作授權給了她的運作團隊的成員。

delegation
[,dɛlə'geʃən]

n 代表團　　　　　　　　　　d2020
The delegation of officials decided to prolong their visit for a week to explore more beautiful places.
官員代表團決定多停留一週，以便探訪更多美麗的地方。

deliberate
[dɪ'lɪbərɪt]

adj 深思熟慮的；故意的　　　　d2021
He does things in a quiet and deliberate manner.
他做事安靜且深思熟慮。

deliberate
[dɪ'lɪbərɪt]

vi/vt 研討，深入商討　　　　d2022
The jury was given as much time as they needed to deliberate on the facts of the case.
陪審團被給予充分的時間來深入商討這個案子的真相。

delicate
['dɛləkət]

adj 纖弱的；精緻的；微妙的；靈敏的　d2023
The father marveled at his daughter's delicate fingers.
那位父親驚歎於他女兒纖細的手指。

demobilize
[di'mobḷ,aɪz]

vt 遣散，使退伍；使復員　　　d2024
I wish that all the world armies get demobilized and the world can live in harmony.
我期望世界上所有的軍隊都能遣散，這樣全世界就能和諧共處。

denote
[dɪ'not]

vt 表示，意味著　　　　　　d2025
His manner denoted confidence and ease around people.
他的架勢透露出自信和在人群中的輕鬆自如。

denounce
[dɪ'naʊns]

vt 公開指責，公然抨擊；譴責　　d2026
She denounced her old way of life and became a good woman.
她譴責自己過去的生活，並成了一個好女人。

deprive
[dɪ'praɪv]

托 雅 學

vt 剝奪，奪去，使喪失 `d2027`
She deprived herself of many creature comforts in order to care for her children.
她剝奪了自己很多小小的物質享受，以便照顧自己的子女。

derivative
[də'rɪvətɪv]

托 雅 學

n 衍生物 `d2028`
The word "decent" is a derivative of a Latin word.
「下降」這個詞是拉丁語的一個衍生詞。

desalination
[dɪ,sælə'neʃən]

托 雅 學

n 脫鹽，海水淡化 `d2029`
Desalination is the process for removing salts and minerals from water or soil.
脫鹽是指從水或土壤裡把鹽分和礦物質剔除出來的過程。

descent
[dɪ'sɛnt]

托 雅 學

n 下降，降下；斜坡；血統，家世 `d2030`
The scientists took careful measurements during the descent of the submarine.
在潛水艇下潛時，科學家們小心地進行了測量。

desolate
['dɛsḷɪt]

托 雅 學

adj 荒涼的；孤獨淒涼的 `d2031`
The death of her dog left her desolate for several weeks.
狗的死去讓她在孤獨中度過了數週。

despise
[dɪ'spaɪz]

托 雅 學 托 雅 學

vt 輕視，蔑視 `d2032`
She despised any thoughts that are different from hers.
她輕視與她不同的想法。

deteriorate
[dɪ'tɪrɪə,ret]

托 雅 學

vt 使⋯惡化，使⋯變壞 `d2033`
The social order deteriorated rapidly, so a curfew was imposed to reduce crimes.
社會治安急速惡化，只好實施宵禁來減少犯罪。

deterioration
[dɪ,tɪrɪə'reʃən]

托 雅 學

n 惡化，變壞；退化；墮落 `d2034`
It takes time and effort to protect antiques from deterioration.
防止古物損壞需要時間與精力。

deterrent
[dɪ'tɝ·rənt]

托 雅 學

adj 遏制的 `d2035`
The judge did not believe the deterrent effect of death penalty on serious crimes.
這位法官不相信死刑對重大犯罪的遏制效果。

D

deterrent
[dɪ'tɝ·rənt]

d2036

n 威懾力量

To discourage poor behavior, the teacher has found that communicating well with parents is the best deterrent for most problems.

要阻止不良行為，老師發現遏制大多數問題最好的方式就是與家長進行良好溝通。

detest
[dɪ'tɛst]

d2037

vt 極端厭惡

She detested yellow wall paper.

她非常厭惡黃色的壁紙。

devastate
['dɛvəs,tet]

d2038

vt 破壞，蹂躪；壓倒，垮掉

The news of the stock market crash devastated the investor.

股市崩盤的消息使投資者崩潰了。

devastating
['dɛvəs,tetɪŋ]

d2039

adj 毀滅性的；驚人的

A devastating typhoon caused hundreds of deaths in a nearby village.

一場毀滅性的颱風造成附近村莊裡數百人死亡。

differentiate
[,dɪfə'rɛnʃɪ,et]

d2040

vi/vt 區分，區別；使不同

Soon April was able to differentiate between the ripe and unripe fruit.

很快，愛普羅就可以區分熟的和生的水果了。

diffuse
[dɪ'fjus]

d2041

adj （文章等）冗長的；漫無邊際的；散開的

The editor told the new reporter that his article was diffuse and pointless.

編輯告訴那位新記者他的文章冗長且無重點。

diffuse
[dɪ'fjuz]

d2042

vi/vt 擴散，傳播

She preferred the light to diffuse in her bedroom.

她更喜歡房間裡的燈光漫射開來。

digress
[daɪ'grɛs]

d2043

vi 脫離主題

The professor was famous from digressing from the topic of his lectures.

這位教授在演講時離題是出了名的。

digression
[daɪ'grɛʃən]

d2044

n 離題

Unfortunately, the most interesting parts of his speech was irrelevant digressions from the topic.

不幸的是，他演講中最有趣的部分是與主題無關的題外話。

dilute
[daɪˈlut]

托 雅 學

vt 稀釋，沖淡

d2045

She diluted the lemonade because it was too strong.

她沖淡了檸檬水，因為它太濃了。

discern
[dɪˈzɝn]

托 雅 學

vt 看出，辨出，辨別

d2046

After 40 years of studying birds, she could discern different species by their song.

經過40年的鳥類研究，她可以通過鳥鳴辨別出鳥的種類。

discharge
[dɪsˈtʃɑrdʒ]

托 雅 學

vi/vt 遣散，解僱，釋放；卸貨，排出；放電；**n** 分泌物

d2047

Some factories in this locality still discharge waste water into the river.

這一地區有些工廠仍把廢水排入河中。

discourse
[ˈdɪskors]

托 雅 學

n 論文；演說；談話；話語 **vi** 講述，著述

d2048

His scholarly discourse on Van Gogh was considered one of the best published that year.

他的關於梵谷的論文被認為是年度最佳的出版物之一。

discreet
[dɪˈskrit]

托 雅 學

adj （言行）謹慎的，慎重的；有判斷力的

d2049

She was discreet about seeking help for the family.

她謹慎地為她的家庭尋求幫助。

discrepancy
[dɪˈskrɛpənsɪ]

托 雅 學

n 相差，差異；矛盾

d2050

A discrepancy in the miscellaneous earnings column remains unaccounted for.

雜項收入欄的帳目有出入，到目前為止仍然無法解釋。

discrete
[dɪˈskrit]

托 雅 學

adj 分離的，不連接的

d2051

These events seem discrete but they are all related.

這些事件看上去不相關，但是它們都是有聯繫的。

disguise
[dɪsˈgaɪz]

托 雅 學

n 假裝；隱瞞；掩埋

d2052

Her happy smile was only a disguise for her sadness.

她喜悅的笑容只是對她憂傷的掩飾。

disguise
[dɪsˈgaɪz]

托 雅 學

vt 假裝；隱瞞；掩埋

d2053

She disguised her surprise by forcing herself to look away.

她強迫自己看別處來隱瞞自己的驚訝。

disperse
[dɪˈspɝs]
托 雅 學

vt 使分散；驅散 　d2054
She dispersed her inheritance between her three children equally.
她將遺產平分給了三個孩子。

dispose
[dɪˈspoz]
托 雅 學

vi/vt 處理，處置；做最後安排，解決 　d2055
The criminal disposed of all evidence that would connect him to the crime scene.
那個罪犯處理了所有能夠把他和犯罪現場聯繫起來的證據。

disposition
[ˌdɪspəˈzɪʃən]
托 雅 學

n 排列，部署；性格傾向；傾向，意向 　d2056
She loved his easy-going disposition.
她喜歡他隨和的性格。

disproportionate
[ˌdɪsprəˈporʃənɪt]
托 雅 學

adj 不協調的，不成比例的；不均衡的，不相稱的 　d2057
Those big feet and hands look disproportionate on such a small man.
那雙大腳和大手在這麼一個小個子男人身上看著很不協調。

disrupt
[dɪsˈrʌpt]
托 雅 學

vt 使混亂，使崩潰，使分裂，使瓦解 　d2058
The unexpected visitors disrupted her normal cleaning routines.
未預料的訪客打亂了她正常的大掃除安排。

dissatisfaction
[ˌdɪssætɪsˈfækʃən]
托 雅 學

n 不滿，不平 　d2059
She wrote to the manager about her dissatisfaction at the store's customer service.
她寫信給經理表達她對商店客戶服務的不滿。

dissipate
[ˈdɪsəˌpet]
托 雅 學

vi 消散；作鳥獸散 　d2060
The mob dissipated immediately after they had completed their mission.
幫派分子完成任務後立刻作鳥獸散。

dissipate
[ˈdɪsəˌpet]
托 雅 學

vt 發散；揮霍 　d2061
The diffuser's new design is more efficient, as it dissipates the aroma evenly.
那個噴霧器的新設計更有效率，因為它可以更均衡地散發香氣。

distend
[dɪˈstɛnd]
托 雅 學

vi 擴張，膨脹；腫脹 　d2062
Dr. Brown's concern rose when the child's abdomen started to swell and distend.
當孩子的腹部開始腫脹時，布朗醫生更擔憂了。

distention
[dɪˈstɛnʃən]

托 雅 學

n 擴張

d2063

The distention of the damage is difficult to determine until all the reports are in.

受損的擴張程度很難鑑定，除非所有的報告都拿到了。

distill
[dɪsˈtɪl]

托 雅 學

vt 蒸餾，用蒸餾法提取；吸取，提煉

d2064

Distilled water is made by boiling water while purified water usually means the water is filtered.

蒸餾水取自沸水，而純淨水通常只表示水曾過濾。

divert
[daɪˈvɝt]

托 雅 學

vt 使轉向，使改道；轉移（注意力）；使娛樂

d2065

The flash of the camera diverted his attention from the ball for a second.

照相機的閃光燈讓他的注意力從球上轉移開了一下。

dole
[dol]

托 雅 學

n 賑濟物，施捨物

d2066

After the storm flooded the area, thousands of people were living on the government's dole.

在暴風雨淹沒那個區域後，成千上萬人靠政府的賑濟物過活。

domain
[doˈmen]

托 雅 學

n （活動，思想等）領域，範圍；領地

d2067

His wife did all the cooking, but he considered the yard his domain.

他的妻子做飯，而他將院子視為他的領地。

dormant
[ˈdɔrmənt]

托 雅 學

adj 休眠的；靜止的，平靜的；潛伏的，潛藏的

d2068

The volcano on the island is believed to be dormant so let's hope so.

島上的火山被認為是休眠的，所以讓我們希望是如此吧。

drowsy
[ˈdraʊzɪ]

托 雅 學

adj 昏昏欲睡的，催眠的；沉寂的

d2069

After taking pain medication, the patient fell into a drowsy sleep.

吃完止痛藥，病人陷入了昏昏欲睡中。

duly
[ˈdjulɪ]

托 雅 學

adv 及時；恰當地，充分地

d2070

His objection to the new rule was duly noted by the secretary.

他對新規則的反對意見被秘書及時地記錄下來。

E

ecosystem
['εko,sɪstəm]

n 生態系統   e2001

An ecosystem refers to all the animals and plants in a certain area.

生態系統涉及特定區域裡所有的動物與植物。

eccentric
[ɪk'sɛntrɪk]

托 雅 學

adj 古怪的，反常的；**n** 古怪的人   e2002

The professor was known to be eccentric in his dressing.

這位教授因穿著古怪而出名。

eclipse
[ɪ'klɪps]

托 雅 學

n （日、月）蝕   e2003

A solar eclipse occurs when the moon partially or fully blocks the sun during its passage between the earth and the sun.

當月亮在太陽與地球之間的軌道部分或全部遮住太陽時，日蝕就會發生。

ecstasy
['ɛkstəsɪ]

n 狂喜，心醉神迷，忘形   e2004

She was in ecstasy for coming in first at the pageant.

她因選美比賽獲得第一名而狂喜不已。

eddy
['ɛdɪ]

n 渦流，漩渦   e2005

The Niagara River has a swirling eddy from the strong water current.

尼亞加拉河的激流中間有迴旋渦流。

edible
['ɛdəb!]

adj 可食用的   e2006

I didn't know that the stem of the plant was edible too.

我並不知道那種植物的根也是可食用的。

edifice
['ɛdəfɪs]

n 大型建築物，大廈；巨大而複雜的組織   e2007

The White House is probably the most photographed edifice in the United States.

白宮可能是美國出鏡率最高的大廈。

elasticity
[ɪ,læs'tɪsətɪ]

n 彈力，彈性   e2008

Sally maintains her muscular elasticity by exercising regularly.

沙莉通過規律運動來保持肌肉的彈性。

elicit
[ɪˈlɪsɪt]
托 雅 學

vt 引出，抽出，引起　e2009
His pleas elicited compassion from the judge.
他的請求引起了法官的同情。

eligible
[ˈɛlɪdʒəbl̩]
托 雅 學

adj 符合條件的；（尤指婚姻等）合適（意）的　e2010
He is a decent guy with a stable job, making him an eligible bachelor.
他是一個正派的小夥子，工作又穩定，這讓他成為一個適合結婚的單身漢。

eliminate
[ɪˈlɪməˌnet]
托 雅 學

vi/vt 除去，淘汰；排（刪、消）除；削減（人員）　e2011
She eliminated several of the afternoon chores to give herself more time to relax.
她取消了下午的好幾件雜務以便多給自己一點兒時間放鬆一下。

elite
[eˈlit]
托 雅 學

n 精華；精英；優秀分子　e2012
It was a party held for elite investors, so not everyone was invited.
那是一個為精英投資者所舉辦的派對，所以並不是每個人都受邀。

elixir
[ɪˈlɪksə]
托 雅 學

n 萬能藥；長生不老藥　e2013
Vitamin drinks are advertised as the elixir for prolonging life.
維生素飲料被廣告成延年益壽的萬能藥。

elliptical
[ɪˈlɪptɪkl̩]
托 雅 學

adj 橢圓的；省略的　e2014
The discovery of the elliptical orbit of planets was made in 1609.
西元1609年發現了行星的橢圓軌道。

eloquence
[ˈɛləkwəns]
托 雅 學

n 雄辯；口才；修辭　e2015
He always spoke with words of eloquence and it was a real pleasure to hear his speeches.
他有雄辯的口才，聽他演說是一件令人享受的事。

eloquent
[ˈɛləkwənt]
托 雅 學

adj 雄辯的，有口才的；動人的　e2016
His eloquent words swayed the jury.
他雄辯的口才讓陪審團動搖了。

embark
[ɪmˈbɑrk]
托 雅 學

vi/vt 乘船，上飛機　e2017
She embarked on the ship in order to do some sightseeing.
她搭上船好遊覽觀光。

E

embassy
['ɛmbəsɪ]

n 大使館；大使及其隨員
The embassy hosted a formal dinner for the local dignitaries.
大使館為當地的顯要人物舉辦了正式的宴會。

e2018

emblem
['ɛmbləm]

n 象徵；徽章
The lion and the unicorn appear on the royal emblem of England.
在英國皇家徽章上刻有獅子和獨角獸。

e2019

emboss
[ɪm'bɔs]

vt 製成浮雕，用浮雕裝飾；使隆起，使凸出
The company president likes to emboss his initials on his personal stationery.
那位公司總裁很喜歡把他名字的首字母製成浮雕，印在他的個人文具上。

e2020

emerge
[ɪ'mɝdʒ]

vi 顯現，浮現；暴露；形成
The butterfly emerged from its cocoon slowly.
蝴蝶慢慢破繭而出。

e2021

eminent
['ɛmənənt]

adj 著名的，傑出的，卓越的
The eminent pianist agreed to play an encore.
那位著名的鋼琴家同意返場再演奏一曲。

e2022

empirical
[ɛm'pɪrɪkl̩]

adj 經驗主義的；實證的
The empirical evidence of the theory has been proven through many laboratory experiments.
該理論的實驗證據已被實驗室的許多實驗證實。

e2023

encompass
[ɪn'kʌmpəs]

vt 包含，含有
This team encompasses all the excellent characteristics of elite performers.
這個團隊含有優秀選手們的所有優良品質。

e2024

encompass
[ɪn'kʌmpəs]

vt 包圍，圍繞
Unfortunately, he was overcome by the disease, as the cancer encompassed his entire body.
不幸的是，他被病痛纏著，因為癌症擴散到了他整個身體。

e2025

encyclopedia
[ɪn,saɪklə'pidɪə]

n 百科全書
Even with the Internet, she still liked to go and check the encyclopedia for information.
即使有網路，她仍喜歡翻百科全書找資料。

e2026

endeavor
[ɪn'dɛvə]
托 雅 學

n/vi 努力，盡力   e2027
He endeavored to make better grades that semester.
他努力在那學期取得好成績。

endorse
[ɪn'dɔrs]
托 雅 學

vt 支持，贊同；背書，簽   e2028
The former governor endorsed the candidate recommended by his political party.
前州長支持那位他的政黨推薦的候選人。

endow
[ɪn'daʊ]
托 雅 學

vt 資助；賦予，授予   e2029
Music endows someone with a totally different sense.
音樂賦予人一種完全不同的感受。

ensemble
[ɑn'sɑmbl]
托 雅 學

n 全體；合唱曲   e2030
He played in a small string ensemble every Saturday.
每星期六他都在一個小型的弦樂合奏團演奏。

ensue
[ɛn'su]
托 雅 學

vi 跟著發生，繼起   e2031
A fight ensued after the little boy smashed the little girl's new toy.
在小男孩打碎小女孩的新玩具後，打架就跟著發生了。

entail
[ɪn'tel]
托 雅 學

vt 使必需   e2032
The rules for renting the apartment entail standards of cleanliness and being a responsible neighbor.
租用公寓的規則需要潔淨的標準和做個負責的鄰居。

entail
[ɪn'tel]
托 雅 學

vt 使蒙受，使承擔   e2033
His disgraceful behavior will more than likely entail the most severe consequences for him.
他不光彩的行為必將使他自己承擔嚴重的後果。

enterprise
['ɛntə,praɪz]
托 雅 學

n 事業，企（事）業單位；事業心，進取心   e2034
He was known for his diligence and enterprise as a business owner.
身為一個公司老闆，他以勤勞和進取心為人所知。

entitle
[ɪn'taɪtl]
托 雅 學

vt 給以權利（或資格），授權，給…稱號（題名）   e2035
The deed entitled her to rent the property to whoever she wanted.
該契約授權她將房產租給任何她想租的人。

entity
['ɛntətɪ]

n 實體；存在（物）；組織，機構；本質
The design was strange; the garden and the house were treated as two completely separate entities.
那個設計很奇怪，花園和房子被當作是兩個完全分開的實體。

e2036

entrepreneur
[ˌɑntrəprə'nɝ]

n 企業家；承包人
The young entrepreneur started his first company at the age of 25.
這位年輕企業家在25歲時就創業了。

e2037

envisage
[ɪn'vɪzɪdʒ]

vt 想像，設想；展望，正視
She envisaged a time when her kids would grow up and get married.
她想像著孩子長大並結婚的那一刻。

e2038

ephemeral
[ɪ'fɛmərəl]

adj 短暫的，瞬息的，曇花一現的；朝生暮死的
The ephemeral pleasure of watching fireworks is that they only last for a very short time.
觀賞煙花的短暫愉悅就在於，它們只持續很短時間。

e2039

epidemic
[ˌɛpɪ'dɛmɪk]

adj 流行性的，普遍的；傳染的
Polluted water stagnating in the sewer will shortly add the peril of epidemic disease.
停滯在下水道裡的污水很快就會增加傳染病的危險。

e2040

epidemic
[ˌɛpɪ'dɛmɪk]

n 流行病；傳播
There's an epidemic happening throughout Southeast Asia and many people died.
有一種流行病在東南亞肆虐，許多人因此喪命。

e2041

episode
['ɛpəˌsod]

n 一段情節；片斷；（連續劇的）一集
She recorded an episode of her favorite show for later viewing.
她錄了一集自己最喜歡的電視劇，準備以後再看。

e2042

epoch
['ɛpək]

n （新）時代；曆元
The golden epoch of Hollywood filmmaking was between the 1930s and 1960s.
好萊塢電影的黃金時代在1930至1960年間。

e2043

equilibrium
[ˌikwə'lɪbrɪəm]

n 平衡，均衡；均衡論
They rearranged the cargo to bring the ship back into equilibrium.
他們重新整理貨物以使船隻恢復平衡。

e2044

equivalent
[ɪ'kwɪvələnt]

托 雅 學

adj 相等的，等價的；**n** 相等物，等價物　e2045

The worth of the diamond was equivalent to his annual salary.

那顆鑽石的價值相當於他一年的工資。

erratic
[ɪ'rætɪk]

托 雅 學

adj 不穩定的；不依常理的；**n** 古怪的人　e2046

Because his behavior is sometimes erratic, it is often difficult to communicate with him.

跟他溝通時常會有困難，因為他行事不依常理。

erroneous
[ɪ'ronɪəs]

托 雅 學

adj 錯誤的，不正確的　e2047

The scientist's findings turned out to be erroneous due to a miscalculation.

因為計算錯誤，科學家的研究發現證明是錯誤的。

escalate
['ɛskə,let]

托 雅 學

vi/vt 逐步擴大，逐步升高，逐步增強　e2048

The diplomat worked hard to keep tensions from escalating between the two countries.

外交官努力避免兩國緊張情勢的逐步擴大。

escort
['ɛskɔrt]

托 雅 學

n/vt 護衛，護送；（在社交場合）陪伴異性的人　e2049

Her escort walked her down the red carpet at the ball.

她的舞伴陪她走下舞會的紅地毯。

esteem
[ɪs'tim]

托 雅 學

n 尊敬，尊重；**vt** 尊敬，尊重；認為　e2050

The generosity of the family was highly esteemed by the villagers.

這家人的慷慨讓全村村民尊敬。

ethnic
['ɛθnɪk]

托 雅 學

adj 種族的；人種學的　e2051

According to the annual census, ethnic households indicate diverse cultures in the city.

根據一年一次的人口普查，不同種族的家庭展現了這座城市中的多元文化。

etiquette
['ɛtɪkɛt]

托 雅 學

n 禮儀，禮節，成規　e2052

The girls took all the academic subjects as well as lessons in etiquette.

那些女孩修習所有的學科以及禮儀課程。

eviscerate
[ɪ'vɪsə,ret]

托 雅 學

vt 去除⋯內臟；抽取精華，挫傷元氣　e2053

The fisherman used a sharp knife to eviscerate the fish.

那個漁夫用一把鋒利的小刀去除了魚的內臟。

E

exalt
[ɪg'zɔlt]

vi/vt 提升，提高，讚揚，使得意 e2054

The king exalted the brave commoners to the rank of knighthood for their brave conduct during the battle.

這些平民在戰爭中表現英勇，國王將他們提升為騎士。

excavate
['ɛkskə,vet]

vi/vt 挖，挖開，鑿通 e2055

They carefully excavated the newly discovered city.

他們小心翼翼地挖掘最新發現的城市遺跡。

excess
[ɪk'sɛs]

adj 過量的，額外的；**n** 過量；超額；無節制 e2056

An excess of snow this winter caused a massive power outage in our city.

這個冬天過量的積雪導致我們的城市大規模停電。

excessive
[ɪk'sɛsɪv]

adj 過多的；過分的；額外的 e2057

He used an excessive amount of spice in his chili.

他在辣椒中加了過量的調味料。

excessively
[ɪk'sɛsɪvlɪ]

adv 過分，極端地 e2058

It was excessively wasteful of me moneywise to buy three different handbags today!

就金錢而言，我今天買了三款手提包，實在是過度浪費。

excursion
[ɪk'skɝʒən]

n 短途旅行，遊覽；遠足 e2059

They took an excursion into the woods every weekend.

他們每個週末都到樹林裡進行遠足旅行。

excursion
[ɪk'skɝʒən]

n 離題；偏移，漂移 e2060

Your comments are an excursion from the theme.

你的話偏離了主題。

exemplary
[ɪg'zɛmpləɪ]

adj 可仿效的，可做模範的 e2061

His exemplary behavior has been his greatest asset in moving up the corporate ladder.

他那可做模範的行為是他在公司內提升自己地位的最大資產。

exemplify
[ɪg'zɛmplə,faɪ]

vt 舉例證明；示範；作⋯的範例（榜樣） e2062

He exemplified courage and honor when he rescued the girl from the fire.

當他從火災中救出小女孩時，他就是勇氣和榮譽的典範。

exempt
[ɪgˈzɛmpt]
托 雅 學

adj 免除的
Foreign visitors are exempt from paying any taxes.
外國觀光客是免稅的。

e2063

exempt
[ɪgˈzɛmpt]
托 雅 學

vt 使免除，豁免；免稅
Kevin is exempted from doing the housekeeping today, since he helped twice last week.
凱文今天可以免除家務，因為他上週幫了兩次忙。

e2064

exhilarate
[ɪgˈzɪləˌret]
托 雅 學

vt 使高興，使愉悅，振奮
The swimming program will exhilarate and energize you all.
這個游泳訓練課程將振奮和激勵你們所有人。

e2065

exile
[ˈɛksaɪl]
托 雅 學

n 流放；被流放者
Napoleon died in exile from France.
拿破崙在從法國流放途中去世。

e2066

exile
[ˈɛksaɪl]
托 雅 學

vt 流放，放逐
The King was exiled by his own people many years ago.
國王許多年前被自己的國人放逐。

e2067

exotic
[ɛgˈzɑtɪk]
托 雅 學

adj 異國的，外來的；**n** 外來物，舶來品
He bought his grey parrot at the exotic pet store.
他在外來寵物店買到了這隻灰鸚鵡。

e2068

expenditure
[ɪkˈspɛndɪtʃɚ]
托 雅 學

n （時間等）支出，消費
The school board approved the expenditures required by the principal.
學校董事會批准了校長所要求的支出。

e2069

expire
[ɪkˈspaɪr]
托 雅 學

vi 滿期，到期；斷氣
Don't forget to renew your contract before it expires next month.
別忘了在下個月到期之前更新你的合約。

e2070

explicit
[ɪkˈsplɪsɪt]
托 雅 學

adj 詳述的，明確的；坦率的；外顯的
Sometimes demonstration, not explicit verbal instruction, is the best way to teach.
有時候演示才是最好的教法，而非直接明確的言語指導。

e2071

exploit
['ɛksplɔɪt]

托 雅 學

e2072

n 功績（動）；業績
He has had many exploits during his youth.
他年輕的時候曾有過許多功勳。

exploit
[ɪk'splɔɪt]

托 雅 學

e2073

vt 開拓，開發；剝削
She hated to see poor people exploited by the government.
她痛恨看到窮人被政府剝削。

exquisite
['ɛkskwɪzɪt]

托 雅 學

e2074

adj 精緻的，細膩的；敏銳的
Her performance of the aria was exquisite.
他的曲調表演非常細膩。

extinct
[ɪk'stɪŋkt]

托 雅 學

e2075

adj 絕種的；熄滅了的
The dodo bird became extinct in the 17th century.
渡渡鳥在十七世紀絕種了。

extinguish
[ɪk'stɪŋgwɪʃ]

托 雅 學

e2076

vt 熄滅；結束；壓制；使黯然失色；償清
She extinguished the candles one by one until the room was in complete darkness.
她把蠟燭逐根熄滅，直到房間完全變暗。

extract
[ɪk'strækt]

托 雅 學

e2077

n 摘錄；vt 取出；榨取；摘錄
The following information is extracted from the monthly paper.
以下資訊摘自月報。

F

figurehead
['fɪgjɚˌhɛd]

托 雅 學

n （有名無實的）傀儡；首領

f2001

Many outsiders knew that the rebel tribal leader was just a figurehead with no real power over his territory.

許多局外人都知道反叛的部落首領只是一個傀儡，在自己的領地上並沒有實權。

---

fabricate
['fæbrɪˌket]

托 雅 學

vt 捏造，編造（謊言、藉口等）；建造，製造

f2002

That young lady quickly fabricated an excuse and intended to get past the custom.

那位年輕小姐很快地捏造了一個理由，企圖通過海關。

---

fabrication
[ˌfæbrɪ'keʃən]

托 雅 學

n 製作，構成；捏造；偽造物

f2003

After touching the bag, she immediately recognized that it was a cheap fabrication rather than one of high quality.

在觸摸了包包後，她馬上察覺到那是個便宜的偽造物，並非高級材質的包包。

---

facility
[fə'sɪlətɪ]

托 雅 學

n 靈巧，熟練；天賦

f2004

Both his brothers shared a facility for languages.

他的兩個哥哥都有語言天賦。

---

facility
[fə'sɪlətɪ]

托 雅 學

n 設備，設施；便利條件

f2005

The new sports facility could host soccer, baseball, and rugby games.

新的運動設施可主辦足球、棒球和橄欖球比賽。

---

famine
['fæmɪn]

托 雅 學

n 饑荒，饑餓

f2006

The Red Cross sent food supplies to Somalia during the famine.

紅十字會在饑荒時把食物補給送到索馬利亞。

---

feast
[fist]

托 雅 學

n 節日；宴會

f2007

I had a great time last night at the feast.

昨晚的宴會讓我非常愉悅。

---

feat
[fit]

托 雅 學

n 功績，偉業；技藝

f2008

He was known for his feats of bravery during combat.

他因為作戰期間的英勇功績而出名。

feeble
[ˈfibl̩]

托 雅 學

adj 虛弱的，無力的

f2009

His feeble attempts at an apology only made her angrier.
他道歉的嘗試很無力，這讓她更生氣。

fend
[fɛnd]

托 雅 學

vi/vt 保護；謀生

f2010

The mother bird fed her chicks until they were old enough to fend for themselves.
母鳥餵她的小鳥直到它們大到可以自己謀生。

feud
[fjud]

托 雅 學

vt 長期鬥爭，爭吵不休

f2011

I really don't want to feud with you anymore over a trivial matter.
我真的不想再因為一件無關緊要的小事和你爭吵不休了。

fickle
[ˈfɪkl̩]

托 雅 學

adj 善變的，靠不住的；反覆無常的，變幻莫測的

f2012

Her fickle nature didn't keep him from pursuing her.
她善變的性格並沒有妨礙他對她的追求。

fidelity
[fɪˈdɛlətɪ]

托 雅 學

n 忠實，誠實，忠誠；保真度

f2013

He was known for his fidelity to the rules.
他以對規則的忠誠而聞名。

filth
[fɪlθ]

托 雅 學

n 污穢，汙物；淫猥

f2014

The women sweep away the filth on the sidewalk each day.
那些婦人們每天清掃人行道上的汙物。

flabby
[ˈflæbɪ]

托 雅 學

adj 肥胖的，肌肉鬆弛的；無活力的，優柔寡斷的

f2015

Without regular exercise, you will have a flabby body.
如果不定期運動，你將全身肌肉鬆弛。

flare
[flɛr]

托 雅 學

vi/vt 閃耀，（使）閃亮

f2016

The torch that the soldier held in the dark flared beautifully, and filled the area with light.
士兵在黑暗中高舉的火把美麗地閃爍著，並讓那個區域充滿亮光。

flatter
[ˈflætɚ]

托 雅 學

vt 奉承；使高興；自命不凡

f2017

He flattered himself saying that he was the best dancer in our class.
他鼓吹自己是班上最好的舞者。

F

flaunt
[flɔnt]

托 雅 學

vt 炫耀，誇耀，誇示

f2018

By all accounts, the countess takes every opportunity to flaunt her wealth and buys every luxury item she can.

據大家所說，那位伯爵夫人利用一切機會炫耀她的財富，購買她所能買到的每一樣奢侈品。

flee
[fli]

托 雅 學

vi 逃走；逃避

f2019

The bank robber decided that the only way to evade capture was to flee from the country.

那個銀行搶匪決定，躲避追捕的唯一辦法就是從這個國家逃走。

fleet
[flit]

托 雅 學

n 艦隊，船隊

f2020

The number of whaling fleets is decreasing since the whaling industry is no longer lucrative.

捕鯨船隊的數量正在減少，因為捕鯨業已不再賺錢了。

fleeting
['flitɪŋ]

托 雅 學

adj 疾馳的，飛逝的，短暫的，閃現的

f2021

Susan said her boss has fleeting moments when she thinks he's almost human but most of the time he's like a bear with a sore head.

蘇珊說她老闆有幾個短暫的瞬間，讓她覺得他幾乎是有人性的，但大多數時候他都脾氣暴躁。

flirt
[flɝt]

托 雅 學

vi/vt 揮動，擺動；調情，玩弄；**n** 賣弄風騷者，調情的人

f2022

The man flirted with the lady in a playful way.

那個男人用開玩笑的方式與那位小姐調情。

fluctuate
['flʌktʃʊ,et]

托 雅 學

vi/vt 使…波動；使…起伏

f2023

The gas prices tend to fluctuate up and down every weekend.

油價每週有上下波動的傾向。

fluctuation
[,flʌktʃʊ'eʃən]

托 雅 學

n 波動；變動

f2024

Recent fluctuations in the money market have caused uncertainty of the economy in other areas.

貨幣市場的近期波動已導致其他區域經濟的不穩定。

fluff
[flʌf]

托 雅 學

vt 抖鬆，拍鬆；搞壞，弄糟

f2025

While you are making the bed, please fluff up the pillows.

鋪床時，請把枕頭拍鬆。

flutter
['flʌtɚ]

托 雅 學

n 興奮，激動；慌亂

f2026

The sudden arrival of the police caused quite a flutter in the pub.

員警的突然到來在酒吧引起了一陣騷亂。

F

flutter
['flʌtɚ]
托 雅 學

vi 振翼；飄動
f2027
The bird fluttered on the window sill.
那隻鳥在窗臺上振翼。

foam
[fom]
托 雅 學

n 泡沫；**vi** 起泡沫
f2028
My cappuccino is always served with a thick head of foam.
我的卡布奇諾總是有著厚厚的泡沫。

foliage
['folɪɪdʒ]
托 雅 學

n 樹葉；植物
f2029
The foliage was so thick in the jungle that they had to use machetes to get through.
叢林裡的樹葉太厚了，以至於他們要使用大砍刀來通行。

foment
[fo'mɛnt]
托 雅 學

vt 激起，煽動（麻煩等）
f2030
Really it's a shame that some fanatics disturb world peace by fomenting religious conflicts.
令人遺憾的是，部分狂熱主義者藉著煽動宗教衝突，干擾世界和平。

foremost
['for,most]
托 雅 學

adj 最先的；最初的；主要的；**adv** 首要地
f2031
The safety of the passengers and crew was foremost in the mind of the pilot.
乘客與全體機務人員的安全是機長主要的考慮。

forfeit
['fɔr,fɪt]
托 雅 學

n 沒收物，罰金
f2032
The forfeit for each basketball player involved in the fight was $6,000.
參與打架的每一個籃球隊員都被判罰款6000美元。

forfeit
['fɔr,fɪt]
托 雅 學

vt 沒收；喪失，失去
f2033
The boy forfeited his right to play games when he broke his promise to his parents.
那個男孩因為違背對父母的承諾喪失了玩遊戲的權利。

forge
[fɔrdʒ]
托 雅 學

n 煉冶場；鍛爐；鐵匠鋪
f2034
The blacksmith's forge makes horse shoes for the stallion.
那個鐵匠的鍛爐製作種馬的馬蹄鐵。

forge
[fɔrdʒ]
托 雅 學

vi 穩步前進
f2035
Let's all forge ahead today and report no later than this evening.
我們今天全部穩步前進，最遲在今天傍晚前彙報。

319

forge
[fɔrdʒ]
托 雅 學

vt 鍛造；偽造
It is a punishable crime to forge a signature.
偽造簽名是會被處罰的罪行。

f2036

formidable
['fɔrmɪdəbl]
托 雅 學

adj 強大的；令人敬畏的；可怕的；艱難的，艱巨的
It is a formidable challenge for anyone to climb Mt.Everest.
對任何人來說，攀登珠穆朗瑪峰都是一項艱巨的挑戰。

f2037

formula
['fɔrmjələ]
托 雅 學

n 公式；規則；分子式；藥方；複數＝formulae
This company's winning formula includes professionally trained personnel and excellent services.
這家公司的獲勝公式裡包含了受過專業訓練的人員和優秀的服務。

f2038

formulate
['fɔrmjə,let]
托 雅 學

vt 用公式表示；制定，規劃；設計；系統地闡述
The school plans to formulate a dress code for both teachers and students.
學校打算要制定老師及學生的著裝要求。

f2039

fort
[fort]
托 雅 學

n 堡壘，要塞
The fort that was being built over the past 40 years was made to protect the villagers.
過去四十多年一直在建造的堡壘是用來保護村民的。

f2040

fossil
['fɑsl]
托 雅 學

n 化石
I was collecting some seashells at the beach and discovered an old fossil preserved in a rock.
當我正在沙灘上撿貝殼時，我發現了一個被保存在岩石裡的古老化石。

f2041

fossilize
['fɑsl,aɪz]
托 雅 學

adj 偶然的，意外的；幸運的，吉祥的
Geologists study how animals, plants and other organisms, fossilize over the course of many, many years.
地質學家研究動物、植物和其他生物，是如何在許多年的過程中變成化石的。

f2042

fraction
['frækʃən]
托 雅 學

n 碎片；小部分，一點兒；分數
He bought the used car for a fraction of the price he would have paid for a new one.
他買這輛二手車只用了他本來要買一輛新車的一部分價錢。

f2043

fracture
['fræktʃə]
托 雅 學

n 裂縫（痕）；骨折
The doctor set the boy's bone fracture before he put the cast on.
醫生先把男孩的骨折復位，然後才把石膏敷上。

f2044

F

fragment
['frægmənt]

n 碎片，小部分；片斷　　f2045

She picked up the fragments of the broken jar and glued them back together.

她撿起破罐子的碎片並將它們黏回去。

frantic
['fræntɪk]

adj 狂亂的，瘋狂的　　f2046

The group members were frantic when they discovered their director was missing.

當他們發現主管失蹤時，小組成員都瘋了。

freight
[fret]

n 貨物，貨運；運費　　f2047

The seller has to pay the costs for shipping freight.

賣方必須支付運費。

fret
[frɛt]

vi/vt （使…）煩惱　　f2048

Mia's teacher advised her not to fret over the entrance examination next week.

米亞的老師建議她不要使自己煩惱下週的入學考試。

friction
['frɪkʃən]

n 摩擦，摩擦力　　f2049

He changed the oil in his car so that friction wouldn't damage the moving parts.

他換了車裡的油，這樣摩擦就不會破壞車子的運轉零件了。

fringe
[frɪndʒ]

adj 邊緣的，外部的　　f2050

A fringe group is responsible for the attack.

一個外部的團體負責發動攻擊。

fringe
[frɪndʒ]

n 邊緣；（窗簾）緣飾；額前垂髮　　f2051

She walked from the interior to the fringe of the forest and once again yelled.

她從黑暗的森林裡頭向外面的邊緣走去，並再次叫喊。

fringe
[frɪndʒ]

vt 在…上裝以緣飾；以穗裝飾　　f2052

The hat is fringed with many intricate little decorations.

帽子的邊緣有許多複雜精細的飾品做裝飾。

frugal
['frugl]

adj 節儉的，儉省的　　f2053

He liked to buy used clothing because he was frugal.

他喜歡買舊衣服，因為他很節儉。

fumigate
['fjumə,get]
托 雅 學

f2054

vt 燻製；香薰；用煙燻消毒
They had their house fumigated for termites.
他們讓人把房子煙燻了一遍以消除白蟻。

furnace
['fɜ·nɪs]
托 雅 學

f2055

n 爐子，熔爐，火爐
They added a few more logs to the furnace to keep the house warm for the night.
他們在火爐裡多加了些木頭，讓房子保持整夜暖和。

furnish
['fɜ·nɪʃ]
托 雅 學

f2056

vt 供應；裝備；佈置
The interior designer furnished this place with a number of creative elements.
室內設計師運用了許多有創意的元素來裝飾這個地方。

fury
['fjʊrɪ]
托 雅 學

f2057

n 狂怒，暴怒；猛烈
He feared his father's fury when he found out about the broken window.
他害怕父親發現破窗後的暴怒。

fuse
[fjuz]
托 雅 學

f2058

n 保險絲，導火線；熔線
When the lights went out in the house, he checked the fuse box.
當屋子裡的燈熄滅時，他檢查了保險線盒。

fuse
[fjuz]
托 雅 學

f2059

vt 熔化，熔合
The scientist tried to fuse two materials together to make a new type of fuel.
科學家嘗試融合兩種原料來產生一種新型燃料。

fusion
['fjuʒən]
托 雅 學

f2060

n 熔合物；結合，熔合；核聚變
The citizens voted to build a fusion reactor outside the town in order to power the county.
為了給縣裡提供電源，市民投票在鎮外建造一個核聚變反應堆。

fuss
[fʌs]
托 雅 學

f2061

n 忙亂；大驚小怪
When I think about the fuss my mother always made over me as a child, I always smile to myself.
當我想起我還是小孩時母親對我的一切都大驚小怪，我都對自己微微一笑。

fuss
[fʌs]
托 雅 學

f2062

vi/vt 忙亂；大驚小怪
Oh please, don't you even fuss over such a small misunderstanding.
喔，拜託，請你不要連這麼小的誤會都大驚小怪。

G

gale
[gel]
托 雅 學

n 狂風，大風　　　　　　　　　　　g2001
The aged woman could hardly move forward in a strong gale.
老婦人在狂風中幾乎無法向前行進。

galvanize
['gælvə,naɪz]
托 雅 學

vt 通電；鍍鋅；刺激　　　　　　　　g2002
The factory will galvanize the steel rods to prevent them from rusting.
工廠會給鋼管鍍鋅，以防它們生銹。

garment
['garmənt]
托 雅 學

n 衣服，服裝，衣著　　　　　　　　g2003
She took the dirty garments off the toddler to wash them.
她把這個學步兒身上的髒衣服脫掉拿去洗。

garnish
['garnɪʃ]
托 雅 學

n 裝飾，裝飾品　　　　　　　　　　g2004
The green onion garnish on the steamed fish gives it a fresh look.
蒸魚上的青蔥裝飾讓魚看起來很新鮮。

garnish
['garnɪʃ]
托 雅 學

vt 給上餐桌的食物加裝飾，點綴　　　g2005
The chef garnished the potato salad plate with parsley.
廚師用西芹點綴馬鈴薯沙拉的盤子。

gaudy
['gɔdɪ]
托 雅 學

adj 俗麗的，華而不實的；n 盛大宴會　g2006
She loved big pieces of jewelry, but her daughter thought it looked gaudy.
她愛大件珠寶，但她的女兒認為它看起來太俗麗。

gauge
[gedʒ]
托 雅 學

n 標準尺寸；規格；量規，量表；vt 測量　g2007
The policeman uses a radar gun to gauge the speed of all passing motorists.
員警用雷達槍來測量往來車輛行駛的速度。

generic
[dʒɪ'nɛrɪk]
托 雅 學

adj 非註冊商標的；通用的，非特有的　g2008
Some generic medications can be bought over the counter nowadays.
一些通用藥品如今在櫃檯就可以買得到。

genesis
['dʒɛnəsɪs]

托 雅 學

n 發生，起源；創世紀

g2009

His speech was the genesis of a new grassroots political movement.

他的演說就是新基層民眾的政治運動的起源。

genetic
[dʒə'nɛtɪk]

托 雅 學

adj 起源的，發生的；遺傳學的

g2010

Her family's medical history revealed a genetic disease.

她的家族病史揭露了一個遺傳性疾病。

genial
['dʒinjəl]

托 雅 學

adj 和藹的，親切的，友善的

g2011

His genial, slow personality sometimes kept people from realizing how smart he was.

他的和藹和慢性子有的時候讓別人看不出來他有多聰明。

genius
['dʒinjəs]

托 雅 學

n 天才；天賦，天資

g2012

She was a genius in the field of robotics.

在機器人學這個領域裡她是個天才。

genre
['ʒɑnrə]

托 雅 學

n 類型；流派；體裁

g2013

The short story is a popular genre in literature.

短篇故事是文學裡很受歡迎的類型。

genuine
['dʒɛnjʊɪn]

托 雅 學

adj 真正的，千真萬確的；名副其實的

g2014

Her concern for his welfare was genuine.

她對他財富的關切是千真萬確的。

gist
[dʒɪst]

托 雅 學

n 主旨，要點

g2015

The reporter soon understood the gist of the story.

那位記者很快就理解了這個故事的要點。

glacier
['gleʃə]

托 雅 學

n 冰河

g2016

The glacier was a popular place to ski in winter and early spring.

冰河在冬天和早春的時候是個受歡迎的滑雪場地。

glamour
['glæmə]

托 雅 學

n 魅力，魔法；**vt** 迷惑

g2017

He was drawn to the city by the glamour and excitement of the night life.

他受到這個充滿魅力和刺激的夜生活的吸引而來到這個城市。

G

glare
[glɛr]

托 雅 學

n 強光；怒視；炫耀；vi 怒目而視；發射強光　g2018

He glares aggressively at his opponent to show his utmost determination to win.

他朝對手怒目而視，表示出他想贏的最大決心。

glaze
[glez]

托 雅 學

n 釉，上光；光滑面；（眼睛的）翳；vi 變為光滑；變呆滯　g2019

The glaze in her eyes showed that she drank too much.

她眼神中的呆滯顯現出她喝多了。

glaze
[glez]

托 雅 學

vt 裝以玻璃；上釉於　g2020

The worker glazed the window frames for the entire house near the final stage of construction.

在接近最後工程階段，工人給整棟房子的窗戶裝上玻璃。

glitter
['glɪtə]

托 雅 學

n 光輝，燦爛；小發光物；vi 閃閃發光；閃耀　g2021

She used glitter to make her paper fairy wings sparkle.

她用小發光物來裝飾紙做的小仙女的翅膀，讓它發光。

gloss
[glɔs]

托 雅 學

n 光彩，光澤；粉飾，假像；注釋　g2022

I really think the gloss of the new partnership has worn off rather quickly.

我真的認為新夥伴的光彩已經迅速地消失了。

gloss
[glɔs]

托 雅 學

vt 使有光澤；掩蓋過失，粉飾　g2023

Her speech glossed over the scholarly achievement of the late president.

她的演講粉飾了前校長的學術成就。

glossy
['glɔsɪ]

托 雅 學

adj 光滑的，有光澤的，油亮的　g2024

The glossy magazine cover features a talented designer who has just landed a major deal.

油亮的雜誌封面上印著一位天才設計師，他剛剛搞定一筆大交易。

gracious
['greʃəs]

托 雅 學

adj 親切的；寬厚的，仁慈的；大方的；雅致的　g2025

Contestants always try to present themselves in the most gracious way during a beauty competition.

選美參賽者總是儘量把她們最雅致的一面表現出來。

graft
[græft]

托 雅 學

n/vt 嫁接，移植，接枝　g2026

The farmer grafted two different types of scions onto the tree as an experiment.

農民在那棵樹上嫁接了兩種不同的幼枝當實驗。

grand
[grænd]
托 雅 學

adj 盛大的，豪華的；重大的，主要的　　g2027
They got married in this magnificently grand church in 1980.
他們1980年在這個華麗宏偉的教堂結婚了。

grandeur
['grændʒə]
托 雅 學

n 莊嚴，偉大；壯觀　　g2028
The sunset over the grand Canyon is a strong example of both beauty and grandeur.
大峽谷的落日是兼具美麗與壯觀極好的例子。

granite
['grænɪt]
托 雅 學

n 花崗岩，花崗石　　g2029
She chose granite countertops for the kitchen.
她選擇用花崗岩做廚房的檯面。

graphite
['græfaɪt]
托 雅 學

n 石墨，石墨電極　　g2030
She used soft graphite pencils to draw her sketches.
她用軟石墨鉛筆來畫素描。

gravity
['grævətɪ]
托 雅 學

n 嚴肅，莊重；嚴重性；重要性　　g2031
Do you realize the gravity of the situation?
你意識到了事情的嚴重性嗎？

gravity
['grævətɪ]
托 雅 學

n 重力，引力　　g2032
The gravity on Jupiter is about 16 times greater than that on Earth.
木星上的重力比地球上的約大十六倍。

gravy
['grevɪ]
托 雅 學

n 肉汁，肉湯　　g2033
She loved the gravy that her father made every Thanksgiving.
她喜歡她父親每年感恩節時所烹飪的肉湯。

graze
[grez]
托 雅 學

vi 吃青草；**vt** 放牧；擦傷；掠過；**n** 擦傷處　　g2034
The goats were grazing contentedly in the pasture.
山羊滿足地在牧場吃草。

grease
[gris]
托 雅 學

n 動物脂，油脂，潤滑脂；**vt** 抹油，潤滑　　g2035
It's reported that pork grease increases the chances of high blood pressure.
豬油據說會增加患高血壓的幾率。

gregarious
[grɪ'gɛrɪəs]

托 雅 學

adj 社交的，合群的；群居的　　g2036

The doctor was popular with his patients for his gregarious and kind personality.

這位醫生因為合群和仁慈的個性在病人中很受歡迎。

grieve
[griv]

托 雅 學

vt 使悲傷，使傷心　　g2037

I know you are sad, but please do not grieve too much over your dead pet.

我知道你對於死去的寵物很難過，但還是別過於悲傷。

grim
[grɪm]

托 雅 學

adj 嚴酷的，令人害怕的；不愉快的，討厭的　　g2038

When he talked to me, he had a very grim look on his face.

他和我說話時，表情非常嚴酷。

G

grope
[grop]

托 雅 學

n/vt 摸索，探索　　g2039

Since all the street lights were out last night, I had to stumble and grope my way home in the dark.

因為昨晚的路燈都不亮了，所以我必須蹣跚而行在黑暗中摸索回家的路。

growl
[graʊl]

托 雅 學

vi （狗等）嗥叫，咆哮　　g2040

The dog growls at me for no reason whenever I walk by him.

每當我經過那只狗的旁邊，它總是沒理由地對我咆哮。

grudge
[grʌdʒ]

托 雅 學

vt 懷恨，嫉妒；吝惜　　g2041

Many people grudge his overnight success.

很多人嫉妒他在一夜之間成功。

grumble
['grʌmbl]

托 雅 學

vi 抱怨，發牢騷　　g2042

She grumbled about the chilly weather.

她對這個寒冷的天氣猛發牢騷。

guild
[gɪld]

托 雅 學

n 同業公會，協會，行業協會　　g2043

Lisa's mother used to be an active member of the Parent-Teacher guild of the school.

麗莎的媽媽曾經是這所學校親師協會的活躍分子。

gullible
['gʌləbl]

托 雅 學

adj 輕信的；易受騙的　　g2044

He teased his gullible sister by telling her outrageous lies.

他的妹妹容易上當受騙，他老是毫無忌憚地撒謊跟她開玩笑。

gulp
[gʌlp]

g2045

n 吞嚥，（喝下）一大口
Sammy was so nervous that she took a gulp of water and started coughing uncontrollably.
珊米太緊張了，以至於她喝下一大口水後就開始控制不住地咳嗽。

gulp
[gʌlp]

g2046

vi 哽住；喘不過氣
All of a sudden, he gulped and couldn't say another word.
忽然之間，他喘不過氣來，連話都說不出。

H

haggle
['hægl̩]

托 雅 學

vi （尤指在費用上）爭論不休，討價還價　`h2001`
He haggled with the dealer over the price of the car for a while before coming to an agreement.
他跟經營商就車的價格爭論了半天之後，才最終達成了協定。

halt
[hɔlt]

托 雅 學

n 止步，停步，停止前進　`h2002`
At the sound of the horn, the parade comes to a halt.
號角聲一響，遊行隊伍就停止前進了。

halt
[hɔlt]

托 雅 學

vi/vt 止步，（使…）停止；遏止　`h2003`
The government hopes to halt tax fraud.
政府希望能夠遏止逃漏稅。

hamper
['hæmpɚ]

托 雅 學

n 洗衣籃；**vt** 妨礙，阻礙　`h2004`
The laundry hamper was overflowing with dirty clothes.
洗衣籃積了一堆的髒衣服。

haphazard
[,hæp'hæzɚd]

托 雅 學

adj 偶然的，隨意的，無計畫的　`h2005`
His filing system was haphazard and disorganized.
他的檔案整理得毫無計畫、混亂不堪。

harass
['hærəs]

托 雅 學

vt 使煩惱；不斷騷擾　`h2006`
The lady was routinely harassed by her boss, so she looked for a new job.
這位女士不斷受到她老闆的騷擾，所以她尋找了新的工作。

harassment
['hærəsmənt]

托 雅 學

n 騷擾，擾亂；煩惱，煩亂　`h2007`
The social worker showed great compassion for the victim of sexual harassment.
那位社工人員對性騷擾的受害者表示出極大的憐憫。

harmonious
[har'moniəs]

托 雅 學

adj 和諧的，協調的　`h2008`
The relations between our neighboring countries are mostly harmonious.
我們鄰國之間的關係多數是相當和諧的。

329

harmony
['hɑrmənɪ]
托 雅 學

n 協調，和諧，融洽
The band played in perfect harmony.
這個樂團的演奏極其和諧。

h2009

---

harness
['hɑrnəs]
托 雅 學

n 馬具，輓具；vt 治理；利用
Our farm harnesses solar energy to power our entire facility.
我們的農場利用太陽能源來供給我們整個設施的用電需求。

h2010

---

haul
[hɔl]
托 雅 學

vi/vt 拖曳；拖運；用力拖
I have to haul all my unwanted clothes to the thrift store.
我必須把我所有不想要的衣服都拖運到舊貨店去。

h2011

---

haven
['hevən]
托 雅 學

n 避難所；聖地
Switzerland is a tax haven for foreigners.
瑞士是外國人的避稅聖地。

h2012

---

havoc
['hævək]
托 雅 學

n 大破壞，浩劫
The frightened cat wreaked havoc in the kitchen.
那隻嚇壞了的貓在廚房造成一場大浩劫。

h2013

---

hazard
['hæzəd]
托 雅 學

n 危險，危害；冒險；障礙物
The golf player hit his last shot into the water hazard.
那個高爾夫球選手把他最後一桿球打進了水障。

h2014

---

hazard
['hæzəd]
托 雅 學

vt 冒險；拼命
The crew hazarded their lives to work on a fishing boat off the coast of Alaska.
船員們冒著生命危險在阿拉斯加外海的漁船上工作。

h2015

---

hazardous
['hæzədəs]
托 雅 學

adj 危險的
Hazardous chemicals need to be stored safely to prevent fires and explosions.
危險的化學品應該存放到安全的地方，以防起火或爆炸。

h2016

---

haze
[hez]
托 雅 學

n 薄霧，霧霾；朦朧
A thick haze of toxic smoke from the fire three days ago still hangs over the neighborhood.
三天前火災的毒氣霧霾持續籠罩著鄰近地區。

h2017

haze
[hez]
托 雅 學

vi/vt 模糊，朦朧
h2018
The sky hazed over before it started to pour.
下大雨前天空變朦朧了。

heave
[hiv]
托 雅 學

vi/vt （用力）舉，提，拉，扔，拖；嘔吐；發出；**n** 舉起
h2019
She did heave a sigh of relief when she found the plane had been delayed.
當她發現班機已經被延遲了時，的確發出了一聲如釋重負的歎息。

heaven
['hεvən]
托 雅 學

n 天；天空；天堂；上帝；神
h2020
Western children are told that people go to heaven when they die.
西方小孩被教導人死後會上天堂。

H

hereditary
[hə'rεdə,tεrɪ]
托 雅 學

adj 世襲的；遺傳的
h2021
His color blindness was a rare hereditary defect passed on by his mother.
她從母親那裡傳下來的色盲是罕見的遺傳性缺陷。

heritage
['hεrətɪdʒ]
托 雅 學

n 遺產，繼承物；傳統
h2022
She was proud of her rich cultural heritage.
她對自己豐富的文化遺產感到驕傲。

heterogeneous
[,hεtərə'dʒinɪəs]
托 雅 學

adj 異種的；異質的；由不同成分形成的
h2023
The students made a heterogeneous mixture of sand and water.
學生們做了由沙和水組成的異質混合物。

hibernate
['haɪbə,net]
托 雅 學

vi （動物）過冬，冬眠
h2024
Many bears hibernate when it begins to turn cold.
天氣變冷時，很多熊就開始冬眠。

hibernation
[,haɪbə'neʃən]
托 雅 學

n 冬眠
h2025
The squirrels stored acorns before their winter hibernation.
松鼠在冬眠前儲存橡樹果。

hinge
[hɪndʒ]
托 雅 學

n 樞紐；鉸鏈
h2026
The hinge of the gate was broken during the earthquake.
這個門的鉸鏈在地震期間被弄壞了。

hinge
[hɪndʒ]
托 雅 學

vi 依…而定

h2027

The direction of the project will hinge on our CEO's decisions in the next few days.

這項計劃的方向將會依執行長接下來幾天的決定而定。

homogeneous
[ˌhoməˈdʒɪnɪəs]
托 雅 學

adj 同種類的，同性質的，有相同特徵的；均勻的

h2028

She pureed the tomatoes into a smooth homogenous mixture for the soup.

她為了湯把蕃茄煮爛成糊狀的均勻的混合物。

homonym
[ˈhɑməˌnɪm]
托 雅 學

n 同音異義字；同形同音異義字

h2029

Fluke is a homonym that can mean a whale's tale or a stroke of luck.

Fluke是同形同音異義字，一個意思是鯨魚的尾巴，另一個是指純屬僥倖。

hound
[haʊnd]
托 雅 學

n 獵狗；卑鄙的人；**vt** 用獵狗追，追逐

h2030

The boy's parents hounded his teachers so that they would give their son special treatments.

那個男孩的父母追逐著他的老師們，以便他們可以給兒子特殊的待遇。

hover
[ˈhʌvɚ]
托 雅 學

vi （鳥）盤旋，翱翔；（人）逗留在附近，徘徊

h2031

The humming bird hovered above the flower briefly before flying away.

蜂鳥在飛走之前在花朵上方短暫地盤旋。

humanity
[hjuˈmænətɪ]
托 雅 學

n 人類；人性；人情

h2032

His extensive medical research will certainly benefit humanity.

他廣泛的醫學研究必定會造福全人類。

humanity
[hjuˈmænətɪ]
托 雅 學

n 複數＝人文科學

h2033

My son is taking courses in humanities at university.

我的兒子在大學修人文科學的課程。

humiliate
[hjuˈmɪlɪˌet]
托 雅 學

vt 使羞辱，使丟臉

h2034

He was careful not to humiliate his students when he corrected them.

當他糾正學生的錯誤時，會小心不讓學生感到丟臉。

hybrid
[ˈhaɪbrɪd]
托 雅 學

adj 混合而成的

h2035

These are examples of hybrid dogs of various species around the world.

這些是世界上各種品種混合而成的狗的代表。

hybrid
[ˈhaɪbrɪd]

n （動植物的）雜種；合成物 `h2036`
The liger is a hybrid of a female tiger and a male lion.
獅虎獸是母老虎和公獅子的雜種。

hydrogen
[ˈhaɪdrədʒən]

n 氫 `h2037`
Hydrogen is the most abundant element in the universe.
氫是宇宙中最豐富的元素。

hygiene
[ˈhaɪdʒin]

n 衛生 `h2038`
She taught kids how to brush their teeth so that they would have good dental hygiene.
她教孩子們正確的刷牙方式，這樣他們才會有好的牙齒衛生。

H

hypothesis
[haɪˈpɑθəsɪs]

n 假說，假設；前提 `h2039`
Her hypothesis about the effectiveness of the fertilizers was correct.
她對肥料的有效性所做的假設是正確的。

hypothetical
[ˌhaɪpəˈθɛtɪkl̩]

adj 基於假設的；作為假設的 `h2040`
The prosecutor's hypothetical version of how the murder occurred carried a lot of weight with the students.
檢察官對謀殺案發生過程的假設對學生們產生了很大的影響。

hysterical
[hɪsˈtɛrɪkl̩]

adj 情緒異常激動的，歇斯底里的 `h2041`
The girl's parents were hysterical when they heard of their son's death.
女孩的父母在得知自己兒子的死訊後變得歇斯底里。

ideology
[ˌaɪdɪˈɑlədʒɪ]

托 雅 學

n 意識形態，（政治或社會的）思想意識
Communist ideology rejects the idea of private property.
共產主義的意識形態反對私有財產。

i2001

ignite
[ɪɡˈnaɪt]

托 雅 學

vt 點火，引燃
He ignited his cigarette with a match.
他用一根火柴點燃了香煙。

i2002

illiterate
[ɪˈlɪtərɪt]

托 雅 學

adj 文盲的；未受教育的；**n** 文盲
A large percentage of the population is illiterate in this country owing to poverty and limited opportunities for education.

i2003

illuminate
[ɪˈlumə,net]

托 雅 學

vt 照亮，照明；用燈光裝飾；說明，闡釋
Sally went to see her professor during office hours, hoping to illuminate the homework problem he was struggling with.
莎莉在辦公時間去見她的教授，希望能闡釋在作業上碰到的問題。

i2004

illustrate
[ˈɪləstret]

托 雅 學

vt 舉例說明，闡明；圖解，加插圖
She illustrated a hand-made birthday card for her children.
她給孩子的手製生日卡上加插圖。

i2005

immerse
[ɪˈmɝs]

托 雅 學

vt 使…沉浸在；使…浸沒；給…施洗禮
She went to Paris to immerse herself in French culture.
她去了巴黎，使自己沉浸在法國文化中。

i2006

imminent
[ˈɪmənənt]

托 雅 學

adj 迫在眉睫的；即將發生的
The tallest buildings downtown were in imminent danger of being bombed.
市區裡最高的建築物有立即被轟炸的危險。

i2007

immobilize
[ɪˈmobɪ,laɪz]

托 雅 學

vt 固定
The airlines had to immobilize their aircraft on the ground due to the tornado warnings.
由於風暴預警，航空公司只能讓航班滯留在機場。

i2008

impair
[ɪm'pɛr]

托 雅 學

i2009

vt 損害，損傷；削弱，減少
Drinking too much alcohol can impair your judgment.
飲用過多的酒精會削弱你的判斷力。

impart
[ɪm'part]

托 雅 學

i2010

vt 傳授，給予；告知，通知
The tutor passionately imparted his knowledge of English to his pupil.
這位老師熱切地將他的英語知識傳授給他的學生。

impartial
[ɪm'parʃəl]

托 雅 學

i2011

adj 公正的，無偏見的
The judge was famous for remaining perfectly impartial to both sides in the trial.
這位法官因為在審問中對雙方都保持公正而有名。

imperative
[ɪm'pɛrətɪv]

托 雅 學

i2012

adj 強制的；緊急的
It is imperative that you correctly complete your homework every night.
你每天晚上必須正確完成你的作業。

imperial
[ɪm'pɪrɪəl]

托 雅 學

i2013

adj 帝國的，帝王的；（度量衡）英制的
The palace staff worked overtime in preparing for the imperial visit.
皇宮的工作人員加班準備著帝王的造訪。

impetus
['ɪmpətəs]

托 雅 學

i2014

n 推動（力），促進
Growing up in poverty gave him the impetus to go to college.
在貧窮中長大給了他上大學的推動力。

implement
['ɪmpləmənt]

托 雅 學

i2015

vt 貫徹，實現，執行
She worked hard to implement the new curriculum standards in the school.
她努力執行學校的新課程標準。

implicate
['ɪmplɪ͵ket]

托 雅 學

i2016

vt 牽連，扯上關係
He was implicated in the scandal by several e-mails that he'd written.
因為之前寫過的幾封電子郵件，他被牽連進了醜聞。

implication
[͵ɪmplɪ'keʃən]

托 雅 學

i2017

n 含意，暗示，暗指；牽連
He was troubled by the implication that his business partner might have been unfaithful.
他對於別人暗指他商業夥伴可能不忠這件事情感到不安。

implicit
[ɪm'plɪsɪt]

托 雅 學

adj 含蓄的；固有的；無疑問的；絕對的　i2018

A commitment to high academic standards was an implicit understanding in her family.

為了取得高學歷而付出的要求在她家裡是不言自明的。

impose
[ɪm'poz]

托 雅 學

vi 利用；欺騙；打擾　i2019

She worked hard to find a place to live so that she didn't impose on her aunt longer than necessary.

她努力工作以找到住的地方，如此一來就不必長期打擾她的阿姨了。

impose
[ɪm'poz]

托 雅 學

vt （把…）強加給；征（稅）　i2020

The landlord has tried to impose fines on tenants, but many tenants refuse to pay them.

這個房東試圖把罰款強加在承租者身上，但很多承租者拒絕付給他們。

imposing
[ɪm'pozɪŋ]

托 雅 學

adj 莊嚴的，雄偉的　i2021

The stately homes in England are certainly grand and imposing residences.

英國富麗堂皇的家庭建築真是氣勢宏偉，莊嚴壯麗。

impromptu
[ɪm'prɑmptju]

托 雅 學

adj 事先無準備的；即席的，即興的；**n** 即興之作　i2022

He threw an impromptu party in the office for his secretary's birthday.

他為他的秘書即興在辦公室辦了一個派對。

improvise
['ɪmprəvaɪz]

托 雅 學

vi 即興創造，即興發揮，臨時做　i2023

Sometimes when Jenny is baking she will improvise to save a trip to the grocery store.

在烘焙糕點時，珍妮有時會即興發揮，省得再跑一趟雜貨店去買。

inaugural
[ɪn'ɔgjərəl]

托 雅 學

n 就職演講；開幕詞　i2024

The President's inaugural was considered one of his best speeches.

總統的就職演說被認為是他最好的演講之一。

inaugurate
[ɪn'ɔgjə,ret]

托 雅 學

vt 開始；使…就職　i2025

The new president was inaugurated on Jan. 20th by the Chief Justice of the Supreme Court.

新總統在一月二十日由最高法院的首席法官任命就職。

incandescent
[,ɪnkæn'dɛsnt]

托 雅 學

n 白熱（光）的；白熱化的，強烈的，激情的　i2026

She was incandescent with rage when she caught her boy friend cheated on her.

當她發現男朋友出軌的時候，憤怒到了極點。

incessant
[ɪn'sɛsnt]

`adj` 連續的，持續不斷的　　　　i2027

She moved out to the country to escape the incessant noise of the city.

為了逃離持續不斷的噪音，她遷居到了鄉下。

incidentally
[ˌɪnsə'dɛntlɪ]

`adv` 附帶地，順便提及　　　　i2028

Incidentally, the conference begins at 8 o'clock in the morning.

順便提一下，研討會在早上八點開始。

incline
[ɪn'klaɪn]

`vi`/`vt`（使⋯）傾斜；（使⋯）傾向於　　　　i2029

She inclined her head to one side in order to hear him better.

她把頭斜到一邊好聽清楚他（說什麼）。

incur
[ɪn'kɝ]

`vt` 招致，惹起；遭受　　　　i2030

She knew that leaving a messy kitchen would incur her mother's wrath.

她明白留下髒亂的廚房會招致母親的憤怒。

indifference
[ɪn'dɪfərəns]

`n` 冷淡，不關心；無足輕重　　　　i2031

The mother seemed to show complete indifference to her children so much so that her family became concerned.

這位母親顯得似乎完全不關心自己的孩子，這引起了她家人的擔憂。

indigenous
[ɪn'dɪdʒɪnəs]

`adj` 本土的，土著的　　　　i2032

Palm trees are indigenous to warm, tropical climates.

棕櫚樹是溫暖的熱帶氣候區的本土植物。

indignant
[ɪn'dɪgnənt]

`adj` 憤慨的，憤慨不平的　　　　i2033

The restaurant manager gave the indignant guests a free meal after they found a bug in the food.

當發現食物中有蟲子之後，餐廳經理給憤慨的客人免費用餐。

indignation
[ˌɪndɪg'neʃən]

`n` 憤怒，憤慨　　　　i2034

The little girl responded with indignation when she was blamed for her brother's mistake.

當這個小女孩因為她弟弟的過錯而被責備時，她的反應很憤怒。

indomitable
[ɪn'dɑmətəbl]

`adj` 不認輸的；不氣餒的　　　　i2035

She survived the imprisonment, through faith and an indomitable spirit.

她通過信仰和不認輸的精神在監禁中存活下來。

induce
[ɪn'djus]

托 雅 學

vt 引誘，勸使；引起，導致；感應；催生嬰兒

i2036

She was two weeks past her due date, so the doctors decided to induce the baby.

她已經比預產期晚了兩個禮拜了，所以醫生決定要催生嬰兒。

indulge
[ɪn'dʌldʒ]

托 雅 學

vi 縱情；**vt** 放縱（感情）；放任

i2037

She indulged herself in a piece of chocolate after a hard day at work.

她在辛苦工作一天之後縱情享受了一塊巧克力。

inept
[ɪn'ɛpt]

托 雅 學

adj 笨拙的；無能的，不稱職的

i2038

He was a wonderful athlete, but inept at mathematics.

他是個優秀的運動員，但是數學能力不行。

inertia
[ɪn'ɝʃə]

托 雅 學

n 不活動，惰性；慣性

i2039

It is not easy to overcome the inertia of an object that has great mass, but it can be done with enough force.

要克服有巨大質量物體的慣性並不容易，但只要有足夠的力量就可以完成。

infect
[ɪn'fɛkt]

托 雅 學

vt 傳染；感染

i2040

You had better clean your wounds thoroughly before they become infected.

你最好在傷口受到感染之前徹底地清理一下。

infectious
[ɪn'fɛkʃəs]

托 雅 學

adj 傳染的，傳染性的，有感染力的

i2041

This illness is still infectious even after all the symptoms are gone.

即便所有症狀都消失了，這個疾病仍然是會傳染的。

inferior
[ɪn'fɪrɪɚ]

托 雅 學

adj 下等的，下級的；劣等的，差的；**n** 下級，晚輩

i2042

The wine steward considered the previous year's vintage to be inferior to this year's.

侍酒師認為去年的葡萄酒比今年的還要差。

inferiority
[ɪnfɪrɪ'arətɪ]

托 雅 學

n 下等；次等；劣質；自卑感

i2043

Her inferiority complex made it hard for her to make friends at school.

她的自卑感讓她在學校很難交朋友。

infest
[ɪn'fɛst]

托 雅 學

vt 大批出沒於；侵擾

i2044

The gardener worked hard not to let caterpillars infest his rose garden.

園丁辛勤工作，以防蟲子大量出沒於他的玫瑰園。

infinite
['ɪnfənɪt]

托 雅 學

i2045
adj 無限的；極大的
That young businessman seems to have infinite wealth, but nobody knows where it came from.
那個年輕的企業家看來有無限財富，但無人知道財富從哪裡來的。

---

infirmary
[ɪn'fɝmərɪ]

托 雅 學

i2046
n 醫務所，醫務室，小醫院
After she fell off the horse, she spent the night in the camp infirmary.
她從馬上摔下來之後那晚是在營隊醫務室裡度過的。

---

inflate
[ɪn'flet]

托 雅 學

i2047
vi/vt （使…）充氣；（使…）膨脹；（使…）得意
The boy asked his father to inflate the basketball because the air pressure was too low.
這個男孩要他爸爸給籃球充氣，因為氣壓太低了。

---

inflation
[ɪn'fleʃən]

托 雅 學

i2048
n 通貨膨脹，物價飛漲
The country's inflation is beginning to steadily rise again.
那個國家的通貨膨脹再次開始穩固增加。

---

inflict
[ɪn'flɪkt]

托 雅 學

i2049
vt 使…遭受，使承受
The tornado inflicted massive damage on the small town.
龍捲風使得小鎮承受了巨大的傷害。

---

ingenious
[ɪn'dʒinjəs]

托 雅 學

i2050
adj 機敏的；有獨創性的；精緻的
Eli Whitney invented an ingenious machine called the cotton gin for separating cotton seeds from cotton fibers.
艾利‧惠特尼發明了一台具有獨創性的機器，名為軋棉機，其功用是將棉花纖維與棉花籽分開。

---

inhabitant
[ɪn'hæbətənt]

托 雅 學

i2051
n 居民，住戶
Native Americans are believed to be the first inhabitants of North America.
美國原住民被認為是北美最早期的居民。

---

initiate
[ɪ'nɪʃɪt]

托 雅 學

i2052
vt 開始，創始，發動；啟蒙；使…入門；引入
They were lucky enough to receive sponsorship, which allowed them to initiate the project right away.
他們夠幸運能接受贊助，讓他們立刻開始啟動這個計畫。

---

initiative
[ɪ'nɪʃətɪv]

托 雅 學

i2053
adj 創始的
What are the President's initiative thoughts regarding these issues?
總裁對這些議題的最初想法是什麼呢？

insolent
['ɪnsələnt]

adj 粗魯的，無禮的　　　　　　i2054

Alice's son is very insolent to people when she takes him out in public.

愛麗絲帶兒子出席公共場合時，他對人非常粗魯無禮。

instantaneous
[ˌɪnstən'tenɪəs]

adj 瞬間的，即刻的　　　　　　i2055

We got an almost instantaneous response to our ad for a nanny.

我們登的招聘保姆廣告幾乎得到了即刻回復。

insulate
['ɪnsəˌlet]

vt 隔離，孤立；使…絕緣　　　　i2056

The mother tried hard to insulate her baby from others to protect it from the dangers of the world.

這位母親努力將寶寶與其他人隔絕，以保護他免於世界的危險。

intact
[ɪn'tækt]

adj 完整無缺的，未經觸動的，未受損傷的　　i2057

The explorers discovered several ancient scrolls that seemed to be completely intact.

探險家發現了幾個似乎完好無損的古老卷軸。

integral
['ɪntəgrəl]

adj 構成整體所必需的；完整的；組成的　　i2058

Sincere and unconditional love from parents is an integral part of a happy childhood.

雙親真摯和無條件的愛是構成快樂童年必需的一部分。

integrity
[ɪn'tɛgrətɪ]

n 正直，誠實；完整，完全　　i2059

The bank president was known for her integrity and straight forward manner of dealing with people.

這位銀行總裁因她的正直和與人相處的坦率之道而聞名。

intellect
['ɪntl̩ˌɛkt]

n 理智；智力，才智　　i2060

Despite his impressive intellect, he had great difficulty remembering names.

儘管他擁有令人欽佩的才智，記住他人姓名對他來說也是一件難事。

intellectual
[ˌɪntl̩'ɛktʃʊəl]

n 知識份子　　i2061

She used to hang around a group of intellectuals in her youth.

在她年輕的時候曾經與一群知識份子混在一起。

intelligible
[ɪn'tɛlədʒəbl̩]

adj 可理解的，明白易懂的，清楚的　　i2062

This manual is highly intelligible and easy to follow.

這份操作手冊是非常明白易懂的，很容易照著做。

interim
['ɪntərɪm]

托 雅 學

`adj` 中間的;暫時的,臨時的;`n` 過渡時期,暫定

i2063

Representatives of the two parties signed an interim agreement until the final contract is completed.

雙方陣營代表簽訂了臨時協議,直到最後的合約完成為止。

intermittent
[ˌɪntəˈmɪtnt]

托 雅 學

`adj` 間歇的,斷斷續續的

i2064

Their favorite TV show was interrupted by intermittent reports on the severe weather.

他們最喜歡的電視節目被間歇插入的嚴酷天氣報告打斷了。

interpret
[ɪnˈtɜˈprɪt]

托 雅 學

`vi`/`vt` 解釋,說明;口譯,翻譯

i2065

The archaeologist called in a linguist to interpret the new tablets they discovered.

這位考古學家請來語言學者翻譯他們發現的新刻寫板。

intervene
[ˌɪntəˈvin]

托 雅 學

`vi` 干涉,干預;插入,介入

i2066

Jim intervened in the argument before it became a fight.

吉姆在爭論變為打架前進行了干預。

intervention
[ˌɪntəˈvɛnʃən]

托 雅 學

`n` 干預

i2067

The family decided it was time for an intervention for their drug-addicted relative.

全家決定是時候該干預他們吸毒成癮的親戚了。

intimidate
[ɪnˈtɪməˌdet]

托 雅 學

`vt` 脅迫,威脅(某人做某事)

i2068

The defense lawyer tried to intimidate the witness on the stand.

辯護律師試圖脅迫那個小攤上的目擊證人。

intricate
['ɪntrəkɪt]

托 雅 學

`adj` 錯綜複雜的,難以理解的

i2069

She was able to knit intricate patterns into her sweaters and scarves.

她能夠在毛衣和圍巾上編織複雜的圖案。

intrigue
[ɪnˈtrig]

托 雅 學

`n` 陰謀;`vt` 密謀;詭計取得

i2070

The man intrigued his way into the board of directors.

這個男人使用詭計一路晉升到董事會。

intrigue
[ɪnˈtrig]

托 雅 學

`vt` 激起…的興趣,吸引,著迷

i2071

He was deeply intrigued by her sense of humor.

他被她的幽默感深深吸引。

341

intrinsic
[ɪn'trɪnsɪk]

托 雅 學

adj （指價值、性質）固有的，本質的，內在的　i2072

Moral education should focus on raising intrinsic motivations rather than relying on superficial rewards.

道德教育應該著重於提升內在的動機而非依賴膚淺的獎勵。

invade
[ɪn'ved]

托 雅 學

vi/vt 入侵，侵略，侵襲，侵擾　i2073

Britain has not been invaded by another nation since the year 1066.

自從1066年起，英國就沒被其他國家入侵了。

invalid
[ɪn'vælɪd]

托 雅 學

adj 有病的；傷殘的；無效的　i2074

The will was declared invalid because it didn't have a signature.

這份遺囑被宣告無效，因為上面沒有簽名。

invalid
['ɪnvəlɪd]

托 雅 學

n 病人，傷殘人　i2075

It is the government's responsibility to develop and maintain programs to care for invalids.

發展及持續照顧傷殘人士的計畫是政府的責任。

invaluable
[ɪn'væljəbl]

托 雅 學

adj 非常寶貴的，無價的　i2076

The help she has given in accomplishing this task has proven to be invaluable.

她對完成這項任務的協助被證實是非常寶貴的。

invariably
[ɪn'vɛrɪəblɪ]

托 雅 學

adv 不變地，永恆地；總是　i2077

This area has four distinct seasons invariably each year despite of the influence of global warming.

儘管全球變暖有影響，這個地區還總是四季分明。

invert
[ɪn'vɝt]

托 雅 學

vt 倒置，倒轉，顛倒　i2078

He wanted to invert the cake onto the plate, but he carelessly dropped it.

他想把蛋糕倒出來放在盤子上，但不小心掉在地上了。

invincible
[ɪn'vɪnsəbl]

托 雅 學

adj 所向無敵的；不屈不撓的　i2079

Her admiration made him falsely believe himself to be invincible.

她對他的崇拜讓他錯誤地以為自己是所向無敵的。

involuntary
[ɪn'vɑlən,tɛrɪ]

托 雅 學

adj 不由自主的，無意識的　i2080

Your digestion and your breathing are involuntary muscle movements that your nervous system does on its own.

你的消化和你的呼吸都是無意識的肌肉運動，神經系統自行去做的。

irrigate
['ɪrə‚get]

i2083

vi/vt 灌溉，修水利；沖洗
A system of canals drew water from a nearby river to irrigate crop fields.
水道系統從附近的河流引進河水來灌溉農田。

irrespective
[‚ɪrɪ'spɛktɪv]

i2081

adj 不考慮的；不顧的
Doctors should provide their best care to all patients, irrespective of the person's social class.
醫生應該給所有的病患提供最好的照料，而不考慮其社會地位。

irrevocable
[ɪ'rɛvəkəbl]

i2082

adj 不可逆的；不能取消的
His decision to sign the contract was irrevocable.
他要簽約的決心已經不可能逆轉了。

irrigation
[‚ɪrə'geʃən]

i2084

n 灌溉；沖洗法
Improving irrigation in Africa helps alleviate hunger and encourage economic growth.
改進非洲的穀物灌溉有助於減輕饑荒並鼓勵經濟增長。

itinerant
[ɪ'tɪnərənt]

i2085

adj 流動的，巡迴的
The itinerant lecturer is always traveling for weeks at a time around the globe.
巡迴演說家往往要連續幾個星期進行環球演講。

I

jeopardize
['dʒɛpəd,aɪz]

托 雅 學

vt 使瀕於危險境地；危及；冒…的危險　j2001

The scandal has jeopardized his political reputation in the party.

那個醜聞已危及他在黨內的政治聲譽。

jeopardy
['dʒɛpədɪ]

托 雅 學

n 危險　j2002

By driving drunk, he placed all his passengers in a great deal of jeopardy.

因為酒醉駕車，他置所有乘客於極大的危險之中。

jolt
[dʒolt]

托 雅 學

n 震驚；顛簸，震動　j2003

When the bus driver braked hard, I woke up with a jolt as I'd been cat napping on the ride home.

我本來在回家的車上打盹，司機一個急煞車，一下子把我震醒了。

junction
['dʒʌŋkʃən]

托 雅 學

n 連接；交叉路口；樞紐站；中繼線　j2004

The city installed a new stoplight at the junction of Smith Road and Jackson Road.

這個城市在史密斯跟傑克森路交叉路口設了一個新的紅綠燈。

justification
[,dʒʌstəfə'keʃən]

托 雅 學

n 辯護；辯解；藉口　j2005

Juries rarely accept insanity as a justification for violent crimes.

陪審團很少接受精神失常作為暴力犯罪的藉口。

justify
['dʒʌstə,faɪ]

托 雅 學

vi/vt 證明……為正當（或有理、正確），為……辯護　j2006

She justified her decision to move out of her parents' house.

她證明搬離她父母居所的決定是正確的。

juvenile
['dʒuvən!]

托 雅 學

adj 青少年的，幼稚的；n 青少年，少年讀物　j2007

The parole officer loved to help juvenile delinquents rebuild their lives.

假釋官喜歡幫助青少年罪犯重建他們的生活。

K

ken
[kɛn]

托 雅 學

n 視野，眼界；知識範圍　　k2001

Beyond one's ken relates to complex issues that are beyond one's comprehension, knowledge or understanding.

在視界之外指的是有些複雜的問題超出了人的理解能力和知識範圍。

kin
[kɪn]

托 雅 學

adj 親屬關係的，同類的　　k2002

The new receptionist is kin to the General Manager of the company.

新來的接待員是這家公司總經理的親戚。

kin
[kɪn]

托 雅 學

n 家族，親屬，血緣關係　　k2003

She has gone to live with her husband's kin.

她住到丈夫的親戚家裡去了。

K

lapse
[læps]

托 雅 學

n 失誤；流逝；喪失；下降

After a lapse of five years, Joshua's grief over his wife's death still haunts him.

時間流逝，五年過去了，約書亞還無法從失去妻子的傷痛中平復過來。

I2001

lapse
[læps]

托 雅 學

vt 失效；偏離；流逝；陷入

After a hard day at work, he frequently lapsed into his former introverted ways.

在辛苦工作一天之後，他常常陷入往常內向的狀態。

I2002

lash
[læʃ]

托 雅 學

n 鞭子；鞭打；睫毛；諷刺

They each received 10 lashes for being guilty of sexual harassment.

他們每人都因為性騷擾遭受10次鞭打的處罰。

I2003

lash
[læʃ]

托 雅 學

vt 鞭打；擺動；捆紮

The tiger's tail lashed the tree stump like a whip.

老虎的尾巴像鞭子一樣鞭打在樹墩上。

I2004

latent
['letnt]

托 雅 學

adj 潛在的；休眠的；隱性的；不易察覺的

He discovered he had a latent talent for acting.

他發現自己有潛在的演戲天分。

I2005

latitude
['lætə,tjud]

托 雅 學

n （言語、行動）自由範圍

Her parents allowed her little latitudes in their family's religion.

她的父母在信仰方面幾乎沒有給她什麼自由。

I2006

latitude
['lætə,tjud]

托 雅 學

n 緯度；緯度地區

A lot of the world's high-income countries are located far away from the tropical latitudes.

世界上許多高收入國家都離熱帶緯度地區很遠。

I2007

launch
[lɔntʃ]

托 雅 學

n 發射；下水；發行

They celebrated the launch of his first album that night.

那天晚上他們一起慶祝他第一張專輯的發行。

I2008

launch
[lɔntʃ]

托 雅 學

vi 發射；使（船）下水，發動

I2009

The presidential candidate launched a new campaign early this week.

總統候選人在本週頭幾天發動了一場新的選舉運動。

lave
[lev]

托 雅 學

vt 沖洗；洗滌

I2010

Soaking my feet in water will lave my blisters.

把腳泡在水裡可以沖洗那些磨出的水泡。

lavish
['læviʃ]

托 雅 學

adj 非常慷慨的；浪費的

I2011

He threw several lavish parties every spring break.

每年春假他都會辦些奢華的派對。

lavish
['læviʃ]

托 雅 學

vt 濫用；揮霍，浪費

I2012

He used to lavish time and money on collecting rare stamps.

他曾揮霍時間與金錢收集稀有郵票。

layman
['lemən]

托 雅 學

n 外行

I2013

This video was filmed for both experts and laymen alike.

這部影片適合專業人士和外行觀看。

legal
['ligl]

托 雅 學

adj 法律的，法定的；合法的，正當的

I2014

Only Congress has the legal authority to declare war.

只有國會有合法權利來宣告開戰。

legend
['lɛdʒənd]

托 雅 學

n 傳說，傳奇

I2015

The legend of King Arthur says that he and his knights sat at a round table.

在亞瑟王的傳說裡，他和他的騎士們都圍著圓桌而坐。

legislation
[,lɛdʒɪs'leʃən]

托 雅 學

n 制定（或通過）法律；法律（規範）

I2016

The new immigration legislation was struck down by the courts.

新的移民法規被法院駁回。

legitimate
[lɪ'dʒɪtəmɪt]

托 雅 學

adj 合法的；合理的，合乎邏輯的

I2017

The company accepted the workers' legitimate demands.

這家公司接受了這些工人正當合理的要求。

lethal
['liθəl]

托 雅 學

adj 致命的；毀滅性的
One bite from a rattlesnake can be lethal.
被響尾蛇咬到可能致命。

12018

liability
[ˌlaɪə'bɪlətɪ]

托 雅 學

n 傾向；義務；負債
Reports revealed that the Jackson family had liabilities of over one million dollars.
報告顯示，傑克森家族欠下了超過一百萬美金的負債。

12019

liable
['laɪəbl]

托 雅 學

adj 易於……的；可能的
The car is liable to break down at any moment.
這輛車隨時都有可能會壞掉。

12020

liaison
[ˌlɪe'zɑn]

托 雅 學

n 私通；聯絡（處）
The city government hired a community liaison to help explain their policy and procedures to the neighborhoods.
市政府雇用社區聯絡處來協助對鄰近地區解釋政策與程式。

12021

liberty
['lɪbətɪ]

托 雅 學

n 自由，自由權；特權
My parents gave me a great deal of liberty.
我父母親給我很大程度的自由。

12022

litigation
['lɪtə'geʃən]

托 雅 學

n 訴訟，官司
The singer has been in litigation with her previous record company for 6 months.
這位歌手已經和她之前的唱片公司打了六個月的官司了。

12023

locality
[lo'kælətɪ]

托 雅 學

n 地區，現場；方位
They moved to another locality where industries were less concentrated.
他們搬到另一個工業相對不集中的地區。

12024

locomotive
[ˌlokə'motɪv]

托 雅 學

adj 運動的；火車頭的；經常遷移的
Unlike feet, the heart is not a locomotive organ and it never stops beating.
和腳不一樣，心臟不是運動器官，它從不停止跳動。

12025

locomotive
[ˌlokə'motɪv]

托 雅 學

n 機車，火車頭
The museum is holding an exhibition of steam-powered locomotives.
博物館正在舉行蒸汽火車頭展覽。

12026

lofty
['lɔftɪ]

adj 崇高的，高尚的；高傲的；極高的   I2027
As a nurse, she tried hard to live up to her own lofty ideals of patient care.
身為護士，她很努力地實現病患照護的崇高理想。

lubricate
['lubrɪ,ket]

vi/vt 潤滑，加潤滑油   I2028
He lubricated the door hinges because they were squeaking.
門開始在嘎嘎作響，所以他在門的鉸鏈上加了潤滑油。

lucrative
['lukrətɪv]

adj 賺錢的，有利可圖的   I2029
My boss's new contract has opened more doors of opportunity into a lucrative market.
老闆的這紙新合約開啟了他進軍有利可圖的市場的大門。

ludicrous
['ludɪkrəs]

adj 滑稽的；荒唐可笑的   I2030
Her teenage boys ate a ludicrous amount of food everyday.
她青春期的兒子每天吃的食物數量都多得荒唐可笑。

L

lull
[lʌl]

n 暫時平息，暫時呆滯時期，暫時平靜   I2031
It feels awkward when there is a lull in the debate.
在激烈的辯論中忽然一陣間歇，令人覺得很尷尬。

lull
[lʌl]

vi 平息；停止；減弱   I2032
The snowstorm lulled overnight, so we may be able to drive to work tomorrow morning.
暴風雪在一夜之間平息了，所以我們明天早上可以開車去上班了。

lull
[lʌl]

vt 使安靜，使…睡著；使緩和；使放鬆警惕   I2033
The motion of the car soon lulled the baby to sleep.
車子的運動很快就讓寶寶睡著了。

luminous
['lumənəs]

adj 發光的，夜光的；有見識的；明白易懂的   I2034
The tree was luminous with Christmas lights.
樹因為聖誕燈飾在發光。

lure
[lʊr]

n 吸引力；魅力；誘惑物   I2035
Few boys can resist the lure of her beauty.
幾乎沒有男孩能抵擋她美貌的誘惑。

lure
[lʊr]

托 雅 學

vt 引誘，吸引

12036

They tried to lure him with money but failed.
他們試圖用錢財來引誘他，但失敗了。

luster
['lʌstɚ]

托 雅 學

n 光澤

12037

She polished the silverware because it had lost its luster.
她擦拭銀器，因為它們已失去光澤。

luxurious
[lʌg'ʒʊrɪəs]

托 雅 學

adj 奢侈的，豪華的

12038

They spent a week in the most luxurious hotel on the island.
他們在島上最奢華的旅館待了一個星期。

luxury
['lʌkʃərɪ]

托 雅 學

n 奢侈，華貴；奢侈品

12039

Her husband's family enjoyed a higher level of luxury than what she had grown up with.
她丈夫的家庭比她的成長環境更奢侈。

M

magistrate
['mædʒɪs,tret]

n 地方行政官，地方法官，治安官　　　　m2001
The magistrate will be presiding over the trial of the murderer next Monday.
這位地方法官下週一將主持該名謀殺犯的審判。

magnify
['mægnə,faɪ]

vt 放大，擴大；誇大，誇張　　　　m2002
His bifocal glasses helped magnify small print for his failing eyes.
他的雙焦距眼鏡為他視力下降的眼睛把小字放大。

magnitude
['mægnə,tjud]

n 大小，數量；巨大，廣大　　　　m2003
The earthquake was of such a high magnitude that it leveled all the buildings in the city.
這場地震的震級是如此巨大，把城市裡所有的建築物都夷平了。

malign
[mə'laɪn]

vt 誹謗，污蔑　　　　m2004
The director was furious that one of his peers had the gall to malign him publicly.
導演很生氣，他的一位同行竟敢公然誹謗他。

mandate
['mændet]

n 授權；命令　　　　m2005
The new government claimed to have the mandate from its constituents to push for formal and legitimate independence.
新政府宣稱有選民授權，打算推動正式且合法的獨立。

mandatory
['mændə,torɪ]

adj 強制的，必須執行的；法定的　　　　m2006
Filing your taxes before April 15 every year is mandatory.
每一年的四月十五日前填報稅單是必須執行的。

maneuver
[mə'nuvɚ]

n 機動；運用，操作　　　　m2007
He learned many advanced aerial maneuvers in flight school.
他在飛行學校學會了許多高級的飛行操作。

maneuver
[mə'nuvɚ]

vt 操作　　　　m2008
Just be careful when you try to maneuver the car into such a small parking space.
如果你試圖操作車輛並開進這麼小的停車位上，要小心謹慎。

maniac
['meni,æk]

n 發燒友，購物狂

m2009

From all accounts, Laura is a shoe shopaholic maniac.
據大家所說，蘿拉是個熱衷買鞋的購物狂。

manifest
['mænə,fɛst]

vt 表明，證明，顯示

m2010

Her depression manifests itself how well she slept.
她的憂鬱程度顯示了她的睡眠品質。

manifestation
[,mænəfɛs'teʃən]

n 表明；表現；顯現，化身

m2011

The artist sculpted Romeo and Juliet as the manifestation of true love.
藝術家把羅密歐與茱麗葉塑造成真愛的化身。

manipulate
[mə'nɪpjə,let]

vt （熟練地）使用，操作；（巧妙地）處理

m2012

Opposable thumbs allow humans to manipulate tools.
對生拇指讓人們能夠熟練地使用工具。

manure
[mə'njʊr]

n 肥料；糞肥

m2013

The dairy farmer used manure from his cows to fertilize his crops.
畜牧場主用乳牛的糞肥來給農作物施肥。

martyr
['mɑrtə]

n 烈士；殉難者

m2014

St. Stephen was the first martyr of Christianity.
聖史蒂芬是基督教第一位殉道者。

masculine
['mæskjəlɪn]

adj 男性的，似男性的；陽性的

m2015

She tried to soften the masculine features of her face with make-up and a feminine hair style.
她試著用化妝品和女性的髮型讓她臉上似男性般的五官變柔和。

massacre
['mæsəkə]

n 殘殺，大屠殺

m2016

The International Court of Justice is now investigating whether the tyrant played a role in the massacre.
聯合國國際法庭正在調查這個暴君是否參與了大屠殺。

massacre
['mæsəkə]

vt 殘殺，集體屠殺

m2017

Hundreds of thousands of civilians were ruthlessly massacred in a series of armed conflicts.
多次武裝衝突中，成千上萬平民無情地遭到集體屠殺。

matrimony
['mætrə,monɪ]

托 雅 學

n 結婚，婚禮　　　　　　　　　　m2018
The bride and groom were betrothed in holy matrimony.
新娘和新郎在神聖的婚禮上訂了婚。

meddle
['mɛdḷ]

托 雅 學

vi 干涉　　　　　　　　　　　　m2019
He didn't like other people to meddle in his affairs.
他不喜歡別人干涉他的私事。

mediate
['midɪ,et]

托 雅 學

vi 調解，調停　　　　　　　　　m2020
She was used to mediating between her sister and her mother who did not get along.
她母親和姐姐關係不和，她已經習慣給她們調停了。

mediocre
['midɪ,okə]

托 雅 學

adj 平庸的；二流的　　　　　　m2021
The team had a mediocre season losing almost as many games as they won.
這球隊本賽季表現平庸，輸的比賽和贏的一樣多。

memorandum
[,mɛmə'rændəm]

托 雅 學

n 備忘錄，備忘便條　　　　　　m2022
The secretary sent out a memorandum to the company detailing the procedures for ordering office supplies.
這位秘書給公司發了一份備忘錄，詳述訂購辦公用品的程序。

M

menace
['mɛnɪs]

托 雅 學

n/vi/vt 威脅，威嚇　　　　　　m2023
The neighbors felt that the aggressive dog was a menace to their children.
鄰居們擔心這隻好鬥的狗會對他們的孩子造成威脅。

mercantile
['mɝkən,taɪl]

托 雅 學

adj 商業的，重商主義的　　　　m2024
Britain was a major mercantile and naval power in the 19th century.
在十九世紀，英國是當時商業和海上的軍事主力。

mercenary
['mɝsn,ɛrɪ]

托 雅 學

n 雇傭兵　　　　　　　　　　　m2025
A mercenary is a trained soldier hired and paid for foreign service.
雇傭兵是訓練有素的士兵，給他們報酬，他們就為外國人服務。

merge
[mɝdʒ]

托 雅 學

vi/vt （使）結合，（使）合併，（使）合為一體　　m2026
The government refused to let the two companies merge because they were too big.
政府拒絕授權這兩家公司合併，因為它們太大了。

merger
[ˈmɝˈdʒɚ]

托 雅 學

m2027

n 合併

The merger of the two hotels created the biggest hotel chain in the hospitality industry.

這兩家的飯店合併後，成為酒店服務業最大的飯店連鎖。

merit
[ˈmɛrɪt]

托 **雅** 學

m2028

n 優點；價值；功績

He thought his opponent's argument had a lot of merits, but he still didn't quite agree.

他認為他對手的論點有很多優點，但他仍不太同意。

merit
[ˈmɛrɪt]

托 **雅** 學

m2029

vi/vt 值得，應得

Bullying on campus has been on the rise, and thus merits the attention of teachers and parents alike.

校園霸淩事件愈來愈多，因此值得師長們關注。

metaphor
[ˈmɛtəfɚ]

托 **雅** 學

m2030

n 隱喻，暗喻

Poems often have various metaphors that inspire our imagination.

詩歌常富含隱喻，激發我們的想像力。

meteorite
[ˈmitɪərˌaɪt]

托 雅 學

m2031

n 隕星，隕石

A meteorite is a solid piece of debris from outer space that impacts the Earth's surface.

隕石是從外太空而來，撞擊地球表面的固體碎片。

meteorology
[ˌmitɪəˈralədʒɪ]

托 雅 學

m2032

n 氣象狀態；氣象學

He studied the meteorology of hurricanes in order to help cities better prepare for these massive storms.

為了要幫助都市為大風暴做更好的準備，他研究熱帶氣旋的氣象狀態。

methodical
[məˈθadɪkəl]

托 雅 學

m2033

adj 有系統的，有方法的，有條理的，辦事有條不紊的

As a methodical assassin, Luke only takes out targets designated by his superior.

路克是很有條理的刺客，只解決雇主指定的目標。

methodology
[ˌmɛθədˈalədʒɪ]

托 雅 學

m2034

n 方法（學）

The advisor seems to be dissatisfied with the methodology used in the thesis, and wants his advisee to revise it.

這位指導教授似乎不大滿意論文的研究方法，所以要他的指導學生加以修改。

metropolitan
[ˌmɛtrəˈpalətn]

托 雅 學

m2035

adj 主要都市的，大城市的

Metropolitan areas are so densely populated that the traffic during peak hours moves slowly.

大城市地區人口相當稠密，高峰時段的交通極不順暢。

metropolitan
[ˌmɛtrə'palətn]

🄝 大主教　　　　　　　　　　　　　　m2036
The metropolitan is in charge of supervising other bishops in the province.
大主教負責管理教區內其他主教。

microcosm
['maɪkrəˌkazəm]

🄝 小宇宙；縮影　　　　　　　　　　　m2037
The tide pool was a microcosm of sea life.
這個潮池就是海洋生物的縮影。

microscopic
['maɪkrə'skapɪk]

adj 顯微鏡的；微觀的　　　　　　　　m2038
These microscopic images from inside the human body enable us to see the organs from a different perspective.
這些人體內的顯微圖片讓我們得以從不同角度觀察器官。

millenarian
[ˌmɪlə'nɛrɪən]

adj （基督教）一千年至福的；（相信）太平盛世　　m2039
（會到來）的；🄝 千禧年信奉者
A millenarian is a person who believes in the coming of the millennium and a time of contented peace.
千禧年信奉者是相信千年到來後會出現太平盛世的人。

M

minuscule
[mɪ'nʌskjul]

adj 十分小的；小寫的　　　　　　　　m2040
Compared to an ostrich, the hummingbird looks minuscule.
相較於鴕鳥，蜂鳥看起來小得微不足道。

mirage
[mə'raʒ]

🄝 海市蜃樓；幻想，妄想　　　　　　　m2041
Desert travelers often get dehydrated and think they see a mirage.
沙漠旅行者經常會脫水，以為他們看到海市蜃樓。

mischief
['mɪstʃɪf]

🄝 損害，傷害，危害；惡作劇，胡鬧；災禍　m2042
She put her dog in a crate during the day so he wouldn't get into mischief.
白天她將狗放置在板條箱裡，所以牠才不會胡鬧。

molecule
['maləˌkjul]

🄝 分子　　　　　　　　　　　　　　m2043
I don't know anything about the structure of the water molecule or its physical properties.
我對於水的分子結構或者物理特性完全不瞭解。

momentum
[mo'mɛntəm]

🄝 動力；要素　　　　　　　　　　　m2044
As the rock rolled down the hill, its momentum increased drastically.
當巨石向下滾動時，它的動力迅速增加。

monopoly
[məˈnɑplɪ]

托 雅 學

n 壟斷，專賣；專利權，專利事業

m2045

The computer company became so popular that they achieved a near monopoly on the personal computer market.

這家電腦公司如此受歡迎，幾乎壟斷了個人電腦市場。

morbid
[ˈmɔrbɪd]

托 雅 學

adj 不健康的，病態的

m2046

He steered the dinner conversation away from the morbid topic of his work as a homicide detective.

晚飯時談他的謀殺案偵探工作不利健康，他轉移了話題。

motto
[ˈmɑto]

托 雅 學

n 座右銘，格言，箴言

m2047

The bishop's motto was "Truth and Love."

這位主教的格言是「誠實與愛」。

mourn
[morn]

托 雅 學

vi/vt 哀悼，憂傷

m2048

Peter is mourning the loss of his best friend.

彼得正在哀悼已逝的好友。

mournful
[ˈmornfəl]

托 雅 學

adj 悲切的；令人悲痛的

m2049

The church service was mournful because the pastor relayed the sad loss of one of his congregation.

教堂禮拜儀式是令人悲痛的，因為牧師傳遞了一個悲傷的消息，他失去了一位會眾。

multiplication
[ˌmʌltəpləˈkeʃən]

托 雅 學

n 增加；繁殖；乘法

m2050

The multiplication tables are of no challenge for the child prodigy.

乘法表對這名神童來說毫無挑戰性。

muster
[ˈmʌstə]

托 雅 學

vt 召集；使振作，鼓起

m2051

The young boy had to muster all his courage when approached by the schoolyard bully.

當校園惡霸靠近時，那個小男孩不得不鼓起他所有的勇氣。

N

nausea
['nɔʃɪə]

托 雅 學

n2001

n 噁心，反胃
Lea felt nausea sweep over her when big waves rocked the boat.
當大浪搖晃著船體時，莉雅感到一陣噁心襲來。

---

necessitate
[nɪ'sɛsə,tet]

托 雅 學

n2002

vt 使成為必要，需要
The freeze broke several pipes and necessitated an overhaul of their plumbing system.
冰凍（的天氣）把一些水管弄破了，使得管路系統的檢修十分必要。

---

negligence
['nɛglɪdʒəns]

托 雅 學

n2003

n 疏忽，大意
The plants were slowly dying because of the gardener's negligence.
由於園丁的疏忽植物正瀕臨死亡。

---

negligible
['nɛglɪdʒəbl]

托 雅 學

n2004

adj 可忽略不計的，微不足道的
The government is convinced that the protest will have a negligible impact.
政府相信這次抗議的影響微不足道。

N

---

neurotic
[njʊ'rɑtɪk]

托 雅 學

n2005

adj 神經過敏的，神經質的；易激動的
She was a little neurotic about keeping her house clean.
她對房子潔癖到了有點兒神經質的地步。

---

neutral
['njutrəl]

托 雅 學

n2006

adj 中立的；中性的，中和的
The judge did not take sides and remained neutral during the debate.
評審在辯論過程中不偏袒任何一方，保持中立。

---

neutralize
['njutrəl,aɪz]

托 雅 學

n2007

vt 抵消，中和，壓住
Alison sprayed air freshener to neutralize the pet odor.
愛麗森噴灑空氣清新劑來壓住寵物身上的異味。

---

nibble
['nɪbl]

托 雅 學

n2008

n 啃；輕咬
She took a nibble from her muffin as she thought.
她一邊思考一邊小口地啃著松餅。

niche
[nɪtʃ]

托 雅 學

n2009

n 合適的位置；壁龕

Everyone has a unique talent, which will help them find their niche in life.

每個人都有獨特的天賦，可以幫他們在生活中找到合適的位置。

nominal
['namənl]

托 雅 學

n2010

adj 名義上的；（金額，租金）微不足道的

His membership in the club was nominal--he rarely went to meetings.

他在俱樂部的會員資格只是名義上的——他很少去參加會議。

nominate
['namə,net]

托 雅 學

n2011

vt 提名，任命

The governor of Virginia was nominated for the presidency at the convention.

維吉尼亞州長在大會中被提名參選總統。

norm
[nɔrm]

托 雅 學

n2012

n 規範，準則；平均數

My son's essay received a mark well above the norm for his class.

我兒子的文章得到一個很棒的分數，遠遠超過了他們班的平均分。

notation
[no'teʃən]

托 雅 學

n2013

n 符號，標注

Brandon made a notation in his notebook to check online for more info.

布瑞登在他的筆記本中做上標注以便上網收集更多資訊。

notch
[natʃ]

托 雅 學

n2014

n 皮帶上的孔；刻凹痕

After losing weight, the man found he could tighten one more notch on his belt.

體重減輕後，那人發現他的皮帶又可以往裡多繫一個孔了。

notorious
[no'torɪəs]

托 雅 學

n2015

adj 臭名昭著的，聲名狼藉的

The movie director was notorious for his bad temper.

那個導演因壞脾氣而臭名昭著。

nuisance
['njusns]

托 雅 學

n2016

n 討厭的人（或東西）；麻煩事

She set traps for the roaches because they were becoming a nuisance.

她給蟑螂設了陷阱，因為它們是討厭的東西。

null
[nʌl]

托 雅 學

n2017

adj 無效的，無價值的

Justin signed a document when not of legal age so it was null and void.

賈斯汀簽署文件時還不到法定年齡，因此它是無效的。

oblivious
[ə'blɪvɪəs]
托 雅 學

adj 健忘的，不以為意的
Some individuals are oblivious to other people's feelings.
有些人對他人感受不以為意。

o2001

obnoxious
[əb'nakʃəs]
托 雅 學

adj 極令人不快的；令人厭惡的；可憎的
She thought her little brother was loud and obnoxious.
她覺得自己的小弟弟太喧鬧，讓人討厭。

o2002

obscene
[əb'sin]
托 雅 學

adj 猥褻的，淫穢的；令人厭惡的，可憎的
The man was accused of showing obscene gestures in public.
這個男人被指控在公開場合做出猥褻的動作。

o2003

obsess
[əb'sɛs]
托 雅 學

vt 使著迷，使煩擾
Teenagers tend to obsess over their looks.
青少年總是煩惱外表的美醜。

o2004

O

obsessed
[əb'sɛst]
托 雅 學

adj 沉迷的，著迷的
Mia is obsessed with Facebook and checks it all the time.
米婭對臉書很著迷，不停地查看消息。

o2005

obsession
[əb'sɛʃən]
托 雅 學

n 著迷，迷住；困擾
His obsession has always been collecting classic cars.
他一直著迷於收集古董車。

o2006

obsolete
['absə,lit]
托 雅 學

adj 已廢棄的，過時的
He upgraded the obsolete software on his mother's computer.
他為媽媽升級電腦中過時的軟體。

o2007

obstruct
[əb'strʌkt]
托 雅 學

vt 阻塞；妨礙；擋住（視線）
The scan showed that cholesterol build-up was obstructing his artery.
掃描結果顯示，膽固醇堆積正在阻塞他的動脈。

o2008

obstruction
[əb'strʌkʃən]

托 雅 學

n 妨礙，障礙物

o2009

The accountant was charged with five counts of obstruction of justice for helping his client falsify his bookkeeping.

那位會計師因為協助客戶做假賬而被指控犯有妨礙司法公正的五項罪狀。

odor
['odəʳ]

托 雅 學

n 氣味，臭味

o2010

When her brother took off his shoes, Lily almost fainted from his foot odor.

莉莉的弟弟一脫下鞋子，腳臭差點沒把她熏倒。

odyssey
['ɑdəsɪ]

托 雅 學

n 遠行，長途冒險旅行

o2011

Astronaut John Glenn's trip to the moon was a space odyssey.

阿姆斯壯‧約翰‧葛蘭的登月之旅是一次太空遠行。

offset
['ɔf,sɛt]

托 雅 學

n 分支；補償；抵消

o2012

Even though the boxer is shorter than his opponent, his speed and strength were an offset to his smaller size.

雖然這位拳擊手比起對手來相對矮小，但他的速度和力氣補償了他體型的不足。

offset
['ɔf,sɛt]

托 雅 學

vt 抵消，補償，彌補

o2013

Grandma's tasty sweet potato soup helped offset my poor attempt at making stew.

外婆可口的地瓜湯彌補了被我做壞的燉菜。

omen
['omən]

托 雅 學

n 徵兆，預兆

o2014

The sunny weather seemed like a good omen.

晴朗的天氣仿佛是個好的兆頭。

opaque
[o'pek]

托 雅 學

adj 不透明（光）的；難理解的，晦澀的

o2015

Because the jargon in the man's speech was opaque, most of the audience were confused.

由於這位演講者所用的專用術語很難理解，所以很多聽眾都感到很困惑。

optimum
['ɑptəməm]

托 雅 學

adj 最適宜的

o2016

The English cram school claims that they provide the optimum environment for their students to develop English proficiency.

這個英文補習班宣稱，他們給學生提供最適合培養英文能力的環境。

ordeal
[ɔr'diəl]

托 雅 學

n 嚴峻考驗；苦難，折磨

o2017

The child had been through an extreme ordeal when he lost his parents in a big earthquake.

這個小孩子曾經遭受了極端的苦難，他在一次大地震中失去了父母。

originate
[əˈrɪdʒəˌnet]

vt 起源，發生；首創，創造　　o2018
His theories about philosophy originated in Aristotle's writing.
他關於哲學的理論源自於亞里斯多德的文章。

orthodox
[ˈɔrθəˌdɑks]

adj 傳統的，正統的；習慣的；保守的；東正教的　　o2019
She knew the priest was orthodox in his views.
她知道神父的觀點是傳統的。

outlaw
[ˈaʊtˌlɔ]

n 逃犯，歹徒　　o2020
The outlaw fled the city before they discovered the murder.
在他們發現謀殺案之前，歹徒已逃離城市。

outrageous
[aʊtˈredʒəs]

adj 大膽的；不尋常的；驚人的　　o2021
Her taste in fashion was considered outrageous.
她對時尚的品味非常大膽。

overhaul
[ˌovəˈhɔl]

vt 拆開檢修；全面檢查；趕上　　o2022
The company was disorganized, so they hired a consultant to overhaul their internal communications.
這家公司組織不善，因此他們找來顧問全面檢查內部溝通問題。

override
[ˌovəˈraɪd]

vt 撤銷；推翻；不顧；壓倒　　o2023
The CEO's decision was overridden by the board because they did not want to invest more money in the project.
董事會推翻了執行長的決定，因為他們不想再在這個項目上投資更多的錢了。

overrun
[ˌovəˈrʌn]

vt 蔓延，佔領　　o2024
The sale at the store was so good that they were overrun with traffic.
他們商場的商品賣得非常好，顧客盈門。

oversee
[ˈovəˈsi]

vt 監視，監督；眺望，俯瞰；無意中看到　　o2025
The manager wanted to oversee the new employee because they were not well trained yet.
經理想要監督新進員工，因為他們還不夠訓練有素。

overt
[oˈvɝt]

adj 明顯的；公然的　　o2026
The board of directors gave overt support to the new investment plan.
董事會公開支持這個新投資計畫。

overthrow
[ˌovəˈθro]

vt 推翻，顛覆；推倒

o2027

Many people wanted to overthrow the government because the leader was a tyrant.

很多人想要推翻政府，因為領導者是一個暴君。

overture
[ˈovətʃʊr]

n 提案；序曲

o2028

Stella thought the bouquet of flowers was a grand overture from her neighbor.

斯特娜認為這束鮮花是來自鄰居的盛大序曲。

P

pageant
['pædʒənt]

n. 盛會；遊行；虛飾；露天表演
Caroline watched the street pageant parade through the town.
卡洛琳看著大街上遊行隊伍穿過小鎮。

p2001

paradox
['pærə,dɑks]

n. 似非而是的話；自相矛盾的情況；反論
If a time traveler killed his father in the past, it would create a paradox because he would have never been born.
假如時光旅行者回到過去殺了自己的父親，會造成矛盾，因為那樣的話他根本就不可能出生。

p2002

parameter
[pə'ræmətə]

n. 參數，參量；限制
The parameters of the big debate were agreed to by both parties.
對這場大辯論的限制已經經過雙方同意了。

p2003

paranoia
[,pærə'nɔɪə]

n. 偏執狂，妄想狂；多疑，恐懼
There is so much paranoia because of the virus that has been spreading rapidly.
已經正在迅速傳播的病毒引起了許多恐懼。

p2004

paternity
[pə't3·nətɪ]

n. 父權；父系；父系後裔
The father asked if he could take a paternity test to make sure the child was his.
那位父親詢問他是否可以做一個親子鑒定，以確保這孩子是他親生的。

p2005

patron
['petrən]

n. 贊助人，資助人；老主顧
She always gave generously and was a patron of the art gallery.
她是藝廊的贊助人，總是慷慨解囊。

p2006

patronage
['pætrənɪdʒ]

n. 贊助；惠顧
The pub owner appreciated the patronage of his regular customers.
酒館老闆對經常光顧的客人表示感激。

p2007

penchant
['pɛntʃənt]

n. （強烈的）愛好，嗜好
I have a penchant for perfumes and always buy them at the duty free stores.
我有收藏香水的嗜好，總是到免稅店去購買。

p2008

percolate
['pɝkə,let]

托 雅 學

vi/vt 過濾；使滲入，使浸透 `p2009`

The mother set the coffee pot to percolate on the stove.

媽媽把咖啡壺放到爐子上濾煮咖啡。

percuss
[pə'kʌs]

托 雅 學

vi/vt 敲，叩；叩診；輕敲 `p2010`

When the patient had trouble breathing, his doctor began to percuss his chest.

當病人呼吸困難時，他的醫生開始輕敲他的胸部。

percussion
[pə'kʌʃən]

托 雅 學

n 敲打，衝擊；震動；叩診；打擊樂器 `p2011`

Triangles, flutes, and cymbals, are part of the school's percussion band.

三角鐵、笛子和鐃鈸是學校打擊樂隊的部分樂器。

peril
['pɛrəl]

托 雅 學

n 危機，危險；危險的事物 `p2012`

The cat was in great peril because there were coyotes in the woods behind the house.

這隻貓處於極大的危險中，因為房子後面的樹林裡有土狼。

perish
['pɛrɪʃ]

托 雅 學

vi/vt 死亡；凋謝；毀滅 `p2013`

I did not want my thing to perish in the fire but it was too late to find them.

我不想我的東西在火裡被毀滅，但是太遲了，已經找不到了。

perishable
['pɛrɪʃəbḷ]

托 雅 學

adj 易腐爛的，易消亡的 `p2014`

I keep all my perishable fruits and vegetables in the fridge.

我把所有易腐爛的水果和蔬菜放到冰箱裡儲存。

perpendicular
[,pɝpən'dɪkjələ]

托 雅 學

adj 垂直的；**n** 垂直（線） `p2015`

The tree tops were bent almost perpendicular by the hurricane, many snapping in half.

樹梢幾乎被颱風折成了與地平線垂直的線條，很多還被折斷了。

perplex
[pə'plɛks]

托 雅 學

vt 使困惑，使費解；使複雜化 `p2016`

That novel is so strange that it would perplex even the best literary critic in the nation.

這本小說如此奇怪，使國內最優秀的文學評論家都覺得困惑。

perspire
[pə'spaɪr]

托 雅 學

vt 出汗，流汗 `p2017`

I was nervous and began to perspire while waiting for my interview.

在等待面試時，我緊張得全身冒汗。

pertinent
['pɝ·tnənt]

adj 恰當的；有關的　　　　p2018

That is not pertinent information to this discussion but we can talk about it after class.

這個資訊與我們的討論議題不相關，但是我們可以在下課後來談談。

perverse
[pə'vɝ·s]

adj 墮落的，邪惡的；乖戾的；違反常情的　　p2019

The teacher thought the student's perverse behavior would affect his future success.

老師認為這個學生的乖戾的舉止會影響到他將來的成功。

picturesque
[ˌpɪktʃə'rɛsk]

adj 風景如畫的，迷人的，生動的　　p2020

The village was very picturesque with views of the sea in front and lush forests behind it.

這個村莊風景如畫，前有海洋，後有蔥鬱森林。

pigment
['pɪgmənt]

n 顏料；色素　　　　p2021

I think you can say that the paint has a soft blue pigment in its color hue.

我覺得可以說塗料的色調裡帶有淡淡的藍色素。

pigment
['pɪgmənt]

vi/vt 給⋯著色；呈現顏色　　　　p2022

Lilly pigmented the frosting with fresh cherry juice.

莉莉用新鮮的櫻桃汁給糖霜著色。

pinpoint
['pɪn,pɔɪnt]

n 針尖；極小量；精確位置；一絲（光線）　　p2023

A pinpoint of sunlight comes out from the tiny hole in the brick wall.

從磚牆的小孔透出一絲光線。

pit
[pɪt]

n 坑，陷阱；礦井；果核　　　　p2024

Digging a big pit is one of the easiest ways to bury household waste.

挖個大坑是掩埋家庭垃圾最簡單的方法之一。

plagiarism
['pledʒəˌrɪzəm]

n 抄襲，剽竊作品　　　　p2025

A student was accused of plagiarism on his essay.

有一個學生被指控在寫論文時有剽竊行為。

planetarium
[ˌplænə'tɛrɪəm]

n 天文館；行星儀　　　　p2026

The astrology club is going to the planetarium tonight to see the constellation.

天文社團打算今天晚上去天文館觀看星座。

P

plaster
['plæstɚ]

托 雅 學

n 灰泥；熟石膏；膏藥

p2027

The worker mixed up some plaster to cover the hole he just knocked in the brand new wall.

這個工人把灰泥混合好後塗抹在牆上，以便覆蓋自己剛剛在嶄新的牆面敲出的洞。

plateau
[plæ'to]

托 雅 學

n 高原；平穩時期；學習停滯期

p2028

She was steadily improving at school until one day she hit a plateau.

一直到遇到學習停滯期前，她在學校都穩定地進步。

plausible
['plɔzəbl]

托 雅 學

adj 似是而非的；巧言令色的，貌似可信的

p2029

I suppose it is not plausible that a politician can actually be honest.

我想要一個政治人物真誠其實是不可能的。

plea
[pli]

托 雅 學

n （法律）抗辯；請求，懇求；托詞

p2030

The students made a strong plea for not being assigned homework at Christmas.

學生們強烈請求耶誕節不指派家庭作業。

plead
[plid]

托 雅 學

vi/vt 抗辯；懇求；為…辯護

p2031

A desperate father pleaded for help in finding his missing son on TV.

絕望的父親在電視上懇求協助，來尋找他失蹤的兒子。

pledge
[plɛdʒ]

托 雅 學

n 誓約；保證；抵押

p2032

My father made a pledge to donate to a local charity regularly.

我的父親保證定期捐款給一個當地的慈善機構。

pledge
[plɛdʒ]

托 雅 學

vt 發誓；保證

p2033

The man pledged to take good care of the woman when he proposed to her.

那個男子向那個女人求婚時，保證會好好照顧她。

plight
[plaɪt]

托 雅 學

n 苦難，困境

p2034

Little Johnny felt sympathetic toward the plight of the stray dog that lived in his neighborhood.

小強尼對他家附近的流浪狗的困境感到同情。

plump
[plʌmp]

托 雅 學

adj 豐滿的；鼓起的

p2035

Grapes are in season now, and they look plump and juicy.

現在葡萄正當季，豐滿又多汁。

plump
[plʌmp]
托 雅 學

vt 使豐滿；使鼓起；把⋯弄鼓
p2036
My mother has been busy cleaning the furniture and plumping cushions all day.
我媽今天一整天都在忙著清洗傢俱並讓靠墊鼓起來。

plunge
[plʌndʒ]
托 雅 學

vi/vt （使）突然前衝；（使）投入，插進，陷入；猛衝
p2037
The room was plunged into darkness during the storm blackout.
當暴風雨導致停電的時候，整個房間陷入了黑暗之中。

portray
[por'tre]
托 雅 學

vt 描寫，描述；畫（人物、景象等）
p2038
As a male writer, I am careful about how I portray women in my stories.
身為一位男性作家，我對我故事中女性的描述格外小心。

postulate
['pɑstʃə,let]
托 雅 學

vt 要求；假定，假設
p2039
The archeologist postulated that early humans had had knowledge to make and use tools.
考古學家假設早期的人類已有製造及使用工具的知識。

potent
['potnt]
托 雅 學

adj 有影響的；有說服力的；有效力的；酒勁大的
p2040
The wine was very potent and made me dizzy after just one glass.
這種葡萄酒的酒勁很大，我只喝了一杯就感覺頭暈目眩的 。

P

pounce
[paʊns]
托 雅 學

vi 突襲，猛撲；抓住不放
p2041
A bob cat will stalk its prey and then pounce.
短尾貓會跟蹤它的獵物，然後猛撲上去。

prairie
['prɛrɪ]
托 雅 學

n 大草原，牧場
p2042
My father grew up on the prairie and loved the long grasses and the big open sky.
我爸爸在大草原長大，所以熱愛長草和廣大的天空。

precarious
[prɪ'kɛrɪəs]
托 雅 學

adj 不穩的；危險的；證據不足的
p2043
The situation was precarious and one bad decision could derail the negotiations.
現在的情勢還不穩，任何錯誤決定都會打亂整個談判。

precede
[pri'sid]
托 雅 學

vi/vt （順序、位置或時間上）處在⋯之前；（地位等）優於
p2044
You might want to precede the report with an introduction, making the content more accessible to the audience.
你也許想在報告之前做個介紹，讓觀眾更容易理解你要報告的內容。

precedence
[prɪ'sidns]

托 雅 學

n 領先於⋯的權利；優先權　　　p2045

This legislation took precedence over other business matters because it pertained to the budget.

法律事宜要先於其他商業事務解決，因為這與預算直接相關。

precedent
['prɛsədənt]

托 雅 學

n 先例　　　p2046

The judge was a little rebellious and ruled in favor of the defendant even though there was no precedent for his decision.

這個法官有點背離常規，不斷維護被告，儘管他的判決沒有先例。

precipitate
[prɪ'sɪpətɪt]

托 雅 學

vi/vt 加速；使陷於困境，陷入；水氣凝結成雨　　　p2047

A relative's unexpected arrival only caused the family turmoil to precipitate even more.

親戚的突然到訪只會讓這個家庭更加陷入混亂之中。

precipitation
[prɪˌsɪpɪ'teʃən]

托 雅 學

n 沉澱；倉促；降雨，降雪　　　p2048

The weather forecast advised there's a chance of rain precipitation today.

天氣預報稱今天可能有降雨。

preclude
[prɪ'klud]

托 雅 學

vt 排除；阻止，妨礙　　　p2049

Her injury will preclude her career as a dancer.

她的傷會妨礙她的舞蹈生涯。

predecessor
['prɛdɪˌsɛsɚ]

托 雅 學

n 前輩；前任　　　p2050

His predecessor at the bank was very popular and Doug knew it would take time to gain the trust of his employees.

這家銀行的前任主管很受愛戴，道格知道要獲得下屬的信賴需要時間。

predominant
[prɪ'dɑmənənt]

托 雅 學

adj 佔優勢的；主要的，突出的　　　p2051

The predominant trait of his art is the use of vibrant shades of blue.

他的藝術作品的主要特色就是使用鮮明的藍色色調。

preliminary
[prɪ'lɪməˌnɛrɪ]

托 雅 學

adj 預備性的，初步的　　　p2052

In the preliminary investigation, the police found important evidence but much more time will be needed to determine a suspect.

在初步的調查當中，警方發現了重要的證據，但需要更多的時間來確認嫌犯。

premise
['prɛmɪs]

托 雅 學

n 前提，假設；房屋　　　p2053

The premise for the story is original but it is up to the writer to execute his ideas well.

這個故事的假設是很具原創性的，但是也要看作者如何詮釋自己的觀點。

premise
[prɪ'maɪz]

vi/vt 提出前提；預設，假定　　p2054
The assumption was premised upon our major findings across all the studies.
這項假設的提出是以所有研究的重大發現作為前提的。

premium
['primɪəm]

n 額外費用；獎金，獎賞；保險費　　p2055
I am willing to pay a premium for good coffee.
我很願意為好咖啡多付額外費用。

preponderance
[prɪ'pɑndərəns]

n 優勢；優越；大量　　p2056
A preponderance of evidence points to the fact that the crime was premediated.
大量的證據表明這樁犯罪是有預謀的。

prerequisite
[,pri'rɛkwəzɪt]

n 不可缺少的事物；前提，必要條件　　p2057
This beginner's course is a prerequisite to the intermediate class.
在學習中級課程之前，先修完初學者課程是必要條件。

prerogative
[prɪ'rɑgətɪv]

n 特權；優先權，優勢　　p2058
The politician was advised that it was his prerogative to change his mind on the final vote.
這位政治家被告知，在最後一輪投票中他有改變立場的特權。

P

prescribe
[prɪ'skraɪb]

vi/vt 指示，規定；處（方），開（藥）　　p2059
Her family doctor prescribed her a drug to help her sleep better at night.
她的家庭醫生開了一種藥幫她晚上睡得好些。

preside
[prɪ'zaɪd]

vi 主持；負責；主奏　　p2060
The principal of the school should preside over meetings concerning school affairs.
學校的校長應該要主持有關學校事務的會議。

presumably
[prɪ'zuməblɪ]

adv 推測起來，大概　　p2061
Presumably, all lives were lost at sea when the ship sank.
推測起來，船沉沒後所有人都在大海中喪生了。

presume
[prɪ'zum]

vi/vt 擅自行動；設想；假設，揣測；濫用；擅自做　　p2062
I would never presume to know why you are upset, but good friends can sometimes guess when you are in trouble.
我從來不去揣測你心情不好的原因，但是作為你的好友，我有時候可以猜到你是有麻煩了。

presumptuous
[prɪˈzʌmptʃʊəs]

托 雅 學

adj 冒昧的，放肆的　　　　p2063

It is extremely presumptuous to sit at the head of a table when you are a guest in someone's home.

身為客人卻去坐在餐桌的主位是一種非常冒昧的行為。

pretentious
[prɪˈtɛnʃəs]

托 雅 學

adj 做作的；自負的；自命不凡的　　　p2064

After she acquired a British accent while living abroad, she sounds pretentious to some of her old friends.

在她住在國外並學得英國腔調之後，她在一些老朋友面前顯得自命不凡。

pretext
[ˈpritɛkst]

托 雅 學

n 藉口，托詞　　　　p2065

I told the hostess I had a headache as a pretext for leaving the party early.

我用頭痛當藉口跟女主人說要提早離開那個派對。

prevail
[prɪˈvel]

托 雅 學

vi 取勝，佔優勢；流行，盛行　　　p2066

The times we live in may be difficult, but if we care for one another we can prevail over any suffering.

我們所處的時代也許是困難的，但是如果我們關心彼此，就可以戰勝任何痛苦。

prevalent
[ˈprɛvələnt]

托 雅 學

adj 流行的；普遍的　　　　p2067

Some diseases are more prevalent in certain parts of the world, like malaria in tropical climates.

某些疾病在世界上一些特定地區是較普遍的，例如熱帶地區的瘧疾。

prey
[pre]

托 雅 學

n 被掠食者；獵物；掠食　　　p2068

Mountain lions typically stalk their prey before attacking.

山獅在攻擊獵物前都會先跟蹤。

prey
[pre]

托 雅 學

vi 捕食；掠奪；詐取；折磨　　　p2069

My anxiety about the upcoming test preyed on my mind.

我對即將到來的考試的焦慮讓我心裡受折磨。

primitive
[ˈprɪmətɪv]

托 雅 學

adj 原始的；早期的；未開化的　　　p2070

The first telephone was a very primitive machine and you had to yell quite loudly to be heard.

第一部電話是非常原始的，使用者必須大聲喊才能被聽見。

proficiency
[prəˈfɪʃənsɪ]

托 雅 學

n 熟練，精通　　　　p2071

I was pleasantly surprised by his proficiency at mastering tennis after only a few lessons.

對於他在幾堂課之後網球技術就已如此熟練，我真是又驚又喜。

prolong
[prə'lɔŋ]

vt 延長，拉長；拖延　　p2072

Some treatments can prolong a patient's life but often with terrible and painful side effects.

有些治療雖能延長病患的生命，但通常伴隨著可怕又痛苦的副作用。

prone
[pron]

托 雅 學

adj 傾向於；俯伏的，傾斜的，陡的　　p2073

Many white-collar workers are prone to work over-time because of the increasing competition in their workplace.

隨著工作場所競爭的與日俱增，很多白領傾向於加班工作。

propaganda
[,prapə'gændə]

n 宣傳（機構），宣傳手法；（天主教）傳道總會　　p2074

During World War II, many countries used propaganda in posters, movies, and radio to promote their political position.

第二次世界大戰期間，很多國家用海報、電影和收音機等宣傳手法來宣揚他們的政治立場。

propagate
['prapə,get]

vi/vt 繁殖；傳播，普及　　p2075

The plant is aggressive and will propagate over the entire garden.

這種植物長得很快，很快就會佈滿整個花園。

propel
[prə'pɛl]

托 雅 學

vt 推進，推動；激勵，驅使　　p2076

He was able to propel the boat forward even though the current was very strong.

儘管溪流強勁，他還是能夠推動船使其前進。

prophet
['prafɪt]

托 雅 學

n 預言家；先知；提倡者　　p2077

Some think the CEO of that company is a prophet and can predict changes in the consumer market.

有些人認為這家公司的執行長是個預言家，可以預知消費者市場的變化。

protocol
['protə,kal]

n 協定書；草案　　p2078

The school should establish a new protocol for how to evacuate the school during an emergency.

學校應該制定新的草案，決定如何在緊急情況時疏散學校的人。

prototype
['protə,taɪp]

n 原型；典型，範例　　p2079

The inventor made a working prototype of his new design.

發明家根據新的設計做了一台工作原型機。

provision
[prə'vɪʒən]

n 供應；預備；規定　　p2080

What provision should I make for an unexpected emergency?

我應該怎麼為突發的緊急事故做好準備呢？

P

proximity
[prɑk'sɪmətɪ]

托 雅 學

n 接近，鄰近；親近

I live in proximity to the university.

我住在大學的鄰近地區。

p2081

proxy
['prɑksɪ]

托 雅 學

n 代理人；委託書；代用品

Katie's ailing father sent her to vote by proxy on his behalf.

凱蒂病中的父親派她作為代理人代表他投票。

p2082

pry
[praɪ]

托 雅 學

vi/vt 窺探，打聽

Some people like to pry into the celebrities' private life.

有些人喜歡打探名人的私生活。

p2083

pry
[praɪ]

托 雅 學

vt 撬開

I am trying to carefully pry open my jewelry box.

我正試圖小心翼翼地撬開自己的首飾盒。

p2084

pulp
[pʌlp]

托 雅 學

vi/vt 把…製成漿；變成漿（狀）

The paper factory pulps old books for the purpose of recycling.

造紙廠把舊書化成紙漿，目的是回收再利用。

p2085

puncture
['pʌŋktʃɚ]

托 雅 學

n 刺，穿刺；刺孔

The needle left a puncture mark where it entered the vein in my arm.

當針頭穿入我手臂的血管，留下了一個穿孔。

p2086

pungent
['pʌndʒənt]

托 雅 學

adj （氣味）刺鼻難聞的

I love aged cheese but the smell can often be pungent.

我喜歡成熟的乾酪，只是氣味常常讓人感到刺鼻難聞。

p2087

Q

quaint
[kwent]
托 雅 學

adj 古雅的，精巧的；古怪的   q2001
Tourists think our town is very quaint and full of charm.
觀光客認為我們的城鎮古雅又充滿魅力。

queer
[kwɪr]
托 雅 學

adj 奇怪的，古怪的   q2002
Adam felt queer and confused after being dumped by his girlfriend.
亞當在被他女友甩了以後覺得很奇怪，也很困惑。

quench
[kwɛntʃ]
托 雅 學

vt 熄滅；平息下來；壓制   q2003
People's rage against the government could not be quenched and ended in a riot.
人民對政府的憤怒無法平息下來，最終演變成了大暴動。

query
['kwɪrɪ]
托 雅 學

n 疑問；詢問   q2004
After the scandal, the public has submitted a query about his credibility.
醜聞發生後，大眾對他的誠信提出疑問。

query
['kwɪrɪ]
托 雅 學

vt 懷疑，表示疑慮；詢問   q2005
He has been so autocratic that no one dares to query the motives for his decisions.
他總是非常獨裁，所以沒有人敢質疑他做決定的動機。

quiver
['kwɪvɚ]
托 雅 學

n 顫抖；vi/vt 顫抖，抖動   q2006
The lime flavored gelatin quivered slightly as he raised his spoon to his mouth.
在他拿起湯匙靠近嘴巴時，酸橙口味的果凍微微地顫動。

quota
['kwotə]
托 雅 學

n （生產、進出口等的）配額；（移民的）限額   q2007
The baker was worried that she did not have enough time to finish the 400 cupcakes to meet her quota that day.
麵包師傅擔心沒有充裕的時間完成當天四百個杯子蛋糕的配額。

Q

R

radiant
['redjənt]
托 雅 學

adj 發光的；輻射的；容光煥發的　　r2001
The groom had never seen his wife look as radiant as she did on their wedding day.
新郎從未看到他的妻子像在婚禮那天那樣容光煥發。

radiate
['redɪ,et]
托 雅 學

vi 發射光線；輻射　　r2002
The heat was so intense in summer that it would radiate off from the concrete at night.
那年夏天的高溫是如此強烈，以至於它會在晚間從水泥中散發出來。

radius
['redɪəs]
托 雅 學

n 半徑；有效航程；範圍　　r2003
The radius of a circle is the distance from the center to the outside edge.
圓的半徑是中心到外緣的距離。

raid
[red]
托 雅 學

n/vt 襲擊，搜查　　r2004
The illegal casino was raided and the police arrested many people last night.
這個違法的賭場昨晚被員警突擊檢查，逮捕了很多人。

rally
['rælɪ]
托 雅 學

n 聚集，集會；拉力賽　　r2005
The protesters held a large rally to raise support and awareness for their agenda.
抗議者舉行了一個大的聚會來增加人們對於他們關注議題的支持與意識。

rally
['rælɪ]
托 雅 學

vi/vt 重整，恢復，振作；集合　　r2006
The CEO rallied his subordinates to discuss the principles for the new products' sales drive.
執行長集合了他的下屬討論新產品的銷售方針。

ramble
['ræmbḷ]
托 雅 學

vi 閒逛，漫步；聊天　　r2007
The speaker began to ramble on about his childhood and my attention wandered toward the bar.
演講者開始聊起童年往事，我的心思也轉向酒吧。

rampant
['ræmpənt]
托 雅 學

adj （尤指疾病、社會弊端）猖獗的；無法控制的　　r2008
Crime is becoming rampant, making the residents in the community nervous.
犯罪越來越猖獗，搞得社區居民非常緊張。

374

rarefy
['rɛrə,faɪ]

托 雅 學

vt 使鬆散；使稀薄

r2009

A lack of calcium can cause bones to rarefy which can then cause fractures.

缺鈣會導致骨質疏鬆，進一步引起骨折。

realm
[rɛlm]

托 雅 學

n 王國，國土；領域

r2010

Robin has published several articles in his professional realm.

羅賓在他的專業領域裡發表了幾篇文章。

rebellion
[rɪ'bɛljən]

托 雅 學

n 叛亂，反抗，起義

r2011

By slowing down their pace of production, the workers created a small and effective rebellion against the new pay policies.

生產線的工人降低生產速度，用這樣小規模但又有效的手段來反抗新的薪酬政策。

rebel
['rɛbl̩]

托 雅 學

n 叛逆者，起義者

r2012

He was always a rebel, constantly challenging every authority figure he met.

他就是一個叛逆者，始終挑戰每個他遇見的威權人物。

rebel
[rɪ'bɛl]

托 雅 學

vi 反抗，反叛，起義

r2013

The college students have united to rebel against the government.

這些大學生聯合起來反抗政府。

recession
[rɪ'sɛʃən]

托 雅 學

n 經濟衰退；撤回

r2014

The government should be aware of the signs of economic recession.

政府應該留意經濟衰退的徵兆。

R

reciprocal
[rɪ'sɪprəkl̩]

托 雅 學

adj 相互的；互利的

r2015

The couple shared reciprocal benefits from their chosen careers.

這對夫婦分享他們所選擇的事業上的相互利益。

reckon
['rɛkən]

托 雅 學

vi/vt 計算，總計；估計，猜想；依賴

r2016

I am not sure what time the meteor shower will begin, but I reckon we will have to wait until at least midnight.

我不確定流星雨什麼時候會開始，但我估計我們至少要等到半夜。

reclaim
[rɪ'klem]

托 雅 學

vt 要求歸還，收回；開墾

r2017

The country has reclaimed its land from several foreign invaders during the past 40 years.

這個國家在過去的四十年間從幾個外來侵入者手中收回其領土。

reconcile
['rɛkənsaɪl]

vi/vt 使和好，調解，使調和；使一致

r2018

The accountant attempted to reconcile the bankers' accounts and had trouble finding receipts for her expenses.

會計師嘗試調解銀行家的帳戶，但她找不到消費的收據。

reconciliation
[rɛkən,sɪlɪ'eʃən]

n 調解；協調；和解

r2019

I hope that my parents and I will soon achieve reconciliation for my plans for college.

我期待與父母能在我的大學規劃這件事上達成某種和解。

recur
[rɪ'kɝ]

vi 再發生；反復出現

r2020

The dead dog had recurred in the boy's dreams for a long time.

死去的小狗很長一段時間反復出現在男孩的夢裡。

recurrent=recurring
[rɪ'kɝ-ənt=rɪ'kɝ-ɪŋ]

adj 經常發生的；週期性的

r2021

I have a recurrent dream at least twice a week about falling.

我一個星期裡至少兩次重複夢到墜落。

redeem
[rɪ'dim]

vt 補救；維護；付清；兌換

r2022

Jessica works hard in order to redeem the image of her father after his massive gambling debts.

在父親欠下巨額賭債後，潔西卡努力工作以挽救她父親的形象。

reel
[ril]

n 捲筒，線軸

r2023

Movies are spun onto a reel and then played in theatres across the country.

電影在播放前都被捲成一個捲筒，然後在全國的各個電影院裡放映。

reel
[ril]

vi/vt 捲，繞

r2024

After reeling in the big fish, the fisherman called his friends to help him carry it to the market.

在捲收了魚竿線把大魚釣上岸後，漁夫叫他的朋友來幫忙把那條魚扛到市場。

referendum
[,rɛfə'rɛndəm]

n 全民公投

r2025

The government decided to vote on a referendum on homosexual marriage.

政府決定將對同性戀婚姻進行全民公投。

refraction
[rɪ'frækʃən]

n 折射；曲折

r2026

Physicists tell us that the sky is blue because of a force acting on sunlight called refraction.

物理學告訴我們天空是藍的，是因為一種叫折射的力量作用在陽光上。

refrain
[rɪ'fren]

托 雅 學

n （詩的）疊句；副歌

r2027

She loved the song, and she sang along with the refrain all the time.

她愛這首歌，她一直跟著唱副歌。

refrain
[rɪ'fren]

托 雅 學

vi 節制；避免，制止

r2028

Grown-ups should refrain from smoking or drinking in front of children.

大人應該避免在孩子面前抽煙或喝酒。

refute
[rɪ'fjut]

托 雅 學

vt 駁斥，反駁，駁倒

r2029

The world-famous physicist and cosmologist Stephen Hawking recently refuted the existence of black holes.

最近，舉世聞名的物理學家及宇宙論者史蒂芬·霍金駁斥了黑洞的存在。

regenerate
[rɪ'dʒɛnərət]

托 雅 學

vt 恢復；使再生

r2030

Scientists are always striving to regenerate human body cells.

科學家們一直致力於使人體細胞恢復活力。

regeneration
[rɪ,dʒɛnə'reʃən]

托 雅 學

n 再生，新生；重建，改造

r2031

Cathy is enjoying a regeneration of her interest in fitness and yoga.

凱西正享著她對健身和瑜伽興趣的重生。

regime
[rɪ'ʒim]

托 雅 學

n 政體，制度

r2032

During his regime, the King was benevolent to all of his subjects.

這位國王在他統治期間對他的人民很仁慈。

R

rehabilitate
[,rihə'bɪlə,tet]

托 雅 學

vt 使復興，使恢復原狀；復原

r2033

His surgery went well, but he will have to rehabilitate his leg for several months before he can walk long distances.

他的手術進展順利，但是他的腳還要經過好幾個月的復原才能長距離走路。

reign
[ren]

托 雅 學

n 統治時期

r2034

The queen had a long reign, ruling for more than sixty years.

女王在位期間很長，超過六十年。

reign
[ren]

托 雅 學

vi 佔優勢

r2035

The dictatorial emperor has reigned in the country for three decades.

這位獨裁的君主已經統治這個國家三十年了。

377

reiterate
[ri'ɪtə,ret]

托 雅 學

vt 反復地說，重申

r2036

Please listen while I reiterate the terms of the new policy to you.

當我給你們重申新政策的條目時，請注意聽。

rejoice
[rɪ'dʒɔɪs]

托 雅 學

vi 欣喜，高興

r2037

The birth was unusually difficult, so all the hospital staff began to rejoice with the family when the doctor told them the baby was fine.

那次生產極其困難，因此當醫生說寶寶健康時，全醫院的員工也都為他們高興。

relapse
[rɪ'læps]

托 雅 學

n 再度惡化；舊病復發；故態復萌

r2038

Her cancer was gone for now, but she knew that there was a real possibility that she could have a relapse.

她的癌症暫時控制住了，但是她知道復發的可能性很大。

relic
['rɛlɪk]

托 雅 學

n 遺物；遺跡；聖人遺物

r2039

The holy relics attract many foreign tourists to this small town every year.

聖人的遺物每年都吸引了很多外國遊客來到這個小鎮。

remittance
[rɪ'mɪtns]

托 雅 學

n 匯款

r2040

The country club called today and asked for full remittance of membership dues by the end of this month.

鄉村俱樂部今天打來電話要求在本月底前對應繳會費全額匯款。

remnant
['rɛmnənt]

托 雅 學

adj 剩餘的，殘留的

r2041

Cathy's hobby is using remnant cloth to make small bags.

凱西的業餘愛好是利用多餘的布料來製作小包。

remnant
['rɛmnənt]

托 雅 學

n 剩餘（物），零料；遺跡

r2042

My elementary school had changed so much that I only recognized a remnant of the old swing set on the playground.

我的小學變了太多，以至於我只認得操場上舊秋千的遺跡了。

remorse
[rɪ'mɔrs]

托 雅 學

n 懊悔；自責

r2043

The teacher had a sense of remorse for scolding the students seriously.

這位老師對於嚴厲地責備了學生感到懊悔。

remunerative
[rɪ'mjunə,retɪv]

托 雅 學

adj 付酬的，有報償的

r2044

If you volunteer you may eventually be rewarded with remunerative employment.

如果你當志願者，最終會為你贏得付酬的職位。

renaissance
[rə'nesns]

n 文藝復興時期；復興 `r2045`

Kevin claims that the best era of art is the Renaissance.

凱文認為藝術最美好的時代是在文藝復興時期。

rendezvous
['randə,vu]

n 約會，約會地點，熱門聚會場所；**vi** 會面，相會，集合 `r2046`

They divided the shopping list among them and agreed to rendezvous in the parking lot in two hours.

他們按照清單分別去採購，並約定好兩小時後在停車場碰頭。

renovate
['rɛnə,vet]

vt 修復；翻新 `r2047`

The college has renovated all girl's dormitories recently.

這所大學近來翻新了所有的女生宿舍。

renovation
[,rɛnə'veʃən]

n 新；整修；恢復活力 `r2048`

Ben and Brad worked very hard to finish the home renovation.

班和布萊德為了完成他們家的整修而努力工作。

repel
[rɪ'pɛl]

vt 拒絕；使厭惡 `r2049`

These candles you buy are supposed to repel mosquitoes.

你買的這些蠟燭應該可以驅蚊。

repertoire
['rɛpə,twar]

n 可表演項目；全部本領 `r2050`

The repertoire of the orchestra is worth listening.

這個管弦樂團的全部曲目都值得一聽。

reproach
[rɪ'protʃ]

n/vt 責備，指責 `r2051`

We know mistakes happen. You can't reproach children for everything they do wrong.

我們都知道犯錯在所難免，孩子犯錯不要一味責備。

repute
[rɪ'pjut]

n 美名；聲望；名譽 `r2052`

He was considered an employee in good repute so when the time came, they promoted him.

他被認為是有好名聲的員工，因此當機會來臨，他們就晉升了他。

resonance
['rɛzənəns]

n 洪亮；共鳴；引起共鳴的力量 `r2053`

Mr. Park's words have resonance and his students are very fond of him.

派克先生的話有引起共鳴的力量，他的學生都很喜歡他。

retain
[rɪˈten]

托 雅 學

vt 保持，保留，保有

r2054

The police only needed to retain him so that he could identify the suspect.

員警只需拘留他以讓他指認出嫌疑犯。

retort
[rɪˈtɔrt]

托 雅 學

n/vi/vt 報復；反擊，反駁

r2055

The editor gave a scathing retort to the journalist's excuse for missing his deadline.

主編嚴厲地反擊記者錯過他截稿期限的藉口。

retreat
[rɪˈtrit]

托 雅 學

vi （被迫）退卻，後退

r2056

When the enemy approached, the army was forced to retreat from the ridge.

當敵人靠近時，軍隊被迫從山脊撤退。

retrieve
[rɪˈtriv]

托 雅 學

vt 重新得到，取回；挽回，補救；檢索

r2057

The dog trainer is training the hound to retrieve the prey by the riverside.

馴犬師正在訓練這隻獵犬取回河邊的獵物。

revere
[rɪˈvɪr]

托 雅 學

vt 尊敬；崇敬

r2058

The Maya civilization revered the snake deity as a gift to civilization.

瑪雅文明崇敬蛇神，視其為文明的禮物。

reverent
[ˈrɛvərənt]

托 雅 學

adj 虔誠的；恭敬的；尊敬的

r2059

There was a reverent bowing of heads for all the brave heroes that fateful day.

在生死攸關的那一天，許多人都為所有的勇士英雄們獻上了虔誠的一鞠躬。

revival
[rɪˈvaɪvl]

托 雅 學

n 復興；再生；再流行

r2060

There has been a revival of country music thanks to new talented stars.

感謝這些才華橫溢的新星，鄉村音樂再次流行起來。

revive
[rɪˈvaɪv]

托 雅 學

vi/vt 恢復；（使）復蘇

r2061

He needed a whole pot of coffee to revive himself after staying up all night working.

在整晚熬夜工作之後，他需要一整壺的咖啡來恢復精神。

rhetorical
[rɪˈtɔrɪkl]

托 雅 學

adj 辭藻華麗的，修辭的；反問的

r2062

The politician remarked that the interviewer had asked him a rhetorical question.

員警說，那位記者問了他一個反問句。

rift
[rɪft]
托 雅 學

r2063

n 裂痕，裂縫

The stone wall construction created a rift between the once friendly neighbors.

豎起的石頭牆使原來友好的鄰里關係產生了裂痕。

ritual
['rɪtʃʊəl]
托 雅 學

r2064

adj 宗教儀式的，典禮的；**n** （宗教）儀式，典禮

Miranda rejected all the religious rituals for her wedding.

米蘭達拒絕在她的婚禮上出現任何宗教儀式。

robust
[rə'bʌst]
托 雅 學

r2065

adj 強健的，雄壯的；精力充沛的；濃的

The new coffee had a very robust flavor that was too strong for some of the customers.

這種新咖啡有很濃的味道，對一些顧客來說太重了。

roost
[rust]
托 雅 學

r2066

vi 棲息，歇息

The chickens like to roost on straw beds in their coop.

小雞們喜歡在窩裡的稻草床上棲息。

rugged
['rʌgɪd]
托 雅 學

r2067

adj 崎嶇不平的，多岩石的

The plains of north Texas are rugged and dry lands.

德克薩斯州北部的平原地勢崎嶇，土地乾燥。

rumble
['rʌmbl]
托 雅 學

r2068

n 隆隆聲；**vi** 發出持續而低沉的聲音

The old car rumbled all the way to Seattle.

這輛老爺車在前往西雅圖的路途中一路發出隆隆聲。

R

rupture
['rʌptʃə]
托 雅 學

r2069

vt 斷裂，裂開；破裂

He was rushed to the hospital because the fall had ruptured his spleen.

他被送到醫院，因為摔跤已經造成他的脾臟破裂。

rustic
['rʌstɪk]
托 雅 學

r2070

adj 鄉村（人）的；淳樸的；用粗糙木材做成的

There are a lot of rustic diners in the small town.

這個小鎮有很多簡單的小吃店。

rustic
['rʌstɪk]
托 雅 學

r2071

n 鄉下人

A crowd of rustics swarmed into the theater to see their beloved actor.

一群鄉下人蜂擁到戲院去看他們深愛的男演員。

S

sabotage
['sæbə,taʒ]
托 雅 學

n./vt. 陰謀破壞
s2001
Lisa went out of her way to sabotage her ex-boyfriend's wedding.
莉莎用盡一切方法，只為了破壞她前男友的婚禮。

salvage
['sælvɪdʒ]
托 雅 學

n. 海難救助；搶救，挽救
s2002
The salvage operation on the shipwreck has been halted owing to heavy sea ice conditions.
由於海上浮冰情況嚴重，海難的搶救行動已經中止。

sanction
['sæŋkʃən]
托 雅 學

n. 處罰，制裁
s2003
The U.S.has threatened to impose further sanctions on Iran if it does not stop its nuclear program.
美國揚言，若伊朗不停止核計畫，將對其進行進一步制裁。

sanction
['sæŋkʃən]
托 雅 學

vt. 批准，同意，支持，認可
s2004
The committee voted to sanction the small country for not signing the climate treaty.
委員會投票通過，同意小國家不需簽署氣候協議。

sanity
['sænətɪ]
托 雅 學

n. 神志正常；心智健康
s2005
Lauren said she could hardly keep her sanity with so much work to do.
蘿倫說她有太多的工作要做，搞得她都快無法保持頭腦清醒了。

sarcasm
['sɑrkæzm]
托 雅 學

n. 諷刺，挖苦；諷刺語，挖苦話
s2006
Parents should avoid any tone of sarcasm when talking with their children.
父母在與孩子談話時，應避免任何挖苦的語氣。

saturate
['sætʃə,ret]
托 雅 學

vt. 浸透；滲透使飽和，使中和；使充滿
s2007
Ellie wanted to saturate her tired feet with soothing lotion.
艾麗想給疲憊的雙腳塗滿潤膚霜放鬆一下。

savor
['sevɚ]
托 雅 學

n. 滋味，風味；風趣，愛好
s2008
The savor of the roast chicken appealed to both adults and children alike.
這隻烤雞的風味受到大人小孩的喜愛。

savor
['sevə]
托 雅 學

vi/vt 具有…味道，帶有…性質；品嘗，欣賞；（使）有風味　s2009
The religious leader's words of wisdom deserve to be savored by all.
這位宗教領袖字字珠璣，值得我們細細品味。

scalpel
['skælpəl]
托 雅 學

n 手術刀　s2010
The surgeon skillfully used a scalpel during the operation.
外科醫生手術時手術刀使用得非常熟練。

scenario
[sɪ'nɛrɪ,o]
托 雅 學

n 情節；劇本；事態，局面；方案　s2011
The teacher developed several scenarios for students to practice speaking.
那位老師設計好幾個情境，讓學生做口語練習。

scorn
[skɔrn]
托 雅 學

n/vt 輕蔑，藐視　s2012
The millionaire scorns whoever lives in that poor neighborhood.
那個富豪藐視那些住在那個貧困社區的人。

scour
[skaʊr]
托 雅 學

n 擦淨，沖刷　s2013
Before the Chinese New Year, we gave the whole house a scour.
我們在過年前把整個房子擦淨了。

scrutinize
['skrutn,aɪz]
托 雅 學

vt 細看，細讀；詳察，仔細觀察（或檢察）　s2014
Our company accountant will always scrutinize employee expense receipts.
我們公司的會計總是會仔細檢查員工的開支收據。

S

scrutiny
['skrutnɪ]
托 雅 學

n 周密的調查；仔細看；監視；選票複查　s2015
A candidate for political office must accept that his family and his past will be subject to intense scrutiny during the campaign.
競選期間，政黨候選人必須同意家人及自己的過去接受嚴密監督。

seam
[sim]
托 雅 學

n 縫，接縫　s2016
The weakly welded seam of the boat broke open and caused it to sink.
這艘船的接縫焊接不良，最後裂開導致沉船。

secular
['sɛkjələ]
托 雅 學

adj 世俗的，現世的；長期的，不朽的；修道院以外的，在俗的　s2017
Secular missionaries travel far and wide preaching the gospel.
修道院以外的傳教士走到遠方，廣布福音。

seduce
[sɪ'djus]

托 雅 學

vt 誘惑，引誘

The lady attempted to seduce the gentleman but failed.

那位女士嘗試著引誘那位紳士，結果失敗了。

s2018

septic
['sɛptɪk]

托 雅 學

adj 膿毒性的，腐敗性的

The nurse told Elliot to keep his gash clean to prevent a septic infection.

護士告訴艾略特要保持傷口清潔以防化膿感染。

s2019

serrate
['sɛrɪt]

托 雅 學

adj 有鋸齒邊的，鋸齒狀的

My Siberian husky has sharp, serrate teeth and can chew through rope in no time.

西伯利亞愛斯基摩犬有著鋒利的、鋸齒狀的牙，眨眼功夫就能夠咬斷繩子。

s2020

shabby
['ʃæbɪ]

托 雅 學

adj 簡陋的，破舊的；卑鄙的；不公平的

The couch was old and shabby with tufts of the stuffing coming through tears in the upholstery.

這個沙發又老又破舊，裡面好幾綹填充物從墊襯物的破洞中跑出來。

s2021

shaft
[ʃæft]

托 雅 學

n 軸；杆狀物；礦井；電梯井；通風井

The helicopter cannot take off because there is a problem in the propeller shaft.

因為螺旋槳軸出了點問題，直升機無法起飛。

s2022

shrewd
[ʃrud]

托 雅 學

adj 機靈的，敏銳的；精明的

Though Ashton's grandma was ninety years old, she was still shrewd when it came to money.

艾希頓的祖母雖然九十高齡，但碰到錢的事情還是很精明。

s2023

siege
[sidʒ]

托 雅 學

n 包圍，圍攻；圍困

The siege continued throughout the night until the hostages were released.

圍困持續了一晚，直到人質釋放才停止。

s2024

signify
['sɪgnə,faɪ]

托 雅 學

vi/vt 表示，意味；要緊，有重要性

Some Christians decorate a tree in their home to signify everlasting life.

有些基督徒會在家中佈置一顆樹，意味著不朽的生命。

s2025

slander
['slændɚ]

托 雅 學

n/vt 誹謗，詆毀

The newspaper had so many wrong facts about the candidate in the article that it bordered on slander.

這份報紙有許多關於候選人錯誤的訊息，近乎誹謗。

s2026

slate
[slet]

托 雅 學

n 板岩，石板瓦；候選人名單，提名名單　s2027

The slate of the candidates will be announced next week.

候選人名單會在下周公佈。

slaughter
['slɔtɚ]

托 雅 學

n/vt 屠殺，宰殺　s2028

The hunter was arrested because he illegally captured and brutally slaughtered wild animals.

獵人因為違法捕捉與濫殺野生動物而被捕了。

slumber
['slʌmbɚ]

托 雅 學

n 睡眠；沉睡狀態　s2029

She was deep in a happy slumber when her terrible alarm clock rang at 5:00 a.m.in the morning.

她正在甜甜的夢鄉沉睡，這時嚇人的鬧鐘聲在清晨五點響起。

slump
[slʌmp]

托 雅 學

vi/vt （突然或沉重地）倒下；暴跌；使倒下　s2030

The sales slumped during the economic recession.

銷售量在經濟蕭條時暴跌。

smuggle
['smʌgl]

托 雅 學

vi/vt 走私；偷運　s2031

The border patrol is always looking for suspicious people who might try to smuggle illegal drug into the country.

邊境巡邏隊總是在搜尋可疑的人物，他們可能會企圖走私非法藥品進入該國。

sober
['sobɚ]

托 雅 學

adj 清醒的；認真的；冷靜的；適度的　s2032

He had been out drinking all night, but he became sober immediately when the call came from the hospital.

他外出喝了一整晚酒，但當他接到醫院的來電時，馬上清醒了。

S

solder
['sadɚ]

托 雅 學

vt 焊，焊接，焊合；使連在一起，使聯合　s2033

Whenever I break anything metal I have to solder the pieces back together if I possibly can.

每次我打破了金屬製品，如果可能的話，我就必須把碎片重新焊接在一起。

solemn
['saləm]

托 雅 學

adj 莊嚴的，隆重的；嚴肅的　s2034

The two boys made a solemn vow not to tell their parents about breaking the neighbor's window.

這兩個男孩鄭重發誓，絕不告訴他們的父母打破鄰居窗戶的事。

solicit
[sə'lɪsɪt]

vi/vt 請求，懇求；引發，誘發；（妓女）拉客　s2035

The poor student solicited financial aid from the school.

那名窮學生請求學校經濟援助。

solidarity
[ˌsɑləˈdærətɪ]

托 雅 學

n 團結

s2036

The solidarity of our nation helps us resist the threat from the neighboring countries.

全國人民的團結幫助我們抵抗了鄰國的威脅。

solidify
[səˈlɪdəˌfaɪ]

托 雅 學

vi/vt 團結；凝固

s2037

The milk went sour and solidified after two weeks.

牛奶在兩周後變壞凝固了。

solitude
[ˈsɑləˌtjud]

托 雅 學

n 孤獨，隱居；冷僻（處），荒涼之地

s2038

Tim enjoys his life of solitude and has always preferred to live alone.

蒂姆喜歡隱居生活，總是喜歡自己獨居。

sovereign
[ˈsɑvrɪn]

托 雅 學

adj 有主權的；有統治權的；**n** 君主，國王，統治者

s2039

The King was sovereign over all territories until a parliamentary system was established and the monarch became more of an ambassador.

這個國王統治全國領土直到議會制度被確立，此時君主變成了大使。

sovereign
[ˈsɑvrɪn]

托 雅 學

adj 獨立的，有主權的

s2040

During the international conference, the question of whether the country that claimed its independence last year is a sovereign nation remained unanswered.

在國際會議中，這個去年宣佈獨立的國家是否為有主權的國家的問題仍然無解。

spacious
[ˈspeʃəs]

托 雅 學

adj 廣闊的，寬敞的

s2041

The new campus is quite spacious for 400 students.

新校園對於四百名學生而言是相當寬敞的。

spatial
[ˈspeʃəl]

托 雅 學

adj 空間的，佔據空間的

s2042

We can never overemphasize the importance of spatial ability for science.

空間能力對科學的重要性再強調也不為過。

specimen
[ˈspɛsəmən]

托 雅 學

n 標本，樣本

s2043

The scientist collected a specimen of the beetle from the jungle for identification and study.

科學家們從叢林中收集了一種甲蟲的樣本進行鑒定與研究。

spectrum
[ˈspɛktrəm]

托 雅 學

n 譜，光譜，頻譜；範圍，幅度；系列

s2044

As a candidate, he may appeal to people across a wide spectrum of political beliefs.

作為一個候選人，他可以吸引政治信仰範圍廣泛的民眾。

spur
[spɝ]
托 雅 學

n 靴刺，馬刺；刺激，刺激物；vi/vt 刺激，激勵
He spurred his players to fight harder in the competition.
在比賽中他激勵他的球員更加努力地戰鬥。
s2045

stagger
['stægɚ]
托 雅 學

n 搖晃不穩的動作；蹣跚
The old lady walked downstairs with a stagger.
那位上了年紀的女士蹣跚走下樓來。
s2046

stagger
['stægɚ]
托 雅 學

vi/vt 搖晃著移動；蹣跚
He drank too much and began to stagger as he walked toward the door.
他喝太多了，當他朝門口走去時已步履蹣跚。
s2047

stale
[stel]
托 雅 學

n 變質的，不新鮮的；陳舊的，陳腐的
These fruits are stale. You should not eat them.
這些水果已經變質，你不應再吃。
s2048

stationary
['steʃən,ɛrɪ]
托 雅 學

adj 靜止的，固定的
The train moved slower and slower until it was stationary.
火車移動得越來越慢，直到完全靜止。
s2049

stationery
['steʃən,ɛrɪ]
托 雅 學

n 文具
She was a writer and loved to buy unique stationary to write letters to her friends and family.
她是一個作家，喜歡買獨特的文具來給朋友以及家人寫信。
s2050

stipulate
['stɪpjə,let]
托 雅 學

vi/vt 規定，約定
The rule stipulates that all members must wear uniforms in choir performances.
規則規定所有成員必須在合唱表演時穿制服。
s2051

stoop
[stup]
托 雅 學

n 彎腰，曲背
My brother always walks with a stoop in a strange way.
我哥哥走路彎腰，姿勢也很奇怪。
s2052

stoop
[stup]
托 雅 學

vi/vt 彎腰；卑躬屈膝；自貶，墮落
He didn't think his friend would stoop so low.
他不認為他的朋友會這麼墮落。
s2053

S

strand
[strænd]

托 雅 學

s2054

n 股，絞，綹，串

A strand of hair fell in the little girl's face until she brushed it away with her hand.

一絡頭髮落到了小女孩的臉上，直到她用手把它撥開。

streamline
['strim,laɪn]

托 雅 學

s2055

vt 使成流線型；使有效率；使簡單化；使合理化

The CEO wanted all the employees to streamline the SOP if necessary.

這個執行長希望所有員工在必要時能簡化標準作業程序。

sturdy
['stɝdɪ]

托 雅 學

s2056

adj 堅定的，不屈不撓的；強健的，結實的

The house was old but sturdy because it had been built by a great architect of the 1920s.

這個房子雖然古老但卻很牢固，因為它是由一位1920年代的偉大建築師所建造。

stylize
['staɪ,laɪz]

托 雅 學

s2057

vt 使風格化，獨具風格

My daughter always likes to stylize her look.

我女兒總是喜歡把自己打扮得獨具風格。

submerge
[səb'mɝdʒ]

托 雅 學

s2058

vi/vt 沉沒，淹沒；潛入

They wanted to watch the submarine submerge itself into the sea.

他們想要觀看潛水艇潛入海中。

subordinate
[sə'bɔrdnɪt]

托 雅 學

s2059

adj 次要的，從屬的；下級的

He was subordinate to the company manager, but the CEO thought he was talented and always asked for his opinion on new products.

雖然他是公司經理的下屬，但是執行長認為他很有才華，總是詢問他對於新產品的意見。

subordinate
[sə'bɔrdnɪt]

托 雅 學

s2060

n 下屬

As a new recruit, Shelby's a subordinate of her platoon commander.

作為剛入伍的新兵，謝爾比是排長的屬下。

subside
[səb'saɪd]

托 雅 學

s2061

vi 退落；消退；消失

His injury was not serious and that the pain would subside in a few hours.

他的傷勢不嚴重，疼痛感也將在幾小時後消失。

subsidiary
[səb'sɪdɪ,ɛrɪ]

托 雅 學

s2062

adj 輔助的，補充的；**n** 子公司；輔助者

The clothing store is a subsidiary of a much larger corporation.

這個服裝店是一間規模更龐大的公司的子公司。

subsidize
['sʌbsə,daɪz]

vt 發給津貼，補貼，資助；收買，賄賂拉攏，向…行賄　　s2063

Understandably, his wife doesn't want to subsidize his gambling debts.

可以理解的是，他的妻子不想補貼他的賭債。

subsidy
['sʌbsədɪ]

n 補貼，補助金，津貼費　　s2064

The government gave a substantial subsidy to the car manufacturer to save it from failing during the recession.

政府給予汽車製造商大量的補貼，以避免他們在經濟衰退時破產。

subsistence
[səb'sɪstəns]

n 生存，活命；存在，內在性　　s2065

The decline in salmon has led to fishing restrictions and affects fishermen who live along the river and depend on the salmon for subsistence.

鮭魚數量的減少導致了捕魚的限制，對於住沿河以鮭魚為食生存的漁民也造成影響。

substantial
[səb'stænʃəl]

adj 實質的；相當的；顯著的；堅固的；富裕的　　s2066

The accountant noticed a substantial increase in revenue last month.

會計注意到上個月的收益有顯著的增加。

subtle
['sʌtl]

adj 精巧的，巧妙的；細微的，微妙的　　s2067

The flavor of the white wine was subtle and perfect with the meal.

白酒的風味很精巧，和餐點是完美搭配。

succumb
[sə'kʌm]

vi 屈服，委棄；被壓垮　　s2068

The cold-blooded manager finally succumbed to the pressure from the public opinion.

那個冷血的經理最終屈服於輿論的壓力。

suffice
[sə'faɪs]

vi 充足，足夠；**vt** （食物等）使（某人）滿足　　s2069

No words would suffice to express my gratitude to your generous support.

沒有言語可以表達對您慷慨支援的感激。

sufficient
[sə'fɪʃənt]

adj 足夠的，充分的　　s2070

The little boy found the number of presents for his birthday more than sufficient.

小男孩發現他的生日禮物數量足夠多。

summon
['sʌmən]

vt 召喚；傳訊；鼓起（勇氣），振作（精神）　　s2071

She walked up and down the street looking for the dog while her mother went to summon the rest of the family to help.

當她走遍整條街道尋找那隻狗時，她媽媽則去召喚其他家人來幫忙。

S

supplant
[sə'plænt]

托 雅 學

vt 排擠掉，取代

s2072

A new wave of advanced technology will soon supplant original products that were once unveiled to rousting applause.

一股先進技術的新浪潮將很快取代那些也曾在公眾面前亮相並博得掌聲的原有產品。

supposedly
[sə'pozdlɪ]

托 雅 學

adv 大概，臆測，按照推測，據信

s2073

Well supposedly from all the positive feedback, the new restaurant is doing really well.

據說從各方面積極的回饋來看，新餐廳運營得非常好。

surge
[sɝdʒ]

托 雅 學

n 巨浪；洶湧；澎湃

s2074

The sudden surge of waves scared the vacationers away.

突然而來的巨浪嚇跑了度假的遊客。

surge
[sɝdʒ]

托 雅 學

vi/vt 洶湧；澎湃；蜂擁而至

s2075

The waves began to surge higher and higher as the storm approached the beach.

當暴風雨接近海灘時，海浪越來越洶湧高漲。

surplus
['sɝpləs]

托 雅 學

adj 過剩的，剩餘的；**n** 過剩，剩餘；餘款，餘額

s2076

Finn has been trying to lose his surplus weight by jogging for an hour every night.

芬恩努力想減掉多餘的體重，所以每晚都慢跑一小時。

suspend
[sə'spɛnd]

托 雅 學

vi/vt 懸（浮），掛；暫停，取消；推遲

s2077

The company suspended production of the new shoes because they weren't selling well.

因為銷售不佳，公司暫停新鞋的生產。

suspense
[sə'spɛns]

托 雅 學

n 掛念；懸念；焦慮；暫時停止

s2078

The hysterical husband shouted, "Don't keep me in suspense any more."

歇斯底里的丈夫大喊：「不要讓我一直這樣牽腸掛肚的了！」

suspension
[sə'spɛnʃən]

托 雅 學

n 暫停，中止，停學；懸掛，懸吊

s2079

His suspension from the school was a very harsh punishment.

他被停學是很嚴厲的處罰。

swamp
[swamp]

托 雅 學

n 沼澤，濕地

s2080

It is rumored that three ferocious crocodiles inhabit this swamp.

諭傳說有三隻兇猛的鱷魚在這個沼澤地中棲息。

swamp
[swɑmp]

vi/vt 浸沒;(使…)應接不暇　　　s2081

David is still swamped with work and has to call off the dinner plan on short notice.

大衛的工作仍應接不暇,只得臨時取消晚餐計畫。

sway
[swe]

n 搖動;影響力　　　s2082

The opinions made by our CEO hold sway; even members of the board have to listen to her.

我們執行長的意見極具影響力,就連董事會成員都要聽她的話。

sway
[swe]

vi/vt 搖動;傾斜;使搖動　　　s2083

The cherry blossoms are swaying back and forth in the wind, with bees flying to collect nectar.

櫻花正隨風左右搖動,蜜蜂在一旁飛舞采蜜。

symmetry
['sɪmɪtrɪ]

n 對稱(性);勻稱,整齊　　　s2084

There was a pleasant symmetry in the arrangement of the furniture in the dining room with two matching Chinese cabinets on either side of the table.

飯廳的傢俱安排顯現出舒適的對稱,兩個中式的櫥櫃分別被擺放在餐桌的兩旁。

symposium
[sɪm'pozɪəm]

n 討論會,專題報告會;專題論文集　　　s2085

The scientists were excited about the physics symposium because they would hear a presentation from an eminent physicist.

這些科學家對於物理學的討論會很興奮,因為他們會聽到一位傑出物理學家的演講。

synthesis
['sɪnθəsɪs]

n 綜合,合成　　　s2086

This work of art is considered a synthesis of both eastern and western traditions.

這個藝術作品是東西方傳統的綜合。

synthesize
['sɪnθəˌsaɪz]

vt 綜合;合成　　　s2087

The musical director discovered a way to synthesize sound for the symphony performances.

音樂總監發現了一種為交響樂演出合成聲音的方法。

synthetic
[sɪn'θɛtɪk]
托 雅 學

adj 合成的,人造的;綜合的　　　s2088

Her pants were not cotton, but made from a synthetic material like rayon or spandex.

她的褲子不是棉製的,是用一種類似於人造纖維或彈性纖維的合成材料製成的。

S

tackle
['tækl]

托 雅 學

vi/vt 處理，解決；抱住，抓住   t2001

The government is determined to tackle the rising rate of unemployment.

政府已經決心要來解決失業率攀升的問題了。

tactic
['tæktɪk]

托 雅 學

n 策略；戰術   t2002

My parents tried several tactics to get me to go to college.

我父母試了好幾個策略讓我上大學。

tangle
['tæŋgl]

托 雅 學

n 糾纏，纏結；混亂；**vi/vt**（使）纏繞，變亂   t2003

I have to select elastic bands for my hair carefully because they tangle with my hair easily.

我必須小心選擇彈性髮帶，因為我的頭髮很容易和它們糾結在一起。

temper
['tɛmpɚ]

托 雅 學

n 脾氣；韌度   t2004

My four-year-old daughter has a temper and will scream and cry when she gets frustrated.

我四歲的女兒脾氣暴躁，而且當她沮喪時會尖叫大哭。

temper
['tɛmpɚ]

托 雅 學

vt 調和，使緩和；使回火   t2005

Criticism can be tempered with reason.

批評可以用理性來調和。

temperament
['tɛmprəmənt]

托 雅 學

n 氣質，性格，性情；資質   t2006

He had an even temperament and never seemed too emotional toward or too detached from the people around him.

他的性格平和，似乎從來不曾太過情緒化，也不曾對周圍人太過疏離。

temperate
['tɛmpərət]

托 雅 學

adj 氣候溫和的；心平氣和的   t2007

My hometown is known for its temperate climate.

我的家鄉以氣候溫和聞名。

tempo
['tɛmpo]

托 雅 學

n 節奏；行進速度；（音樂的）速度   t2008

The tempo at the beginning of the music was andante, which implies an unhurried feel to the piece.

音樂一開始的節奏是行板，意味著這首曲子悠閒的氛圍。

temptation
['tɛmp'teʃən]

t2009

n 引誘，誘惑；誘惑物
He did not have the money for the carton of milk and felt a strong temptation to steal it.
他因為沒錢買盒牛奶而沮喪，而且感到一股強烈的誘惑要去偷。

tentative
['tɛntətɪv]

t2010

adj 試探性的；暫時的；猶豫不決的
We had tentative plans to go to a movie, but we can certainly go to dinner with you instead.
我們暫時的計畫是去看電影，但我們一定可以與你一起吃晚餐。

terrace
['tɛrəs]

t2011

n 平臺，陽臺，露臺
They stepped out of the stuffy ballroom onto the terrace to look at the stars.
他們走出悶熱的舞廳，走上露臺看星星。

terrain
['tɛren]

t2012

n 地面；地域，地帶；地形，地勢
The terrain in West Texas is barren but very beautiful.
德州西部一帶雖荒蕪卻非常漂亮。

territorial
[,tɛrə'torɪəl]

t2013

adj 領土的，有地盤意識的；區域的
Wild animals can be very territorial in regards to their habitats.
關於棲息地，野生動物可能會是非常有地盤意識的。

territory
['tɛrə,torɪ]

t2014

n 領土，版圖；領域，範圍
The northern territory of Alaska is amazing but very dangerous to travel in.
阿拉斯加的北部地方真令人驚奇，但在那兒旅行非常危險。

testify
['tɛstə,faɪ]

t2015

vi/vt 作證，證明；表明；說明
As a witness to the crime, he was asked to testify during the trial.
身為犯罪事件的目擊者，審判期間他必須出庭作證。

testimony
['tɛstə,monɪ]

t2016

n 證據，證詞；表明，說明
The testimony of the wife of the defendant seemed unreliable to the jury.
被告的太太所說的證詞對陪審團而言似乎是不可信的。

textile
['tɛkstaɪl]

t2017

adj 紡織的；**n** 紡織品
She worked in a textile mill, making bolts of cotton fabrics to be sold in bulk to manufacturers.
她在紡織廠工作，製造成匹的棉布大量地賣給製造廠商。

texture
['tɛkstʃɚ]

托 雅 學

n （織物）質地；（材料）構造，結構；肌理

The texture of the outfit is as smooth as silk.

這套衣服的質地就跟蠶絲一樣細緻。

t2018

thaw
[θɔ]

托 雅 學

n 解凍；（敵對國）關係緩和

There is finally a slight thaw in relations between him and his father.

他和他父親之間的關係終於稍有緩和。

t2019

thaw
[θɔ]

托 雅 學

vi 解凍；使變得友好

After sitting on the kitchen counter for a few hours, the frozen chicken leg started to thaw out.

冷凍雞腿放在廚房灶臺上幾小時後開始解凍。

t2020

therapy
['θɛrəpɪ]

托 雅 學

n 治療；物理療法

Physical therapy usually helps sports injuries.

物理治療通常對運動中受的傷有幫助。

t2021

thermal
['θɝml̩]

托 雅 學

adj 熱的，熱力的；保熱的；**n** （小規模的）上升氣流

The paramedic wrapped the boy in a thermal blanket after pulling him out of the icy water.

從冰水中救出小男孩後，護理人員用一條保暖毯子包住他。

t2022

thermometer
[θɚ'mamətɚ]

托 雅 學

n 溫度計

She looked at the weather thermometer hanging outside the window and sighed when she saw how hot it was already.

她看著掛在窗外的溫度計，當她知道天氣多熱時，不禁歎了一口氣。

t2023

thermostat
['θɝmə,stæt]

托 雅 學

n 恒溫（調節）器

The house was frigid so she went to the thermostat to turn up the heat.

房子裡非常寒冷，所以她到溫控器那裡把暖氣溫度調高。

t2024

threshold
['θrɛʃhold]

托 雅 學

n 門檻；入門，開端

He stood on the threshold of the house, waiting for the courage to ring the door bell.

他站在門檻上，等待鼓足勇氣後去按門鈴。

t2025

throb
[θrab]

托 雅 學

n 跳動；**vi** 跳動；抽痛

My stomach has been throbbing with pain ever since we left the airport.

從我們離開機場後，我的胃就一直在抽痛。

t2026

thrust
[θrʌst]
托 雅 學

`t2027`

n 插；推力；刺
The woman was stabbed with the thrust of a knife.
這個婦人被刀尖刺傷。

---

thrust
[θrʌst]
托 雅 學

`t2028`

vi/vt 刺，插入；揮
Before the invention of guns, soldiers could only defend the country by thrusting swords at their enemies.
在槍被發明之前，軍人只能夠通過對他們的敵人奮力揮刀來保衛他們的國家。

---

torque
[tɔrk]
托 雅 學

`t2029`

n 轉（力）矩，扭（力）矩
Are you aware of how much torque you'll need when you try to open the jar?
你意識到要打開那個瓶蓋需要多少扭力嗎？

---

torrent
['tɔrənt]
托 雅 學

`t2030`

n 奔流，激流，洪流
Heavy torrents of rain washed away the crops and devastated farms in the area.
大洪流沖走了農作物並且摧毀了這個地區的農場。

---

tournament
['tɝnəmənt]
托 雅 學

`t2031`

n 錦標賽
The basketball team trains hard every day in order to be ready for the tournament.
為了備戰錦標賽，籃球隊每天都努力地訓練。

---

tow
[to]
托 雅 學

`t2032`

n 拖，牽引
Nina thanked Jason for giving her car a tow when it broke down.
妮娜感謝傑森在她的汽車壞掉時幫她拖車。

---

tow
[to]
托 雅 學

`t2033`

vi/vt （用繩、鏈等）拖（車、船等）
The police towed my car because I parked it on the street.
因為我把汽車停在街上，所以它被員警拖走了。

T

---

trait
[tret]
托 雅 學

`t2034`

n 特徵，特點，特性
The best trait that my friend's son possesses is his devotion to his football team.
我朋友兒子所擁有的最好的特性就是他對足球隊的投入。

---

traitor
['tretɚ]
托 雅 學

`t2035`

n 叛徒；賣國賊
The company knew that someone had given detailed information to their competitor but they did not know who the traitor was.
公司知道有人把一些詳細的資訊給了他們的競爭對手，但是不知道叛徒是誰。

transaction
[træn'zækʃən]

n 辦理，交易，事務；複數＝會報，學報

t2036

The financial transaction has been finalized now that all contracts have been signed.

既然所有合約已簽署，這筆金融交易也已完成。

transcend
[træn'sɛnd]

vt 超出，超越（經驗、知識、能力的範圍等）

t2037

The professor was a good speaker and managed to transcend the scientific community and appeal to a broader audience.

那位教授是個優秀的演說家，試圖超越科學界，吸引更多聽眾。

transcontinental
[ˌtrænskɑntə'nɛntl̩]

adj 橫越大陸的

t2038

The transcontinental flight went from Asia to Europe in much shorter time.

這個橫越大陸的航班以更短的時間從亞洲飛到歐洲。

transient
['trænʃənt]

adj 短暫的，轉瞬即逝的；臨時的，暫住的

t2039

This city has a large percentage of transient population of temporary workers.

這個城市打零工的暫住人口比例很大。

transmission
[træns'mɪʃən]

n 播送，發射，傳送

t2040

The transmission of communicable diseases often takes place in highly populated cities.

傳染性疾病的傳播通常發生在人口高度集中的城市裡。

transmit
[træns'mɪt]

vi 發射信號；傳輸

t2041

It's convenient that we can transmit documents through e-mails.

我們通過電子郵件來傳送檔真的很方便。

transparent
[træns'pɛrənt]

adj 透明的，透光的；易理解的，明顯的

t2042

The dress was made from a fine white silk and was slightly transparent in the sunlight.

這條裙子是由細緻的白絲綢布做的，而且在陽光下略顯透明。

transplant
[træns'plænt]

n/vi/vt 移植（植物、組織、器官等）；遷移

t2043

The gardener decided to transplant the bush from the direct sunlight to the shade of the tree.

園丁決定將灌木叢由陽光直接照射處遷移到樹蔭下。

trauma
['trɑmə]

n 外傷，傷口；創傷

t2044

Luella said it would take forever to get over the trauma of her near drowning.

盧埃娜說，要想從那次溺水給她造成的創傷中恢復需要很長的時間。

traverse
['trævɚs]

托 雅 學

vt 橫越，橫切，橫斷

t2045

The hikers traversed the ridge before descending along a safe path into the valley below.

在沿著安全路徑下降至山谷前，那些登山者先橫越山脊。

tread
[trɛd]

托 雅 學

vi/vt 踩，踏，踐踏

t2046

At parties, John often treads on his dancing partner's feet accidentally.

在派對上，約翰常常不小心踩到舞伴的腳。

treaty
['tritɪ]

托 雅 學

n 條約；協議，協商

t2047

They signed a well written treaty at the end of the war that would hopefully bring a long and profitable peace.

他們在戰爭結束時簽署了一份擬得很好的條約，希望帶來長久有利的和平。

trek
[trɛk]

托 雅 學

n 長途跋涉；**vi** 長途跋涉，徒步旅行

t2048

My husband suggests that we trek different mountains every year.

我先生提議我們應該每年去不同的山徒步旅行。

trench
[trɛntʃ]

托 雅 學

n/vi/vt（挖）溝，（挖）戰壕

t2049

During the war, the soldiers trenched deep holes as shelters.

戰爭期間，士兵們挖很深的戰壕作為避難所。

trespass
['trɛspəs]

托 雅 學

vi 未經許可進入私人土地，擅入

t2050

There was a sign in front of the old abandoned mansion that warned people not to trespass around the ruined building.

在那座古老的無人居住的大宅前面豎著牌子，警告人們不要擅自闖入這所廢棄的建築。

tribute
['trɪbjut]

托 雅 學

n 貢品；頌詞，稱讚；（表示敬意的）禮物

t2051

The magazine paid tribute to their retiring editor by publishing a profile of his life and work.

該雜誌刊登退休編輯的生平及作品簡介來表達對他的敬意。

triumph
['traɪəmf]

托 雅 學

n 勝利，成功

t2052

It was a great triumph to win a gold medal in the relay race.

在接力賽中贏得金牌真是一個大勝利。

triumph
['traɪəmf]

托 雅 學

vi 得勝，戰勝

t2053

After a long struggle, the little boy finally triumphed over his stage fright.

經過了長時間的掙扎，那個小男孩終於戰勝了他的舞臺恐懼。

T

truce
[trus]

托 雅 學

n 休戰，休止

t2054

Okay, let's call a truce and agree to disagree without anymore arguing.

好吧，讓我們休戰吧，即使有不同意見也不要再爭論下去。

tuck
[tʌk]

托 雅 學

vt 捲起，塞進

t2055

All students are asked to tuck their uniform shirts into their pants.

學生們被告知他們必須將襯衫塞進褲子裡。

tumble
['tʌmbl]

托 雅 學

n 摔跤，跌倒；vi/vt （使…）摔倒；打滾，翻騰

t2056

He took a tumble on the playground and got a small cut on his forehead.

他在操場跌了一跤，前額有個小傷口。

tundra
['tʌndrə]

托 雅 學

n 苔原，凍原，凍土地帶

t2057

The tundra is a bleak, treeless area of frozen subsoil and sparse vegetation in the Northern Hemisphere.

凍原是指位於北半球的一片荒涼蕭疏、植被稀少的積凍底土。

turf
[tɝf]

托 雅 學

n 草地，跑馬場，泥炭

t2058

Ryder likes playing football on the new turf in the college stadium.

萊德喜歡在大學體育場內新鋪設的草地上踢球。

turmoil
['tɝmɔɪl]

托 雅 學

n 騷動，混亂

t2059

Andrea said she was sorry for creating such turmoil in her life.

安德莉亞說她非常抱歉對她的生活造成了這樣的混亂。

turnpike
['tɝn,paɪk]

托 雅 學

n 收費高速公路，收稅關卡

t2060

At the turnpike, we exited the highway and made our way towards the lights of town.

在收費高速公路處，我們離開了高速公路，朝著小鎮的燈光駛去。

typify
['tɪpə,faɪ]

托 雅 學

vt 作為榜樣，作為典型；代表，作為…的象徵

t2061

Doesn't the selection of English chocolates typify the British love of good confectionary?

英式巧克力的選擇不就代表了英國人對美味糖果的熱愛嗎？

U

---

ultimatum
[ˌʌltə'metəm]

u2001

n 最後通牒
His mother issued a final ultimatum, and when he still wouldn't clean his room, she took away his video games.
他媽媽給他發了最後通牒，如果他再不收拾房間，他的電玩遊戲機就會被媽媽沒收。

---

ultrasonic
[ˌʌltrə'sɑnɪk]

u2002

adj 超音波的；**n** 超音波
Tom asked the doctor to give him an ultrasonic liver scan.
湯姆要求醫生給他做肝臟超音波掃描檢查。

---

ultraviolet
[ˌʌltrə'vaɪəlɪt]

u2003

adj/n 紫外線（的）
Sunscreens protect your skin from being harmed by ultraviolet rays.
防曬霜保護你的皮膚免受紫外線傷害。

---

unanimous
[jʊ'nænəməs]

u2004

adj 全體一致的，一致同意的
The committee is unanimous in recommending Mr. Smith for the job.
委員會一致推薦史密斯先生做這份工作。

---

uniformly
[junɪ'fɔrmlɪ]

u2005

adv 相同地；一貫
As expected, the party uniformly selected the former President to be their new leader.
正如預期的一樣，這個黨派一致選了前總統當他們的新領袖。

---

unify
['junə,faɪ]

u2006

vt 統一，使統一
The King unified the small states into one nation with his kindness and patience.
這個國王用仁慈和耐心統一了這些小邦而成為一國。

---

unilateral
[ˌjunɪ'lætərəl]

u2007

adj 單方面的
Her parents did not support her unilateral decision to divorce.
她的父母不支持她離婚的單方面決定。

---

uninhabited
[ˌʌnɪn'hæbɪtɪd]

u2008

adj 無人居住的，杳無人跡的
Robinson Crusoe lived on an uninhabited island or so he thought!
魯濱遜住在一個無人居住的島嶼上，或者說他自己是這麼認為的。

unravel
[ʌn'ævl̩]
托 雅 學

vt 拆散，解開；解釋，闡明；解決　u2009
I am trying to unravel my gold necklace so that I can wear it tonight.
我正試著解開我的金項鍊，這樣我今天晚上就能戴它了。

upbringing
['ʌp,brɪŋɪŋ]
托 雅 學

n 教養；養育，撫育　u2010
Grady had a perfect upbringing on his parent's farm.
格雷迪在父母的農場裡得到了完美的教養。

upheaval
[ʌp'hivl̩]
托 雅 學

n 劇變；激變；動亂；動盪　u2011
She thanked her husband for being patient and supportive during her emotional upheavals.
她感謝她的丈夫在情緒動盪的時期對她的耐心和支持。

urbanization
[,ɝbənɪ'zeʃən]
托 雅 學

n 都市化，城市化　u2012
Slowly but surely our quiet little town is beginning to take on a feel of urbanization.
慢慢地但又確定無疑地，我們安靜的小鎮正開始呈現出一種都市化的氣息。

utter
['ʌtɚ]
托 雅 學

adj 徹底的，完全的　u2013
The student showed an utter passion for gaining knowledge.
這名學生表現出極強的求知欲。

utter
['ʌtɚ]
托 雅 學

vi/vt 說，發出（聲音）　u2014
When the police broke the door open, the smuggler sat on the floor, too shocked to utter a word.
當員警破門而入時，走私犯跌坐在地板上，太震驚以至於說不出話來。

utterly
['ʌtɚlɪ]
托 雅 學

adv 完全地，徹底地，絕對地，全然地，十足地　u2015
I was utterly amazed that I scored top marks on my French test.
我徹底地驚訝了，我居然在法語考試中得分最高。

V

vaccinate
['væksə,net]

托 雅 學

vt 給…接種預防針;接種…疫苗

v2001

It is a requirement to be vaccinated against measles when entering some countries.

進入某些國家是需要接種麻疹疫苗的。

vaccine
['væksin]

托 雅 學

n 疫苗

v2002

The vaccine has not been approved for use on children aged 3 to 10 years old.

這種疫苗還未通過許可在3歲到10歲的孩子身上使用。

valve
[vælv]

托 雅 學

n 閥;電子管,真空管;心臟的瓣膜

v2003

The main water valve to the house was broken long ago.

這個房子的主要水閥很久以前就壞了。

vanity
['vænətɪ]

托 雅 學

n 虛榮心,浮華

v2004

She suffered from vanity and was always concerned about the clothes she wore.

她因虛榮心而受罪,總是在意自己穿的衣服。

vanquish
['væŋkwɪʃ]

托 雅 學

vt 征服,擊敗;克服,抑制,控制

v2005

Please let me try to vanquish your fears.

請讓我嘗試克服你的恐懼。

vegetation
[,vɛdʒə'teʃən]

托 雅 學

n 植物,草木

v2006

The desert showed no sign of vegetation anywhere.

這片沙漠沒有任何植物存在的跡象。

velocity
[və'lasətɪ]

托 雅 學

n 速度,速率

v2007

The train was moving at a high enough velocity to split a car into pieces.

火車行駛速度非常快,足以將車子撞得支離破碎。

vengeance
['vɛndʒəns]

托 雅 學

n 報復,報仇,復仇

v2008

He sought vengeance against the drunk driver who killed his son.

他要找撞死他兒子的酒駕者報仇。

V

ventilate
[ˌvɛntl'et]
托 雅 學

vt 使通風；給…裝通風設備 `v2009`
The house was not ventilated, with all the doors and windows being shut for a long time.
這個房子因長久以來門窗緊閉而不通風。

venture
['vɛntʃə]
托 雅 學

vi/vt 冒險；大膽表示 `v2010`
They ventured through a part of the desert where no one has ever been before.
他們冒險越過這個以前從沒有人去過的沙漠。

venturesome
['vɛntʃəsəm]
托 雅 學

adj 冒險的；危險的；好冒險的 `v2011`
The venturesome investor played the stock markets gambling on high risk stocks.
那個好冒險的投資者對高風險的股票玩了一把股市賭博。

verbal
['vɝbl]
托 雅 學

adj 用言辭的，用文字的；口頭的；動詞的；能言善道的 `v2012`
She was a verbal little girl and loved to talk to anyone who would listen.
她是一個能言善道的小女孩，喜歡對任何願意聽的人說話。

verdict
['vɝdɪkt]
托 雅 學

n 結論，裁決 `v2013`
Judge Jones asked the jury to read their verdict to the court.
瓊斯法官請陪審團當庭宣讀裁決。

verge
[vɝdʒ]
托 雅 學

n 邊，邊緣；接近…之際，快要 `v2014`
The police were on the verge of solving the case.
警方就快要破案了。

verge
[vɝdʒ]
托 雅 學

vt 瀕臨 `v2015`
Under such heavy pressure from work, both her physical and mental state verged on collapse.
在如此大的工作壓力之下，她的身體和心理狀態都瀕臨崩潰了。

versatile
['vɝsətl]
托 雅 學

adj 通用的，多功能的；多才多藝的，多方面的 `v2016`
I love to buy tools for my kitchen that are versatile and inexpensive.
我喜歡購買便宜的多功能廚房用具。

verse
[vɝs]
托 雅 學

n 韻文，詩；詩節，詩句 `v2017`
She quoted a few verses from Byron's *Don Juan* for her script writing class.
她在劇本寫作課裡引用了幾句拜倫的《唐璜》中的詩句。

vessel
['vɛsl̩]

托 雅 學

v2018

🔟 容器；血管；輪船
I have sailed on a boat many times, but I've never been on a large shipping vessel.
我搭過小船很多次了，但從未搭過大型運輸船。

---

veteran
['vɛtərən]

托 雅 學

v2019

🔟 老手，老兵
She was a veteran of the war in Afghanistan and was ready to retire from the army.
她在阿富汗戰爭中是個老兵，而且準備從軍中退休了。

---

veto
['vito]

托 雅 學

v2020

🔟/🔠 否決
The President threatened to veto any budget that was not balanced.
總統威脅要否決任何未獲得收支平衡的預算案。

---

vibrate
['vaɪbret]

托 雅 學

v2021

🔠/🔠 （使）振動，（使）搖擺
The strings of the piano would ring and vibrate when she sang as loud as she could.
當她用力大聲唱歌時，鋼琴的弦會發出聲響和震動。

---

vice
[vaɪs]

托 雅 學

v2022

🔟 邪惡；惡習
Gambling is a bad vice that can eventually ruin your life.
賭博是最終可能毀了你一生的惡習。

---

vicinity
[və'sɪnətɪ]

托 雅 學

v2023

🔟 鄰近，附近
There is a good restaurant in the vicinity that serves fine French food.
附近有家供應美味法國食物的餐廳。

---

vicious
['vɪʃəs]

托 雅 學

v2024

adj 惡毒的，兇殘的，邪惡的
He told a vicious lie about his rival.
他講了一個關於他競爭對手的惡毒謊言。

---

vie
[vaɪ]

托 雅 學

v2025

🔠 爭奪；競爭
The lead singer of the band will always vie for the attention of the audience.
樂隊的首席歌唱家總是奪取聽眾們的關注。

---

vigilance
['vɪdʒələns]

托 雅 學

v2026

🔟 警戒性，警覺；靈敏
The President has asked fellow Americans to keep up their vigilance.
總統已經要求美國同胞們繼續保持警戒性。

V

403

vigilant
['vɪdʒələnt]

托 雅 學

adj 警惕的，警覺的　　　　　　　　v2027

The police asked residents to be vigilant about personal safety because of the recent attacks.

由於最近的各種襲擊，員警要求居民們提高警惕，注意人身安全。

vigorous
['vɪgərəs]

托 雅 學

adj 精力旺盛的，茁壯的　　　　　　v2028

The students became more vigorous after their PE class.

體育課後，學生們更加精力旺盛。

virtual
['vɜ·tʃʊəl]

托 雅 學

adj 虛擬的；有效的；實質上的　　　v2029

Tommy checked online for the virtual book.

托米上網查找一本虛擬書。

virtually
['vɜ·tʃʊəlɪ]

托 雅 學

adv 實際上，事實上；幾乎　　　　　v2030

She was so hungry that she had virtually eaten everything in the fridge by the time I arrived home.

當我到家時，她已經餓得把冰箱裡的東西幾乎吃完了。

virtuous
['vɜ·tʃʊəs]

托 雅 學

adj 品行端正的；自命不凡的　　　　v2031

The late President was highly respected for his virtuous style of representing the people.

已故總統因代表人民的正直統治風格而深受愛戴。

viscosity
[vɪs'kasətɪ]

托 雅 學

n 粘性，粘度　　　　　　　　　　v2032

Viscosity describes a fluid's resistance to flow such as slow moving honey.

粘性用來形容某種液體的流動阻力，比如緩慢流動的蜂蜜。

viscous
['vɪskəs]

托 雅 學

adj 黏滯的，黏稠的，黏性的　　　　v2033

Viscous lava came out of the volcano in explosive eruptions.

黏稠的熔岩來自火山的爆炸性噴發。

void
[vɔɪd]

托 雅 學

adj 空虛的；沒有的，無效的；**vt** 使…作廢/無效　　v2034

I decided to void the deposit check because I did not want to live in that apartment.

我決定將訂金支票作廢，因為我不想住在那間公寓。

volatile
['valətḷ]

托 雅 學

adj 易揮發的，易發作的，不穩定的　v2035

The chemicals they were researching were volatile and they could easily explode if not handled properly.

他們正在研究的化學物質有揮發性，而且如果不小心處理會很容易爆炸。

voracious
[vo'reʃəs]

adj 狼吞虎嚥的；貪婪的

v2036

The boys had voracious appetites during football season because they were training so much.

在足球季這些男孩都有狼吞虎嚥的胃口，因為他們的訓練真的很密集。

vulgar
['vʌlgɚ]

adj 粗俗的，庸俗的

v2037

His manners were vulgar, but it was easy to see that he had a gentle soul.

他的舉止非常粗俗，但可清楚看出他有溫柔的內心。

V

W

wager
['wedʒɚ]
托 雅 學

n 賭注，用錢打賭　　　　w2001
My father and my father-in-law decided to place a small wager on the game to make it a little more exciting.
我父親和公公決定就這場比賽打個賭，使它看起來更有興致。

warrant
['wɔrənt]
托 雅 學

n 正當理由；許可證，委任狀　　　　w2002
The police issued a warrant for my arrest because I did not pay my traffic tickets.
員警發出了逮捕我的執行令，因為我沒有繳交通罰單。

warrant
['wɔrənt]
托 雅 學

vt 保證，擔保　　　　w2003
The salesman warranted the car for six months after the purchase date.
業務員給這台車售後6個月保修期。

wary
['wɛrɪ]
托 雅 學

adj 小心的，謹慎的　　　　w2004
We were told to be wary of strangers while travelling in Madrid.
我們被告知在馬德里旅行的時候要小心陌生人。

weary
['wɪrɪ]
托 雅 學

adj 疲倦的，令人厭煩的；vt 使疲倦，使厭倦　　　　w2005
His arguments about the definition of art began to weary the audience.
他對藝術定義的辯論開始讓觀眾厭倦。

wedge
[wɛdʒ]
托 雅 學

n 楔，楔形　　　　w2006
We put a wedge under the broken door to keep it open.
我們在這扇壞掉的門下塞了個楔子好讓它一直開著。

wedge
[wɛdʒ]
托 雅 學

vt 楔牢，楔入；擠進　　　　w2007
They wedged a wad of cardboard under the uneven table to stabilize it.
他們用一疊厚紙板楔在這個不穩的桌子下好穩住它。

weld
[wɛld]
托 雅 學

n 焊接，焊縫；vi/vt 焊接　　　　w2008
Workers are trying to weld the damaged steel beam back together.
工人們試著將毀損的鋼樑焊接起來。

whim
[hwɪm]

托 雅 學

n 一時興起，心血來潮；怪念頭，奇想；狂想，幻想

On a whim the young man smiled at the pretty young lady.

年輕人一時興起，朝著那位年輕漂亮的女士微笑了一下。

w2009

withdraw
[wɪð'drɔ]

托 雅 學

vi/vt （使）撤離；退出；領取；收回（說過的話）

Mr. Lee withdrew all the money from his bank account so he could pay for his medical emergency expenses.

李先生把所有的錢從銀行帳戶取了出來，以便支付醫療緊急費用。

w2010

withdrawal
[wɪð'drɔəl]

托 雅 學

n 撤走；退出組織；提款；（說過的話）收回

The government made an official withdrawal of troops from the battlefront.

政府正式撤走前線的軍隊。

w2011

wither
['wɪðɚ]

托 雅 學

vi 枯萎；**vt** 使衰弱

A bouquet of tulips will wither quickly if you don't keep the water fresh.

如果不保持使用新鮮的水，一束鬱金香將很快枯萎。

w2012

withhold
[wɪð'hold]

托 雅 學

vt 隱瞞，不給

We strongly suspected that he was withholding evidence.

我們強烈懷疑他在隱瞞證據。

w2013

withstand
[wɪð'stænd]

托 雅 學

vt 抵抗，經受住

The villagers build shelters in their homes that can withstand the deadly winds.

村民在家裡搭蓋可以抵擋狂風的遮蓋物。

w2014

wring
[rɪŋ]

托 雅 學

vt 擰，擠，扭，榨

Tom wrings sweat from his wet shirt every time he plays basketball.

湯姆每次打籃球都能把濕透的上衣擰出汗來。

w2015

W

國家圖書館出版品預行編目資料

新多益高分核心字彙：3000個一定要記住的必考單字 / 尤菊芳著.
-- 初版. -- 臺北市：商周出版：家庭傳媒城邦分公司發行, 2016.02
　面；　公分. -- (不分類；BO0239)
ISBN 978-986-272-970-0(平裝附光碟片)
1.多益測驗 2.詞彙
805.1895　　　　　　　　　　　　　　　　105000600

BO0239
新多益高分核心字彙 3000個一定要記住的必考單字

作　　　　者／尤菊芳
責 任 編 輯／李皓歆
企 劃 選 書／簡伯儒
版　　　　權／黃淑敏

行 銷 業 務／張倚禎、石一志
總　編　輯／陳美靜
總　經　理／彭之琬
發　行　人／何飛鵬
出　　　版／何飛鵬
法 律 顧 問／台英國際商務法律事務所 羅明通律師
出　　　版／商周出版司
　　　　　　臺北市104民生東路二段141號9樓
　　　　　　電話：(02) 2500-7008　傳真：(02) 2500-7759
　　　　　　E-mail: bwp.service@cite.com.tw
發　　　行／英屬蓋曼群島商家庭傳媒股份有限公司　城邦分公司
　　　　　　臺北市104民生東路二段141號2樓
　　　　　　讀者服務專線：0800-020-299　24小時傳真服務：(02) 2517-0999
　　　　　　讀者服務信箱E-mail: cs@cite.com.tw
　　　　　　劃撥帳號：19833503　戶名：英屬蓋曼群島商家庭傳媒股份有限公司城邦分公司
　　　　　　訂購服務／書虫股份有限公司客服專線：(02) 2500-7718；2500-7719
　　　　　　服務時間：週一至週五上午09:30-12:00；下午13:30-17:00
　　　　　　24小時傳真專線：(02) 2500-1990；2500-1991
　　　　　　劃撥帳號：19863813　戶名：書虫股份有限公司
香港發行所／城邦（香港）出版集團有限公司
　　　　　　香港灣仔駱克道193號東超商業中心1樓
　　　　　　E-mail: hkcite@biznetvigator.com
　　　　　　電話：(852) 25086231　傳真：(852) 25789337
　　　　　　E-mail：hkcite@biznetvigator.com
馬新發行所／Cite (M) Sdn. Bhd.
　　　　　　41, Jalan Radin Anum, Bandar Baru Sri Petaling, 57000 Kuala Lumpur, Malaysia.
　　　　　　電話：(603) 9057-8822　傳真：(603) 9057-6622 E-mail: cite@cite.com.my
美 術 編 輯／簡至成
封 面 設 計／簡至成
製 版 印 刷／鴻霖印刷傳媒事業有限公司
總　經　銷／聯合發行股份有限公司 新北市231新店區寶橋路235巷6弄6號2樓
　　　　　　電話：(02) 2917-8022　傳真：(02) 2911-0053

■2016年2月3日　初版1刷　Printed in Taiwan

ISBN　978-986-272-970-0
定價399元　HK$133

城邦讀書花園
www.cite.com.tw